Further praise for the author—

Sparhawk's Angel
"Ms. Jarrett successfully mixes genres to bring forth an unusual, delightful, and precious reading experience. 5★s."

—*Affaire de Coeur*

"This reviewer can't wait to see where Ms. Jarrett takes us next! 5♥s."

—*Booklovers*

"Miranda Jarrett performs magic in this very special romance. 4½."

—*Romantic Times*

"...lighthearted and utterly charming romance..."
—*The Paperback Forum*

"...another delightful Sparhawk book..."
—*Rendezvous*

1996 RITA finalist Reviewer's Choice Award Winner, *Sparhawk's Lady*
"...a hero to die for and a heroine who is his perfect match. Another keeper."
—award-winning author Theresa Michaels

"...a splendid story, superbly written. 5*."
—*Affaire de Coeur*

One kiss, she told herself.

One kiss to let herself pretend she was seventeen again. She swayed against Anthony as she opened both her lips and her soul to him.

"Catie."

Slowly she opened her eyes, bewildered and bereft. What would make him stop now?

"Catie, look at me," he said. "I do not know how it can be possible, and yet it must be so."

He searched her face, and the first wisp of fear began to curl in Catie's stomach. "Years ago, the night before I sailed for London, there was a girl I met in a tavern near the water."

"You are mistaken, sir." Catie jerked free, her heart pounding.

Relentlessly he followed. "A little serving girl afraid of her own shadow and still unaware of what her pretty face could do to a man."

"No," said Catie, her eyes wild as she backed away from him. "No."

"Yes, Catie," he said softly. "You are that lass."

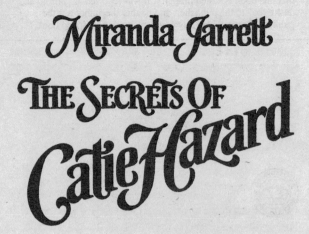

Miranda Jarrett
THE SECRETS OF CatieHazard

Harlequin Books

TORONTO • NEW YORK • LONDON
AMSTERDAM • PARIS • SYDNEY • HAMBURG
STOCKHOLM • ATHENS • TOKYO • MILAN
MADRID • WARSAW • BUDAPEST • AUCKLAND

ISBN 0-373-28963-4

THE SECRETS OF CATIE HAZARD

Copyright © 1997 by Miranda Jarrett

This edition published by arrangement with Harlequin Books S.A.

® and TM are trademarks of the publisher. Trademarks indicated with ® are registered in the United States Patent and Trademark Office, the Canadian Trade Marks Office and in other countries.

Printed in U.S.A.

Books by Miranda Jarrett

Harlequin Historicals

Steal the Stars #115
*Columbine #144
*Spindrift #174
Providence #201
*Mariah's Prize #227
*Desire My Love #247
*Sparhawk's Lady #271
*The Sparhawk Bride #292
*Sparhawk's Angel #315
*Gift of the Heart #341
*The Secrets of Catie Hazard #363

Harlequin Books

Christmas Rogues 1995
"Bayberry and Mistletoe"

*Sparhawk Family Saga

MIRANDA JARRETT

was an award-winning designer and art director before turning to writing full-time, and considers herself sublimely fortunate to have a career that combines history and happy endings, even if it's one that's also made her family regular patrons of the local pizzeria. A descendant of early settlers in New England, she feels a special kinship with her popular fictional family, the Sparhawks of Rhode Island.

Miranda and her husband—a musician and songwriter—live near Philadelphia with their two young children and two old cats. During what passes for spare time she paints watercolor landscapes, bakes French chocolate cakes and whips up the occasional last-minute Halloween costume.

Miranda admits herself that it's hard to keep track of all the Sparhawk family members, and she has prepared a family tree to help, including which characters appear in each book. She loves to hear from readers, and if you write to her and enclose a self-addressed, stamped envelope, she'll send you a copy of the family tree along with her reply. Her address: P.O. Box 1102, Paoli, PA 19301-1145.

For Angela, Deborah, Margaret and Karen,
the cream of the crop of the sixth floor,
and most especially for Tracy,
who never believed that Yankee love stories
were an oxymoron.
With much respect and fondest wishes
Au revoir, guys.

Chapter One

All evening long the gold-haired gentleman had been watching her, watching her as surely as a hawk watches a rabbit, and there wasn't a thing, not a blessed thing, that Catie could do to stop him.

No matter that he laughed at the ribald jests his two friends were telling, or raised his tankard in their noisy toasts, or roared his approval of the blind fiddler's tunes along with the others crowded into the Crossed Keys tonight. Through it all, Catie felt the man's green-eyed gaze always on her as she moved among the tables, trailing her, following her, never leaving her for an instant.

And, with all her heart, Catie willed him to stop. Couldn't he tell she wasn't like other serving maids? Her kerchief was tied modestly high across her bodice, her hair drawn back tightly beneath her cap. She didn't whisper her name to the sailors at her tables, and she didn't make plans to go out walking along the wharf with them in the moonlight. She didn't squander her wages on strong drink and fripperies like the others, but instead sent as much as she could spare back home to her mother on the farm. She was a good lass, always had been. No one could say otherwise, or accuse her of being bold or slatternly.

Until now.

She swallowed hard and tried to concentrate instead on not dropping the four empty tankards clutched in her hands. Yet still she could not quite look away from the table nearest the fire. In all her seventeen years, she'd never seen a gentleman like this one, with his gleaming blond hair and his even white teeth and the fine linen ruffles at his cuffs, falling just so over his wrists. Not that he was a dandy or a fop. His face was tanned too dark for that, his shoulders were too broad and the hands below those ruffled cuffs too large and strong.

"You can just put your eyes back into your foolish head, Catie Willman," snapped Rebeckah as she shoved Catie aside at the bar, pushing her tray of empty tankards forward to be filled by the keep first. "Them handsome gentlemen ain't for the likes o' you."

After a year of serving the tables beside Rebeckah, Catie knew better than to try to push her way in front of the older woman, just as she knew she'd waited a moment too long to defend herself.

"A cat may look at a king, Rebeckah. There's no sin in that." But even to Catie's own ears, the retort sounded wistful, not defiant, the way she'd intended, and the nervous little shrug of her narrow shoulders didn't help, either.

And Rebeckah wasn't a merciful woman. She squinted at Catie scornfully and laughed, showing the gaps between her tobacco-stained teeth.

"Kings, y'say? Fat lot you know of it, Miss Priss!" she taunted. "Right royal rogues is closer to the truth, come here tonight to take their sport among the common folk, a pox on the three o' them. Handsome as sin and twice as wicked, and all the gold in their pockets won't make them Sparhawks better than they are."

"Sparhawks?" echoed Catie faintly. Even on the backwater farm where she'd been born, they'd heard of the Sparhawk family. The Sparhawks were Newport gentry, shipowners and captains, who lived with their fine, beautiful ladies in grand houses at the other end of town. No wonder she'd never seen the gold-haired man here before. She couldn't help stealing another glance his way.

But this time he caught her. He cocked his head back a fraction, just a fraction, and smiled, slow and lazy enough to make Catie's cheeks flame and her mouth fall open in a silent O of amazement.

Rebeckah shoved her again, this time hard enough that Catie nearly dropped her tankards. "I told you to quit your gawking, you silly little cow!"

Catie yelped, her side smarting where the other woman's elbow had jabbed her. "And I tell you he was the one to stare at me first!"

"*You?*" Rebeckah's brows shot up with cruel disbelief. "One of them Sparhawks fancyin' a rabbity little chit like you? The only man ever looks *your* way, Miss Priss, is old Ben himself!"

Automatically Catie's gaze darted to the front hall, where the tavern's owner sat perched on his tall stool to greet the customers. Master Hazard *was* old, nearly twice her own age, with wispy auburn hair that trailed beneath his curled snuff wig and hands that always seemed damp when he brushed against her.

"Oh, aye, that's *your* admirer," continued Rebeckah relentlessly, leaning closer so Catie wouldn't miss a word. "An' even old Ben only smiles your way on account o' you being so eager to work yourself to the very bone."

"That's not true, none of it!" cried Catie. "And I swear to you, Mr. Sparhawk has been watching me, all night, too!"

But still Rebeckah's barbs struck painfully close to the mark. Why should she believe what Catie said about the fair-haired gentleman, when Catie could scarcely believe it herself?

Rebeckah's eyes were glittering with malicious triumph. "Then prove it. Go to him now an' ask if he wants his glass refilled. If he's been oglin' you, he'll welcome the chance to see you close. Go on, show me."

"Oh, I couldn't," said Catie hastily. "Besides, that's your table, not mine, and I wouldn't—"

"Go on, Miss Priss," goaded Rebeckah. "Unless you're afraid you'll cross old Ben. Unless you're scared. Unless you're *lying.*"

Her heart pounding, Catie thumped the empty tankards onto the counter and spun about, her striped petticoat swirling around her ankles. If she hesitated for even a moment, she'd lose her nerve, and she couldn't afford to do that. Swiftly she threaded her way among the tables and chairs, smoothing her apron with quick, anxious fingers as she went, heading directly to the table where the green-eyed gentleman waited.

He watched her come, his expression remaining almost languidly charming, while her own cheeks grew hotter still. She stopped before him with awkward abruptness, and barely remembered to bob the hint of a curtsy. Her heart was racing, and her mouth was so dry she prayed she'd be able to speak at all.

And at the last moment, to her horror, she realized she couldn't. She swallowed convulsively, opened her mouth, and nothing, absolutely nothing, came out.

"Good day to you, lass," he said, saving her from herself without a hint of mockery. "Or good evening, considering the hour."

"Whichever Your Lordship wishes," she said, finally finding a reedy, breathless voice to pass as her own. "That is, in truth it's night, but if it pleases you to call it day, then so it is."

She hadn't thought it possible to blush any deeper, but after that half-witted speech she found she most certainly could, sinking deeper into mortified misery as her whole face burned, clear to the tops of her breasts.

But still he didn't tease or ridicule her. Instead he merely nodded, the lazy smile that curved his lips meant for her alone. "What an agreeable creature you are," he marveled softly, "willing to turn night into day and back again merely because I wish it."

"Aye, Your Lordship." She wasn't sure what else was proper. This close to the firelight, his eyes were greener than she'd realized from across the room, shadowed beneath the sweep of his lashes—green cat's eyes, and she the little mouse with the racing heart, caught in their spell.

"Might I bring Your Lordship more rum?" she asked at last, struggling to return the conversation to the more usual topics. Surely she'd convinced Rebeckah by now. The sooner she left this table, the better. "Or is it something finer Your Lordship's drinking this night?"

"'Your Lordship?'" repeated the next man at the table, one of the two younger, black-haired, and quite drunk Sparhawks. "Your ruddy *Lordship?* Damnation, Anthony, no wonder you've been eying this wench all evening!"

Instinctively Catie moved back. Long ago she'd learned from her stepfather to keep an arm's distance between herself and men who'd drunk too much, but by edging away from one Sparhawk she'd moved closer to the first, the fair one they were calling Anthony. Before she could protest—before she noticed, really—he'd taken her hand and begun lightly tracing his finger along her bare arm, from her wrist to the inside of her elbow and back.

"She's merely displaying inestimable judgment of my true worth, that's all, cousin," he said, his lazy, green-eyed gaze never wavering from hers as his touch trailed across her skin. "As well as proving beyond question why the ladies smile more favorably in my direction than in yours. Isn't that so, pet? Ah, a lass as wise as she is lovely."

She knew she should pull her hand free. With any other man, she'd have done so already.

But not with him. The gentleness of his touch disarmed her, the feather-light caress across her skin leaving her speechless with startled pleasure.

"Alas, sweet child, I'm not your lordship, or anyone else's, either," he continued. "Merely plain Anthony Sparhawk, of Franklin County in Massachusetts Bay, and these two worthless rogues are my cousins Jonathan and Joshua. Your servant, ma'am."

"Nay, but I am the one serving you!"

He chuckled, a rich, deep sound that warmed Catie even over the din of the taproom. "It's only an expression, sweet. A politely meaningless turn of phrase. Though I'd be most honored to turn the tables—ah, another expression, eh?—for so pretty a serving lass."

Confused, Catie looked away, down, as the immaculate linen of Anthony's ruffled cuff fell across her own red, rough little hand with its bitten nails. It was all nonsense, him calling her pretty and lovely, the sort of claptrap drinking men always said in taverns when the rum was doing the talking. She wasn't lovely and never would be. But oh, from a man this gentle, this charming, this beautiful, how she wished it were true!

"'Ere now, Catie, where's our rum?" demanded an irritated male voice behind her. "Or be you too busy playin' patty-hand with them fancy cockerels t' serve us honest laborin' men?"

There was nothing gentle about the hand that suddenly snaked around her waist now, yanking her away from Anthony and nearly off her feet. Zeb Harris was a regular customer, a hawser in the shipyard, and he and his four friends all roared with laughter as Catie stumbled, barely catching herself on the edge of their table.

"Off with you, you little hussy, an' fetch our rum,"

growled Zeb as he smacked her backside. "Else I'll complain t' Master Hazard."

"Oh, n-no, Zeb, you needn't do that!" stammered Catie hastily, at once humiliated and contrite and strangely close to tears. "I'll fetch it right now, I promise. 'Twas wrong to keep you waiting, Zeb, and I vow it won't happen again!"

But as she turned to hurry to the bar, she ran instead squarely into the broad chest of Anthony Sparhawk. Lord, she'd no notion he'd stand so tall, nearly a head more than herself.

"Oh, sir, forgive me, I didn't mean to—"

"Hush now, no harm's done," he said, smiling as he gently steadied her with his hands on her shoulders. "Far mightier foes than you have tried to do me in, and I always prove remarkably hardy. And mind you, no more apologies, either."

Mutely Catie nodded. The light pressure of his palms was as oddly unsettling as his fingertips had been on her wrist, yet once again she felt incapable of pulling free.

"Enough of your dawdlin', you lazy little hussy!" roared Zeb impatiently. "Now leave your fancy boy be till later, an' fetch my rum!"

Catie felt Anthony tense, though his face didn't lose its smile as he looked over her head to Zeb. "The *lady,*" he said pointedly, "doesn't wish to hear your insults, any more than you deserve her attentions."

In an instant the taproom fell silent. Every eye was turned toward Catie and the two men, every ear strained to hear Zeb's reply.

Zeb shoved back his chair as he rose to face Anthony. "Catie Willman ain't no lady," he said belligerently. "She's a ha'penny rum-shop wench that's paid t' do as I say. An' you'll keep your fine nose out o' my say-so, if you don't want it broken."

"Shall I now?" asked Anthony with a mildness that fooled no one. "And here I was going to offer you the exact same advice."

Trapped between them, Catie looked frantically from Zeb to Anthony and back again, her hands twisting in her apron as she felt the hostility flaring on either side of her. The two men were matched in height, but Anthony, in his blue superfine jacket and embroidered waistcoat, was a gentleman, and what could such a gentleman know of tavern brawls? Zeb's muscular arms were larger from toiling in the shipyards than most men's thighs, and his strength was combined with both a notoriously short temper and a fearsome long knife that everyone in the Crossed Keys knew well to avoid.

Everyone, that is, except the Sparhawks. The two dark-haired cousins had come to stand behind Anthony, their good-natured drunkenness vanished as they curled their hands into fists at their sides. The tables around them had emptied with an unimaginable speed, with men clambering over chairs and benches to find a safer place—something Catie wished she could do, as well.

"You must not do this, Mr. Sparhawk," she said urgently, drawing herself up as tall as she could to appeal to Anthony. "I'm just as Zeb says, a serving lass, nothing more. I'm not worth *this!*"

"Hidin' behind the chit's petticoats, are you now, my lord?" taunted Zeb, mimicking Catie. "'Feared you'll soil yourself, are you, my lord?"

At last Anthony's smile vanished, his dark brows coming together in a single line as he guided Catie to the side and out of the way.

"Mind yourself, pet," he ordered, swiftly shrugging his arms free from his jacket and tossing it over the back of a chair. "This will be but the work of a moment."

"But Mr. Sparhawk, sir, you'll—"

"It's Anthony, sweet, just Anthony. None of this mistering between us." The quick, fleeting grin, almost boyish, was for her alone, as was the self-mocking wink. "Not now, and certainly not later."

"Anthony, is it?" taunted Zeb, shifting back and forth on his feet in anticipation. "Ah, Anthony's such a right manly name!"

From the corner of her eye, Catie saw Ben Hazard come trotting across the room, his round face puckered with anxious concern. No wonder, thought Catie— they all knew how dearly the last fight Zeb began had cost the tavern in broken crockery and chairs. And if the board that granted the keepers' licences learned that a party of Newport's finest young gentlemen had been injured here in a brawl, then the Crossed Keys could be ruined forever.

"Gentlemen, gentlemen, please!" cried Ben, his hands outstretched in his most conciliatory manner, to include both Zeb and Anthony. "Surely we can consider other, more peaceful ways to settle this dispute, eh?"

With a frown, Anthony glanced his way, and in that fraction of a second of inattention Zeb lashed out, his huge bunched fist flying through the air so fast that Catie shrieked. But though Zeb was fast, Anthony's reflexes were even faster. Suddenly Zeb buckled over, his arms flailing ineffectually as he gasped for breath, Anthony standing over him with his legs widespread and scarcely a single gold hair disarranged. With an indignant roar, one of Zeb's friends seized a spindle-back chair and swung it at Anthony, who twisted and ducked as Jon Sparhawk lunged forward. Amid the crash of splintered wood, the three of them toppled to the floor in a tangle of flailing arms and legs, knocking over a table and sending spoons flying and bottles and plates shattering.

"Catie, here!" shouted Rebeckah, dodging forward to grab Catie's hand and pull her clear. "Quick now, come with me!"

She shoved Catie over the counter of the bar and scrambled after her, slamming the grate back down for extra protection.

"Zeb and the others will kill those gentleman, I know it!" cried Catie as she and Rebeckah crouched together on the floor behind the bar, listening to the barrage of oaths and grunts and breaking wood.

"Nay, they won't, not by half." Unperturbed, Rebeckah eased the cork from the bottle of brandy she'd filched from the bar and drank deeply. "Gentry or common-bred, most men be the same as curs in the street when it comes to a good scrape."

"But they're—"

"No, they ain't," said Rebeckah flatly. "I told you them Sparhawks'd come down here for a bit o' sport, an' by Mary, they found it with Zeb an' his lads."

Unconvinced, Catie wrinkled her nose and tried not to imagine what was happening to Anthony Sparhawk's beautiful face. She'd seen too many fights not to.

Rebeckah cackled and poked Catie in the side. "But what the devil were you about, setting that gentleman off like that?"

"I did no such thing!" said Catie indignantly. She shielded her head with her arms as an empty bottle struck the grate above them and bits of slivered glass showered down. "I only went to that table because you dared me! You saw how it was!"

"Oh, aye, else I never would have believed it. Plain Miss Priss teasin' them Sparhawks into takin' on Zeb." Rebeckah shook her head as she took another long swallow of the brandy, then frowned as she cocked her head toward the door. "There come the watchmen. That'll put an end to th' sport for tonight, and us left to do the tidyin'."

At the sound of the harsh wooden rattle carried by the night watch, the sounds of the fight abruptly ended, replaced by running footsteps and shouted warnings as the combatants—and the customers—fled. Quickly Catie rose to peek through the grate, eager to see how Anthony had fared.

"That pretty man be long gone," said Rebeckah, rising more slowly as she recorked the brandy and slid it into her pocket with a fond pat. "Nor will he show his face round here again. His sort never do. Nay, by morn he'll forget he was even here, save for the bumps an' scrapes."

Forlornly Catie saw that Rebeckah was right. The taproom was empty, the floor littered with splintered furniture, puddles of spilled drink, and smashed dishes. Even the tavern's most prized possession, the colored engraving of the king, swung crazily from its single nail over the fireplace. Catie tried to tell herself it didn't matter, that *he* didn't matter, but, miserably, she knew she was lying.

"Best forget him, same as he's done with you," advised Rebeckah philosophically. "Besides, you're headed for trouble enough. Here comes ol' Ben, an' he don't look pleased."

One look at Ben Hazard's furious face, his cheeks livid and his thin lips pressed tightly together, and Catie knew with a sinking feeling that Rebeckah was right once again.

"Rebeckah, go to the kitchen and fetch cloths and pails to clean up this wretched mess," he ordered with an angry flick of his hand. "Nay, Catie Willman, you stay. I've words to say to you."

With obvious relief, Rebeckah scurried off, leaving Catie to face Ben's wrath alone. "I didn't mean to cause any trouble, sir," she began uneasily, "and if that's what—"

"For God's sake, girl, have you no wits?" With disgust he pulled off his wig and slapped it on the counter. "This—this *shambles* is the least of my trouble this night! I thought we had an understanding, Catie."

"An understanding, sir?" said Catie faintly.

"Aye, Miss Cate, and don't pretend we didn't. Before this, I'd believed that by your interest in this trade and your willingness to work at it you would be equally willing to share the profits, as well as the toil."

"Forgive me, Master Hazard, but I do not—do not follow you." It was exactly, horribly, as Rebeckah had predicted, the only role for plain, dutiful Catie Willman.

Ben sniffed and scowled and twisted his mouth to one side. "How can I make it more clear, Catie? A tavern needs a woman's eye to make it respectable and prosper, and I judged you able to fill that role. I've grand plans, Catie, enough to make us both proud. But the wife of a tavern owner must be a sober, hardworking woman, and after tonight—"

"The *wife?*" repeated Catie, her voice turning suddenly squeaky. "But you haven't asked for me, any more than I've agreed to accept you!"

"If I haven't spoken before this, it was because I did not feel such idle words were necessary between us." Impatiently he thrust his fingers through his wispy hair, still matted flat by his wig. "Be honest, Catie. What better offer are you likely to have?"

Tears of frustration stung her eyes. If she was honest with herself, the way Ben asked, then she'd have to admit that his offer was a handsome one, a chance to improve her station far beyond what she'd dreamed when she ran away from her stepfather's farm.

Yesterday, even this afternoon, Ben's offer would have been enough. But that would have been before she heard the sweet, empty praise of Anthony Sparhawk, and discovered how much her poor, parched heart ached to hear such words again, sweet words meant for her alone.

And with no answer she could bring herself to speak, she turned and fled. She ran through the taproom and the kitchen and out the back door to the yard, and she didn't stop until she reached the well, to lean against the rough bricks.

She didn't want to be sober and plain and capable, and she didn't want to work her life away as Ben Hazard's wife. She was only seventeen, and she wanted to be pretty and merry and praised by a gentleman with golden hair and red silk flowers on his waistcoat. She wanted—oh, Lord help her, she didn't know what she wanted, and with a muffled sob she buried her face against her forearm.

"Did they blame you for that foolish row, pet?" asked Anthony softly. "'Twas hardly your fault that we Sparhawk men regard such scrapes as entertainment."

Startled, Catie swiftly raised her head. He was standing there in the shadows on the other side of the well, his jacket and waistcoat gone, one sleeve of his fine linen shirt torn in a strip from the shoulder.

"Mr. Sparhawk!" Self-consciously she rubbed away her tears with the heel of her hand instead of taking the handkerchief he offered. "Oh, dear Lord, look at you! Are you hurt? I can take you into the kitchen and—"

"No, lass, I swear I'm none the worse for wear." He stepped into the moonlight to show he'd no hideous bruises or blackened eyes. "And for the last time, it's Anthony, not Mr. Sparhawk."

"Anthony, then." She frowned and clucked her tongue with dismay. "But look what's become of your beautiful clothes!"

"Ha! Old rags, not to be missed." Dramatically he held his arms out straight at his sides so that the tattered fabric fluttered in the breeze. "You know, I was afraid you wouldn't come."

She hoped the shadows hid her flush of pleasure.

He had come back, no matter what Rebeckah said, and he'd come back to see *her*. "Why did you take my side against Zeb?"

"What, because you're a serving girl in a sailors' tavern?" He let his arms drop back to his sides and walked around the well to join her. "Ah, that you must blame on my grandfather's teachings. His own chivalrous inclinations were wonderfully universal, an indubitable doctrine I espouse as my own, as well."

To her shame, she hadn't the faintest idea what he'd just told her. Such grand language the gentry used!

"But why?" she asked hesitantly, praying another question would not displease him. "Why me?"

"Because I wished it, pet. Because you're fresh and pretty, with marvelous, solemn eyes that shine like polished pewter." He was studying her intently, almost frowning, like an artist composing a painting. "You color most charmingly, too, you know, especially by moonlight."

"But I'm not pretty," she protested. "It's very gallant of you to say that foolishness about my eyes, but I know they're just gray, just as I know my face is too round and my hair's drab and straight. I *know* I'm plain. Everyone tells me so."

"Then everyone may go to the devil." Gently, easily, he drew her close, guiding her arms around his waist. "Someday you'll be more beautiful than all of them put together."

"But I—"

"Hush now, and listen to me." He cradled her face in his hands, stroking her cheeks with his thumbs. "The loveliest flowers are often the ones that take the longest to blossom. I can see the promise of real beauty in this charming little face already, and don't let anyone tell you otherwise."

For an endless moment, Catie let the sweetness of his words wash over her, before she forced herself to break away. "We can't stay here. Someone may see us from the tavern." Someone like Ben Hazard, she added mentally. How she'd hate for him to spoil this moment with his grumpy face! "Come, across here to the stable."

Shyly she took his hand. Anthony Sparhawk wasn't like the other men from the tavern that she'd always avoided. He was a gentleman, and he had defended her against Zeb. How could she not trust him?

"I was born on a farm," she explained as she led him across the shadow-filled yard to the stable that shared the well with the Crossed Keys, "and when I cannot bear the city crowds and noises any longer, I come here to be alone with the beasts. Mr. Freeman— he's the ostler—he understands, and lets me come and go as I please."

Carefully she unfastened the latch and slipped inside, pausing for Anthony to follow her up the ladder to the loft. Her feet slipped deep into the mounded hay, the fragrance musty and redolent of summer. She knelt beside the narrow window and looked out at the harbor and the ships at the moorings.

"When all the sails are furled like that, I think the masts look like trees," she said dreamily, the breeze from the harbor cool on her cheeks. "A whole magic, silvery forest on the water."

She heard the straw rustle as he came to kneel beside her. "How old are you, pet?"

"Seventeen," she admitted, hoping he wouldn't

think her a child. "But I've been working in Newport on my own since last spring."

"That makes seven years between us. Was I ever as young as you, I wonder?"

She turned and smiled. "Of course you were," she said. "Seven years ago."

"Of course." Gently he tugged off her white linen cap, letting her fine, pale hair spill over her shoulders. "In the morning I'll be sailing in one of those ships for England. After years of fighting the French for king and country, my grandfather's at last seen fit to reward me with a lieutenancy in a real regiment. My commission's waiting in London."

"London?" said Catie unhappily as she shook her hair back from her eyes. He might as well have said the moon. "When will you come back?"

"Ah, that only God in His mercy can answer. One year or ten, or maybe not at all." He spoke with such a brave melancholy that it tore at her heart, and impulsively she slipped her arms around him, eager to take the sorrow from his blue eyes.

"You must not talk that way," she said fiercely, pressing her cheek against the fine linen of his shirt. "You will come back, I know it."

He sighed, letting his hands settle around her waist to hold her against his chest. "A good soldier's life isn't his own, pet, and he never knows when it may be forfeit."

"But that's so sad!" cried Catie, pushing herself back so that she could search his face. With all his grim talk of war and soldiering, she had meant to comfort him, but she was the one who felt safe here, his arms around her making a special haven in the warm, fragrant straw. "How can you bear to sail from home, knowing you may not live to return?"

With infinite care, he slowly traced the bow of her upper lip. "You can help me bear it, sweet," he said, his voice deep and low. "Give me a memory to take with me."

He kissed her then, as lightly at first as his touch had been, brushing his mouth across her lips until they parted willingly for him. If he wished to take the memory of her kiss with him into battle, then she'd give it gladly. How, really, could she not?

But in the first instant, disappointment stung her, for he tasted unmistakably of rum. How could he share this same rare joy that she felt if his senses were clouded by liquor? Then he deepened the kiss, his mouth warm and sure, and she forgot the rum and everything else in the heady new sensations swirling through her.

Drawn into his passion, she scarcely noticed that he'd lowered her back into the rustling pillow of the straw, or that somehow her skirts had become tangled above her knee as he caressed the soft skin above her stockings and garters until she sighed into his mouth with pleasure.

But still she started when she felt his hand roam higher, and clumsily she tried to move away and push down her skirts.

"You—you must not," she gasped raggedly as she broke off their kiss. "No, Anthony, please."

"Yes, sweet lass, yes," he murmured, his breath warm on her ear. "I told you I was a chivalrous man, and I mean to prove it. You'll have your pleasure from me, be sure of that."

And Catie gasped, her protests forgotten as he kept his promise. She had no words to describe the delicious heat that filled her body as he kissed her and touched her again, or experience to warn her what would come next as her body arched with instinctive wantonness.

Another moment, her ravished senses pleaded with her conscience, *only another precious moment more.*

The pleasure spiraled dizzily upward, and her conscience fell silent. Lost in her own world, she didn't try to stop him as he shifted on top of her. He was a gentleman, her Anthony, and she would trust him not to harm her.

She *would* trust him; and then came the sharp, sudden hurt that ended that trust and the pleasure with it, and the helpless little cry tore from her heart when she realized too late what he'd done, what she'd done, and now could never undo.

Afterward he smiled down upon her as he stroked her cheek with the back of his hand and called her his own sweetest pet, coaxing her to smile, too. But she didn't smile; nor did she weep, either, not even when he heard the ribald, drunken bellow from the street and with an oath rolled off her to one side. All she did was close her eyes so that she would not have to see the shame of his nakedness.

"*Damn* Jon," muttered Anthony as he buttoned the fall of his breeches and bent to peer from the window into the street below. "He'll bring the whole bloody watch back here again."

He turned back to her, shaking his hair back from his face as he shoved his shirttails back into his waistband. "I must go now, pet," he said hurriedly. "I've still much to do, packing and such, before I sail, and besides, it's high time I stopped my sot of a cousin from braying like a jackass at the moon.''

She'd sat up by then, tucking her petticoats tightly over her legs and hugging her bent knees to her chest. She could not understand why there was no blood on her shift to prove she'd been a maid, and miserably she wondered if that was a sign of her wickedness and sin.

He fumbled in his pocket, his fingers jingling coins together. He held them out to her as he bent to kiss her farewell, silver coins shining in the moonlight that had lost all its magic.

"Go," she said softly, lowering her face to avoid his lips. Now she was only a fool, but if she took his money she would be something far worse. "Just—just go."

And without another word, he left. She listened to the ladder from the loft creak beneath his weight, and heard the thump of the latch as he let himself out, the echo of his footsteps fading down the street while one of the horses in the stalls below stirred and nickered sleepily.

Alone in the silence, she closed her eyes. No matter how tightly she curled herself, the cold, empty hollowness deep inside wouldn't go away. It was bad enough that she'd lost her maidenhead here in the straw like a common strumpet, to a man who'd never bothered to learn her name. But worse still was knowing that when Anthony Sparhawk took the innocence of her body, he'd also destroyed the innocence of her heart,

and her future with it. And that she would never be
able to forget.

Or forgive.

Chapter Two

Eight years later

*Newport
Rhode Island
December 1776*

The streets that should have been alive with people at this time of the morning were as quiet and still as if it were midnight. Houses and shops were shuttered. The market house was empty. Even the church bells failed to toll the hour. Only the raucous mewing of the gulls that wheeled over the lifeless ships in the harbor proved it was indeed day, rather than night.

Uneasily Major Anthony Sparhawk of His Majesty's Royal Welsh Fusiliers scanned the silent houses, sensing the hostility of the eyes that watched from behind the shutters. How many rifles and muskets and pistols were hiding there, too, ready to offer the only welcome he and his men could expect?

He rode at the head of his regiment, their bright red uniforms and tall fur caps making a brave show for the secret watchers on this cold, gray December morning. So far, they'd taken the island without a single casualty, and a blatant display of the king's forces like this was calculated to keep it that way. Besides, Rhode Islanders had never been as extreme in their politics as the mob in Boston were. Here, surely, King George would have more friends than enemies.

A day for rejoicing, thought Anthony. Hadn't they managed to capture the best harbor in the northern colonies? Perhaps at last the British luck was changing for the better. No wonder every brass button was proudly polished, every man's hat cocked to the same degree, every musket and bayonet held at the same precise angle, as they marched in practiced unison through the Newport streets Anthony remembered so well.

Eight years had passed since he was here last. To his eyes, the town looked much the same, and yet everything—*everything*—had changed.

He was a major now, an officer in one of the finest regiments in the army. And because the land where he was born, the New England he still thought of as his home, was in open rebellion against the king he'd sworn to serve, he was also now the enemy.

He tightened his chilled fingers around the reins, striving to get the blood flowing through his hands again. Like the rest of the British troops, he'd been soaked to the skin by an icy rain when they landed from the transports at Weaver's Cove, and two nights spent on a windswept hillside had left him feeling the ache in every one of the old wounds that marked his body. He'd be thirty-three his next birthday, and this wretched campaign against the American rebels had made him feel every day of it.

As if to mock his age even more, the youngest officer in the regiment, a lieutenant from Dorset whose voice had barely broken, came racing up to ride beside him.

"General Ridley's compliments, sir, and he says to tell you that you're to be quartered at...quartered at..." Peterson gulped and referred nervously to the crumpled paper in his hand. "At a tavern in Farewell Street. That's three streets to the north, sir, and—"

"I know perfectly well where Farewell Street lies," snapped Anthony irritably. He'd already received these orders once this morning, before they broke camp, and he didn't need to have them repeated as if he were in his dotage. "And I know the tavern in question."

"Of course, sir," said Peterson immediately, his cheeks flushing. "Forgive me, sir. I should have recalled your familiarity with the rebels' town, sir."

Anthony didn't answer. Oh, aye, he knew this town well, too well. Hadn't he spent half his summers here as a boy, clambering up and down the entire island with his Sparhawk cousins? It was the reason he'd been chosen as one of General Ridley's adjutants for the duration of the action in Rhode Island. A considerable honor, that, though one he hadn't particularly wished to receive.

Still the young lieutenant hung doggedly at Anthony's side, refusing to be dismissed. "The general said I was to take you to your quarters directly, sir. Your baggage is already there. Afterward he expects you to report to him, sir."

Briefly Anthony glared at the younger man, then swung his horse away from the ranks to follow. He'd

rather see his men properly cantoned, but being one
of Ridley's staff officers carried a whole different set
of responsibilities. If the general wished him to report
to the tavern now, he had no choice but to obey.

Ridley had made no secret of his reasons for quartering Anthony there, instead of with the rest of the
general's staff. Anthony was expected to make the
most of his colonial background and strive to win the
confidences of the tavernkeeper and his people, reporting whatever he learned.

Gathering information, Ridley had delicately called
it. Spying, Anthony had thought with disgust. Listening at keyholes in a public house seemed a low, dirty
task for a king's officer. But those were his orders,
and if such foolishness would help put down the rebels, then it was his duty to do it.

A pair of guards had already been posted on either
side of the door to the tavern, marking it as officers'
lodgings, and his regiment's flag—dark blue centered
with the three plumes of the Prince of Wales—hung
limply from the staff over the doorway. With disgust,
Anthony wondered how many of the local townspeo-
ple, particularly those sympathetic to the rebels, would
dare cross that threshold to reach the taproom on the
other side.

Briefly he paused on the steps, letting Peterson
swallow his impatience. Unlike many taverns that had
begun life as a private home, this one had clearly been
built to the purpose, a large, imposing public house
with a gambrel roof and an elaborately carved pedi-
ment, complete with a pineapple for hospitality over
the door. According to the gilded signboard, the tavern
was now called Hazard's, and from the fresh coat of

dark red paint and the new kitchen ell to the rear, Mr. Hazard had clearly prospered.

But to Anthony's surprise, no one came to greet them as they stepped inside. Whatever Hazard's politics, it was poor business to keep guests waiting. Anthony unhooked his cloak and walked into the front room off the hall to warm his hands over the fire. The furnishings were elegant enough to grace a private parlor: mahogany chairs cushioned in leather, tavern tables with polished brasses, a *chinoiserie* mirror over the mantel and framed engravings on the walls. From the kitchen drifted the aroma of roasting, seasoned beef, tempting enough to make Anthony's mouth water in anticipation. No ordinary rum shop, this, he thought with approval; lodging here would be infinitely more comfortable than a water-soaked tent on a windswept hillside.

That memory alone was enough to make Anthony lean closer to the fire, relishing the warmth clear through his body. "Have you met this host of ours, Peterson?" he asked. "He's being so dilatory in his greeting that I'm beginning to suspect the fellow doesn't exist."

"He doesn't," said a woman behind him, her voice brittle with hostility. "At least he doesn't any longer. My husband died two years ago of apoplexy, and thankful I am that he's spared the sight of this house overrun with red-coated soldiers."

"Then perhaps, ma'am," answered Anthony, "it is also well that he died before he saw his colony turned traitor to His Majesty."

Before he turned to face her, Anthony drew himself up to his full height, determined to let the woman feel the full impact of that officer's uniform. In the black riding boots with the silver spurs, he stood over six feet, and in his immaculately cut red coat with blue facings and regimental lace over the white waistcoat and breeches, his sword hanging at his hip and the rose-colored sash of a staff officer around his waist, he was confident that he cut a far more imposing figure than any of his counterparts among the shabby American forces.

"Your servant, ma'am," he said, and smiled, depending on the reliable charm of that smile to complete the work of the uniform. With women, anyway, it generally did.

But not, apparently, with this one. "My servant, or my oppressor?" she asked acidly. "You must be one or the other, for I can't see how you could possibly be both."

"Mistress Hazard," said Peterson hastily, "may I introduce Major Anthony Sparhawk of the Twenty-third Regiment, adjutant to General Ridley. Major Sparhawk, Mistress Catharine Hazard, proprietress of this establishment."

Anthony smiled again and bowed slightly in acknowledgment, while she in her turn did nothing. Blast her impertinence, he thought irritably. Not only was it an insult to the crown he represented, but such rudeness stung his pride, as well. Mrs. Hazard was a beautiful woman, and beautiful women seldom scorned him like this.

In peacetime she'd be too young to be a widow, perhaps only in her middle twenties, and far too young for the responsibility of running so large a tavern. Her hair was the pale color of new wheat, her eyes a solemn gray that was at odds with a mouth that could, he suspected, blossom into ripe, lush temptation under more auspicious circumstances. She dressed with a peculiar blend of respectability and elegance in a flowered wool gown with a kerchief of sheer embroidered lawn tied over the front, a starched apron around her small waist and a gold locket in the shape of a heart pinned to the front of her bodice.

"You will forgive me, Major Sparhawk, if I have left you too long to enjoy this fine fire and this handsome, comfortable room," she said, her sarcasm impossible to overlook. "I am somewhat shorthanded today, you see. A number of my people fled when they heard you and your brethren had come to save us from ourselves."

"It is seldom the way of war to be agreeable, ma'am," said Anthony evenly, determined to keep his temper. He knew she was baiting him, but the knowledge didn't make it any easier to bear. "Perhaps you should be grateful instead that our coming was so peaceable, and that none of your people were wounded or killed in the process."

She cocked one eyebrow and tipped her head, her gray eyes narrowing skeptically. "Grateful? Oh, I'd be a good deal more grateful if I weren't expected to offer food and shelter to you and your men. I'm told I'll have two dozen soldiers sleeping on mats in my attic alone."

"You will receive just compensation for the quarters, ma'am," said Peterson promptly, "and the men will receive their usual provisions, both fresh and salt. I thought I'd explained that well enough before."

But Anthony doubted she even heard the lieutenant,

her gaze was so fixed on him. "What of my four maid-servants, major? They are accustomed to attending gentlemen and ladies of the better sort, not a troop of rough soldiers."

"You have my assurance, ma'am, that the women will be unharmed," said Anthony. If the maidservants were half as prickly as their mistress, then his men were the ones who'd need defending, not the other way around. "There will be no problems with my men. I give you my word upon it, both as a gentleman and an officer."

To his surprise, Mrs. Hazard abruptly lost her studied composure as bright pink patches appeared on either cheek. "Your word as a gentleman, sir? As an officer?"

"Yes, ma'am," he said, intrigued by the change the blush made in her face, "my word as both, and you've no reason to doubt either."

"Indeed." Her mouth twisted into a tight little smile that made no sense to Anthony, and then, with a sudden flurry of petticoats, she turned on her heel. "If you will but follow me, Major, I'll show you to your room."

Anthony gathered his hat and cloak, nodded to Peterson, and followed her to the staircase, still wondering what he'd done or said to make her blush so becomingly. He wished he knew for certain; he'd like to do it again.

Sorting through the jingling keys on her ring, she walked up the stairs briskly before Anthony, giving him an unintentional but appealing display of her ankles. Her yellow thread stockings matched her gown, the worked flowers the same pink and blue, and he smiled to himself. No matter that the British army had invaded her town, Mistress Hazard had still found the time and presence of mind this morning to match her stockings to her gown when she dressed.

"I have put you here in the green room, Major," she said as she unlocked the door and pushed it open, standing to one side to let him pass. "I trust it will suit?"

"How could it not, ma'am?" Anthony tossed his hat and cloak on the bed, noting with satisfaction that his trunk and saddlebags had already arrived. Like the rest of the tavern, the room was simply but elegantly furnished, the tall-posted bed hung with the dark green chintz that must have given the room its name. "We poor soldiers seldom have such grand quarters."

Her glance alone managed to scornfully dismiss his comment for the gallantry it was. "According to the lieutenant, you'll have a cord of wood for your fire delivered here each week. I suggest you draw your curtains tightly around the bed at night, Major Sparhawk. Clearly your dear king is unfamiliar with Rhode Island winters, else he would have granted his officers three cords instead of one."

With her arms folded over her chest, she walked across the room to the window. She moved gracefully, the ring of keys swinging from her waist and clinking with each step. "I thought you would prefer this room in the front, where you and your guards can see who comes and goes and make sure none of us wicked rebels tries to escape."

But this time Anthony wasn't listening to her gibes. The weak winter sun was slanting through the window, lighting the full curve of her cheek in a way that seemed oddly familiar. He thought again of how she'd blushed, and that, too, helped drag up some fragment of a memory.

"We've met before, Mrs. Hazard, haven't we?" It was less a question than a statement, and he frowned as he stepped closer to her, trying to find her place in his past. "Here in Newport, long ago. At a party, perhaps, a dance or assembly?"

"You're mistaken, Major," she said quickly, too quickly for it to be anything but a lie. Restlessly she touched her fingers to the polished gold locket on her bodice. "You and I would never have been guests at the same houses."

He waved his hand impatiently, as if to brush aside her denial. "I told you it would have been long ago, long before this rebellion. I was sickly as a lad, and my grandparents sent me here to take the sea air. Even after my health improved, I returned from affection alone. I stayed with my uncle, Captain Gabriel Sparhawk. Perhaps at his house, we might have—"

She stared at him, openly incredulous. "You truly have no shame, no loyalties, do you? For you to *dare* to speak of a gentleman as fine and good as Gabriel Sparhawk, a gentleman I've been honored to know both in business and in friendship?"

Anthony's frown deepened. "And why should I not speak of my own uncle?"

"Why not, indeed, considering everything else that has befallen him and his poor wife these last days?"

"I do not—"

"No, you do not and you did not," she said sharply, her eyes flashing. "Or will you pretend that you didn't know your uncle was on your general's list of rebels to be taken prisoner? At least his true friends saw to it that he escaped in time, he and Mistress Sparhawk and their last daughter Rachel. At least now they're safe from *you*."

Anthony listened, considering how much of her raving to believe. In Boston and on Long Island he'd seen himself how cunning the rebels could be at manipulating emotions with half-truths for their own purposes, and Mrs. Hazard could well be doing exactly that.

He had not heard from his uncle or his cousins for years, but given the mails between old England and new, that was hardly unusual. As soon as he learned that the regiment was bound for Newport, of course he'd thought of his relatives there, but it was inconceivable that a gentleman as intelligent and respected as his uncle Gabriel would have let himself be swayed to support treason.

For whatever reason, then, the Hazard woman was lying. But what the devil did she hope to gain by doing so?

"My uncle and his family would never have cause to fear me," he said, carefully watching Mrs. Hazard's face. "He must know that, but if you tell me where I might find him, I'll be happy to reassure him and my aunt myself."

Instantly the woman's face shuttered against him. "Forgive me, Major Sparhawk, but in truth I cannot say."

"Cannot," he asked, "or will not?"

"Either one amounts to much the same thing, doesn't it, Major?" She smoothed the sleek wings of her hair with her fingertips, making sure no loose strands trailed from beneath her cap. "Now, if there's nothing more you'll be requiring from me, I have other matters to tend to."

She left him by the window, her head bowed to avoid meeting his eyes as she began to close the door after her.

"One last question, Mrs. Hazard," called Anthony, and reluctantly she looked back. He smiled slowly, almost teasingly, holding her attention for a fraction longer than was necessary.

"Mrs. Hazard, ma'am. You've been so good as to house my men in your attic and my junior officers in your lesser rooms, and you've been especially kind to grant me this splendid chamber for my own use. But where, ma'am, will that leave you to lay your own weary head this night?"

"Your concern touches me, Major Sparhawk. Where shall I sleep?" She smiled with an insolence that challenged his own. "In my own bed, behind a locked door, with a loaded musket on the pillow beside me. Good day to you, Major. And may the devil rot your red-coated soul in the black hell you deserve."

The door clicked shut, and Anthony smiled. If she wanted a battle from him, then a battle she'd get. He'd make her his second, more personal, Rhode Island campaign, another chance to subdue another rebel. And before he was done, he meant to make her surrender every bit as complete.

An hour later, her heart still beating too fast, Catie watched from the window of her bedchamber as Anthony Sparhawk finally left the tavern with two other officers, his unpowdered golden hair gleaming in the moment before he settled his hat. With a muffled groan, Catie closed her eyes and sank into the nearest chair, and wondered at the impossibly cruel trick that fate had played upon her.

At least she'd had some warning from the young lieutenant. If she'd walked into the front room to find *him* there without it, she felt sure, she would have fainted dead away from the shock. He was, if anything, more handsome than she'd remembered, his face more ruggedly masculine, and the easy, inborn charm that had been her undoing so long ago was there still, too.

A week ago, she would have laughed at anyone who told her that Anthony Sparhawk would come back into her life. Didn't she have more than enough Sparhawks in it already?

It was Gabriel Sparhawk who had long ago loaned Ben the money to buy Hazard's, with the stipulation that the tavern serve only Sparhawk rum, and even after her husband paid back the debt, Gabriel had remained involved with the business as a silent partner. After Ben's death, Catie had come to regard Gabriel as a friend, as well, a trusted and powerful business advisor who helped make certain she could keep the tavern in her name. With his support, she'd been able to prosper where most other widows would have foundered and failed.

But she'd gained more than mere bookkeeping from the Sparhawks. Through the example of the old captain's wife, Mariah, Catie had learned to speak and act like the gentry, and to match her manners and clothing to theirs. Soon more and more of the tavern's custom-

ers had been gentry, as well, drawn by curiosity and
the Sparhawks' recommendations and won by Catie's
hospitality.

Yet not once in all that time had either Gabriel or
Mariah mentioned a nephew named Anthony, and
Catie had secretly rejoiced. It made perfect sense: Anthony had chosen to be a soldier, and soldier's lives
were notoriously short.

But not, it seemed, short enough. What were the
phenomenal odds that Anthony Sparhawk's regiment
would be among those sent to subdue the American
colonies, and then, even more unlikely, one of the
three sent to invade Newport? Before this, the island
had been considered impregnable, protected by nature
and defended by the fort on Goat Island, and no one
had seriously thought the British would even attempt
to take the best harbor in New England.

But dare they had, and, worse yet, they'd succeeded,
and now here she was, with Anthony Sparhawk beneath her roof. Once before, he'd come close to ruining her life, and now—Lord, he could bring her
whole careful world crashing down around her.

With trembling fingers Catie unfastened the locket
from her bodice and opened it. Inside one half lay
curled a wisp of her daughter's silvery baby hair, tied
with a red thread, while on the other was the portrait
Catie had had painted of Belinda two years ago, on
her fifth birthday. The artist had perfectly captured the
little girl's serious smile and the wide green eyes that
looked upon the world with a wisdom beyond her
years.

So much like her mother, everyone said, the very
image of Catie. Ben had always laughed and said what

a blessing it was that his darling Belinda hadn't favored her father instead.

But Belinda did favor her father, thought Catie miserably. Lord help them both, she *did,* more than anyone could ever have dreamed possible.

"Mrs. Hazard, there be— Oh, forgive me, mistress, but the door was open." Self-consciously Hannah ducked her head, giving Catie time to compose herself. Hannah had worked for Ben Hazard long before he hired and then wed Catie, and the older woman's cookery was one of the main reasons that he had prospered.

"No harm done, Hannah," said Catie as she dabbed at her eyes with the corner of her apron and forced herself to smile. "'Twas my fault, leaving the door ajar like that. With all these wretched Britishers underfoot, I'll have to change my ways, won't I?"

"Yes, ma'am," said Hannah with obvious relief. Though she was at least thirty years Catie's senior, Catie was the mistress, and mistresses were supposed to be the strong ones that everyone else depended upon.

But where, thought Catie unhappily, was *she* supposed to turn for comfort?

"Yes, indeed, Hannah," she said, closing the locket with a soft click to repin it to her bodice. "There are many things that must change, whether we wish them to or not."

Hannah's glance followed the locket. "You're fretting over your little girl, aren't you?" she said sympathetically. "I'm sure Miss Belinda's worrying over you, as well. But you did right to send her away, mistress. A house full o' rough men's no place for a sweet angel like Miss Belinda.''

Catie nodded, her smile tight. It wasn't the score of rough men under her roof that she feared so much as the one very polished major. When two nights ago, at the first news of the invasion, she sent Belinda from Newport to stay with a married couple she knew near Nantasket, she'd had no idea how wise a precaution it would prove to be.

She rose briskly, determined to put aside her own worries. "Now, Hannah, I want you to make sure that you keep the cellar locked, and that you leave nothing—*nothing*—unattended in the kitchen as long as we must house these particular guests," she warned. "While that puppy of a lieutenant assured me his men will receive daily rations from their quartermaster, I don't believe for a minute they'll be able to resist trying to steal a taste of your cooking."

"Don't know a man what can, mistress," said Hannah proudly. "But any of them lobsterbacks come creepin' into my kitchen, an' they'll answer to my cleaver."

"We should have had you and your cleaver on the beach at Weaver's Cove instead of that fool militia," said Catie wryly, only half jesting. Certainly she and Hannah would have made a better show of defending their home. "Now, as for supper—"

"Beggin' your pardon, mistress," Hannah interrupted, "but Cap'n Jon's still waitin' downstairs at the back door. That's why I came up here, to tell you."

"Captain Sparhawk's here? *Now?*" Without waiting for an answer, Catie gathered her skirts and hurried down the back stairs to the kitchen. Jon Sparhawk was known to be a brave man, a daring man, but he was tempting fate to come to Hazard's when it was so full of British soldiers.

Yet when she reached the kitchen, the room was empty, Hannah's pie crust sitting half-crimped in its pan on the table, the back door closed and latched. Puzzled, Catie went to bolt the door. Perhaps Jon Sparhawk had left to avoid one of the British guards, or perhaps, more likely, he'd simply realized how foolish it was for him to come to the tavern now.

The man's hand closed over Catie's mouth before she could scream, his other arm locking around her waist to drag her back from the door and window beside it. Frantically Catie plunged against him, struggling to break free, but the man only tightened his grip further, pinning her arms against her sides. He was so much bigger than she was, so much stronger, and, terrified, she instinctively seized the one defense left to her: as hard as she could, she bit the palm of his hand.

With a yowl of pain, the man released her. Stumbling forward, Catie grabbed the rolling pin from the table and wheeled round to face him.

"For God's sake, Catie, did you have to *bite* me?" demanded Jon Sparhawk indignantly as he cradled his wounded hand.

"Did you have to scare me out of my wits?" Catie glared at him, the rolling pin still in her hand. In all the time she'd known Jon, he'd never dared treat her this way, and she didn't like it, not at all. "With everything else that's happening in this town, I certainly don't need you creeping about my house playing footpad!"

"I'm not 'playing' at anything, Catie. No one in

Newport is.'' He scowled down at the bright red marks
Catie's teeth had left in his hand. ''I didn't want you
to scream and raise a fuss, that was all. Did you know
your yard is full of those British bastards?''

''They're in my yard, my attic, and my best bed-
chambers,'' said Catie with disgust. She tossed the
rolling pin back on the table, dipped a rag in the water
bucket and held it out to Jon for his hand. ''They're
probably under the very bedsteads, as well, if I cared
to look. How else would I know your cousin is one
of them?''

Jon looked up sharply. ''Then it is Anthony?''

''Of course it is,'' said Catie, praying she'd be able
to keep her voice even. Though she had known Jon
for years, he had never made the connection between
Ben Hazard's wife and the nervous serving girl she'd
been at the Crossed Keys, and she had no wish for
him to realize it now. ''I wouldn't have sent the message to you if it wasn't your cousin. There is, you
know, a certain family resemblance.''

''Oh, aye, no doubt of that,'' he said. ''Even though
Anthony's turned traitor, his face would still mark him
as a Sparhawk.''

He dropped into the chair beside the table, the skirts
of his coat falling back so that Catie could see the
pistols in his belt, silver-mounted and deadly elegant.

Purposefully she looked away. No matter what the
circumstances, she didn't approve of guns in her
house, but she didn't wish to challenge Jon on it now.
''He thinks we're the ones who are the traitors, Jon.''

Wearily Jon shook his head. His jaw was stubbled
black, his eyes ringed from sleeplessness, and his

clothes so rumpled that Catie doubted he'd been home to sleep since the British landed.

"Anthony wouldn't say that if he'd stayed here at home, where he could see how bad things have become. He'll come round to our side. You'll see. Once he learns how Father's been driven away—"

"He knows already." Catie's hands tightened into fists at her sides. "Though he pretended not to, and tried to trick me into saying more. Not a quarter hour past, he left for the general's headquarters."

Jon swore, long and furiously. "To my father's house, you mean."

Catie nodded. "The only loyalty your cousin has now is to that blessed red coat of his."

"Then they've poisoned him against his own people," he said flatly. "There's no other explanation. I cannot believe—"

"Believe it, Jon, for it's true," said Catie vehemently. "Two minutes in your cousin's company and you'd see for yourself. He's not an American any longer. He's one of them now, the worst kind of arrogant British officer, and he doesn't care a fig for what happens to you or your parents."

Jon's expression hardened, the lines carved deep on either side of his mouth. "Then we'll have to treat him with the same high regard, won't we?"

He lowered his voice to a conspirator's rough whisper. "As long as he's under your roof, Catie, I want you to watch him. Listen to his conversations, note who comes to see him, charm him into trusting you. Then tell me whatever you learn."

Startled, Catie drew back, her hands clasped tightly together at her waist. She hadn't expected Jon to ask her to do *that,* and she didn't want to, not at all. To charm Anthony Sparhawk no, she couldn't do it.

"I can't, Jon," she said, faltering. "I just—I *can't.*"

"Oh, aye, you can, Catie, and you will," said Jon firmly. "You'll have chances to be near him that none of the rest of us will. It's not that much to ask. Think of all the men risking their very lives for the cause."

But if she did as he asked, her own life would be at stake, too. Already Anthony had nearly recognized her. The more time she spent in his company, the more likely it was that he'd be able to remember who she was. And once he did, her carefully ordered world would collapse like a wobbly house of playing cards.

"You don't know what you ask, Jon," she said miserably, unable to explain. "I can't—"

"You will do it, lass," said Jon, and the harsh edge in his voice warned Catie to obey. "Not just for the cause of freedom. You'll do it for my father and my mother, as well. After all my family's done for you, Catie Hazard, you *will* do this for us."

Her conscience twisting the fear around her heart, Catie stared down at the pistols at his waist. Such guns weren't an affectation with Jon; he'd use them if he had to. She thought again of how he'd trapped her earlier, and now she shivered at the thought of what he could have done. This was the other side of the Sparhawk family, the ruthless, violent side that she'd heard whispered of, but had never seen in the front room at Hazard's, the side that had made them their fortunes as privateers and in a score of other risky ventures.

Including, she realized now, her own.

Her shoulders drooped, and she touched the locket

with her daughter's picture. For Belinda's sake, she didn't want to do as Jon asked, but for Belinda's sake, too, she knew she had no choice.

"Very well," she said softly. "But I'll send word to you, mind? You must promise me not to come here again. It's too dangerous."

Jon's heavy brows curled down with contempt. "War *is* dangerous, Catie. If I hadn't wanted to do what I could against the British here in Newport, why, I would have taken the children and scurried off to Providence with my parents."

"I almost wish you had," said Catie wistfully, thinking not only of Jon's family, but of Belinda, too. His three children had dozens of doting aunts, uncles, and grandparents to watch over them, but she and Belinda had only each other. "You know that's what Betsey would have wished."

His face grew studiously emotionless, the way it always did when he spoke of the pretty young wife he'd lost in childbirth two years before. "Betsey wished for many things."

"This is one wish you could grant her," said Catie gently. "All I'm saying is that I—that *we*—must be careful, Jon, very careful. Your cousin Anthony is not a man to take lightly."

"And you be careful, too, Mrs. Hazard." Unexpectedly he smiled, almost ruefully. "I know what I'm asking, Catie, and what it must cost you. You're the most kindhearted woman I know, and here I am trying to turn you into a low, sneaking spy."

But Catie's smile in return was bleak. He *didn't* know what he asked, and, God willing, he never would. As for being low and sneaking, she'd crossed that boundary long ago.

"It won't be that hard for me, Jon," she said softly. "I'm wonderfully good at keeping secrets."

Chapter Three

"**Y**ou've done well, Major Sparhawk, very well," said General Ridley as he leaned back in his chair, making a little tent of his spread fingers on the mound of his belly. "Don't think for a moment that I don't appreciate the importance of your contribution to this campaign. That little cove you suggested for the landing was a capital choice, sir, a capital choice. We've taken the best harbor in the north, one of the richest cities, too, and not a single man lost. I'd like to see Howe say the same, eh?"

He chuckled, his watery blue eyes glancing around the room, past Anthony, with smug pleasure. "And I ask you, Major, have you ever seen more handsome quarters! A house fit for a gentleman, this one, even an English gentleman, eh?"

Anthony nodded curtly, not trusting himself to say or do more. The house that the general had appropriated for his headquarters *was* the grandest one in town, as was proper. The pale winter sun filtered through tall windows hung with red damask that matched the coverings on the chairs. The mahogany tea table was set with a delicate service of Canton ware, the translucent porcelain rimmed with gold, and more of the china filled the two tall cupboards that flanked the fireplace. The wall paneling and the mantelpiece were the finest work of Newport woodworkers, as was the stairway in the front hallway, where candles had already been lit in the polished brass sconces.

Without doubt, the house was as fit for an English general as it was for an English gentleman, the best of everything. As it should be, Anthony told himself grimly. As it *must* be.

"Pity to think of all this wasted on a rebel rascal," continued Ridley. "Too bad we let the old rogue slip away from us, else I would have packed him off to London for trial. Still and all, he won't be able to cause us any more trouble here. His name was Sparhawk, too. Kin of yours, y'think?"

"A distant connection," said Anthony, as evenly as he could. "An uncle."

Blast it all, the Hazard woman had been *right*. How could a man who had served the king as well as had Gabriel Sparhawk—a man who'd fought under the British flag in at least three wars—now join with that ragtag pack of rebels? And what in blazes had become of his aunt and cousins? Unconsciously Anthony gripped the carved arm of his chair, struggling to control the emotions that roiled within him.

Ridley grunted, idly rubbing his thumb across one of his waistcoat buttons. "Uncle, eh? Someone told me he'd been a privateer in the old Spanish war. Damned successful at it, too, from the look of this place." The general's gaze wandered beyond the top of Anthony's head. "You know my wife's parlor in

Bath. Do you think she'd fancy that looking glass there, the gilt one with the gewgaws on the top? There's a dispatch ship sailing for home tomorrow, and I thought I'd send dear Chloe a little gift to keep me well in her thoughts.''

Anthony twisted in his chair to look over his shoulder, more to mask his feelings than to appraise the looking glass. Though Ridley's own orders had been explicit about looting, he wasn't overparticular about helping himself. It was common enough knowledge among the other officers, and cause for more than a few jests, about how crowded dear Chloe's parlor would be by the end of the war.

But this time Anthony wouldn't be among those laughing, not when his aunt Mariah's looking glass was to be the plunder. Damnation, they must have fled with only the clothes on their backs, for everything else in the house to have been left exactly as he remembered it.

But would good could come of remembering? Better, so much better, to forget his uncle's desk as it had been, piled high with shipping manifests and bills of lading, and how Uncle Gabriel would always find the time to break away from his work to talk to him and to Jon, to show them some rare coin from China or explain how the jiggling needle of a compass worked, the three of them standing there together, with the summer sun slanting in through the tall window and the sweet fragrance of Aunt Mariah's gingerbread drifting up from the kitchen.

"Yes, I do believe the looking glass would suit Chloe," the general was saying. "It's nearly a match for the one I sent her from Boston."

Slowly Anthony turned back in his chair. How that woman at the tavern must be laughing by now, her silver-gray eyes fair bubbling over with mirth at his expense. She'd been right about his aunt and uncle, of course, while he'd been appallingly wrong in his assumptions. What a pompous, blustering, ignorant fool he must have seemed to her!

Abruptly he shoved back his chair and rose, his sword swinging back against his thigh. "I'm certain Mrs. Ridley will be most pleased with whatever gift you make to her," he said with a curt bow. "But if you'll be so good as to excuse me, General, there are a good many other matters that need my attention."

Ridley's brows rose toward the front of his wig with mild surprise. "I'd say that such matters are my decision, sir, not yours." He waved his hand back toward the chair. "And I say you stay until I dismiss you. Unless in your present choler you find my company intolerable, eh?"

It was all the reproof Anthony needed. He'd always been known as a moderate man, one who kept his temper in check. At least he had been before now. Swiftly he bowed again and sat, mentally cursing the woman who'd let him make such a fool of himself. If she'd been more honest with him, if only she hadn't been so damnably coy, then perhaps—

"You'd do well to watch yourself, Sparhawk," continued the general, subtly replacing the air of a genial country squire with something harder, sharper and far more astute than his enemies would have dreamed possible. At once Anthony was on his guard. Off the battlefield, Ridley seldom showed this side to his subordinates, and its appearance now could mean nothing good.

"Sir," said Anthony. It was the only possible answer.

"Sir yourself, man, and listen to me." Impatiently he drummed his thick-knuckled fingers on the top of the desk. "You know I trust you, Sparhawk. You've been with me for more years than I care to count, damn me if you haven't, by my side through all the worst of this wretched campaign. Breed's Hill, Long Island, especially that miserable showing at Lexington—not once have you given me cause to doubt your loyalty."

"Yes, sir," said Anthony stiffly, already guessing what was coming. "Thank you, sir."

"Why else d'you think I've made you my adjutant here, eh? But there's plenty of others here who say otherwise, and I can't say I fault 'em for it." He leaned forward, his gaze shrewdly appraising. "You don't want me in this house, do you, Major? You're thinking I don't belong here. You're thinking I'm taking the place of that blackguard uncle of yours, and you're thinking of him instead of your king."

"But, sir, I can—"

"No, sir, you hear me out," ordered Ridley, each word crackling with authority, and antagonism, too. "I was sent here to put down this rebellion, and I mean to do it. But, by harry, how can I be expected to subdue these damnable colonials when I've someone who sympathizes with the bloody rascals in the fore of my own regiment, eh?"

Anthony inhaled sharply. "Are you challenging my honor, sir, or my loyalty to my king?"

"What, and have it said that I'd called out one of my own officers?" retorted Ridley. "I'm too clever for that nonsense, Sparhawk, and so are you. But what else will people think, eh? This town as much as belonged to your people, scoundrels that they are, yet you turned your back on them as pretty as kiss-my-hand. Who's to say you won't do the same to us in return?"

Anthony lunged forward, the rank between them forgotten as his long-simmering temper finally boiled over, and he struck his fist down hard on the desk, inches away from the general's face. "*I* say it, and to hell with the man who dares say otherwise!"

"How dare you—"

"Sweet Mary, Ridley, if you slander me and then can't explain your meaning any better than that, then I—"

"Remember yourself, Sparhawk!" barked Ridley. "At once, sir!"

The order shattered Anthony's anger, years of training racing to silence him. Orders were to be obeyed; every good soldier knew that.

So what the devil was he doing now? Two steps behind him the general's sentries had rushed through the door with their muskets raised, the gleaming barrels aimed at him, at *him*, and in that horrible moment he realized how close he was to facing a court-martial and the end of everything he'd worked so hard for.

Breathing hard, he jerked his hand back as if he'd been burned and shook his head in disbelief, appalled by what he'd done. Once again he'd lost control. To threaten his superior before witnesses, to raise his voice and bellow like a madman—for the sake of this one insane minute, his career might be over and done, and his life with it.

He drew himself up as tall as he could, his eyes staring impassively ahead. "Forgive me, sir. I do not know what came over me, but I give you my word that it will not happen again."

"The devil it won't." Furiously Ridley glared at Anthony as he waved the sentries from the room. "Your unforgivable behavior here only proves that I'm right to doubt your allegiances."

"But sir, I assure you that—"

"I want none of your assurances, Sparhawk," snapped the general, his face purple above his neck-cloth. "I want your loyalty. Now you watch yourself, watch every last bloody step you take. Because I'll be watching, too, and next time, an outburst like that will break you. Do you understand me, Major Sparhawk?"

"Perfectly, sir," said Anthony, and this time, when he bowed to take his leave, the general didn't stop him. "Good day, sir."

But instead of feeling relief at having escaped the punishment he deserved, Anthony continued to smolder with anger as he stalked through the still-empty streets. By the time he reached Hazard's, he felt close to strangling with blind fury and frustration. The winter sun had set, and supper, such as it was, would be served soon, but the very notion of sitting down to dine with the other officers was more than he could stomach. Instead, he turned to the stable in back, ordering the black gelding that he'd brought from Boston to be saddled.

"Now what shall I fetch for the others, Major?" asked the groom, trying to look around Anthony and out the door into the yard. "How many more do you reckon be riding wit' you?"

Anthony swung himself up into the saddle. "There are no others," he said, gathering the reins in his fingers. "I'll be riding alone."

The man stared up at him, openmouthed with surprise. "Alone, sir?"

"Alone," repeated Anthony curtly, and turned the gelding's head toward the street.

He understood the groom's surprise. He carried no weapon beyond his dress sword, and even half-hidden by his cloak, his uniform coat, glittering with lace and polished buttons, would stand out wherever he went. For him to travel unattended on this island was risky enough; to do so after dark was madness. But tonight Anthony *was* mad, or close to it, and as soon as he reached the edge of town he let the gelding have his head, urging the horse to race wildly into the darkness.

He headed south, then west, following the curve of the coast as the road became little more than a worn path. The way hadn't changed over the years, and he followed it effortlessly, without having to consider his route. Overhead, pale clouds scudded across the stars and the silver moon in the icy-clear winter sky. The wind was cold here, near the sea, as cold as it had been when they landed, two days before, but tonight Anthony scarcely felt it.

At last he came to the last of the land, a rocky outcropping called Damaris Point, jutting into the sea, and he jerked the tired horse to a halt. Here he was alone; here, at last, he could think.

Damnation, he *was* English. How could the general say otherwise? Since he left the colonies, he'd come to think and act and feel like a true English gentleman, one born in London's shadow, instead of in a house of peeled logs on the banks of the Connecticut River. He had learned to prize the neat, well-drilled precision of a line of soldiers in battle over the strike-and-run Indian fighting he'd practiced as a boy. He had put aside the rough ways of the frontier and instead perfected the hard-edged confidence of an officer in the most powerful army in Europe. His honor was his guide, his king his master, and in his well-ordered London world, that had always been everything.

Yet he was still a Sparhawk, too. He couldn't deny that, either. Staring out beyond the rocks and waves, Anthony pulled off his hat and stuffed it beneath his coat, letting the salt-filled wind from the water whip against his face and clear away the confusion in his thoughts.

Of course he'd been shocked by the news of his uncle's treachery. How could he not have been? In those early, homesick years, he'd written to his Newport relatives as often as he could, whenever he heard of a ship bound for the colonies. But because he moved so often with his regiment, he had had no permanent address of his own where they in turn might write to him. Without replies, his own correspondence had dwindled and then finally stopped. Otherwise, he might have known of his uncle's dangerous inclinations, and wouldn't have been taken so completely by surprise.

Aye, surprise, that was it. His uncle's decision to embrace the traitors' cause was unfortunate, even lamentable, considering it had brought about his ruin, but that was no reason for Anthony to destroy himself, too. His duty was to protect the decent, loyal subjects of the king and to subdue the rascals who'd broken the peace of the land. If that included his uncle, then so be it. His duty to the crown must come first, and the rest would follow. That was what his grandfather had taught him so long ago, and his grandfather had always been right.

Autumn was slow in coming that summer he turned eight. It was the middle of September, yet only the very tops of the maple trees had begun to turn from green to red, and there were still tall stalks of snapdragons— rose, white, palest yellow—nodding around the base of the sundial in Grandmother's garden. A long summer, but a peaceful one, too, the first that Anthony could remember when the Frenchmen and their Iroquois allies hadn't threatened the wide valley around Plumstead. Otherwise Grandfather would never have brought him out to these woods to hunt, far from the big house or any of the lesser farms. Most likely he wouldn't have been on these lands at all, but off with the rest of the militia, fighting with the other king's men against the French.

Anthony shifted his musket from one shoulder to the other and stole another glance at Grandfather. Grandfather was about the oldest gentleman Anthony knew, his long hair snow-white beneath the flat brim of his hat with the old-fashioned sweeping plume, but he was also the wisest and the bravest gentleman, too. Everyone in the valley said so. Though he'd given over being the leader of their county's militia, Anthony heard how they still called him Captain Sparhawk instead of Master Sparhawk or just plain Kit, though only Grandmother did that. They all came to him whenever they had a problem, too, and day or night, there always seemed to be someone waiting in the hall to see Grandfather.

But not today. Today Anthony had Grandfather all to himself, and he couldn't quite believe his good luck.

"Here, lad," said Grandfather, holding back a branch for Anthony. "We'll stop here for a moment, then onward to home."

Anthony nodded, the shy little ducking of his head that he always used around Grandfather, and obediently clambered up the big rock before them. Beneath his tired legs, the stone felt smooth and warm from the sun, and with a contented sigh he settled as close to the older man as he dared.

Grandfather drank deeply from the wooden canteen, then handed it to Anthony. "Your grandmother will be glad to see us tonight, won't she?" he said, cocking his head toward the three wild turkeys they'd shot, now lying on the rock beside them, with their feet bound together for carrying. "You're a good companion, Anthony. You know the rare virtue of silence."

Anthony flushed with pleasure, and prayed Grandfather would never guess that his silence came from being tongue-tied with awe, rather than from virtue.

Grandfather was studying him closely, his expression thoughtful. "You're like your father, you know. He wasn't full of empty talk, either, but there wasn't a better man in the forest or in a fight. If you turn out like him, you'll do well by yourself, and by his memory."

Anthony handed him back the canteen, desperately wishing he'd hear more about his father. He'd been only a baby when his parents died, and he remem-

bered nothing of either of them. "I want to be like him," he said wistfully, "'specially if he was like you."

Grandfather grunted. "Ah, well, Richard was more like your grandmother, small and dark, the way her people were. You're more pure Sparhawk. The green eyes mark you, lad, like it or not. Cat's eyes, eh?"

His smile was bittersweet as he rested his hand on Anthony's shoulder, the weight heavy, but comforting, too. "There won't be much I can do for you, Anthony. Your father was my youngest son, and by English law and entail there's little to come your way."

"I don't care," said Anthony promptly, and at that moment he didn't. "I'm a Sparhawk, and that's enough."

Grandfather laughed. "A good answer, that. But think well before you make such pledges. My father, and his father before him, were good, honorable men, strong men. There's a responsibility to being in this family, you know, and it isn't easy. In this valley, we've always been the ones to watch over those who can't, to guard and treasure what we love most and believe in. Can you understand that?"

Anthony squinted a little as he looked up at Grandfather. The setting sun was bright around the old man's shoulders, almost like a halo. "I think I do," he said slowly. "You want me to help everybody and keep them safe from the French and make sure we all can be free, loyal Englishmen, the same way that you do?"

Grandfather laughed again, softly, and pride was warm in his eyes. "If you do half that much, Anthony, then you'll do well indeed. Here, I've something for you.'' He reached inside his hunting pouch and held out his open hand to Anthony. *''A small trinket, I know, a bit of silver I've had fashioned for trading with the Abenaki, but still, it might serve as a reminder for you.''*

It was a small silver disc, polished and gleaming against his grandfather's lined, worn palm. Etched into the silver was a fierce bird with spread wings, perched on a stick or branch and surrounded by tiny stamped hearts.

''A hawk on a spar,'' explained Grandfather as he traced his finger across the design. *''A spar's part of a ship's mast, you know, or maybe you didn't. A spar with a hawk. Spar-hawk, eh? There's a pin on the back, too, so you won't lose it.''*

Anthony held his breath as Grandfather bent to pin the silver circle to his hunting shirt. He'd never had anything so beautiful or so wonderful in all his life.

''There now, Anthony,'' said Grandfather. *''Wherever you go, you look at this and you'll always remember what we said this day.''*

Anthony slipped his hand inside his cloak and touched the same pin on his waistcoat, there where he always wore it. With time, the silver had grown scratched and flattened, but the magic of that afternoon—and the message—had never dulled.

To be strong and watch over those who were weak, to guard and protect what he loved and treasured most—that was why he'd become a soldier in the first place, and why, too, he was here now. He must take care to remember that. With Ridley, he had let his reason and his judgment become clouded. He must not let it happen again.

And yet, strangely, it wasn't his grandfather's voice that echoed in Anthony's conscience now, or the sharp taunts that had come from Ridley, but a softer, more passionate voice.

You truly have no shame, no loyalties, do you?

He swore to himself, ordering the woman's words from his thoughts. But what remained was the woman herself, the way the winter sun had gilded her face as she stood by the window, her bowed head framed by the squares of the panes. Catharine Hazard could deny whatever she wished. He was certain they'd met before, and not just in passing. He thought again of her neat ankles in the colored stockings, and how—

Abruptly the gelding shied away at the sound of the musket shot, reduced by the wind to a dry, muffled crack, and Anthony pulled hard on the reins to wheel the frightened horse away from the sea. It was then that he heard the second shot, and felt the sharp, sudden bolt of pain rip through his upper left arm. Fifty yards to the west lay the dark shadow of low, scrubby pines, more than enough to shelter a man—or men—and their muskets.

Anthony swore again, cursing his own carelessness as he struggled to control the terrified horse. He dug his heels hard into the gelding's sides and bent low over the animal's neck, striving to make himself as small a target as possible as he raced back toward Newport.

Not that Anthony expected his assailants to follow. Rebels never did. Yet when at last he reached the town, he felt more relieved than he knew he had any right to, and he didn't slow the gelding until Hazard's swinging signboard was in sight.

The groom was slow coming from the stable, sleepily shoving his shirt into his breeches as he trotted forward to take the reins. Anthony winced as he swung his leg over the horse and slid to the ground, the impact jarring like a bolt straight to his arm. He knew the wound wasn't a bad one, especially considering what it might have been, but his sleeve was wet and clammy with blood and his knees felt weak, and he prayed he'd be able to walk across the yard to the doorway without keeling over facefirst onto the paving stones.

Carefully he placed one foot after the other, holding his injured arm beneath his cloak as naturally as he could. If he wobbled now, the groom would merely believe he was in his cups, which was far better than letting the man spread stories about how the redcoat major had been fool enough to get himself shot.

Anthony gritted his teeth from the effort, his forehead glazed with sweat even on this cold night. He was almost to the back door now, where his manservant, Routt, would be waiting for him in the kitchen. Routt would know what to do; he'd mended far worse than this.

Inside the kitchen, Catie hurried to the window at the sound of the horse in the courtyard and peeked through the shutters. One flambeau was always kept burning for the sake of any late travelers, and by its dancing light she made out the tall shape of Major Sparhawk as he climbed from his horse. With a self-conscious shake of her skirts, she stepped back from the window and took a deep breath to calm herself. She'd been preparing for this moment all evening. So why, then, was she as nervous as a cat on coals?

She heard him try the door, discover it locked, swear to himself and knock instead. She almost smiled at that muttered oath, for the very human irritation behind it made him somehow less daunting.

"Who is it?" she asked. Though she knew full well who was there, she decided it wouldn't hurt to make him wait that extra half minute.

"Major Anthony Sparhawk," he said, his voice rumbling deep through the barred oak door. "Damnation, woman, open the bloody door!"

This time she frowned, not caring to have the oaths directed at *her*. It would serve him right if she left him out in the cold all night. But she had her promise to Jon to keep, and, setting her face in a smile she drew the bolt and swung open the door.

"Good evening to you, Major," she said pleasantly as he brushed past her with a rush of icy air. "Though, faith, 'tis well past midnight. Do all you English officers keep London hours?"

Anthony ignored her, in no mood or condition for banter. "Where's my man?"

She closed the door and stood beside it, her hand still resting on the latch. He was hatless, his neat queue torn apart from the wind in a way that left his golden hair loose and wild around his face, dashing and dangerous, enough to make her feel once again like a giddy seventeen-year-old girl.

What Jon asked of her, she thought woefully, oh, what Jon asked!

"Your Mr. Routt?" she repeated, as offhandedly as she could. "I sent him to bed."

Anthony wheeled around to face her, his long, dark

cloak swirling around him. "You'd no right to do that. Routt reports to me, not you."

"I've every right in the world, when he's cluttering up my kitchen, getting himself underfoot with my cook," she said defensively. "I sent him to his bed an hour ago, along with the rest of my own help. We've precious few customers tonight, thanks to you, and I saw no reason to make them all wait up."

"That still doesn't give you the...give you the..." Lord help him, he couldn't remember. All he knew now was that the fireplace was drifting upward at a crazy angle, and if he didn't sit down directly he was going to fall down, here at her feet. He groped for the chair that must be behind him, his uninjured hand tangling clumsily in his cloak.

"Let me help you." In an instant she was there at his side, her arm around his waist as she guided him into the chair. "Here you are, no harm done."

But as soon as he was seated, Catie drew back, frowning down at the blood smeared on her hand and sleeve. Before he could protest, she gently lifted his cloak back over his shoulder to reveal the torn, bruised wound where the ball had ripped through his arm.

He grimaced, but didn't flinch. At least for now, the fireplace had stopped spinning. "Not pretty, is it?"

"Not in the least." To his surprise, she didn't flinch, either. Deftly she unfastened the clasp at the neck of his cloak and pulled it off. "Is a jealous husband after you already?"

"Something like that." He flexed his fingers and grimaced, noting how the blood still oozed fresh from the wound. "Send for my servant, Mrs. Hazard, so I can stop cluttering up your kitchen, as well."

She looked at him sharply. "Don't you wish me to summon a surgeon?"

"What, and have the news common on every street corner, with every rebel in town claiming credit for having done this?" He shook his head with disgust at his own foolishness. "No, thank you, ma'am. For now, I'd rather stake my luck on Routt."

Catie bent closer to him, her arms akimbo as she studied the wound. At least now she had something safer than politics to discuss with him. "You don't need Mr. Routt just yet. I can tend to this well enough myself."

He glanced at her skeptically and tugged his neck-cloth loose with his thumb. "How do I know you won't put arsenic in the dressing, and thus be rid of one more wretched redcoat?"

"You don't know. You'll simply have to trust me." Without waiting for an answer, Catie went to one of the wall cabinets and took down a wooden box filled in readiness with neatly rolled bandages and lint, scissors, needles and waxed thread. Next she hung a kettle of water over the coals to boil, and laid a clean towel and a dish of soap on the table beside Anthony.

Yet as Anthony watched her preparations, his doubts grew. The only other woman to nurse him had been his own grandmother, when he was still a boy. And considering how this woman had practically spat at him this afternoon, trusting her now hardly seemed wise.

He pushed himself up from the chair, leaning heavily on the edge of the table. "A lady such as yourself needn't do such—such tasks."

"You won't escape that way, sir," she said softly.

How could a man as tall and strong as this one be so clearly terrified of *her?* Jon had been right when he'd called her kindhearted. Perhaps because she'd been something of a stray herself, no mongrel was ever turned from her door without a plate of scraps. She'd always been tender that way, and she doubted she could ever bring herself to harm any creature, beast or man, enemy or not.

Yet even so, the hazy reality of what he was to her pricked uneasily at her conscience. Was she being kind to him only because he was a man in sore need of her help, or in spite of it?

Anthony thought of the long retreat from Lexington to Charlestown, when he first learned that the people they'd come to protect didn't want protecting. The rebel marksmen had stayed hidden in houses and behind walls, like the one who'd fired at him tonight, and like that unseen man, the Massachusetts rebels had almost always found their mark. His regiment had formed the rear guard of the retreat, and over the musket fire and screams of the wounded and dying he had shouted at his men until he was hoarse, to hold their lines steady, to reload, to fire, to be brave.

But by the time they reached Charlestown, more than two hundred British soldiers had been wounded or killed outright, and those marked as missing, those left behind, had found no mercy at all at the hands of the enemy, even hands that seemed as gentle as Catharine Hazard's. Better to leave now, to find Routt. Aye, Routt he could trust.

"Mrs. Hazard," he protested weakly, trying to rise. "Please, ma'am, I'd prefer—"

But at once he began to sway, and barely in time

Catie grabbed his uninjured arm to guide him back down into the chair.

"I've tended far more grievous efforts than your piddling little scrape, Major Sparhawk," she said, with more gentleness than she'd intended. With his handsome uniform disheveled and stained with blood and his face taut with pain, he bore little enough resemblance to the proud, haughty officer who'd belittled her hospitality earlier. "You're hardly the first gentleman that's sat there begging to keep his sins secret. When a woman runs a tavern, sir, there's nothing she won't see."

"Nothing?" His upper lip beaded with sweat, Anthony smiled faintly, mortified by his own weakness. "I thought this was a respectable house."

"It is," she said promptly as she rolled up her cuffs. Though she knew he was only half listening, she continued talking, hoping that it would help take his mind off the pain. "You won't find any more genteel than Hazard's in all Newport County. But the better-bred the custom, the greater the mischief. Gentlemen are always getting into scrapes of one sort or another beneath my roof, and then begging me to keep the scandal down. And I do. Can you take off your coat yourself, sir, or shall I help you?"

She would have bet the tavern that he'd do it himself, and he did, working so hard to master the pain that by the time he'd finally eased the tattered sleeve from his wounded arm, she was certain he was going to faint. Most men she'd known would have. But he didn't, and grudgingly she gave him credit for being able to back up his bravado.

"Now, this sorry rag I will leave to your man to

put to rights," she said as she took the blood-soaked coat from him.

With his face rigid with hard-won control, all Anthony could do was nod.

"Then what can I fetch you from the bar? We've brandy, sack, canary, whiskey, peary—"

"Rum." The single word came out as a harsh growl, and Catie realized that his fainting was still a definite possibility. She hurried to the taproom, filled a tankard with more rum than water, and put it into his hand. "There you are, the best Rhode Island rum there is. At least your taste's still Yankee even if your colors aren't."

He closed his eyes and drank deeply, and while he did, Catie ripped away the linen of his shirt's sleeve. The ball had gone straight through his arm, and though the swelling and bruising made for a hideous-looking wound on both sides, it did not take her long to clean and cover it with an oiled poultice to help drain away the poisons.

Though the rum was strong and she worked as swiftly as she could, she knew she'd hurt him further. There wasn't any way to avoid it. Yet not once had he cried out or complained, his only sign of pain the way his fingers whitened around the tankard of rum.

"You're a fortunate man," she said softly as she wrapped a linen bandage around and around his arm. "Another inch to the side, and the ball would have struck the bone."

He sighed—an exhausted, drawn-out exhalation—now that the worst was past. "Another eight inches, and it would have found my heart. I'll warrant that's where the bastard was aiming, and lucky I was that my horse shied when he did."

Automatically Catie's glance shifted to the broad expanse of his chest, trying to imagine the heart beneath it stilled forever. For the first time, she noticed the little silver circle, unlike any official medal or badge she'd seen, pinned to the breast of his waistcoat.

"What is that?" she asked curiously. "I'd say it was perilously close to a stout Yankee eagle, save that it's worn on a British uniform."

"Yankee, yes, but a hawk, not an eagle." He took another long drink from the tankard, grateful for the way the rum eased the pain. "It's the Sparhawk mark that my grandfather used on all his dealings with the Indians. He gave the pin to me when I was a boy, and I've kept it since as a kind of charm. Not that it brought me much luck this night."

"Oh, but it has," said Catie quickly. "Think of how close this shot came to being mortal!"

"You believe in degrees of luck, then?" he asked wryly. "Too bad I was shot, but at least I wasn't killed outright?"

He looked at her over the rim of the tankard. Now that the task of cleaning the wound was done, she was once again achingly aware of him as the man who had haunted her thoughts and dreams for so many years. But reality was so different from dreams: reality was the curling gold hair on the muscled forearm that rested so close to hers, reality was the stubble of beard above the lips that had once kissed hers, reality was the blood-spattered uniform that made him her enemy.

"You were riding when you were struck?" she asked, striving to turn her thoughts back to where they belonged. At least this might be something that would interest Jon.

He sighed ruefully, rubbing his palm across his forehead. "What an easy mark I must have been, too, there in the moonlight with the sea around me. I was south of the town, near a place called Damaris Point. Or so it was called once. Do you know it?"

She nodded, her throat constricting. Of course she knew it. Damaris Point was Sparhawk land, land that Jon would know even better. Could Jon have done this, then, aimed and shot to kill his own cousin?

Not his cousin, but a Tory officer. Not another Sparhawk, but the enemy. Remember that, Catie, remember, or else you'll be lost once again!

"Ah, forgive me, Mrs. Hazard," he said softly, misunderstanding her silence. "I forget myself. Of course you'd know Damaris Point. A good tavernkeep knows everything, doesn't she? All the better to advise her guests, even the ones who don't wish to be advised."

Swiftly she turned away, busying herself with washing her hands. "You're not forgetting yourself, Major, as much as speaking nonsense."

"It wasn't nonsense when you told me about my uncle," he said. "I didn't believe you, perhaps because I didn't want to. But you were indeed right about his...his *allegiances*. I wonder, Mrs. Hazard, did you laugh at me behind my back as I left for the general's headquarters?"

"Oh, no," she said, remembering how she'd watched him leave, with Belinda's picture clasped tight in her fingers. "However could I laugh at such a thing?"

"No?" He turned his head to look at her, his green

eyes searching and his expression quizzical, and she almost gasped aloud. That expression, the angle of his jaw as he leaned his head to one side to study her, even the small hint of a smile that curved the corners of his mouth—all of it was so much like her dear little daughter that she could have wept.

No, Catie, not your daughter alone. His daughter, too, the daughter you made together...

"No," she said, as firmly as she could. She pushed her stool away from him and rose, bundling the soiled linen in her hands. "You need your rest, Major. Shall I fetch Mr. Routt now to help you up the stairs to your room?"

"Stay a moment," said Anthony softly, and before she could pull away he had covered her hand with his own. Such a little hand, he thought, for all the work it must do. She didn't look like the stern tavernkeeper now, not with her pale eyes so full of sadness. What could make her so unhappy? Had she a lover fighting far from home, or was this still grief for her husband? In all the years he was a soldier, he'd never stayed in one place long enough for any woman to mourn his leaving with genuine regret. What would that be like, to have a woman like this one waiting and worrying for him?

She tugged her hand free, curling it against the other as if to protect it. From him, he thought grimly, from him, and wisely, too. He was here beneath her roof expressly to betray her, and he couldn't have sworn that she wouldn't do the same to him.

"It's late, Major Sparhawk," she said, avoiding his gaze as she restlessly fingered the heart-shaped locket. "You should rest."

"Am I not permitted, then, to thank you for what you've done?"

She bent to bury the coals in the fireplace for the night, her face in profile against the glow of the dying fire, and once again he tried to think of where he'd known her before.

"I told you, sir, what I've done for you I've done for many others, as well. I've looked to your wound the best I can, but you must still guard against a fever or putrid discharge."

He smiled, as much to himself as to her, as he accepted her rebuff. "You sound more like a surgeon than a tavernkeeper."

"A good hostess must be many things to prosper," she said, her expression carefully composed as she turned toward him again with the black iron shovel still in her hands. "If there's nothing else you wish from me, sir, I'll bid you good-night and fetch your Mr. Routt."

His smile faded. "No, ma'am, that is all," he said softly. "That is all."

Chapter Four

Catie pulled her cloak more tightly around her shoulders, the cold air hitting her face as soon as she stepped out the kitchen door. In these short days of December, dawn was still a good two hours away, and the courtyard remained every bit as dark as it had been at midnight. She knelt to set the wooden trencher down, gently rapping it three times on the paving stones, the way she did every morning. But before the second tap the cats had already begun to appear, quick gray and black shadows racing toward the dish of scraps.

"There now, you greedy kits, there's enough for everyone," she scolded fondly as two of the cats tussled over a piece of turkey skin. "Don't I always see that there's plenty?"

She smiled wistfully, imagining how Belinda would have insisted on true justice, swatting the quarreling pair apart with a broom and awarding the turkey to a third, meeker cat instead. Fairness was very important to Belinda's eight-year-old idea of how the world should be, almost as important as rising so early every morning to be here at her mother's side.

Every morning, that is, until this week, thought Catie wretchedly. Nothing fair about that, or this war, either.

"You'll be singin' a different tune before this winter's out, mistress, see if you won't," grumbled Hannah behind her, thumping a heavy iron kettle for emphasis. "You won't be tossin' good food out for those wicked beasts once all them filthy lobsterbacks pick this poor island clean."

"And I say the British will be gone long before that happens," said Catie as she came back inside. "Why should they stay? There's no other army here for them to fight, and no American ships will be foolish enough to wander into a harbor full of British frigates. I say they'll stay here only long enough to boast that they've conquered us properly, and then they'll be off to fight somewhere else."

Hannah scowled and shook her head, unconvinced. "Beggin' pardon, mistress, but them soldiers are a mean, ugly lot o' men, an' I can see 'em stayin' here forever, just to be contrary."

"Well then, Hannah, I'll pray that you're wrong and that I am right." Though hadn't she already done exactly that all this long sleepless night, praying that one red-coated officer in particular would leave? With a sigh, Catie pulled the hood of her cloak over her cap and looped the covered basket with the jam cakes over her arm. "If anyone asks for me, Hannah, you haven't the faintest notion where I've gone."

"But I do, mistress." The cook's scowl deepened into a frown of unhappy concern. "Anyone who knows you can guess you're off t'see Belinda. Them jam cakes only make it certain.''

"No, it doesn't," said Catie, "and I've no intention of telling you any more, one way or the other. That way, you can answer truthfully if you're asked.''

Briskly she pulled on her mittens, hoping the gesture would mask the dismay she felt. Was she really so dreadfully transparent? Three days ago she'd been determined not to risk visiting her daughter for a fortnight, or at least until the situation here in town was more settled. But then, that had been before Anthony walked through that door, needing her help, needing her—

No. He had not sought her, nor had he wanted her assistance. She was the one who hadn't been able to resist forcing her care, her concern, upon *him.* And he wasn't Anthony. He was Major Sparhawk, a Tory officer cantoned in her home, an enemy she'd promised to spy upon. The sooner she remembered that and forgot everything else, the better for her, and Belinda, too.

She gave her head a little toss, trying to shake away the shameful memory. "You'll have to make do with what we have in the cellar, Hannah, at least until the market opens again. Not that we'll have that many guests—*paying* guests—at table. Still, I've every intention of returning to greet them all at dinner, and so you may tell them if they ask.''

But Hannah refused to let Catie change the subject. "I do wish you'd be takin' one o' the lads from the stable with you, mistress. The notion o' a lady like you alone in the street with all them soldiers—well, it chills me t' the quick. At least a pistol, mistress. Take one o' the master's old guns to protect yourself.''

"Oh, yes, and shoot myself for good measure. All the king's men would quiver with terror at the sight of me with a gun, that's for certain.'' Catie smiled grimly. "This is my town, Hannah, my home, and my life, and none of it is King George's affair. I refuse to let myself be cowed into hiding by a great pack of bullying Tories.''

Brave, patriotic words indeed, thought Catie proudly as she closed the door after her. But with each hurried step through the dark, deserted town, the bravery evaporated and the patriotic words faded into no more than an empty bluff as her heart pounded and her hands grew damp inside her mittens.

Patriot or not, she wasn't a complete fool. She knew what she was doing was impulsive at best, sliding down the scale to out-and-out dangerous. She kept to the narrower side streets and hugged the edges of the houses and shops, where her footsteps would make less sound than on the paving stones, sometimes so close to the walls that her skirts brushed the clapboards and snagged against the bricks. Twice she heard men's voices and a clanking of muskets that she guessed belonged to the British sentries, and both times she managed to dart through alleyways to avoid them.

By the time she finally reached the edge of town, dawn was a pale glow through the bare trees on the horizon, and Catie quickened her steps with a sigh of relief, glad to be rid of Newport. The little gossip she'd heard said that the British troops were concentrated in the town and around the harbor, and that they weren't bothering with the more isolated farms scattered across the island.

But to be certain, she decided to leave the road and cut across the fields instead, and with her skirts bunched in one hand and the basket in the other, she climbed over the low stone wall that marked the boundary of the Arnold farm. The stubbled grass glistened with the heavy frost, crunching brittle beneath her feet as she cut out across the empty fields.

When at last she saw the smoke curling from the old stone chimney of the Pipers' house, the sun had risen and stretched into a lemon-colored band across the pale winter sky. Catie's fingers and toes were numb from the cold and her cheeks stung with it, but she was nearly running the final steps through the orchard, almost desperately eager to see her daughter again.

To her joy, Belinda was outside, helping Abigail Piper draw a bucket of water from the well. Catie called her name, and the little girl's head rose at once, her face was so bright with the same excitement that Catie herself felt that she could have wept with joy. Only three days they'd been apart, but that was three days longer than they'd ever been separated before.

"Belinda, here!" she shouted, dropping the basket to the grass to wave her hands. "I'm over here!"

Without another glance at Abigail, Belinda began to run to Catie, her skirts flying high around her legs and her white linen cap falling back from her hair. She threw herself into Catie's outstretched arms like a small, wriggling puppy, linking her arms tightly around her mother's waist and burying her face against her breasts.

"Oh, Mama, you said you'd come, and you did!" she cried, her words tumbling over themselves with happiness. "Mrs. Piper said you wouldn't, not for a fortnight at least, but I knew you wouldn't leave me that long, and you didn't! You *didn't!*"

She shoved herself back, impatiently shaking her hair back from her face. "You have been feeding the cats, Mama, haven't you?" she asked, her heart-shaped face turning serious. "You made certain the little ones got their share, too? The Pipers have cats here in the barn, but they're so fat from mice that they pay no mind at all to the scraps I bring them."

"Of course I feed them," said Catie promptly. "I even give them extra to make up for their disappointment at not seeing you. Hannah scolded me for it."

"Well, good." Belinda beamed. "I mean to make Hannah cross at me, too, starting first thing tomorrow morning. Now I'll go fetch my things from the house so we can leave."

"Belinda, sweet, wait a moment."

"Why should I?" The girl's smile widened to show the gap where she'd lost her last baby tooth. "The sooner we leave, the sooner we'll be home. You'll see, Mama, I kept everything neat in the bag, all folded tidy and neat, the way you did. I wouldn't take anything out, even though Mrs. Piper said I should, because I knew I'd only have to put it back when you came for me."

"Oh, Belinda," murmured Catie, her heart sinking. "We must talk."

How could she tell her the danger wasn't past, that she'd only come to visit? Gently she reached out and took the girl's rough little hand, smoothing back a lock of Belinda's hair. Her daughter's hair was so different from Catie's own, not fine and silvery, but thick and gold and full of sunshine.

Her father's hair, thought Catie wretchedly. Her father's hair, and his green eyes, with their impossibly long lashes, and the same bowed curve of his smile, too, all of it unmistakably Anthony's. Lord, was it only her shame that made her find his mark everywhere on her daughter's innocent face, or would others see the resemblance, too?

"I can't take you home, lamb," she said as gently as she could. "Not just yet, though I promise—"

"But why *not*, Mama?" cried Belinda, stunned enough that her voice squeaked upward. "You said it wouldn't be long. You said I'd only have to stay here until Newport was safe again!"

"And it's still not, Belinda, not yet," said Catie hurriedly, hating herself for the pain she saw in her daughter's eyes. "You're much better off here with the Pipers, away from all the trouble in town."

"But I don't care, Mama," said Belinda urgently. She was trying so hard to be brave and not cry, her fingers clutching around Catie's. "I don't care about the Pipers and I don't care about the trouble. I want to go with you. I want to go *home!*"

Catie sighed unhappily. "I'm sorry, love, but I can't take you just yet. You're much safer here. The town's too full of redcoats, hundreds and hundreds of them, plus Hessians—Germans—besides. Why, there's even a good score of Britishers in our own house, thumping up and down the front stairs as if it's their private parade ground."

But Belinda scarcely heard her, her face crumpling

with fear and disappointment and resentment, too, as she jerked her hand away from Catie. "You don't care what happens to me, not really! You say you want to keep me away from the soldiers, but there's been soldiers here, too, bunches of them, and you don't even *care!*"

Catie looked at her sharply. "Soldiers here, Belinda? When?"

"Yesterday noon, Mrs. Hazard." Abigail Piper joined them, the musket slung across her back in grim counterpoint to her welcoming smile. The Pipers had three sons serving in the south with General Greene. Abigail often vowed she would have gone for a soldier herself if Owen would let her, and somehow Catie didn't doubt it. "A whole party of the nasty devils came poking about."

"Oh, Belinda, forgive me, I didn't know." Gently Catie drew her daughter back into her arms, and with a little sigh Belinda pressed her head against Catie's side.

"She was safe enough, Mrs. Hazard," said Abigail, shifting the musket butt from her shoulder to the ground, leaning on the long barrel like a staff. "And brave as can be into the bargain. We were both sick abed and powerfully ill, weren't we, Belinda?"

Catie frowned, slipping her hand beneath Belinda's chin to feel if she was warm. "Ill?"

"We were only playing, Mama." Belinda sniffed loudly, and she smiled in spite of herself. "When the redcoats tried to come into the house, Mr. Piper told them that Mrs. Piper and me were sick."

Abigail chuckled. "Nothing an army fears more than a good dose of smallpox sweeping through the camp,'' she said cheerfully. ''Owen met them at the door, all harried and long-faced, while Belinda and I lay beneath the coverlets upstairs and moaned as if our last hour had come. We had our faces all dabbed with flour-paste sores, too, in case they dared come peek. Not that they did. Lord, you should have seen them turn tail and run, Mrs. Hazard!''

''But they could come back.'' Protectively Catie tightened her arms around Belinda. The Pipers' ruse had been a clever one, more clever than any she'd have invented herself—in peacetime the Pipers had been smugglers, accustomed to outwitting the authorities, which was one of the reasons Catie had trusted Belinda to them in the first place—but still she couldn't help half considering taking Belinda back with her to Newport after all.

''Nay, they won't come back, not once the word goes round their camp,'' declared Abigail. ''You'll see. The pox is better than a score of muskets.''

Yet her smile faded. ''But you, Mrs. Hazard. Coming out here all by yourself—that wasn't wise, ma'am, 'specially not if things are as bad in town as we heard. Don't want to consider what those redcoats might do to a lady like yourself.''

Catie felt how Belinda shrank closer. Automatically she hugged the girl for reassurance, though she couldn't have said which of them was the more comforted.

''I didn't see a soul the whole way out here, Abigail,'' she said, as much for her daughter's benefit as for the other woman's, ''and I doubt I will on the walk home, either. As for us in town—true, it seems they've put half the infantry under my eaves, but I've officers staying with me, as well, and I pray those fine gentlemen with the gold lace on their coats will make their men behave.''

"Then why can't I go home with you?" pleaded Belinda, twisting to look up at Catie. "If it's safe enough for you, Mama, then why wouldn't I be safe, too?"

Gazing down at Belinda's upturned face, Catie wondered if the girl would be safer in Newport after all. At least she'd be home, where Catie herself could watch over her. Maybe she should take her back today, so that they could have biscuits and chocolate together in Belinda's room before she went to bed, the way they did every night.

"Please, Mama," begged Belinda. "Please."

The little girl blinked, fighting to keep back tears, and the sun turned her eyes green as gemstones.

The same glinting green as Anthony Sparhawk's.

And slowly Catie shook her head, steeling her heart against the tears that now spilled down her daughter's cheeks. She had to; she had no choice. For how could she ever forget that the greatest danger to them both had nothing to do with the war?

She had stayed too long, far longer than she'd intended, and now she was racing back toward Newport against the lengthening shadows and the sinking sun. When she came this morning, she'd almost enjoyed the solitude of the empty fields. But listening to Abigail Piper had changed all that. Now, behind every stone wall and bush, Catie imagined a British soldier lurking, and she longed for the moment when she'd once again be within sight of the Friends' burying ground that marked the edge of town.

Wearily she shifted the heavy basket from one hand to the other. Abigail had replaced the jam cakes with a crock of new butter and fresh eggs packed in straw, and Catie had been most grateful; with the market closed by the British, such common things from a farm were a luxury that she, and Hannah, too, could well appreciate. But now the basket's willow handle dug deep into her palm from the weight of the butter crock, like the heaviness in her heart from leaving Belinda behind.

She shifted the basket yet again, flexing her cold-stiffened fingers within her mittens as dry leaves swirled and skittered against her legs. The wind had changed, coming from the west, and the clouds were thick and low in the sky. Snow clouds, she thought with a sigh as she climbed over a fence, as if she needed one more reason to wish this day done.

And then, quite suddenly, another rose from the coppice before her.

"You there, halt!" The soldier's words echoed across the empty fields in the chilly air, the raised muskets of the other two soldiers silent reinforcement. "You, ma'am, stay where you be!"

"Here on top of this wall?" she asked indignantly, too tired and unhappy to really believe they'd shoot her. "To stay perched here like some straw jack-a-dandy? Is that what you wish of me?"

The soldier's mouth worked as he tried to decide. He was only a corporal, and very young. "Do you be alone, then?"

Catie swept her free arm grandly around her. "Do you see anyone else?"

"We take no chances, ma'am," he said with a great show of sternness, though he motioned for the two men beside him to lower their guns. "Rebels are not to be trusted."

"And who's to say I'm one of them?" demanded Catie, clambering down from the wall. "Where's my uniform? My musket and sword? Or is it your almighty king's orders to charge unarmed women as dangerous to the crown, too?"

"My orders be to trust no one from Newport, man nor woman," he answered stiffly. "I must take you to camp for questioning."

"But I can't go with you. I've a business to tend to, and I'm late returning as it is." Catie sighed with dismay, glancing back over her shoulder to the road she'd almost reached. She took one tentative step away from them, and immediately the muskets rose in unison.

She froze, and sighed again. Cajoling young men into doing what she wished was one of the necessary skills of a tavernkeeper's trade, but right now she was failing miserably.

"Surely you can let me pass, Corporal," she said, striving to be reasonable. "A gentleman of your experience can surely see that I—"

"I'll hear none of your rebel trickery, ma'am!"

"And I've none to offer. Truly, what use could I be to you in your camp? I promise I've no dreadful answers to any questions you might ask. I'm no threat to you, not in the least."

But there was no agreement. Instead, the young corporal's eyes turned hard with hatred. "Oh, aye, all you rebels be harmless. Wasn't you or your kind that killed my mates at Concord an' Lexington, was it?"

She shook her head, appalled that he'd make a connection like that. "I'm sorry for your friends," she began, "but I can hardly be—"

"Orders be orders, ma'am," he said sharply. "You be coming with us."

The camp was nothing more than a flag thrust in the ground beside a springhouse and a dozen men gathered around a fire with their hands outstretched to catch the warmth. No wonder the fire burned so brightly, thought Catie with disgust; the soldiers had wantonly pulled down a rail fence that had been there as long as she could remember to build it.

"We found her running 'cross the field to the north, sir," said the corporal to his sergeant as he gave Catie a little shove into the ring of firelight. "She resisted, sir."

Catie glared at him. "I wished to return to my own home before nightfall, and this man has prevented me from doing so. I'd scarcely call that *resisting*, and if—"

"Search the basket," ordered the sergeant curtly, and the corporal yanked the basket from Catie's arm.

"See here now, that's mine!" sputtered Catie indignantly as the man began to paw through the basket's contents. "You've no right—"

"We've every right, ma'am," said the sergeant sharply. "In the name of the king, and for the safety of his loyal subjects."

"Oh, yes, as if my butter and eggs are a threat to

your precious king!'' She tried to grab the basket back, but before she could, one of the other soldiers seized her arm and roughly pulled her aside. She struggled to free herself, and as she did, the man stepped on the hem of her cloak, jerking the ties tight across her throat and making her stumble clumsily. Tears stung her eyes, both from anger and from fear as she realized how vulnerable her position was. Lord, what was she *doing?*

Jeering laughter circled the campfire, and the sergeant raised his voice over it. ''Such bold talk will gain you little, hussy. If you've nothing to hide, then you've nothing to—''

''Let the woman go, Douglass,'' said Anthony quietly from the height of his horse's back. ''Let her go now.''

Every soldier's face whipped about to look at him. By the firelight Anthony saw surprise, guilt, disappointment, fear and resentment as they all jumped to attention, and he felt his own anger rise in response. He'd been a soldier himself too long to expect more from his men than was reasonable, but the general's orders regarding civilians, no matter what their sympathies, had been clear as day. What would have become of this poor woman if he and Peterson hadn't been drawn from the road by the light of the campfire?

''She was acting suspicious, sir,'' said the sergeant defensively. ''That, and talking treasonous, sir. I thought she might be carrying gunpowder in the basket.''

Anthony let an extra second pass, his gaze stony. ''And what, Sergeant, was she in fact carrying?''

''Butter and eggs, Major Sparhawk,'' said the

woman herself as she pushed her way into the light. "And not even you, sir, can find any sin or danger in that."

Only years of practice kept Anthony's face impassive when he realized who it was.

Lieutenant Peterson was not as reticent. "Mrs. Hazard, ma'am! What in the blue devil—?"

"Have a mind for the lady's sensibilities, Peterson," said Anthony, interrupting him. "Mrs. Hazard, ma'am. I should never have expected to find you here."

"I might well say the same to you, Major," she said, lifting her chin a fraction higher. While most women would have been wailing with fear or weeping with gratitude, Catharine Hazard seemed merely furious. "At least I had a good reason for crossing Mr. Arnold's north field, which is more than can be said of you or your men."

"And, pray, what might that reason be, Mrs. Hazard?" he asked coolly, staring down at her upturned face. "Where were you going at this hour, with your butter and eggs?"

"I wasn't going. I was coming." She was rubbing her arm where the soldier had held it, and with a frown Anthony wondered if the man had hurt her. Despite all her bluster, she was not a large woman, and delicately made. "I spent this day at the house of a friend whose wife and daughter are ill with smallpox. The eggs and butter were small tokens of his thanks, that was all."

Anthony saw how Peterson and the others edged away from her at the mention of the pox. Nor did he blame them. Illness was the last thing an army wanted.

Even Mrs. Hazard would understand that, and in another place Anthony would have joined the rest in keeping a healthy distance from her. But here in Newport, any inhabitants who fell sick with smallpox were by law immediately taken from their homes to a special small sickhouse on an island in the bay, to be nursed there in careful isolation until recovered, or dead.

How careless of Mrs. Hazard to have forgotten. How fortuitous that he himself had remembered. But what—or who—did she hope to protect by lying?

Intrigued, he glanced toward her basket, sitting forgotten at Douglass's feet. "So which is it, Sergeant? Eggs and butter, as the lady maintains, or gunpowder?"

Hurriedly Douglass plunged his hands beneath the checkered cloth and rummaged through the straw packing the basket. Far more slowly he rose, holding three eggs in his hand for Anthony to see for himself.

"Very well, Sergeant Douglass. You were wise to be cautious." Bemused, Anthony kept his surprise to himself. After the smallpox tale, he would have wagered five guineas on the gunpowder. "Return the basket to the lady."

He watched as she took the basket, her mouth curved with a triumph she didn't bother to hide, and that, strangely, made him wish to smile. Without another word or glance to spare for him, she looped the basket over her arm and marched out alone into the dusk, her head still held high and her skirts sweeping like a queen's across the dry grass.

Then, at last, he did smile. Misplaced and foolhardy

though it was, how could he not admire such brazen confidence?

"Mrs. Hazard," he called after her. "I did not give you leave to go."

Catie sighed. She should have known it had all been too easy, and slowly she turned back to face him. "I did not realize, Major Sparhawk, that your leave was necessary for me to return to my home."

"Your home, ma'am, and my quarters, as well. Come." Imperious and disturbingly handsome on the tall black horse, he beckoned to her. "You shall ride with me."

"But I do not wish it!" she protested, horrified by the intimacy of what he proposed. "That is, you are too kind, Major, and I much prefer to walk, for it is— it is such a pleasant evening, and we are so near to town."

"It's an abominably wretched evening, ma'am," said Anthony, guiding his horse toward her, "with a chill that cuts straight to the bone. Peterson can finish here. You are my landlady, and as such, I feel a certain responsibility toward you. Now come."

Wildly Catie shook her head, backing away with the basket clutched before her. "I told you, I do not wish it, and I—*no!*"

Her wail of protest died in midbreath as two soldiers lifted her onto the horse in front of Anthony. She gasped and tried to pull away from him and tug her petticoats over her legs at the same time. The big gelding shied nervously at her scrambling, and with a frightened yelp Catie grabbed a fistful of mane to keep herself from pitching over the horse's neck. She had a dizzying view of the ground spinning far below her, blurred together with the wide, grinning faces of the two soldiers, before she felt the sure, steadying hand at her waist, drawing her back to safety.

"There now, I won't let you fall," said Anthony in a soft, low voice meant to calm both her and the horse. "Didn't I tell you I felt a certain responsibility for your well-being?"

Responsibility was one thing. Being pressed close to the man's chest with her legs sprawled wantonly to one side over his thighs was quite another. Instinctively Catie tried again to edge away from him, but with his arm curled around her waist, her motions served only to make her more painfully aware of his body against hers. In his crimson uniform he was so large and strong and warm and *male,* and beside him she felt small and vulnerable, seventeen once more.

No, she thought frantically. *No.* She'd sworn that she'd never again let herself be that trusting, that weak, that foolish. Never again would she let herself be hurt by any man.

Especially not by the same man who had so carelessly destroyed her innocence.

The basket with the eggs and butter was thrust up into her hand, and she felt the hard muscles of Anthony's thighs shift beneath her bottom as he urged the horse into a walk. One of the soldiers near the fire said something that Catie couldn't quite hear, but the rumble of male laughter was unmistakably crude as they left the makeshift camp.

Anthony felt how she stiffened against him as they cut out across the empty field, toward the road. She was lighter than he'd expected, her body warm and soft beneath her wool cloak, so soft and warm that he had to force his thoughts elsewhere abruptly.

"You don't care for riding, do you, Mrs. Hazard?" he said, his mouth close to her ear. Her hood had slipped back from her pale, wispy hair, and she hadn't bothered to pull it back. "But you can trust Thunder, you know. He may look the brute, but he's the steadiest mount in any regiment in Newport."

"Indeed." The single word was bitten off cleanly, as sharp as the winter evening. "It is not your horse that I mistrust, Major."

"Ah. The one conclusion you leave me is not very flattering."

"It's not meant to be." She twisted to face him, her eyes bright with anger. "First I am stopped from my business and accused of smuggling gunpowder—*gunpowder!*—in my market basket!"

"It was done by the rebel women in Boston," said Anthony testily. "And often, too, as our men learned to their sorrow."

But Catie wasn't listening. "Next you order me thrown across your saddle and carried off quite against my will, exactly, sir, like the red-coated, king-loving, *untrustworthy* bully that you unquestionably are!"

The sound deep in Anthony's throat was as close to a growl as a man makes. "That, ma'am, is hardly the thanks I expected."

"Thanks?" Catie's brows shot skyward as she impatiently shoved the wisps of her hair back from her face. "The thanks you *expected?*"

The look he gave her now beneath the brim of his hat had reduced many a soldier to helpless quivering. "Aye, Mrs. Hazard, thanks. When Peterson and I

came upon you, you were a lone rebel woman surrounded by a group of rough, hostile men.''

''*Your* men, major!''

''I know that, Mrs. Hazard,'' he said curtly, ''just
as I know how sorely the frustration and fear and un-
certainty of this blasted war can try even the best of
them.''

''But I fail to see—''

''No, ma'am, you will hear me out,'' he ordered,
so sharply that this time she fell silent. ''This day
alone I have witnessed two of our men arrested and
charged with rape. If they are found guilty, they will
be hanged. Such is the king's justice, and yet I did not
wish such a fate for those men we just left. Nor, Mrs.
Hazard, did I wish it for you.''

Her only answer was to pull her hood up like a
shield and turn away, preferring to stare steadfastly at
the road before them, rather than to meet Anthony's
eye. He had not expected her to thank him, not really,
but he was surprised at how much he wished she had.

Her anger forgotten, Catie let the sickening truth of
what Anthony had said echo again and again through
her conscience. She didn't doubt him, not for a moment. Hannah, the stable boy, Abigail Piper—they'd
all warned her of the same danger, and still she'd been
too selfishly stubborn to listen. Hadn't she heard
enough in the tavern of the atrocities committed by
both armies to realize the danger she'd courted? Anthony had saved her, and for that he *did* deserve the
thanks that stuck so foolishly in her throat.

Yet even worse was realizing how close she'd come
to having Belinda with her. All too easily she could
imagine what those soldiers might have done to her

beautiful, innocent daughter—unless Anthony had come to her Belinda's rescue, as well. No, not Anthony. Belinda's *father*. Catie bowed her head beneath the twisting turmoil of her emotions.

Thunder's pace quickened as they reached the beginnings of the town, and Anthony let him have his head between the guard posts. The poor devil was likely near starving, thought Anthony, same as he was himself. He glanced over the rooftops to the three-quarter moon, its lopsided circle ringed with a pale halo that meant snow.

"Does your arm grieve you very much?"

He didn't answer, not certain he hadn't imagined the soft, hesitant words, so different in tone and concern from the strident ones she'd used before. With a sigh she turned her face toward his again, the moonlight spilling over her full cheeks.

"I thought you'd keep to your bed today, you know," she said, almost ruefully. She frowned at his arm as if she could see through the sleeve of his coat to the bandage beneath. "I certainly wouldn't have believed you'd go jostling about on horseback, not after seeing what that ball did to you last night."

His expression remained guarded, inflexible. Now was the time to ask her where she'd truly spent her own day, to demand to know who she'd tried to protect. His duty, and his orders, would expect nothing less.

But instead he imagined how much it cost her to offer this commiseration, to let her brusque tavernkeeper's mask slip again as it had last night. Here in the moonlight, he wasn't ready to see that mask shift back into place just yet.

"To be perfectly honest, Mrs. Hazard," he confessed, "my confounded arm has hurt like the devil's own hell the entire day, and only a flask filled by Routt with black coffee and white rum has kept me from royally disgracing myself any number of times."

Her mouth puckered with a concern he found a great deal more charming than he should. "That was most foolish," she chided. "I warned you of fever from such a wound, and then your Mr. Routt's coffee won't be worth a tinker's dam."

"The pain was my penance, Mrs. Hazard," he said with nearly perfect seriousness. "To remind me not to ride out at night alone again in a country where I make such a splendid target."

Her eyes narrowed skeptically. "Precious good your penance did, Major Sparhawk. Or doesn't this darkness qualify as night?"

"Of course it does," he agreed. "But with you as my escort, I feel thoroughly safe."

Yet Catie didn't smile. He had meant to tease her, nothing more, but by doing so he'd unwittingly told the truth, as well. The musket that had wounded him last night would remain silent as long as they were on the same horse. Jon Sparhawk would have seen to that.

Troubled, she searched Anthony's face, willing him to understand all she couldn't say as the gelding came to a halt in the tavern's stable yard.

"No one knows of your wound, Major Sparhawk," she said swiftly. "At least not from my lips. I swear by all that's holy that I have told not a soul. No one, mind?"

Before he could answer, she had slid clumsily down from the horse's back to the paving stones in a tangle of petticoats, and was already hurrying across the yard to her kitchen door.

"Mrs. Hazard!" he called after her as he swung himself down from the horse. He intended nothing more than to say good-evening; there was no sin to be found in that. "Mrs. Hazard, ma'am!"

He watched her slow, hesitate, pause to consider, and finally dart back to him. How many times this night had he watched her turn away from him, yet still, each time, come back?

"You were right to expect my thanks," she said quickly, her cheeks pink beneath the newly lit flambeaux, "and I give them to you now. You could well have saved my life, and I thank you for it."

"Nay, Mrs. Hazard, I should not have asked—"

"My Christian name is Catharine," she said breathlessly, her smile sudden and fleeting. "But friends will call me Catie."

And as she scurried away from him for the last time, he realized two things: that he had still forgotten to wish her a good evening, and that he, Major Anthony Sparhawk of His Majesty's Royal Welsh Fusiliers, was standing with his hat in his hands and grinning like a clod-pated fool.

No, three things, he decided with disgust as he jammed his hat back onto his head. War was full of dangerous surprises, but the greatest threat to him here in Newport would be the little rebel widow with the silver-gray eyes.

Chapter Five

Pausing at the top of the back stairs, Catie balanced the pewter tray full of dirty dishes and half-eaten breakfast against the windowsill. It was not a task she relished, but Dr. and Mrs. Portian were two of her last guests, and if they preferred to dine in their room on account of Mrs. Portian's fragile sensibilities regarding soldiers, then Catie was more than willing to accommodate them.

Deftly she looped her petticoats through the side pocket-slits of her skirt until the hems were knee-high, to keep from tripping, then hoisted the heavy tray back onto her shoulder to head down the narrow, winding stairs to the kitchen. Though it had been years since she regularly carried trays herself, she hadn't forgotten the tricks of parlor maids and serving girls. A good thing, too, since one of the tavern's girls had quit outright when the British arrived and a second had simply vanished with her belongings the next night.

"So there you are at last," said Hannah as Catie set the tray down with a clatter on the kitchen table.

"Halfway t' making supper, I am, while some persons still lie abed with bacon and cocoa."

"We've not so much custom that I can turn guests away because their habits don't suit you, Hannah," answered Catie irritably as she wiped her hands on her apron. She'd tossed and turned all night, groaning into her pillow over how freely she'd behaved with Anthony Sparhawk. "Besides, Dr. Portian always settles his bill without a quibble, and pays hard money, too."

The cook sniffed and shuffled through the plates, poking crossly at the remains of the breakfast with the backside of her wooden spoon. "But look at this, ma'am, look at this, I beg you!" she cried with a wounded air. "I crisped the bacon special as that Mrs. Portian ordered, and back it comes as if I'd heeded her not at all!"

"They leave tomorrow, Hannah," said Catie as she began to scrape the plates herself. "I trust you can bear with them until then, just as I'm certain you'll find another use for Mrs. Portian's bacon."

With a sigh, Catie rubbed her fingertips across her forehead, wishing there were more guests for Hannah to fuss about. In a way, it was a blessing that the two serving girls had left on their own before she had to let them go.

"Oh, aye, ma'am, you can be sure I will," declared Hannah with scowling conviction as she carefully set aside the offending bacon. "But you've another trial before you, ma'am. You've company in the front room. He's been a-waiting for you this quarter hour past."

Catie looked up sharply. "I told you before that when Captain Jon comes he's to—"

"Nay, ma'am, 'tis not Captain Jon," said Hannah. "'Tis that yellow-haired Britisher major."

"Major Sparhawk?" Immediately Catie's fingers flew to her hair, smoothing the loose strands back beneath the ruffles of her cap. "He's waiting to see me?"

Pointedly Hannah's gaze lingered on her mistress's newly tidied hair, long enough to make Catie flush. "Aye, ma'am, Major Sparhawk. The *English* Sparhawk. The one what's staying in the green room, fine as a lord. He's the kind what should be paying his way, ma'am, if you're askin' my thoughts on the matter."

"Which I am not, Hannah," said Catie, as curtly as she could with her cheeks turned a guilty red. Lord only knew who had seen her return on Anthony's horse last night, or what the cook might already have heard. Foolish, thought Catie dismally, foolish, *foolish*, to have behaved like some moon-eyed milkmaid, for all the world to see! "All that you and I have to discuss is what will be offered at the table for dinner tonight, and I shall return directly after I've seen Major Sparhawk."

"Perhaps both matters can be satisfied at once, Mrs. Hazard," said Anthony from the doorway.

Instantly Catie turned to face him, the heat of her cheeks only burning more fiercely. She might have spent a long, sleepless night because of him, but there were no shadows beneath *his* eyes or ill humor in his expression as he smiled at her now.

"I've come with welcome news, Mrs. Hazard," he continued easily. "I was sure you'd wish to know that the market house is once again open."

"It would never have been closed in the first place if your general hadn't ordered it shut," said Catie rebelliously, her arms folded across her chest. At least he'd the sense not to call her by her Christian name, the way she'd practically begged him to do last night. What *had* possessed her? "Though what danger he could see in housewives and farmers haggling over eggs and turnips is beyond me."

"It was for the protection of those same housewives and farmers that the general made his decision," said Anthony. "The rebels have a way of turning even the most harmless gathering into a dangerous place for innocent persons."

He toyed with the hat in his hand, smoothing the silky beaver as he wondered how she managed to look so damnably pretty in the harsh light of morning. Few women did. He'd heard her voice in the passage and followed her here to the kitchen, not meaning to take her unawares, as he evidently had. Not that he regretted it; with an apron around her waist and her homespun skirts tucked high above her ankles, she looked much more like some saucy maidservant than the stern landlady she was trying to be. She *looked* like a Catie.

Last night she'd told him to call her that, not Catharine, not Mrs. Hazard. Just Catie. Dressed like this, the name suited her, even though he'd resolved never to use it. As delightful as it might be, such familiarity was equally certain to bring sorrow with it.

Catie's chin rose higher. How could the man stand there, smiling so charmingly, and say such nonsense as if it were gospel-true? "Oh, la, such protection! Was it *protection* your gallant men offered me last night?"

His smile cocked up crookedly on one side. "Perhaps my men were less than gallant, Mrs. Hazard, but I'd rather hoped I'd made up for their deficiencies myself."

"Beggin' pardon, Mrs. Hazard," said Hannah, not bothering to hide her impatience, "but if the market's open as he said, then there's plenty we'll be needin'. I can't be asked to make fancy dishes from air, you know."

Catie sighed, mentally taking stock of their larder. Even with the number of guests dwindling, there were things that Hannah couldn't be expected to do without.

"Very well, I'll go," she said, untying her apron. Belatedly she realized she'd left her skirts and petticoats shortened, and hastily she tugged them down, her cheeks flushing all over again at how common she must have appeared to Anthony Sparhawk. "I'll go fetch my cloak."

"Excellent, ma'am," said Anthony heartily. "Then I'll have the joy of your company as we walk."

Catie froze. "That's not necessary, Major," she said quickly. "I'm sure you've other duties that need your attention."

"First is to see that all is proceeding peacefully with the reopening of the market, and that I can do as well with you as alone." He didn't bother to add that for him to be seen with her, one of the most respected women in the town, at the reopened market could only help to convince the rest of Newport that the British did wish them well.

He took her red wool cloak from the peg near the door and held it open for her. "Come, Mrs. Hazard.

If you wish, I'll even bring one of my men to carry your purchases home for you."

"That," said Catie swiftly, "most certainly won't be necessary."

Feeling thoroughly trapped, she let him settle the cloak over her shoulders. Better to take no greater notice of his attentions than to give Hannah one more thing to squint and scowl over. She'd walk the short distance at his side if she must, but once at the market, she intended to free herself from him as soon as she could. The last thing she needed or wanted was for people to begin linking them together; the next leap, to connecting Belinda, as well, would then be all too easy to make.

She purposefully ignored his offered arm as they stepped into the street, drawing her hood up instead, and he let the slight pass. He'd made enough stern resolutions to be more wary of her that it was definitely for the best. Yet still he remembered how warm and soft she'd been against him last night, and he couldn't help wishing she'd rest that little mittened hand of hers again upon his arm.

"Snow again," said Catie, wrinkling her nose as she peered up at the dull gray sky. Fat white flakes were swirling around them, and already enough lay on the ground to shroud the walks and dry grass around them. "Pray it doesn't amount to much."

"Amen to that," agreed Anthony. "At least now we've cantoned all the men in decent quarters and no one's left to sleep in tents. Those first two nights were enough for me. I can assure you, Mrs. Hazard, that your hospitality and your bed are a good deal more comfortable than an open hillside in a Rhode Island winter.''

She knew he meant her bed as one belonging to her tavern, and not specifically her own bed, yet still she stiffened defensively. The bed with the pale rose hangings was her sanctuary, her private place, to be shared with no one. But once before she'd shared such a place with him, and the provocative possibilities his words now raised in her mind were shockingly vivid.

'''Hospitality' implies an invitation that was willingly extended, Major Sparhawk,'' she said, her voice brittle. ''I would not consider being forced to shelter a score of invading British soldiers in my home in that way.''

He glanced at her, surprised by the sharpness of her tone. ''I meant no offense, Catie,'' he said seriously. ''I intended it as praise, nothing else, and if I've erred, please forgive me.''

She stopped abruptly, brought to a halt by the sound of her name from his lips. All night long she'd berated herself for being brazen and forward in giving Anthony leave to use her Christian name, but maybe forwardness had nothing to do with it. Long ago he'd never called her anything but empty endearments. Could it be that part of her truly hoped to redeem that lost past by something as simple, and as complicated, as this?

''Forgive me, Catie,'' he said, more softly this time, the words coming out as little clouds in the icy air. ''Please. I didn't mean to slight the good name of either you or your tavern.''

Overwhelmed, she pressed her mittened hand across her mouth, fighting a silent war with herself as she

stared at him. She didn't want his concern and she
didn't want his apologies. There wasn't room for either in her life right now. But, oh, how green his eyes
were with the snowflakes dancing around his face, the
green she'd never forgotten, the green she remembered
anew each time Belinda smiled.

She lowered her head and turned away, drawing her
cloak more tightly around her body as she hurried
down the street and toward the market. Though she
could hear his footsteps quicken to follow, she didn't
look back.

But when she came to the corner of the street, she
stopped and gasped, her own sorrows forgotten in an
instant.

"Oh, dear Lord, look!" she cried, shaking her head
in denial and disbelief. "Oh, what they've done! What
they've *done!*"

On the corner stood a house so old that it might
have sheltered Roger Williams himself over a hundred
years before, and in the lot beside it was an orchard
of gnarled trees—cherry, apple, pear—that had borne
fruit nearly as long. Nearly a century, but no more, for
every one of the trees had been cut to the ground, the
twisted old limbs chopped crudely into rough chunks
now stacked along the trampled snow. Gone, too, was
the neat whitewashed fence that had surrounded the
orchard, torn down and broken into pieces, as well,
and as Catie watched in horror, the party of red-coated
soldiers with leather aprons began to chop into the first
of the tall elm trees that lined the street.

"It's a shame to lose the trees, I know," said Anthony at her shoulder, brusquely returning the salute
of the other soldiers, "but it's worse still to have a

man freeze to death for want of a decent fire. You said yourself that one cord of wood a week would not be enough for me, and most of my men will be fortunate to have a quarter of that for comfort.''

"But those fruit trees had been there since before we were born—before our parents were born!" she cried bitterly. "How can you destroy them with so little thought?"

The harsh edge to his voice was unintentional, but was there just the same. "There's much thought behind it, ma'am, and as much grieving and sorrow. If the traitors of this town had given equal thought to their actions before they rebelled against their king, then these trees—and the lives of many men—would have been spared.''

"Then you are wrong, sir," said Catie furiously. "Most dreadfully, most barbarously wrong! To say that my countrymen would wantonly choose destruction and death on a whim, on an impulse, proves how little you know of our reasons for this war!"

"We each of us have our reasons, ma'am, for whatever choices we make in our lives," said Anthony grimly. Rebel cant was always the same, even when it came from the tempting mouth of Catie Hazard. "But now my choice is to see you safely to the market house, and do that I shall."

Still she didn't look at him, her back so ramrodstraight that he wanted to reach out and shake her.

"Your choice, Major, and the devil take mine," she said curtly. "Is that how it shall be? For a few moments you shall have your way—your *choice,* as you call it—and then when you are done, satisfied, will I be left with the consequences?"

"Consequences," he scoffed, his pleasure in her company this morning fading fast. "You speak in riddles, ma'am. What manner of consequences could come of you and me walking together to the market house?"

"None in the least," she said, walking from his side. "You've no fear of that this day, Major."

She paused as she pulled off her mitten and lightly ran her hand along the bark of one of the doomed elm trees, her finger tracing over the whorls in the bark in a silent farewell. She looked at him then, letting the hood slip back from her face as she kept her hand on the tree. Her expression struck him as a curious mixture of sadness and defiance, and her pale gray eyes were luminous with unshed tears.

She must have a lover serving with the rebels, decided Anthony with a sudden pang of certainty, some man fortunate enough to inspire both her tears and her anger. An absent lover would explain so much.

But, damnation, why were her eyes, her lips, even her tears, so maddeningly familiar?

With obvious effort, she twisted her mouth into something close to a smile and stuffed her hand back into her mitten.

"We mustn't tarry, Major Sparhawk." A swift blink, and the glitter of tears vanished, willed away. "Unless you wish to be the one who answers to Hannah when I don't return with a turkey and a breast of veal at the very least."

In an odd way, Anthony felt he should apologize again, though he hadn't the faintest idea why. Instead he offered his arm to her again, and this time she took it. Her mittened hand upon his sleeve was not warm, the way he'd imagined, but as light and insubstantial as the snowflakes that gathered there, as well. He was still searching for a way to break the uneasy silence between them when they reached the market.

One of Newport's most elegant landmarks, the new market house was a three-story building with open arches on the ground level for the stalls. Though farmers and fishermen and other pedlars had returned at the general's order to sell their wares, their numbers on this gray, snowy morning were far fewer than usual. There was none of the usual laughter and good-natured bantering, no loitering to gossip or exchange news. The customers who came to the carts and stalls beneath the arches today all finished their business as quickly as possible before they scurried back to their homes. General Ridley could make all the pronouncements he wished about life in the town returning to normal; the red-coated soldiers who stood guarding the marketplace against any signs of rebellious behavior made normal life as Newport's people knew it impossible.

Self-consciously Catie let her hand slide from Anthony's arm, aware of the curious looks that the simple gesture was drawing from her neighbors. For a few brief moments, she'd allowed herself the comfort that little touch had brought. It was dangerous, that little touch, that little public intimacy. She'd let herself believe that even in his silence he somehow understood. Whether she'd sensed it or imagined it, a bond had been there between them, and she thought wistfully of all that could never be—could never even begin—between them.

Purposefully she bent to study a basket of winter pippins, seeming to forget Anthony entirely.

"Open thievery, that's what you're practicing, Enos Jonson," she declared to the farmer behind the basket with the shawl doubled over his greatcoat. "Winter pippins, la! How many months have they been a-moldering in your barn before this, I wonder?"

The man drew the stained stem of his clay pipe from his mouth long enough to spit. "A ha'penny less fer th' lot, mistress," he said, "an' that be low as I'll go. These be hard times fer poor men, mistress, hard times."

"You will excuse me, Mrs. Hazard," said Anthony, his deep voice raised just enough to draw Catie's attention, as well as that of every other woman in the market. "But I must share a word with the general."

"Very well, Major Sparhawk, and good day to you." She scarcely bothered to look over her shoulder as she waved her hand in airy dismissal and returned her full attention to the apples. "A full penny less, Mr. Jonson, and be grateful for that. They must be taken to the kitchen door at Hazard's Tavern. Mind you ask for Hannah."

Yet as she counted out the coins in her palm, her thoughts were uneasily following Anthony. True, she had wanted him to leave her, but she hadn't wished it to be like this. What "words" was he having with his general? Was there something she'd inadvertently done or said that he wished to report so quickly?

As she made her way around the market, she tried to force herself to remember what Hannah needed. Eggs, of course, and the turkey, two if they were to be had, and the sticky molasses sweets that were Belinda's particular favorites, even though Catie wasn't sure when she'd be able to see her daughter again. And rice, and—

"No greetings to spare, lass?" asked Jon Sparhawk. "Or do they all belong to my dear cousin now? Quiet now, and keep your wits about you!"

"You—you startled me, Jon, that was all," said Catie nervously. She hadn't meant to jump, but then, she hadn't expected to find him here, either, standing near the back of a farmer's wagon, in the shadows of one of the brick arches. His usual simple but costly clothing was gone, replaced by a nondescript farmer's felt hat with the brim uncocked and an old-fashioned homespun coat with horn buttons. The stubble she'd first seen on his jaw the day of the British landing had darkened into the beginnings of a black beard. But the greatest change in his face came from within, a deep bitterness etched into every feature.

"I can't come calling proper to the tavern any longer, Catie, you know that." He sighed, his gaze restlessly sweeping beyond her. "We'll have to meet however we can. Now what news have you for me, eh?"

She swallowed, wracking her memory for something that Jon might find useful. "There was a party of Britishers camped at Arnold's farm—"

But Jon cut her off impatiently. "Common tattle, lass. I want what you've heard from Anthony."

"He's hardly about to confide state secrets in me, Jon, not after two days' acquaintance!"

His expression darkened. "To my eye, your acquaintance seems quite cozy. Leastways it did last night, when the pair of you rode into town on a single horse.''

Catie flushed, reminded again of how swiftly such news traveled. ''Since it was late, Anthony offered me his protection through the town. That was all, Jon, I swear.''

''Oh, aye, but you call him by his Christian name. That's good, fair Cate, very good indeed.'' He shifted closer, leaning his arm on the pillar behind her as he lowered his voice to a rough, urgent whisper. ''Has he mentioned any of his fellows wounded? Have any of the officers in your house kept to their beds or summoned a surgeon, or have any of your maidservants remarked bloodstains in the linen set aside for laundry?''

Her heart pounding at the decision before her, Catie shook her head to every question. She had promised Anthony that she'd tell no one of his wound, but she had also promised Jon to report whatever she saw or heard to help the rebel cause.

''Think, lass,'' urged Jon. ''Have you heard nothing of any officer being struck by a marksman?''

Again she shook her head, at once hating herself for the choice she'd made.

Jon swore, thumping his palm against the bricks in frustration. ''I was so sure I'd struck him! That bloody red uniform, the horse—there'd never be a better target, or a more deserving one!''

''Then it *was* you,'' she breathed, forgetting herself in her shock at what he'd admitted.

But before Jon could react, a smaller figure with a half-eaten sugar biscuit in his hand dodged beneath the wagon's tall wheel and came to stand at Jon's side.

With his thick black hair and shoulders that were already broad for an eight-year-old, Jeremiah Sparhawk was his father in boyish miniature.

With a warm smile on her face, Catie automatically crouched to the boy's level. Jeremiah was only three months younger than her daughter, and the two had often played together in the yard behind the tavern.

"Belinda likes those biscuits, too, Jere," she said. "How much she'd wish to be here with you to eat one now!"

But the boy didn't grin, as she'd expected. His expression remained wary, and without answering, he slid farther back beneath his father's protective arm.

"You can't blame the lad, Catie," said Jon. "He saw you walk in here pretty as you please with a redcoat officer, and in our house a redcoat is next to the devil himself."

Slowly Catie rose. "Even if that red coat belongs to Jeremiah's uncle?"

"It belongs to King George, Catie, and if Anthony chooses to wear it, then he's no longer kin of ours." Jon patted his son on the shoulder. "Isn't that so, Jere?"

"Yes, sir," said Jeremiah staunchly, still avoiding Catie's eyes. "No true Sparhawk bows to any tyrant king. Not Pa, not me, not Granfer, not Uncle Nick or Uncle Josh, neither. We're all free men, an' we'll fight t' the death to keep our freedom."

"You're very brave, Jeremiah," said Catie softly. Despite the boy's declaration, his anxious fingers had ground the biscuit into crumbs, and she'd have wagered a guinea he had nightmares, too. How could he not? "Your father must be proud of you."

With far less sympathy, she leveled her gaze to meet that father's. "You've taught him well, Jon. Not many children are such ardent patriots."

"Not many children have their grandparents chased from town with a price on their heads," said Jon grimly. "And how many other children have been torn from their sleep in the middle of the night while soldiers searched their little trundle beds for hidden muskets?"

"Did Betsey believe the same?"

"Betsey is—is gone, Catie," he said, that hesitation betraying the depth of a sorrow that time hadn't eased. "It's up to me to decide what's best for our children now. The young ones will stay with my mother and father, and in the spring I'll take Jeremiah with me privateering, as a cabin boy. Then he'll see men wounded and killed fighting for their country and for freedom, and the sooner he understands why, the better."

There was nothing Catie could say to that, beyond sending a little prayer heavenward for Belinda's safety, and poor Jeremiah's, too. To her mind, a ship of war was no place for any child. She didn't doubt that Jon loved his boy as much as she loved Belinda; she had only to see father and son together to know that. But while she had done her best to spare her daughter from the war, Jon Sparhawk was choosing the opposite course for his son. More decisions made by men, she thought unhappily, more lives changed forever by their whims and those of this wretched war.

Jon sighed, and settled his hat lower on his brow as he took his son by the hand.

"Come to me when you've something useful to tell,

Catie,'' he said as he carefully brushed the biscuit crumbs from the front of Jeremiah's waistcoat. "I'll grant you Anthony's a clever man, but he's one who's swayed by a fair face, or at least he was once. Smile his way, and you'll have his secrets—the secrets we'll need to fight these blasted British, lass, and to win. To have this damnable army gone from Newport by Christmas would be a grand thing for us all.''

Reluctantly Catie nodded, trying not to think of Rhode Island's ragtag militia fighting against the British army that had taken the island with such ruthless efficiency, nor of the two cousins who'd chosen such different sides. "How will I find you? Will you be here at the market again next week?''

"Nay, there's too many redcoats here for my taste. Come next Tuesday night to Owen Piper's house. You'll find me and many of the others who still believe in the cause there.''

Cate gasped with dismay. "The Pipers' house? Oh, please, not there!''

Jon shrugged, turning to leave. "Why not? There's no one else in Newport that I'd trust more than Owen Piper. His ruse with the smallpox has made their house the safest on the island. There's not a Britisher here that will dare go near the place.''

"But Belinda is there!'' cried Catie desperately as she seized his sleeve. "I took her to Abigail and Owen for safekeeping when the British landed to take Newport!''

"Then what better place for us to meet, eh?'' Jon's sudden smile was unsettlingly white against his dark beard as he gently eased his arm free of her grasp. "You'll know for certain that your pretty little lass is snug and safe with us. And I'll know, Mistress Cate, that you won't consider putting my cousin before me again.''

"So that's your pretty widow, eh, Sparhawk?" Standing in the shelter of a shop window, General Ridley squinted through the swirling snow to where Catie had just reappeared from behind one of the market's brick archways. "Pity she's shrouded away in that cloak. Can't have a proper look at the chit."

"Mrs. Hazard is hardly a chit, sir," said Anthony, his gaze following Catie with concern. She was moving slowly, clutching the cloak around her body as if she were frozen, and he couldn't forget how upset she'd obviously been earlier. "She's considered a woman of some substance and position in this town. Her tavern is reckoned by many to be the best in the colony."

"Always the gallant, aren't you, Major?" The general blew his nose loudly. "So is the lady as eager as that last pair, in Hempstead?"

Anthony cleared his throat, wishing the general's memory was equally long regarding merit. "Mrs. Carteret and her daughter were altogether different."

"Ha, willing enough to prove their loyalty with a certain king's officer, as I recall," said the general, leering over his crumpled handkerchief. "You were in clover there, man, and don't try to tell me otherwise!"

Anthony didn't. Ridley wouldn't believe that Anthony had turned away the advances of Mrs. Carteret and her plump pigeon of a daughter while he was quartered in their house. It hadn't been easy; Mrs. Carteret had been most insistently ardent, and she'd kept an extra key to his bedchamber. But while Anthony had long since lost interest in such casual intrigues, the rest of his regiment hadn't, and he wondered wearily how many wagers had been already laid down among the other officers regarding him and Catie Hazard.

"You'll recall, sir, that there's a score of other men quartered at the tavern, too," said Anthony instead. "Besides, as charming as my landlady herself might be, I rather thought I'd been placed under her roof for a reason other than to amuse myself."

The general snorted. "No harm in a young bachelor buck like you doing both. Before I wed, I would have played the very devil with these hussies, were I in your boots. By harry, wouldn't I!" He sneezed, loud and moistly, and wiped his nose again. "Well then, Sparhawk, if you haven't rogered the woman yet, I trust at least you've overheard something useful in her barroom."

"Something, yes, sir." With relief, Anthony began the brief report he'd prepared. "Yesterday Mrs. Hazard was gone from the tavern for the duration of the entire day, with her servants evading my questions as to her whereabouts. Quite by accident, I met her returning late in the evening, and I'm convinced she lied about where she'd been. Cleverly, to be sure, sir, but lied just the same."

The general's eyes narrowed shrewdly, and he forgot his cold. "Protecting some rebel nest, eh? No doubt serving as some sort of go-between or messenger. I trust you had her searched?"

Anthony himself had seen the contents of Catie's basket, but there were a dozen other places on a woman's person where a letter or map could be hidden, and inwardly he winced as he realized how careless he'd been. "I was satisfied at the time, sir," he said, hedging. "But I do believe that she might—"

"No 'mights,' Sparhawk," said the general, interrupting curtly. "I want her watched, followed, whenever she leaves the house."

"Yes, sir," said Anthony. "I'll see to it directly."

But even as he agreed, his gaze was riveted to Catie. She had paused at another stall, bending down to study some bundled greens spread for her inspection, when a dark-haired boy darted through the crowd to her. Whoever the boy was, she knew him; for when he slipped something into her palm—a note? a coin?— she took his hand and drew him near enough to kiss him lightly on his cheek. The boy hovered close, listening to whatever she said as she bent over him, until a thickset man with a broad-brimmed hat shielding his face came to rest his hand on the boy's shoulder and lead him away. Catie waved as they left her, a small, hesitant gesture that the man either didn't notice or chose to ignore.

Anthony frowned, disturbed by the tall man's callousness. Catie knew him, that was clear enough. But then, why had the man been in such haste to lead the boy from her, and why, too, did she linger to watch them go, her shoulders bent in a way that seemed at once dejected and wistful?

The boy looked up to speak to the man, and the man glanced downward to listen. As he did, the same wind that swirled the snowflakes caught the broad brim of his hat and lifted it back from his head. Swiftly he caught it with one hand and jammed it back upon his head, but not before he'd given Anthony a clear, open view of his face.

A familiar face, thought Anthony as he struggled to keep his own expression impassive before the general, as familiar as the one he saw each morning in his shaving mirror. And why shouldn't it be? The two were near enough to belong to brothers, as cousins often were.

One dark, one fair.

One who served his king, one who followed his father into anarchy and treason.

And both of them knew Catie Hazard.

"Aye, Sparhawk, 'tis often the vixen that leads the hunter to the den," the general was saying, with no small satisfaction. "Follow her, and I wager we'll have the whole pack of traitorous rogues in our hands at last."

Chapter Six

"It don't look like much o' a night, mistress," said Liam Connor sadly to Catie. "Thin, it is, terrible thin. Though maybe th' company will improve once th' snow don't lie so thick on th' ground."

He rested his fiddle across his knee and reached for his tankard of lime juice and watered rum—all the drink Catie allowed him while he was playing in her front room—as he stared dolefully at the pewter cup on the bench beside him. Three shillings, a ha'penny and two bent farthings weren't much for a fiddler as accomplished as Liam, even on a Thursday night in December, and the nearly empty room angered Catie.

"'Tis no fault of the snow, Liam, as you know perfectly well," she said crossly. "Most nights, snow's good for custom. If a gentleman's spent all day huddled close to his own fire, he'll look for any excuse to leave it come evening. No, I lay all the blame at the door of the British, and may the devil claim them all for ruining my trade."

She sighed, her irritation masking her deeper worries and fears. Between the snow and the soldiers surrounding the tavern, she hadn't been able to slip away to see Belinda again, and though she'd sent little notes and sweetmeats—including the candy stick that Jeremiah had impulsively given to her at the market—it wasn't the same as holding her daughter in her arms or hearing her rippling laughter.

Again and again Catie reminded herself that it was for the best, that notwithstanding Jon's threat, her daughter was safer with the Pipers than in town. Yet still she pored over the labored little notes that Belinda had written in return, each of them ending in a plea to come home. It did not take much for Catie to guess that the rippled blotches on the paper had been caused by Belinda's tears. The ones she shed herself each night were more than a match for them.

But Belinda was not the only one absent from her life. She had neither seen nor heard from Jon Sparhawk since the day at the market. Not that she would have had any news to share with him if she had, for his cousin seemed to have disappeared, as well.

It wasn't that Anthony had changed his quarters. Far from it. She would overhear his voice discussing orders with Peterson as they left in the morning, and she could identify his footfall on the stairs when he returned late at night. But he had not sought her company again, or even contrived an excuse for them to meet in passing in the hallway. She told herself she was relieved, even though she knew well—and guiltily—enough that if that was true she would not have to tell herself any such thing.

She sighed again, forcing herself to count the handful of guests tonight, instead of the number of times Anthony Sparhawk had smiled her way. An even dozen, that was all. Before the British came, this room would have been filled to overflowing with gentlemen, drinking and smoking and laughing and dining and arguing politics and banging their tumblers to Liam's fiddle. There would likely have been a private supper in the back dining room and another party in the card room, plus more gentlemen gathered to play billiards on the special table she'd imported from London for the game just last year.

Oh, aye, she knew how to cater to all the tastes of the Newport gentry, whether it was French wines or Virginia tobacco. But such whims and indulgences were expensive, and for Catie to turn her usual profit required balancing creditors and customers with great delicacy even in the best of times.

Now, scarcely a fortnight after the British had first captured Newport, Hazard's Tavern's best upstairs chambers were empty and the candles in the card room unlit, and here in the barroom only a half-dozen men gathered halfheartedly to sip their punch. Many of her best customers, like Gabriel Sparhawk, had been forced to flee the island before the army, while more and more had taken their families and left since then. Of the ones who remained, most simply preferred not to be questioned by the sentries at the door for the sake of a dram.

Then there was other, real damage done by the soldiers, as well, from the gouges their swords and heavy shoes left in the woodwork to the tiny, untraceable thieveries, things that Catie was sure were disappearing into British knapsacks. And despite Lieutenant Peterson's assurances, she'd seen not a farthing for quartering either the soldiers in her attic or the officers in her best chambers.

Jon Sparhawk had dared to hope the British would be gone by Christmas. Catie prayed he was right. Hazard's wouldn't be able to continue like this much longer if he wasn't.

She sighed softly, rubbing her forearms against the deep chill that not even the fire could diminish. "It's not your fault, Liam, any more than it's mine," she said, shaking her head. "And you needn't fret over that shameful pittance for your evening's toil. I'll make up the difference myself."

Liam frowned, his sparse, sandy brows coming together as he clicked his tongue. "Now, mistress, you needn't do that. You say yourself, 'tis not your fault. It's King George himself who should be payin', not your own dear pocket."

Catie wrinkled her nose wryly. "La, I'd like to see you present your claim to His Majesty," she said, patting the fiddler on his bony shoulder. "Leave it to me to make up your loss, and play me a set of jigs in return, the more spritely the better."

The little man smiled at her with such open devotion that Catie couldn't help smiling wanly in return. Though with his fiddle and his endless memory for tunes, Liam could find work at any tavern or alehouse in town—perhaps even with the army—he would stay with her now, even after she couldn't afford to be as generous as she was tonight.

"Jigs it be, mistress," he said, rubbing the rosin on his bow. "For you and no other."

She dipped him a small curtsy to honor his loyalty before she went to greet the new customer she heard at the door in the hall. Carefully keeping the smile on her face, she caught a quick, horrifying glimpse of herself in the looking glass over the fireplace. Surely the circles beneath her eyes were a false trick of the candlelight. How could she expect to offer guests a respite from their worries when she herself looked so pale and careworn?

"A good evening to you, sir," she called cheerfully as she hurried into the hall with her arms extended in greeting.

The man remained hidden by the open door while he knocked the snow from his boots against the step outside. A thoughtful gentleman, decided Catie, and despite the hour, one not so far into his cups that he'd stopped caring what happened to her floors. A gentleman, clearly, to be welcomed with pleasure.

Purposefully she brightened her smile even further. "A cold night it may be, sir, but here at Hazard's I can promise you warm company and good cheer."

"And good cheer is precisely what I've a need for, Mrs. Hazard," said Anthony as he closed the door behind him. He swung his cloak from his shoulders, scattering snowflakes like diamonds, and handed it and his hat to the waiting serving girl. "That, and a decent fire."

"Major—Major Sparhawk." To suddenly have him before her after days of fancying left Catie nearly speechless and blushing like a schoolgirl. She had never seen him clothed as handsomely as this, in full dress uniform for evening, his scarlet coat heavy with gold lace, his hair braided and powdered and tied with a black silk riband.

"Your servant, ma'am." He bowed neatly from the

waist, and motioned toward the barroom. "A brandy, please, ma'am, before I retire for the evening. That, and a taste of this splendid company you promise."

"Wait, Major, please, a moment!" began Catie anxiously. "That is, you cannot— *I* cannot—"

But he had already swept by her, leaving her to bustle after him into the barroom. "Major Sparhawk, please!"

He stopped at the fireplace and turned, the blue-faced skirts of his coat swinging and his smile expansive as he ignored the hostile stares of the other men in the room and the way Liam's fiddle squeaked to a halt.

"A glass of your finest brandy, Mrs. Hazard," he ordered as he stepped to the bar where Turner, Hazard's keep, stood waiting behind the raised grate. "In a house as well-appointed as yours, ma'am, I expect that shall be very fine indeed."

Catie stood before him, her hands clasped stiffly before her while Turner looked at her expectantly. Anthony might be unaware of the resentment and outright hatred that flowed from the others, but she felt it so acutely it was almost painful. Whatever was he *doing?*

"Major Sparhawk," she began again, "please, do not ask this of me."

"Oh, now I understand, dear lady," he said easily, reaching into his pocket. "I've heard the speech from tavernkeepers before. 'My liquor's good, my measure just, but honest sirs I will not trust.' Here, ma'am, that should be sufficient."

She stared at the coins in the palm of his outstretched hand, and it took all her willpower not to dash them away.

He didn't remember. Why should he? It had meant nothing to him. But once before he had tried to set things to rights with a handful of coins, and then, as now, he'd only succeeded in making them worse.

"It is not a question of credit, Major, but of loyalties." She lifted her chin and prayed her voice would not tremble. At least she knew better than to meet his eye, and instead she stared at the flat knot of gold lace that made up the epaulet on his right shoulder, and the light dusting of powder from his hair that lay across his coat.

"I cannot stop you or your men from claiming my upper rooms as your quarters," she said carefully. "But even with your flag and your guards before my door, I remain in sympathy to the cause of liberty. So it was when my husband lived, and so it shall remain. Call this room what you please—a rebel taproom, a den of traitors—but your Tory money is not welcome here, sir, nor is your custom. Now I wish you a good evening."

She stood very still, her hands still clasped. She couldn't have made her feelings any more clear, and she knew her words would be repeated a hundred times before breakfast tomorrow morning. She hoped they'd reach Jon's ears, too, for Belinda's sake. She had nothing more to say. Now it was up to Anthony to leave, as she'd requested.

So why didn't he?

Instead, he rested one hand on the half-basket hilt of his sword and tossed the coins in his other hand so that they jingled dully against his palm. His smile remained, guarded now, and without the easy charm that had marked it before.

"So, Mrs. Hazard," he said softly. "Because of my uniform, you refuse to serve me my brandy?"

"Yes, sir." She was emboldened now, and her voice barely shook at all. This whole conversation seemed unreal, like a scene from a play presented for her customers' amusement. "That is true. Brandy or anything else."

"Nor will you drink with me?"

"No, sir," she said firmly. "Most certainly not."

"Ah." He slipped the coins back into his pocket. "A pity, that, Mrs. Hazard. Brandy would have made our conversation a great deal more agreeable."

"Conversation, Major?" she asked warily. "To my mind, sir, there's nothing more between us to be discussed."

"Oh, yes, ma'am, I fear there is." Slowly he walked across the room, his booted footsteps heavy on the floorboards, until he stood directly before her.

Too close, thought Catie, too close. Frantically she fought the urge to back away and put more distance between them. But to back away would be to give in, to acknowledge that he was right when he was so clearly wrong, and before so many witnesses she refused to be intimidated.

"*You* fear, Major?" She jeered, trying hard to bluster and bluff. "Surely a king's officer such as yourself would have nothing to *fear* from me."

"I don't, ma'am," he said slowly. "And perhaps neither shall you. I'll leave that for you to decide, once we've discussed Captain Jon Sparhawk."

Catie felt her expression freeze in place. She hadn't expected that from him, not in the least, though it seemed cruelly obvious now that he'd been planning to ask her about Jon from the moment he entered. Likely he hadn't even expected her to serve him, and ordering the brandy had merely been a way to put her off her guard. And it had worked. She couldn't deny it.

"Captain Jon Sparhawk," she repeated, hoping to regain her advantage. He, too, could be bluffing; she must not forget that. "I wonder that you ask me of Captain Sparhawk. To be sure, his family is known to everyone here in Newport, but what I especially can tell you of Captain Jon will be precious little indeed."

"Indeed?" drawled Anthony, all the skepticism in the world contained in that one tiny word. "Perhaps you're too modest, Mrs. Hazard. I'd heard you keep closer company with the captain than that. So close, in fact, that when he comes to call he prefers your kitchen door that is the familiarity of old acquaintance."

"Old acquaintance, or mere convenience, Major." Her attempt at a laugh was brittle. Lord help her, he might know everything. "Hazard's kitchen door is often used by guests who bring their mounts into the stable yard. As I recall, sir, you have done that yourself."

"But the good captain is mistrustful of horses, in the manner of many mariners," countered Anthony easily. "Stables hold few charms for him. But your kitchen, ma'am, your famed hospitality—that is different."

Catie shrugged, feigning a carelessness she did not feel. She'd be the centerpiece of every bit of town gossip for days to come, her careful reputation shredded and tattered, if she let this continue so publicly.

"I feel sure, sir, that these gentlemen grow weary of our discussion," she said, though to judge from the rapt expressions on the faces around her, weariness was hardly an issue. "If they wished to listen to such tedious questioning as this, they would go to the court-house, not come here to Hazard's."

"Truly, ma'am, you are the model of a hostess, always with an eye toward your guests' welfare!" He smiled, but Catie saw how the smile failed to reach his eyes. "Another room, then, Mrs. Hazard, if it pleases you."

It didn't please her one bit, but there was no way that Catie could imagine to refuse him.

"Very well, Major," she said with a quick nod. "May I suggest we retreat to this next chamber, and leave the gentlemen here to their pleasures?"

She stepped aside and gracefully waved her hand toward the far door. Anthony bowed to show his agreement, and waited for her to lead the way. As prettily done as any ballroom quadrille, thought Catie unhappily, as if they were partners in some genteel dance and no more. He could jest all he wanted about fearing this and fearing that, but the honest truth was that she was the one who'd never been more frightened in her life.

She forced herself to smile, gave a quick twitch to her skirts, and with a whisper to Liam to resume the music, she headed toward the next room.

Anthony watched her walk before him, across the hall to the empty, smaller chamber beyond, pausing only to take a candlestick to light the dark room. In the evenings she dressed more like the wives of the gentlemen she served, and tonight she wore a sage-colored caraco jacket sprigged with roses over a dark red quilted petticoat. Her ruffled linen cuffs were simple, but the fabric was so fine as to be nearly sheer, and the kerchief around her shoulders, cut from the same sheer linen, served more to show off the creaminess of her throat and tight-laced breasts than to hide it. Beyond a pair of small garnet earbobs, her only ornament was the little gold locket that she never seemed to be without.

The entire effect was elegant and costly, fit for any Newport lady, or for a London one, for that matter. So Anthony would have told Catie, if she'd been in any mood to listen to his compliments. But he knew better than to say a word, simply from the straight, unyielding line of her back. She was, he guessed with an inward sigh, very angry with him. Whether that anger had spilled over into fury he'd find out soon enough.

She used the candle in her hand to light the others in the wall sconces while he gently closed the door after him. She set the candlestick on the mantelpiece, folded her arms squarely across her chest and, with a sound that might have been either a grumble or a gulp, faced him.

"Here we are, Major," she said. "You wished to— to *interrogate* me?"

He couldn't help bridling at that. "*Interrogate* is too strong a word, Catie. I wish to ask you a question or two about my cousin's whereabouts, that is all."

"That is *all!*" she cried, with a bitterness that took him by surprise. "You shame me before my customers, you imply all manner of improprieties that could ruin me and my trade, and then you say that is *all!*"

"There was no other way—"

"A gentleman would have found one!"

"Then a gentleman would have instantly made you an outcast in Newport," said Anthony sharply. "You worry over what will be said of you now. What would have been whispered instead if you'd come here with me directly, without a chance to make your little speech?"

"That wouldn't have happened!"

"Oh, aye, it would, as you know full well!" he continued relentlessly. "What would the girl who took my cloak and hat tell her mother, who would tell her sister, and so on, until all Newport knew of it? Damnation, at least this way you're allied with my cousin—a sight more popular position in this town than being a loyalist officer, I can assure you—and you've been able to make your blasted rebel beliefs as well-known as if you'd shouted them from your highest window!"

Her head bowed, Catie sagged back against the mantelpiece. He was right, damn him. He always was. *Damn* him.

"I tell you, Catie, that I—"

"No," she said, her voice strained. "You must not call me that again. I gave you leave, I know, but it wasn't right of me to do. I am your enemy. I must not forget that."

"And I, ma'am? What am I?"

Troubled, she looked up at him through her lashes, her chin tucked low. In the candlelight his eyes were shadowed, unreadable, above the firm, fierce curve of his lips, yet still she felt the spell of attraction pulling them closer.

What was he to her? The most beautiful man she'd ever known, temptation and pleasure and sin and ruin in one undeniably perfect package. And despite the awful, sorrowful price she'd paid for her desire once before, she still wanted to be here with him, to hear him say her name and smile her way and—

But what she wanted didn't matter. She must think of her daughter, of Belinda.

"You," she whispered. "You are my enemy."

"Your enemy, ma'am. Your *enemy*." As sudden and terrifying as lightning, he lashed out against the little table beside him, his arm sweeping everything on its surface to the floor with a shattering crash of pottery. He swung back around to face her, his eyes wild.

"Your enemy, ma'am," he said again, his breath a ragged rasp. "Your *enemy*."

"Major Sparhawk, please, I beg you—"

"No, you *will* listen!" he ordered. "This night I dined with my general and my fellow officers, men I have considered as dear and honorable as brothers. Yet the table at which we sat belonged—*had* belonged— to my aunt, the service that bore our dinner was marked with my family's crest, and when we drank to His Majesty's health, the glasses were filled with wine from my uncle's cellar. I may be your enemy, ma'am, but I am my own enemy, as well."

She swallowed, searching his face. Part of her said she should be frightened, that she should leave him now, before his temper and frustration were turned toward her instead of an earthenware bowl. But she wasn't, at least not of his temper.

"But it was your choice, wasn't it?" she asked gently. She could see how hard he was working to compose himself. "No one forced you to become an officer of the king."

He came to stand beside her, resting his hands on the mantelpiece as he stared down into the fire. He hated himself for losing his temper, especially before her; such outbursts were shameful, unworthy of an officer.

"No, dear lady, I paid quite dearly for the privilege of a commission," he said, striving to sound droll instead of desperate. "Close to three thousand pounds, as I recall. Nearly the sum of what my grandfather left me."

"Three thousand pounds is a great deal of money for anyone," she said softly. "Quite dear indeed."

She'd never know how grateful he was for the gentleness of her voice. "The devil only knows if I am enemy or savior, villain or hero, for I've lost all notion of it myself," he said wearily. "How can I know otherwise? I came to this country, my *home,* believing I could do good, serving my king and my country. But instead I am hated by the very people I am ordered to protect, reviled and spat upon and shot at by those who, not so long ago, would have smiled my way."

He turned and slowly reached out to brush her cheek with the back of his hand. "Except for you, Catie," he said. "My dear Mrs. Hazard. You alone have shown me kindness. Only you, sweet lady, have dared to judge me not by my coat, but as a man."

She felt like a deer caught staring at a lantern's flame, trapped in the heat of his gaze as the warmth it brought crept across her cheeks. It wasn't kindness alone that had made her treat him as she had. She understood the loneliness she heard in his voice, for she'd felt it often enough herself.

But that wasn't all of it, either, not by half. Loneliness didn't make her heart race or her body turn heavy with longing, or rouse a memory that she'd thought was long past and forgotten.

As swiftly as she could, she eased herself free and went to crouch down beside the little tea table. With unsteady fingers she began to gather up the shards of broken crockery and place them in the basket from beside the hearth.

Behind her, Anthony's fingers hovered, useless, in the space she'd left, still aching for the velvety curve of her cheek. At last he let his hand drop awkwardly to his side. He knew she felt the same yearning he did; he'd seen it in her eyes. But if she was strong enough to pull away, then so was he.

"I'll pay for that," he said gruffly. "I insist."

She didn't look up. "Of course you shall pay. Even Tories must pay for damages."

Anthony frowned. He didn't like seeing her fuss over the mess he'd made, reminding him again of his shameful outburst. "It's not the same as the brandy."

"I never said it was." She bent a little lower, purposefully concentrating on the task before her. "You ask about your cousin Jon. I have not seen him for nearly two weeks, and that, I swear, is the truth."

Anthony hid his surprise. "Jon's house is locked and shuttered. A neighbor told me he had taken his children and fled to Providence."

"Oh, I hope it is so!" said Catie fervently, thinking again of Belinda. If Jon had gone to join his parents, then he'd expect nothing more from her, or the Pipers, either. "For his children, and for his own sake, as well, it would be the best thing possible."

"It's hard for me to imagine Jon with children at all," admitted Anthony. "When I saw him last, he was still steeling himself to ask for the young lady's hand. Betsey, her name was, I think. Betsey Pattison. How many children do they have?"

"Three. Two sons and a daughter." She scooped the last shards into the basket and briskly rubbed her hands free of the dust. "But Betsey died two years ago, in childbed with the second boy. You did not know?"

Anthony shook his head, barely remembering a bright, merry girl who clapped her hands with delight whenever she laughed. "May heaven keep the poor lass."

"Amen." Catie sat back on her heels and looked up at him over her shoulder. "Jon misses her sorely. First Betsey's death, then this war. You would, I think, find him much changed."

Now, nagged Anthony's conscience, now was the time for him to press further and ask for the names of Jon's associates. She had already volunteered so much that it would seem natural for him to ask after friends that he and Jon had once had in common, friends he suspected were as deeply involved in the rebel cause as the Sparhawk family. Hadn't he come here tonight intending to learn exactly that? It was his duty to ask, and General Ridley was growing impatient for more information.

But instead Anthony found himself studying the double swell of Catie's breasts above her bodice, a sight that was hard to avoid, with her still settled so gracefully on the floor before him. Had Jon done the same—and more—on his kitchen-door visits to Hazard's? Perhaps the explanation for his cousin's calling had nothing to do with the rebellion. A handsome widower left with three young children, a pretty young widow with property of her own—what could be more natural?

Or more depressing, thought Anthony morosely. Not that he had any right to claim Catie's affections, but the thought of his cousin doing just that was more than he could tolerate with charitable feelings. He watched her smooth her pale hair behind her ear with a graceful little turn of her wrist before she touched the locket, her talisman. Or was it a gift from her lover? Anthony's misery grew by the moment. Damnation, why couldn't she call Jon her enemy instead of him?

As the silence between them deepened, he suddenly became aware of the fiddler's lilting song from the other room. It had been a popular tune in London before they sailed, sung everywhere from Vauxhall on down, and he couldn't help but hear the lyrics echo in his head now.

He cleared his throat. She'd probably break another bowl over his head, but he couldn't resist the opportunity that the song offered. At least it would be better than moping over his cousin's claims on her.

"I'd wager a guinea," he said, "that your fiddler fancies himself something of a wit."

Catie frowned, uncomprehending. How had they jumped from discussing Jon to this? "Liam is the best fiddler in Newport, to be sure, but I've never considered him a wit."

Anthony didn't answer, waiting instead for the verse before he cleared his throat again and began to sing in a rough baritone.

One morning, one morning, one morning in May,
I spied a young couple, they were making their way.
One was a lady, so sweet and so fair,
The other was a soldier, a brave volunteer.

"Oh!" gasped Catie indignantly as she scrambled to her feet. "Oh, how *dare* Liam do this to me! He shall soon find himself replaced by that Jamaican who came to me last week with the trained baboon, see if I don't just do it!"

"Wait, Catie, please," said Anthony, unable to help laughing at her sputtering outrage. "Perhaps the poor man plays at another's request. 'Tis still a pretty enough tune."

She glared at him, her gray eyes flashing fire, and Anthony thought how glad he was not to be that luckless fiddler.

"Oh, aye, a tune pretty enough to mock me!" she declared soundly. "You, too, if you'd only stop laughing long enough to realize! I don't even wish to guess what the rest of the horrid words are, and when I'm quite done with Liam, he'll never—"

"Stay, Catie," he said, still chuckling as he gently took her by the arm to hold her back. "I'm certain the man meant no harm."

"Heaven only knows what becomes of that infamous 'lady,'" said Catie, still fuming. "I vow, in every last one of those wretched songs of Liam's, the woman's either a strumpet or she throws herself off a cliff for the sake of some foolish man.''

"Ah, now, what did I say?'' he teased. "You're no more like the song than I. Besides, I promise I'm not anywhere as wicked as the soldier in the song. No 'wife back in London, and children twice times three.' ''

She narrowed her eyes suspiciously. "At least I am not,'' she said, but she didn't pull her arm away from him, either. "I've only your word to account for you.''

He loosened his grasp upon her arm, turning it gently so that the underside of her wrist lay upward. With the lightest of touches, he drew one finger back and forth along the pale blue veins. Though she went very still, again she didn't try to free herself. The devil take his cousin Jon, he thought with a certain amount of triumph, or at least take him as far as Providence. *He* was the one here with Catie now, and slowly he lifted her hand to his lips.

"What greater assurance could you wish, dear lady,'' he said as his lips grazed the back of her hand, "than my word of honor as a gentleman, a Sparhawk at that, and an officer?''

And as your enemy, added Catie's conscience, but the warning was washed away as he turned her hand over in his and kissed her open palm. She shivered with the unexpected pleasure of it, his lips brushing across the soft, sensitive flesh as her curled fingers had no choice but to touch his rough cheek and jaw.

"You *are* as wicked as the soldier in the song,'' she murmured, with only a hint of scolding. "So much for your word of honor.''

And he did look wicked, thoroughly, unrepentantly

wicked, as he glanced up at her from beneath his brows and slowly smiled. She hadn't noticed before that he had a dimple on only one side of his mouth, the right side, like a little bracket to frame his smile. By firelight his eyes were very green and his hair a tawny gold, and the polished crescent of his officer's gorget swung back and forth on the chain around his neck, tapping gently against her wrist. He slipped his hand over hers, covering it, and drew her closer.

"I've missed you, Catie Hazard," he said, his voice a dark, deep whisper, for her ears alone. "Though God knows, for both our sakes, I've tried to keep away."

She swallowed. "But here you are."

"And so," he said as he lowered his face, "it seems, are you."

The next instant, Catie felt the first touch of his lips, and with a little whimper she closed her eyes and gave her mouth to his. In a single moment, eight years fell away. The gentle but demanding pressure of his kiss and the fiery heat of it were everything that she remembered, and more, for memory had never been able to recapture the dizzying pleasure that he alone had brought her.

One kiss, she told herself, this one kiss, was all she would allow herself. One bittersweet kiss, to make up for the long years of her loveless marriage and the dutiful couplings with Ben. One kiss to let herself pretend she was seventeen again, with all the world and its promise waiting for her. One kiss, she told herself, and swayed against Anthony as she opened both her lips and her soul to him.

One kiss...

"*Catie.*"

Slowly she opened her eyes, bewildered and bereft. Why would he pull away, what would make him stop now?

"Catie, look at me," he said with a bewilderment that matched her own. "I do not know how it can be possible, and yet it must be so."

His brows were drawn together as he searched her face, and the first wisp of fear at what he might find began to curl in Catie's stomach. She tried to ease herself free, but he held her too tightly by the shoulders for her to escape.

"You make no sense, Anthony." She laughed nervously. "Besides, I should return to my guests, and you to your men."

He shook his head, refusing to be diverted. "Years ago, the night before I sailed for London, there was a girl I met in a tavern near the water."

"You—you are mistaken, sir." Catie jerked free, her heart pounding. "Too many years have passed since you left for you to be so certain."

"But I am." Relentlessly he followed, reaching for her hand as he reached for the past. "A little serving girl afraid of her own shadow and still unaware of what her pretty face could do to a man, a sweet little miss with silver-gray eyes and a kiss like velvet."

"No," said Catie, her eyes wild as she backed away from him, toward the door. *"No."*

"Yes, Catie," he said softly. "Because you are that lass."

And with a strangled sob, she turned and fled.

Chapter Seven

"There now, mistress," said Hannah as she shoved another piece of wood into the kitchen fire beneath the hanging pots. "That should do until dinner."

The wood in the fire shifted, the half-burned pieces collapsing and tumbling down with a thump and a hissing spray of sparks, so common a sound that Hannah scarcely heard it. But Catie jumped back and gasped as if crackling wood were a musket shot.

Hannah glanced at her curiously. "Are you well, mistress?" she asked. "It's not like you to be so edgy."

Catie forced herself to smile, though her balled hand was still pressed tightly over her racing heart. "'Tis the wind, no more," she said, as lightly as she could. "You know how I am with these winter storms. Hearing the wind rattle and howl around the windows like some wild creature unsettles me."

"Ah, well, if that's all it is," said Hannah with a shrug. "Here I was thinkin' it was that Britisher major that had you so feared."

Catie barely stopped herself from gasping again.

Were her fears really so transparent that even Hannah could guess them? From the moment she fled from Anthony the night before, she had been expecting him to follow. She had never doubted he would. It was only a question of when.

Somehow she willed her voice to be steady. "You fancy too much, Hannah. Why should I be frightened of the British major, or at least more so today than yesterday?"

"Oh, aye, and why not?" Hannah glanced at her slyly and chuckled. "Weren't enough that I heard it from Liam Connor. No, no. The moment I stepped from the door to go to the well, Mrs. Palmer came bustling from *her* own doorway to ask if what she'd heard of Mrs. Hazard was true."

Catie's mouth went dry. They couldn't know, not this fast. They *couldn't*. "I've asked you before not to gossip, Hannah," she said as sternly as she could. "Repeating rumor and idle talk discredits the house."

"But it don't be gossip when it's true, mistress," protested Hannah. "There was a dozen men in the taproom last night who heard you stand up to that Britisher. Fancy him trying to bully you into serving our good liquor to a redcoat officer in Hazard's! But you stood firm, mistress. You told him his custom wasn't welcome, nor his coin. Told him so clear that even a thick-witted Tory couldn't help but understand. You told him proper, mistress, an' the whole town's proud of you."

"Thank you," said Catie faintly, torn between relief and guilt. The whole town would be feeling far less kindly toward her if they knew what else she'd done with the thick-witted Tory. "Though I don't see how I could have done otherwise."

"Ah, but how you would have pleased the master, God rest his soul!" said Hannah warmly, her hands clasped together and her eyes so full of emotion that Catie feared she'd weep. "Poor Mr. Hazard couldn't have done better himself, and that's the honest truth."

The cook snuffled loudly as she fumbled for her handkerchief, giving Catie far too much time to consider the awful irony of her words.

"Things be so changed, mistress," she said as she blew her nose. "Changed, an' not all for the best, an' it makes me sad to think on it. But you've sorrow of your own, mistress, without hearing mine, too. Better I should step over to the stable to see if any of those infernal hens has seen fit yet to lay this day. I know the cold disturbs them, but they'll find themselves in a kettle if they don't change their idle ways soon."

"No, wait, Hannah, please!"

Surprised, the older woman paused with her hand on her cloak, waiting for Catie to explain.

"Need you go this moment, Hannah?" she asked anxiously. However prickly the cook might be, Catie found her company far better than being left alone with her own conscience. "Surely if you waited until dusk, there would be a better chance of finding eggs?"

"At dusk?" scoffed Hannah as she drew her cloak over her shoulders. "Nay, mistress, I've already waited too long on those silly birds."

"But surely—"

"If you're feared of being alone here, mistress, then you've only to ask an' I'll stay," said Hannah, with a kindness rare for her. "But I'd guess that a lady who speaks up to British officers won't be scared by a bit o' wind an' snow rattling the shutters.''

"Of course I won't," said Catie defensively. She'd spent most of her life hiding her feelings, and hiding them well. Why then now, when so much was at stake, had she suddenly become so appallingly guileless? "I was only worrying on your account, Hannah. You complain so much about the ague in your knees that surely the cold must make it worse. Here, hand me the basket and I'll go hunt for the eggs myself."

"You, mistress?" Indignantly Hannah clutched the basket with both hands. "Nay, that would not be proper, not proper at all!"

Before Catie could stop her Hannah had thrown open the door and gone, marching steadfastly into the blowing snow. With a sigh, Catie pushed the door more tightly shut after her, then began to set a tray for afternoon chocolate and biscuits to take up to Mrs. Chalmers, one of their last remaining guests. By Hannah's reckoning, that wouldn't be particularly proper, either, but to Catie, propriety seemed to matter less and less each day.

She sighed as she took the chocolate mill down from the pantry closet shelf. Next week would be Christmas. In any other year, she would have already decorated the public rooms with greenery, polished fruit and bows of colored ribbons for the holidays, but without Belinda here to help her, she hadn't the heart even to begin. Besides, what was the point in spending the time and money she no longer had? There wasn't a single private dinner or party scheduled between now and Twelfth Night. Before the British ruined her trade, her keeping book would have shown nearly every room filled for every night but the Sabbaths.

Behind her she heard the door open again, the wind rushing around her ankles with a ruffling *whoosh* of her skirts.

"For the sake of heaven, Hannah," she scolded without turning. "Close the door directly, before you make the chimney smoke!"

"Am I that much changed, Madame Hazard," asked Jon Sparhawk, his voice hoarse from the cold, "that you mistake me for your cook?"

Catie spun around to face him. "Whatever are you doing here, Jon?" she demanded as, at last, he closed the door the way she'd ordered. "It's not Belinda, is it? She's well, isn't she?"

"She was when I saw her yesterday. Prime as a little rose, that one."

"Then why are you here, Jon, and in the middle of the day, too! Isn't it enough to risk your own neck, without putting mine through the noose, as well?"

"Hush now, Catie, don't be daft." Heavy clots of wet snow dropped from his hat and shoulders as he went to warm himself before the fire. "Those whey-blooded English are all shivering inside today. Even the sentries at your doorstep have crawled off somewhere, if you'd bothered to notice. There's nary a one of the bastards to see me, let alone try to haul me to the gallows."

"I'm not the one who's daft, Jon. You are."

"What I am, Catie, is powerfully tired of hearing you question my reason." He grimaced as the warmth crept back into his chilled fingers. "Are you saying the same to Anthony, too, I wonder?"

Catie winced at the intimacy Jon was implying. "What I say to your cousin is none of your affair," she said, her voice edgy and defensive.

He glanced sharply over his shoulder at her. "Don't turn forgetful on me, Catie."

"How can I, with you always here in my kitchen to remind me?" Somehow she managed to return the gaze of those hard green eyes as she frantically pieced together an explanation he'd accept. If Jon believed she had something to hide, he wouldn't be put off with some tale about the wind, the way that Hannah had been. For Belinda's sake, she didn't dare falter before him.

"I promised to repeat whatever Anthony said that might be useful to our side," she said, striving now to make her manner merely firm, not defensive. "But that is all, Jon. I cannot do otherwise. No respectable tavernkeeper will whisper a guest's conversations wholesale, even if the guest is an unwelcome Englishman."

Slowly he relaxed, his grudging smile white against his black beard. "Old Ben trained you well, didn't he? A woman who refuses to gossip—Lord, Catie, that alone's enough to make me ask for your hand once again. I do believe you've grown prettier, too, if such a thing were possible."

"Jon, be serious." She came to stand beside him, her expression full of concern. "Anthony came here last night asking questions about you. He's searched your house and questioned your neighbors."

Jon's face hardened. "He found nothing."

"I don't know if he did or not. He said you'd fled

to Providence with the children. I wish he'd been right."

"He was, partly. I sent Desire and the baby upriver to my parents, but I kept Jeremiah with me. And ah, Catie, you should have seen how the lad proved his mettle with us last night!"

Catie sucked in her breath, remembering the dread she'd seen in the boy's eyes. "What did you do, Jon?"

"Only what we Newport men should have weeks ago," he declared, his face animated with excitement. "A party of us rowed into Bryce's Cove and crept up the rocks to fire into the house where a pack of the British are quartered. Easiest game in the world, Catie, all of those bastards sitting in their red dress coats like waxworks in the windows. We must have hit a good half score of them before the damned fools realized what was happening. We got clear away, too, though we had to row like blazes beneath their fire."

For one awful, fleeting moment Catie wondered if Anthony had been one of the men sitting too near the window. Lord, dear Lord, if Jon was given a second chance, he would kill his cousin outright.

But of course Anthony had been here, with her. Of course he was safe. Hadn't kissing him been proof enough of how gloriously alive he was?

And why, why, did she care so much?

"This is only the beginning, Catie," promised Jon with a fervor that sickened Catie. "We'll strike them again, and again, and again. The British may have taken this island without losing a man, but by God, they'll have to fight to keep it!"

"Your eight-year-old son may believe that, Jon, but I cannot," said Catie unhappily. "Oh, Jon, don't you realize what you've done? Before this the British only suspected you, but now—now they'll have a reason for hunting you down!''

He looked at her incredulously. ''Do you think I'd want it otherwise, Catie? This is a blasted *war!*''

''But think of your children!''

''I am thinking of them, Catie, and the kind of future I want them to have. Why the devil else would I—''

''Hush, Jon, listen! Someone's coming!''

They both froze, listening to the man's footsteps in the hall. Without a word, Jon grabbed his hat from the table and turned toward the back door, but Catie seized his arm.

''There isn't time,'' she whispered urgently, shoving him toward the pantry closet, still open from when she'd sought the chocolate mill. ''Go in here now. *Now!*''

She had barely shut the closet's door when the one from the hallway swung open behind her. She took a split-second to compose herself before she turned, a pleasant smile on her face.

''Major Sparhawk!'' The pleasant smile fled as confusion stained her cheeks. ''I didn't expect... That is to say...''

Anthony bowed stiffly. Today he was dressed not for fashion but for the weather, with the reveres of a serviceable wool uniform coat buttoned across his chest and thick leather gloves on his hands, and in place of the elegant grenadier's cap was a plain black cocked hat. Though he'd brushed the snow from his shoulders, his cheeks were still ruddy from the wind, and it was clear he'd come to find her here as soon as he returned to his quarters.

"It is I who must make apologies, ma'am," he said with a grim formality. "I intended to call on you directly this morning, but an unfortunate matter has kept me away until now. My rebel cousin, it seems, was most certainly not in Providence last night."

With Catie's heart pounding painfully in her breast, she could not tell which was worse—realizing that Jon's life depended upon her being able to make Anthony leave, or knowing that her daughter's future could be destroyed by what Jon might now overhear.

"An apology isn't necessary, Major, and neither is this call," she said, choosing her words with infinite care. "There was nothing left unsaid in our conversation last night."

"Nothing?" Impatiently he stepped forward and leaned across the table that separated them, his gaze searching her face. "Nothing, Catie? More truly nothing was said, and everything left unanswered."

"Then truly, sir, you are mistaken." Hoping to discourage him by looking away, she began to set the little chocolate cups and saucers on the tray, her nervous fingers making the blue-and-white porcelain rattle against the pewter tray. Where *was* Hannah, anyway?

Her sleeve brushed over the edge of the tray, and a silver spoon flipped onto the floor. Swiftly she bent to retrieve it, thankful for the excuse to duck away from the intensity of Anthony's gaze, even for a moment. But as she knelt, to her horror she noticed the puddles of melting snow that Jon had left, an incriminating path across the floorboards from the back door to the

hearth and finally to the closet. If Anthony came
around the table, he'd be sure to see the trail for himself, and no explanation in the world would stop him
from opening the closet door.

Quickly she rose to her feet, wiping the spoon on
the edge of her apron before she returned it to the tray.
"You must excuse me now, Major," she said, turning
away from him to fetch the hot milk from the hearth,
"but as you can see, I have other responsibilities that
require my attention."

"Damn your responsibilities, Catie, and look at
me!" He reached across the table and caught her wrist,
his gloved fingers holding her fast. "After what we
have been to each other, don't you believe I deserve
more from you?"

She prayed he couldn't feel how she was shaking.
"You are my enemy, Major, nothing more," she said.
"Why can't you understand that?"

"Catie, listen to me! You cannot deny the past as
if it never happened!"

"I can, Anthony, because it didn't!" she cried, her
desperation growing as she dreaded what Jon must
make of this conversation. "I am a decent woman, a
respectable widow, and what you—what you *suggest*
of me—shames both me and my husband's memory!"

"But Catie, I never—"

"No!" She pulled herself free, furiously rubbing her
wrist where he'd held her, to wipe away the memory
of his touch. "Now good day, Major. *Good day.*"

His gaze flickered down to follow her gesture, and
he frowned. "I won't be dismissed like this, Catie,"
he said, and began to come around the table to her

and the guilty trail of melted snow. "I am not some servant that you can send away on a whim."

"No, you must not!" she cried, panicking. She rushed ahead of him and pulled her cloak from the peg behind the door. "If you will not leave me here in peace as I ask, why, then I shall be the one to leave you!"

She threw open the door and raced out into the swirling snow. The snow was deeper than she'd expected, slowing her footsteps and dragging at her skirts, but she didn't stop, walking so quickly that she was nearly running.

Behind her she heard Anthony shout her name to call her back, then a muffled growl that she was sure was an oath, and then...*nothing*. To her surprise, he didn't seem to be following. But she didn't dare slow to make certain, or look back over her shoulder, in case somehow he was there, ready to misinterpret such a glance as encouragement. Instead, she plunged on through the snow, the wind driving the icy flakes against her face and tugging at her cloak.

She had no gloves or mittens, and the cloak she kept by the kitchen door was old and thin, better suited to running back and forth to the well or stable than to walking through the town's streets in a snowstorm. Her thin-soled shoes soon soaked through, and her feet were numb in her sodden stockings. She knew she should find shelter soon, but she'd no notion where she was going, beyond leaving Anthony Sparhawk behind.

Turning down Spring Street to avoid the wind, she saw the tall clapboarded shape of Trinity Church looming before her, even whiter than the swirling

snow. To her relief, the east door was unlocked, and
pulling it open with both hands, she slipped inside.

The church was empty, as she had hoped it would
be on a Thursday afternoon, and though the candles
on the altar and in the chandeliers were unlit, the pale
gray light of the storm filtered through the double rows
of arched windows. From long habit, she headed for
their box pew, the one that Ben had been so proud to
have purchased for his family. Though it was to the
back and behind a pillar, the pew still marked Ben as
a rising man, a successful man, fit to take his place
beside the gentry even in worship.

Shivering, Catie opened the little door to the pew
and slid onto the polished bench. The unheated church
was not much warmer than the street had been, but at
least it was dry and quiet. She slipped her feet from
her wet shoes and tucked them beneath her skirts,
wrapping her hands tightly around her knees.

She didn't try to pray; her conscience wouldn't let
her. By now Anthony must have discovered Jon and
had him arrested. It was her doing—her failure, really—that one cousin must take the other prisoner, that
two men bound so close by blood would now see that
same blood spilled. If only she hadn't kissed Anthony
last night, then he would not have come looking for
her this afternoon. Oh, dear Lord, if only she had been
strong instead of weak!

But though she would not be tried and hanged for
a traitor the way Jon would, she would be punished.
Once the story spread, as it now inevitably would, she
would forever lose her good name and her home and
her livelihood. She would be ruined and shamed, and
her poor innocent daughter with her.

And all of it, all of it, had come from that single night so long ago, when she had dared to dream of love with a golden-haired stranger. With her head bowed beneath her despair, she curled her frozen fingers around the locket with Belinda's picture and tried not to consider the bitter price that the lost dream had cost.

It was in the church that Anthony found her, curled in the corner of the pew. Her hood had fallen back from her damp, tangled hair, and her windburned cheek lay against the rough wool of her cloak. At first, because her eyes were shut, he thought she'd fallen asleep. But the anguish in her face held none of the peace of sleep; nor did the way she clutched the little locket so tightly in her hand.

"Catie," he said softly, not wishing to startle her as he joined her in the pew. "Catie, lass."

Her eyes flew open and she lifted her head, tossing her hair back from her forehead as she stared at him in unwelcoming silence, her gray eyes as wary as a hunted animal's.

But he'd come this far. Too late to retreat. "I was stopped by one of the sentries," he explained. "A question regarding orders that I couldn't ignore."

Still Catie said nothing, afraid she'd say too much. She'd no sense of how long she'd been here in the church, whether minutes or hours. Had the time been brief enough that Anthony might have followed her closely after all, that he'd let Jon escape unharmed?

"Even officers must stop for sentries, you know." He began to smile, hoping she would, too. When she didn't, he self-consciously studied the hat in his hands, now frowning a bit as he brushed the melting snow from the black beaver.

"I would not have let you go otherwise, you know," he said gruffly. "Running off into the snow like that wasn't wise. I meant to stop you."

"And so you'll always follow me, even here?" she asked, her voice no more than a ragged whisper. "Am I to have no sanctuary from you at all?"

He sighed, still concentrating on the hat in his hands. Damnation, he'd known this wasn't going to be easy, but he hadn't counted on her making it so much harder. Without waiting for the invitation that would never come from her, he swung open the little door and joined her in the pew, taking care to leave a decent length of polished wood between them.

"If I believed half the talk in this town about you, Catie Hazard," he began softly, "then I'd swear you could walk down Queen Anne's Square and directly across the water itself. Tavernkeeper and hostess, wife and widow and mother and, aye, a rebel queen, too, yet all of it done well, with rare grace and honor. If you've any faults, I've yet to hear of them."

He saw the fear flicker in her eyes, and saw, too, how in the next instant she forced it away. But still her fingers returned to the locket, and again he wondered enviously whose picture it contained.

"How thorough you have been, Major," she said, so swiftly that the words nearly left her breathless. Of course someone would have told him she had a daughter, but to hear it from him, her daughter's true father, was still enough to shock her with the peril of her situation. "And how flattering, too. But am I to be allowed no secrets of my own?"

"Only one. How is it that such a lady, a paragon of every virtue, a woman known to stand in proud rebellion where others of her sex would cower—how is it that she can still harbor, also, such remarkable cowardice in her heart?"

She frowned, her mouth twisting to one side. "Perhaps such pretty talk shows well in London, Major, but it doesn't with me."

"Pretty talk, is it?" Impatiently he rapped his fingers against the hat in his hand. "But perhaps you are right. Newport isn't London, and you aren't some general's overbred lady. So why then, Catie Hazard, must you always turn tail and run from me?"

"Because you are a king's man," she answered promptly. That much was easy, and true, as well. "Because you wear an officer's red coat, and are my enemy."

"Damnation, Catie, we both know there's more to it than that!"

She glared at him. "Hush, sir, and remember where you are!"

With an effort, he lowered his voice. "Then you remember it, too, Catie, and tell me the truth. I would never wish to bring you harm or suffering. Surely by now you can believe that much of me. So what could I have done to make you try to avoid me like the plague?"

"You do not know?" she whispered, hugging her knees more tightly to her chest. "Even—even after last night, you don't know?"

"Especially after last night." He sighed heavily, reaching out to trail a finger across the back of her hand. "I had thought that discovering we shared a past might bring you closer to me, and not the other way around."

She shivered at the glancing touch, yet didn't shrink away. How could she? In the harsh white light of the afternoon storm, without the soft magic of evening's candlelight, he seemed as world-weary and care-worn as she felt herself, the dashing officer of the night before reduced to the tired, lonely man who now turned to her. Even his golden hair had somehow dulled, and the lines that fanned from his green eyes now seemed almost carved there. Was it really regret that had done this to him, she wondered uncertainly, or merely a man's unhappiness at being rejected by a woman?

With a little sigh, she closed her eyes, forcing herself to focus on the past—that "shared past," he'd called it.

"You ask why I run from you," she began slowly, "and why I should fear you. Perhaps it's because you're a man that you cannot understand, and—"

"Catie, I—"

"No, please, Anthony, I beg you, hear me first." She took a deep breath to steady herself. "When I first saw you, I thought you were the most perfect gentleman that heaven had ever made. When you noticed me, when you spoke to me and smiled, I could not believe my good fortune. Oh, I'd been warned about the traps that men could lay for little country girls— how could I carry ale in a tavern near the docks and not see and hear otherwise?—but you were different. You weren't a rough, wild sailor or a journeyman from a trade. You were a gentleman, and Lord help me, I trusted you."

"You were different, too, Catie," began Anthony.

"There among the smoke and stench of that wretched place, you stood out like the fairest, freshest little country flower."

"I wasn't a flower," said Catie bitterly, the long-buried pain giving the edge to her words. "I was a seventeen-year-old girl near to perishing for kind words and love, without a mother or father to watch over her. And I was a maid, Anthony. Did you even notice that? Fool that I was, I would have given you my heart, but all you took was my innocence."

Appalled, Anthony shook his head, not wanting to believe her though he knew he should. "How would I have known? I'd been drinking cheap rum all night with my cousins. You were a pretty little wench in a low alehouse that served sailors, and when you led me to the loft—"

"You tried to pay me," she said, her voice breaking. "Do you remember that? Once you'd taken your own pleasure, you could not button your breeches fast enough to be gone. A handful of shillings, that was what I'd been worth to you. But I wouldn't take it. You might have used me as your whore, but as long as I didn't take your money, I wouldn't be one."

She was crying now, the hot tears sliding down her cheeks, but she scarcely noticed. "You took so much from me, Anthony. My hopes, my dreams of love and a handsome young sweetheart and a wedding with flowers and dancing and a little house near the water with roses in the garden, and—and, oh, everything that foolish young girls pray for and desire!"

"But you did marry," he protested. "You married Hazard, and bore his daughter."

For a long moment, she looked at him, his face

blurred by her tears. Yet even so, she still could see the features that mirrored Belinda's, the daughter she prayed he'd never realize was his.

"Yes, I married Mr. Hazard," she said with a painful evenness. "I did. But not for love, Anthony. Love was not what bound me to him."

Not for love. The words echoed heavily in Anthony's conscience. A woman as fine as Catie deserved to be wed to a man who loved her, a man whom she would love in return with all the passion and tenderness that were hers to give.

He remembered the special little kindnesses she'd shown to him since he came back to Newport, how she'd tended his arm that first night without betraying him, every sudden, shy smile she'd granted him, and he remembered, too, the sultry promise of her kiss the night before. All this she'd given to a man who was her enemy, the same man who had so unwittingly destroyed her innocence.

He longed to take her in his arms now, to wipe away her tears and stroke her tangled hair away from her face and tell her somehow how sorry he was for everything. But he didn't, instead staring down again at the hat on the pew beside him. How could he dare to offer her comfort, when he had been the cause of her sorrow?

"Will you believe me if I say that I never forgot you?" he said softly. "You were the last woman I kissed before I left my homeland, the last who smiled at me. I thought of you often on the long crossing to England, and even more when I arrived. You'd called me a gentleman, mistaking me for a lord, and though my cousins laughed, I didn't. Do you remember that?"

Still he didn't look at her, smiling instead to himself. "Until I proved myself with my regiment, I was scorned for being a colonial, little better than a savage. I cannot tell you how many times I remembered you then, the sweet-faced little lass with the solemn gray eyes."

Catie felt the tears welling up again, and she wasn't sure why. "You didn't even know my name," she whispered hoarsely. "You never asked."

"Then I was a fool, Catie, as well as a scoundrel," he said, emotion vibrating deep in his voice. "I won't make any excuses, because there aren't any worth making. If I'd bothered to learn your name, then I would have known who you were the moment Peterson introduced us. You've changed, no mistake. You're a lady of standing in this town, a beauty, too, and few would believe how far you've come from where you began. But when I kissed you, I knew. Because no matter how hard you've tried to bury your past, that small, solemn lass I remember is still within you."

Now he came to sit beside her, the long skirts of his red coat settling against her hip on the bench. With great care, he took her chilly little hand in his and carefully wove their fingers together.

"You can accuse me all you wish of making pretty speeches, Catie," he said, "but now I find I haven't half the words I need. You and Newport and a time before this infernal war, who I was and what I've become—it's all of it tumbled together, lass, and you're the one key I have, the only one that matters, to help me sort it out. Will you give me that much, Catie? Together, could we begin again?"

Catie stared down at their twined hands, trying to control the wild, desperate flurry of hope in her heart. Was it possible that he felt the regret—and the attraction—as keenly as did she? Once before, she had trusted him, and found nothing but heartache. But she had changed since then, and she wanted to believe that he had, as well. Another time, *this* time, and everything might be different between them.

And yet beyond the hope and the foolishly quickened pace of her heart, she knew that the bitter certainties of their lives hadn't changed at all. As a woman, she was the one with so much more to lose, and always would be, and with Belinda and Jon and the war around them, the risks were increased a hundredfold.

But oh, how much, how very much, she wished she could trust her heart instead!

She eased her fingers free, instantly missing the warmth of his hand around hers. "I cannot do this, Anthony," she said miserably. "What you ask of me now—I can't do it."

He smiled, and brushed away a loose lock of her hair with such tenderness she almost lost her resolve. "I'm not asking you to do anything alone, sweet. I intend to be there, too, you know."

She shook her head, as much to deny herself as him. "You are a soldier," she said sadly, "and so you know that to bring down a man, you must have a musket or a sword or a cannon's fire. But to destroy a woman takes only words. Words, that is all, and our good names, our lives, are gone."

Impatiently he swept his hand through the air, dismissing her objections. "You, of all women, must not let gossips rule your life."

"Do you really believe I am so different?" she asked forlornly. "You said yourself that in Newport I could walk on water. But how long would that last if my—my association with you, an enemy officer, became known?"

"Do you think so little of me, then?" he demanded, more wounded than angry. "That I'm the sort of braggart who boasts of conquests?"

"Oh, Anthony, I don't know what I think." Lightly she laid her fingertips across the bow of his mouth to silence him. "But to trust again, to risk everything for you—I can't do it."

He took her wrist to hold her hand steady so that he could brush his lips across her fingers, turning her gesture into a kiss. He saw how her eyes widened, and with an inward triumph he heard the little catch in her breath. She could deny her feelings all she wanted, but denying alone wasn't going to make them—or him—go away.

"I won't abandon the field so readily, Catie," he said, his voice husky with longing. "I don't want to lose you a second time."

"I never thought I was yours to lose at all." With a show of more purpose than she felt, Catie pulled her hand free. But her gaze remained locked with his, with those eyes that were fierce with a strange mixture of longing and determination.

"Mrs. Hazard, ma'am!"

"Reverend Wilson!" Swiftly she shoved her feet into her damp shoes and rose, turning toward the minister, who stood in the aisle at the end of the pew, melting snow dripping from his frizzled wig.

"A good afternoon to you, Mrs. Hazard, and—ah, sir." Nervously the minister dipped his head to look over his spectacles at Anthony, the man's mouth pursed with dismay as he studied the unmistakable lace and epaulets of a king's officer. Because of its Anglican teachings, Trinity was the only Newport church or meetinghouse left untouched by the invading army, but still, the presence of a tall English soldier on a weekday afternoon was hardly a welcome sign. "I do not mean to intrude, Mrs. Hazard, but when I heard voices here in the church—"

"Please don't concern yourself, Reverend Wilson, for we're leaving now," said Catie as she drew her hood over her head without looking again at Anthony. "We are done, you see. Quite, quite done."

Chapter Eight

It was after breakfast the next morning that Catie found the thin package slipped beneath the door to her rooms. She had run upstairs to fetch mittens and her heavier cloak, and in her haste she nearly stepped on the flat packet of cream-colored paper.

She picked it up slowly, and because she didn't recognize the handwriting, she closed the door shut after her. No one who worked for her wrote such a hand, and she didn't like the idea that a stranger had come here undetected, to her own private quarters. Just to be safe, she turned the key to lock the door, as well.

Perplexed, she turned the packet over in her hands. Her full name—Mrs. Catharine Willman Hazard—was written formally across the front and underlined with such a grand, swirling flourish that the pen had sputtered with a little spray of ink. Thin red ribbon crisscrossed the packet to bind it shut, and for good measure a thick dollop of red wax sealed the folded edges together. She carried it to the window, tipping it to the light to make out the seal's impression. Pressed into the red wax was a tiny bird, a hawk with spread wings, grasping a stick—the spar of a deep-water ship—in its minuscule claws.

She'd seen that seal often enough on Sparhawk letters, and her heart sank with dread. What trouble had Jon gotten himself into now? she wondered as she hurriedly cracked the seal and slipped the ribbons away. She knew from Hannah that Jon had left her kitchen unharmed the day before, but since then he could have met with a score of misfortunes. Or Belinda—Lord, what if some ill had befallen her daughter at the Pipers' house?

But instead of the dire news Catie expected as she unfolded the stiff paper, a lady's cambric handkerchief slipped out and drifted to the floor. Frowning, she picked it up. The new linen was so fine as to be translucent, with a deep border of handworked lace, Italian perhaps, and doubly dear for having been smuggled into the port. As elegant as the stock in the Newport shops had been before the war, such a handkerchief now was bound to cost a pretty sum indeed. Certainly Catie herself had never owned a handkerchief that was so beautifully impractical, and as she held its featherweight between her fingers, she read the note that had accompanied it.

For the fairest Lady Paragon in all New England, a small Remembrance of yesterday & a Pledge of my Regard & Devotion,
          Yr. O'b't. Srvt. Anthony Sparhawk

She could not accept such a gift from him; she couldn't accept anything. Hadn't he listened to a word that she told him yesterday in the church? She would return the handkerchief as soon as she could, and make it plain to him that she wished no further gifts or letters from him.

Yet even as she fumed over his audacity, she let the delicate linen glide between her fingers. She'd never seen lace so gossamer-fine, a pattern so elegant. Nor had any man given her such an extravagant gift; the trinkets that Ben brought her had always been calculated more to impress others than to please her. But a handkerchief such as this one was meant to be tucked in a sleeve or pocket or beneath a pillow, private places where only the owner would take secret pleasure in its luxury. The owner, and the giver, and in spite of herself Catie blushed as she thought of Anthony imagining the handkerchief resting inside her bodice, beneath her shift, against her breasts.

A small pledge of my regard and devotion...

No, there was no question that the handkerchief must be returned. Tonight, when he returned to the tavern. Swiftly, before she could change her mind, she folded the handkerchief back into the letter and stuffed them both into her pocket. She swung her cloak over her shoulders, tied a knit scarf around her throat for extra warmth and, with her mittens in her hands, hurried down the stairs through the kitchen.

Her errand was an important one. Two days ago she had seen the perfect Christmas present for Belinda in the window of one of the last remaining shops on Thames Street. A miniature blue-and-white porcelain tea service, the tiny pot complete down to a spout that would pour and a lid that would lift, all arranged on a polished pewter tea tray with a piecrust edge; it was the small, precise scale of it that would appeal most to Belinda, who staged endless parties and balls for her favorite lady-doll, the haughty one called Duchess, in the corner of her bedchamber and didn't worry in the least that tea was no longer a proper beverage for patriotic American dolls to sip.

But as a child's toy, the tea set was also appallingly expensive. Catie had nearly gasped aloud when the shopkeeper told her the price, explaining half-apologetically how such miniatures were all the fashion among the titled London ladies, not their daughters.

Catie had soon retreated from the shop then, yet the more she thought of the tea service, the less the cost had seemed to matter. She wasn't a titled lady and she didn't care a fig about London fashions, but she did know that Belinda had suffered much by being sent away from home, and if a blue-and-white porcelain tea set would help make up for that, why then, Catie would see that her daughter had it, even if it took money that Hazard's ledgers said she could ill afford to spare. No matter how the redcoats had ruined her trade, Christmas was still Christmas.

Lost in imagining Belinda's delight at the gift, Catie didn't hear the soldier's call until he repeated it.

"Halt, ma'am!" he called importantly as he stepped forward to block Catie's path with the long barrel of his musket. "You must halt, I say, ma'am, and heed me when I ask your business!"

Catie drew herself up and stared pointedly at the musket. Though she'd almost become accustomed to the sentries posted outside her front door, this was the first time she'd been challenged herself, and she didn't like it one bit. "*My* business is exactly that," she said sternly, "my own affair, and none of yours. Now I'll thank you to let me pass."

"No, ma'am, I will not." He spoke sharply, his words coming in little puffs in the cold air, and Catie was convinced she saw a certain malicious pleasure in his eyes at her discomfiture. "Orders say you're not to leave this house alone."

"Whose orders?" demanded Catie. Like so many of the British soldiers, this one had the wolfish, hardened look of a man who'd seen much fighting, and she knew better than to try to cajole him. "Why should it matter to King George where I walk in my own town?"

"It matters to Major Sparhawk, ma'am. His orders were that you don't leave this place unattended."

"Is that so?" What right did Anthony think he had to restrict her like this? Crossly Catie thought of his note with the handkerchief in her pocket. Did he think her meek compliance could be so easily bought? "What if *I* wish to leave this place?"

"Then I'm to come with you, ma'am." He looked over his shoulder and nodded curtly to the other guard, still at his post beside the tavern's front door. He tipped his musket back against his shoulder, ready to follow her. "As you *wish*, ma'am."

Catie frowned, her exasperation growing by the second. She wasn't sure if Anthony meant the soldier as her escort or her guard, but either way she would feel like the greatest fool in Newport, parading about the streets with a British soldier at her heels. She certainly couldn't go to the little shop with the miniature tea service; the poor shopkeeper would likely faint dead away.

"Very well," she said, with a curt nod to match his. "If those are Major Sparhawk's orders, then you'd best lead me to him, so he can see how splendidly we've both obeyed."

For an instant she saw surprise and doubt flicker across the soldier's face, and she realized he hadn't really expected her to go anywhere. Well, good, she decided. If this man hadn't expected it, then neither would Anthony.

Even though the soldier slowed his steps for her sake, Catie was still breathless from keeping up with him by the time they reached the square before the State House. Each day different companies used the square for exercises, and this morning the trampled snow was occupied by the red uniforms with the blue facings of the Twenty-third regiment, performing their drills before a small, silent group of spectators who were mainly boys and old men. Ordinarily Catie would not have known one group of British soldiers from another, but this was Anthony's regiment, and she recognized the uniforms, just as instinctively, instantly, her eye found Anthony himself, astride his black horse between two other officers at the far side of the square.

She followed her guide to them, telling herself that the reason her heart was racing at such a ridiculous rate was that she'd been forced to walk so quickly. It had nothing whatsoever to do with seeing Anthony again, smiling and chatting with the other officers. But when he turned and saw her standing below him, the brilliance of his smile, an open, uncalculated smile just for her, made her racing heart lurch to a halt.

"I must speak with you, Major Sparhawk," she

shouted resolutely over the rolling din of the fifes and drums. She pointed at the soldier now standing at attention beside her. "This man says that by your orders I am a prisoner in my own home. Is everyone in Newport under such orders, or am I alone—"

Abruptly the drums ceased, and too late Catie realized she was shouting still. Her cheeks hot, she self-consciously lowered her voice. "So am I the only person in this town to have a guard of my own, Major? I assure you it's not an honor I wish, and I've done nothing to deserve it. You *know* that, Anth—I mean, Major Sparhawk. Now I must insist that you change your orders directly."

She had, decided Anthony, never looked more charming, her cheeks bright pink and her silver eyes flashing as she tried to be stern with him. She was different from most women; indignation became her. But as charming as she was, he knew he'd better put an end to her public tirade before she blurted something he'd rather keep private. He swung down from the horse and tossed the reins to the soldier.

"And a fine day to you, Mrs. Hazard," he said, lifting his hat as he bowed to her. "Your servant, ma'am."

Catie's eyes narrowed. "I'm not here to listen to your pretty talk, Major."

"So I've committed that sin again, have I, ma'am?" He sighed dolefully, and looked back to the two other officers grinning behind him. "If you'll excuse me, gentlemen, I believe this lady would like to speak with me alone."

"I most certainly do," said Catie as Anthony took

her lightly by the elbow. "What's the meaning of these ridiculous orders of yours, anyway?"

"They're for your own good, Catie, though I doubt you'll believe me." He led her through the passage between two empty houses and to the small fenced garden beyond. In the summer the garden must have been a pleasant place, filled with flowers, but now only a few desultory brown stalks poked through the snow, and even the gnomon on the sundial was shrouded with its own little drift. "I generally try to give orders for a good reason."

"Oh, pooh," she scoffed. "You're using your position to bully me, and you know it as well as I do."

His good humor began to fade. Blast the soldier who'd been assigned to follow her during this watch! If the oaf had had any wits at all, he should have shown more judgment in his duty; Catie hadn't noticed any of the others assigned to her these last days, at least not to complain about. Besides, Anthony had hoped she'd come to him on another account. "No, I'm not, Catie, and I'd appreciate it if you'd stop trying to treat me like some tradesman who's cheated you."

"If you were, I'd be treating you a great deal worse," she declared, pulling free of him so that she could fold her arms over her chest. "I must stand firm, you know. The whole world preys on widows."

"Oh, aye, such a weak, pitiful little widow woman you are, too," he said dryly. "And that's exactly why I don't want you wandering about Newport unattended."

Unconvinced, Catie looked up at him from beneath her lashes, her chin stubbornly low. This would all be a great deal easier for her if the man weren't so wretchedly handsome. She'd thought that their conversation in the church yesterday would put an end to any such feelings, but to have him standing here before her, his hat in his hand and his blond hair tugging loose from its queue in the breeze and the most taxingly irresistible glint in his green eyes, was more than a woman should be asked to bear.

"I told you before, Anthony," she said. "I don't want anything from you."

He frowned, and the irresistible glint vanished from his eyes. "In this you don't have any choice, Catie. The military situation in this town, on this entire island, in fact, has changed markedly for the worse."

"Situation this, situation that," she grumbled. "If I sound too much like an innkeeper to suit you, then you sound like some puffed-up old Tory officer."

"Right now that's precisely what I am. Catie, listen to me. The night before last, a pack of rebels attacked one of the outlying houses quartering our men, out near Bryce's Cove. Fired in on them without any warning at all, then ran away into the night like the cowardly blackguards they are. Eight men killed outright, Catie, and as many wounded. Is that something you can understand?"

She didn't answer. How could she? All too clearly she remembered Jon's version of the same night, how proud he'd been to be a part of the skirmish, and she remembered, too, how he'd promised there'd be more such attacks against the British troops to come.

She was good at masking her feelings, thought Anthony as he watched her face, very good indeed. But still he'd seen the little catch in her breathing and the way her lips parted, and it was more than enough to betray her.

"You're not surprised," he said. "Perhaps I've told you nothing that you haven't heard before."

She lifted her chin, determined to meet his obvious suspicion. "It's common knowledge in the town, and all such news is discussed in my taproom. Besides, you mentioned it yourself yesterday."

"Then you'll recall that I mentioned my cousin, too." Anthony sighed heavily. "Jon's one of the leaders. He and his fellows had the audacity to send the general a letter this morning, signing their names, bold as brass. Though perhaps you knew that already, too."

"I did not," she said, with a quick extra shake of her head for emphasis. "I wish that Jon hadn't— Oh, how sorry I am to learn this of him!"

Anthony looked down at the hilt of his smallsword, tapping his finger against the silver wire that wrapped the grip. Most of the time now the resemblance between him and his cousin was passing at best, but in certain light, from certain angles—such as this one, thought Catie unhappily—the likeness was strong enough to make them brothers.

"You know I cannot protect him," he said, his sorrow unmistakable, "and if I have the chance, I'll capture him myself. Just as I'm quite sure that if I'd been among the others in the house at Bryce's Cove, he would have shot at me first. The fortunes of war, eh? The damnable fortunes of war."

Wordlessly Catie reached out to rest her mittened hand on his arm. There was little she could say to comfort him, even if she dared, but from the way he slipped his other hand over hers, she knew her simple gesture had been enough.

"I can't help Jon, Catie," he said softly, "but perhaps I can do as much for you. That's the reason for the guard that you find so objectionable. Oh, I know, you're a poor widow toiling night and day to keep a roof over her head. But the truth is, you run a tavern that encourages the worst sort of rebels and the treason they spout."

"No, Anthony, it's not—"

"It is," he said firmly. "You keep rough company, sweet, my cousin Jon included. This way I won't have to worry about you coming to grief."

She pulled her hand away from his arm. "But I'm not your responsibility!"

"I rather think you are." He smiled crookedly; he was, after all, only half lying about the guard. "Fortunately, His Majesty agrees. What better way for me to protect his subjects and put down the rebellion?"

"Don't be ridiculous, Anthony!"

"I've never been more serious, Catie. This way you can go wherever you please—to the market, to call upon your friends, to visit your daughter in the country—and be sure you won't be waylaid or made a hostage by some gang of desperate extremists."

He saw how the next protest died forgotten on her lips, how the emotions she'd kept so tightly reined before now seemed to run wild across her mobile face as she pressed her hand across her mouth. Puzzled, he tried to think of what he'd said that would upset her this way—the market, friends, her daughter—but none of them would frighten her like this. It must have been the threat of being captured, and now he wished he'd been more circumspect. Of course she'd be frightened of that, of course—

"That's not possible," she blurted out. "To visit my daughter, I mean. It's—that's not possible."

Anthony's puzzlement deepened. "I can understand why you sent her from Newport," he said kindly. "You're hardly the first mother to send a child to a safer place during this war. But if you miss your daughter, then by all means visit her. Just take the guard with you."

But Catie only shook her head, her eyes wide with anguished panic.

Suddenly the answer came to Anthony. "You sent her with Jon's children, didn't you?" he asked gently. "She's gone with the others to Providence?"

The relief that flooded Catie's face was answer enough, an answer that left Anthony feeling that too-familiar stab of envy. Why would she trust his wayward cousin with her only child, and yet refuse even the simplest kindness from him?

With a sigh, he settled his hat on his head and gallantly offered his arm to her. Nothing had gone the way he'd hoped when he brought her to this chilly little garden, but then, where he and Catie Hazard were concerned, nothing ever did. "Come, you must be cold. I'll take you back to the others."

"Wait, Anthony, please." Catie tugged off her mitten to reach beneath her cloak and into her pocket, and drew out the slightly crumpled note with the handkerchief. "Here, you must take this back. It's very nice of you to give the lovely handkerchief to me and all, but I can't accept such a gift from you. Surely, after our—our conversation yesterday, you'll understand why not."

He glanced down at the letter in Catie's fingers, the untied red ribbon trailing in the breeze. Perhaps things between them weren't going so very badly after all. "And I say, after our conversation yesterday, I see no other course but to insist you keep my gift."

"But you *must* take it back!" said Catie with dismay. "Didn't you hear anything I told you yesterday?"

"I did, sweet, and better than you seem to have heard it yourself." Idly he began to wrap the trailing ends of the ribbon around her hand, loosely binding the letter to her palm. "You said I'd robbed you of more than your maidenhead. You said you'd never had the chance to be wooed, or petted, or cherished in any way."

"Anthony, please, I didn't mean—"

"Hush, and listen to me," he chided gently. "I can't make you seventeen again, any more than I can undo the past between us. But I am doing my level best to make up the rest to you."

He hooked his fingers in the ribbons around her hand and gently pulled her closer to him. She *was* listening now, her face rapt with breathless attention, and he lowered his voice so that she'd have to listen even more closely.

"I'm trying to make you see what a rare and fine woman you are, Catie Hazard," he said, reaching out to cradle her face in his hands, "and how dear—how very dear—you are to me."

Lightly he brushed his lips across her forehead, her eyes fluttering shut. He moved lower, searching for her mouth, and as their lips met he caught her sigh, a sweet, small breath of anticipation, of pleasure, of surrender, that meant infinitely more to him than words ever could. He'd intended this kiss to be swift and chaste, a pledge of his honor to her, but once he'd tasted her mouth again he realized how impossible that would be. Her kiss was like no other woman's, warm and eager, and he felt himself sinking deeper into all she offered.

He slanted his mouth across hers, seeking more, demanding more, and he felt that magic sigh of hers again, a trembling vibration between them that sang through his entire body. The intensity of his desire shocked him. There was nothing honorable about how he felt now. Now all he wanted was to take her in his arms and make her his forever, here in this snow-covered garden, against the rolling tattoo of drums from the square.

But now would be wrong. Irredeemably, unforgivably wrong. He couldn't forget how badly he'd used her once before, and with a shuddering effort he broke away, his hands still cradling her face. In a moment, he would take her back to the square. In a moment, that other life, the one with Mrs. Hazard and not Catie, would begin again.

"I won't give up, Catie," he said, his voice rough with longing. "No matter what happens, I won't lose you again."

Slowly Catie opened her eyes, as dreamy and unfocussed as if she'd just awakened. "Then you are mad, Anthony Sparhawk," she whispered. "And so, I vow, am I."

"Ah, here you are at last, Sparhawk." General Ridley frowned as he shifted stiffly in the saddle. "Damned chilly place you picked to go merrymaking with your widow."

Impatiently he waited while Anthony remounted his own horse, and waited, too, for him to laugh, or at least smile.

"You see the jest, Sparhawk, don't you, eh?" he prodded. "'Making merry with the merry widow'? Tidy bit of wit, eh?"

"Yes, sir, clever indeed," agreed Anthony, belatedly and without any of the heartiness that he knew the general expected. But he couldn't make himself laugh at Catie's expense, not even for a jest made by the general. Right now it was taking every shred of his self-control not to look back to where he'd left her, at the edge of the square with her guard. Damnation, how he hated having to lie to her about that "escort," and the more he'd come to care for her, the worse the necessary deception seemed. Of course, the goal had always been to make her trust him, but he'd never dreamed how far awry that trust would go.

Dear, sweet, trusting Catie, and inevitably he thought again of how her little sigh as he kissed her had been the most memorable—and intoxicating—surrender of his entire life.

"Answer me, Sparhawk, or have you lost your hearing, as well as your wits?" demanded Ridley irritably. "What the devil did the chit have to tell you?"

"Ah, General, forgive my inattention," said Anthony, hastily scrambling to recover. "It was exactly that question that I was...ah, was considering."

The general's scowl deepened. "I'm expecting an answer, man, not an apology."

"Of course, sir," said Anthony quickly. "My conversation with Mrs. Hazard has confirmed that Jonathan Sparhawk was the leader of the rebel party."

"The rascal signed his name to the deed. What more confirmation do we need?" demanded Ridley bitterly. "I've lost eight men I can't replace, Sparhawk, and I need more than a *confirmation* from you."

Anthony stiffened, the general's sarcasm stinging like a lash to his pride. "And more I have, sir, if you'll but listen," he shot back. "The rebels on this island still manage to travel freely between here and Providence."

"That's impossible," said Ridley. "We've five ships bottling that river up tighter than a cork."

"Blockades or not, General, the rebels still manage to slip past our navy's guards with such ease that they think nothing of ferrying their own children back and forth."

Their own children, and those of their lovers, as well. Even as Anthony spoke, the fleeting memory of Catie's frightened face rose in his conscience. But by now her daughter was safe in Providence. Neither Catie nor her child would be put at risk by what he told the general, and maybe other lives would be saved. That was it. He wasn't betraying her confidence. He was simply helping keep her safe, and doing his duty at the same time.

"Consider the facts, sir," he continued. "How else could the rebels make such a well-timed attack upon our forces at Bryce's Cove unless they considered the river theirs?"

"I knew it!" Eagerly the general leaned across from his horse toward Anthony. "That infernal navy is worthless—worthless! So tell me, Sparhawk, where do the rebels gather? Where do they hide their boats, their guns?"

"I haven't learned that yet, sir, but—"

"But you will learn it, Sparhawk," said Ridley curtly, not bothering to hide either his disappointment or his contempt, "and you will learn it soon."

"Yes, sir, although—"

"Nothing more, Major. Only answers," said Ridley sharply. "The Hazard woman may be a useful source of information to us and an amusing diversion to you, but you would be well-advised not to confuse the two."

"No, sir, but I—"

"Don't discredit yourself by denying it," snapped the general, sweeping his hand dismissively through the air. "D'you think I haven't heard the tales, eh?"

Suddenly Anthony caught sight of Lieutenant Peterson on the horse behind the general. Though the young man was concentrating hard on the review before him, a guilty flush had flooded his cheeks above the collar of his jacket, leaving Anthony in no doubt as to where the general's "tales" had come. Blast the puppy for gossiping like that, and double blast Ridley for believing it!

"I deny nothing, sir," he said warmly, "because I've done nothing wrong."

"Nothing, eh? Then I don't need to remind you that you are an officer to His Majesty the king. Your loyalty to the crown and your duty come first." The general drew back, his expression as cold as the winter day. "Do you understand, Major Sparhawk?"

For a moment longer than was wise, Anthony met the older man's eyes, determined to prove to the general that he was neither traitor nor coward. He had chosen his allegiance long ago, and turned his back on his family to do it. How could Ridley question his loyalty now? He was a king's man, and always would be.

But what, then, could he be to Catie Hazard?

"Yes, sir," he said curtly, shoving his doubts aside. "I understand."

Catie was scarcely inside the door before Hannah came rushing up to her.

"Oh, mistress, thank the heavens you've returned!" she said, her full cheeks quivering. "While you were gone, a man came asking for you."

"A man?" repeated Catie, still too much under the blissful spell of Anthony's kiss to think clearly. "What man?"

"A wild, rough man, a sailor by the look of him," said Hannah, clucking her tongue at the memory. "Not a gentleman at all, and certainly not the sort of man who comes calling on a lady like you, mistress."

The lovely warm feeling was beginning to break away and scatter, as insubstantial and fleeting as a cloud. "Did this man leave his name?"

"Nay, mistress, he'd leave nothing but his message, saying he'd had it direct from Cap'n Jon himself."

The warm feeling was quite gone now, and the chill that grasped her heart instead was largely fear. "Do you recall his message, Hannah?"

"Oh, aye, mistress, 'tis not the sort of message soon forgotten." The cook swallowed twice and licked her lips to prepare herself. "He said to tell you Cap'n Jon knows everything that you've been doing. He was quite particular about that. 'Jon Sparhawk knows everything that you've been doing,' he said, 'and now he wants you to remember your little daughter before it's too late.' That's just what he said, mistress. 'Remember your little daughter.'"

Slowly Catie dropped onto the long kitchen bench. As if she'd ever forget Belinda, or Jon's threats concerning her safety or the promises, foolish promises, that she'd made to help him.

As if she'd ever forget Anthony...

"He left after that, mistress, just walked out the door without so much as a goodbye or farewell." Anxiously Hannah twisted her apron in her hands as she searched Catie's face for reassurance. "You're not in trouble, mistress, are you? With Cap'n Jon, I mean?

With a groan, Catie closed her eyes, feeling Anthony's letter, with the handkerchief, rustle against her thigh. "Oh, Hannah," she said softly. "This time, I'm afraid I am."

Chapter Nine

Swiftly Catie folded the scrap of paper over and over into a tiny, flat square before she pressed it into Hannah's hand. She had spent all night deciding what to write, yet still her fingers had trembled as she held the pen.

"You must give this either to Captain Jon or to the other man, the one who came here yesterday," she said, holding her hand over Hannah's. "One of them is bound to be at the market house this morning."

Troubled, Hannah shook her head. "I don't like this, mistress," she said. "Not that I don't be willing to help you—I am that—but creeping about like this don't seem right."

"I wouldn't ask you if there were any other way, Hannah," said Catie with a sigh. "But the British soldier will insist on accompanying me if I try to go myself, and for Jon's sake, I can't risk that."

"Oh, mistress." The older woman stared woefully at the message in her hand.

"No harm will come to you if you're stopped, Hannah," said Catie gently. "Even if the British somehow take the message from you, it won't mean anything to them.''

Nothing to them, thought Catie, but everything to her. All night she'd lain awake to contrive the two simple words of the message: *I remember*. Strange to think how many things those words could mean. If the note fell into Jon's hands, he would believe she'd taken his warning to heart. She remembered her promise to help him, she remembered all that the Sparhawk family had done for her in the past, she remembered, most of all, that her daughter's safety depended on the rebels' success.

But to Catie herself, the terse little message meant so much more. She remembered the unmistakable tenderness in Anthony's eyes when he'd explained how he wished to protect her. She remembered how he'd listened to her in the church and, better yet, how he'd heard every word in a way she hadn't even imagined herself. She remembered his gift and the pledge that had come with it and how he'd refused to take any of it back, and she remembered, too, how this morning she'd tucked the lace-trimmed handkerchief into her bodice for luck. But most of all she remembered the way she'd felt when they kissed, the heady sweetness of it mingled with a fierce passion that had made her whole body sing.

I remember. Once before, long ago, she'd believed no other man could be like Anthony Sparhawk. Now she was beginning to believe it again. But was she remembering everything the way she should, or only as she longed for it to be?

''Is there any other message, mistress?'' asked Hannah as she looped her arm through her market basket.

"If I see Cap'n Jon, that is, and not that other nasty sailor-man."

"If you see Jon, tell him to take care, and watch after himself," she said softly, thinking of how Jon seemed so determined to risk his life again and again. "There are many who wish him harm, though I expect he knows that already. And one other thing, too, Hannah."

Catie's fingers touched her locket. "Pray ask him to tell Belinda that I miss her and love her very much," she said wistfully, "and that I'll come for her the first minute I can."

"And high time, too. I know when you took her away you thought 'twould only be for a few days, and here it is nigh on a month!"

"Not quite," said Catie sadly. "Twenty-two days, that is all, though I vow it seems like ten times that."

"Surely by Christmas," said Hannah, clucking her tongue in sympathy. "Surely we'll have the little lass home by then."

"I don't know, Hannah," said Catie, thinking of all the complications that lay behind such a simple wish. "May heaven help me, I don't."

And it wasn't until later, when Catie was able to retreat to her own rooms upstairs, that she felt the tears well up. She had arranged the little blue-and-white tea set on a toy table that she'd taken from Belinda's room, placing it before the fire as she imagined her daughter would do herself. Seeing it there, Catie could almost hear her daughter's serious little voice as she offered tea to Duchess.

But suddenly she could hear another voice there beside her daughter's, a deep male voice, warm and kind and tinged with the elegance of London. For the first time, she pictured Anthony crouched down beside his daughter, their two heads, with the same gold hair, bending over Duchess's new tea tray, Anthony somehow holding the tiny cup in his hand like a giant's.

Father and daughter, their relationship undeniable; Catie had worked so hard to keep them apart, yet now that she'd imagined the unimaginable, she kept returning to the image again and again, as unable to turn away from its beckoning lure as a drunkard from rum. Father and daughter and mother, too, a family with love at its center and not deceit and lies, a chance to begin her life all over again.

Yet as tempting as it was to dream, she knew it was just that, a honey-sweet, idle dream that could never become reality, and alone in her cold bedchamber she struggled to fight back her tears. Weeping could change nothing, she told herself fiercely as she balled her hands into tight fists in her lap, digging her nails into her palms to keep back the tears. Better to think of a way to solve her own troubles than to long for a man to do it for her. Better still to think of a way to bring Belinda safely home than to sit here and cry by herself.

But as she turned to wipe her hand across her eyes, she noticed the flat package halfway under her bed where it had slid across the floor from the door. This time she recognized the thin red ribbons, just as she recognized the hand that had written her name across the front. This time, too, she didn't hesitate to open the slender package, her heart racing as she unfolded the stiff paper.

To her disappointment, no note slipped free, but she

gasped when she unwrapped the second sheet of paper and saw the gloves that lay inside. Pale yellow kidskin the color of new butter and just as soft, with a delicate scroll of slightly darker silk embroidered around the cuff; she'd had no notion that such gloves could even be purchased in a Newport shop. Clearly they were intended for the finest of ladies, the kind who never raised a white, unblemished finger for any sort of labor, and wryly Catie looked down at her own hands, red and chapped from all the extra scullery work she'd undertaken these last weeks.

Yet still the gloves looked to be the right size, and gingerly she slipped one hand inside. Her fingertips touched something that rustled, and with a little frown she withdrew a piece of paper cut into a lopsided heart. Emblazoned across it was a single sentence: *You hold my heart in your hand.* There was no signature, not that Catie needed one as she pictured Anthony struggling first to cut the heart freehand and then to tuck it inside the narrow gloves. As beautiful as the gloves were, it was that awkward little heart that touched her the most, and made her smile, as well.

He *was* trying to woo her. No man bent on seduction alone would ever have tipped his hand so openly with that misshapen heart. Her smile widened with pure pleasure, and even alone as she was, she blushed as she ran her fingers lightly across the heart.

She wished she could see him, now, to let him know how much this gift had pleased her. He could be anywhere on the island this afternoon, but he most certainly wouldn't be found in her rooms. Swiftly, before she could change her mind, she reached for her cloak and the small fur muff she usually reserved for Sundays. With the muff to warm her hands in the thin yellow gloves and to protect the precious paper heart tucked inside, she headed down the stairs to the front door. She told herself she'd walk to meet Hannah, who still hadn't returned from the market and shops, but secretly she hoped to cross paths with a certain British officer, as well.

The afternoon was chilly and gray, and the snow that remained in the streets was dingy with trampled mud. Though the British had not even been here a month, their mark was everywhere. Every third house was shuttered and closed or simply abandoned when their owners had fled. These empty houses had become the first targets of the soldiers in their endless search for firewood, and fences had been ripped up and orchards and garden trees cut down. Even the shutters themselves were ripped from their hinges, and some of the more humble houses had even had their clapboarding pried and peeled away, leaving the beams beneath exposed to the wind and snow. Ships trapped in the harbor stood idle and empty, with neither destinations nor crews. Cargoes sat abandoned on the wharves, hogsheads splitting from the damp and their contents rotting.

All this Catie knew, and it pained her deeply to see Newport dying by degrees, a bit more each day. And yet, though nothing had changed for the better in the town, this afternoon she could scarcely keep the smile from her face as she walked toward the market house. Even the soldier who walked behind her, a red-coated shadow she'd never lose, failed to dampen her spirits today.

She soon spotted Hannah, trudging down the sidewalk with a boy following behind her to carry her purchases, and Catie quickened her steps to meet her.

"It looks as if you had good luck, Hannah," she said, glancing at the packages in the boy's arms and the basket looped over the cook's. "Did you find everything you sought?"

"Nay, mistress, I did not," said Hannah sourly. "So late in the day, there's naught left in the stalls but rubbish and trash, an' that priced so dear you'd think the moldiest turnip be pure gold. I nearly come to tears, thinking of the sorry table we set now at Hazard's. It's all the fault of them British, o' course, may the dear Lord rot them all with pox."

"But you must have seen some friends or acquaintances there," prompted Catie carefully, all too aware of both the soldier behind her and the boy with the market basket. "Surely, Hannah, you found time for a moment or two of conversation?"

"Not so that you'd speak of it, mistress." She nodded and winked so broadly that Catie almost winced. "But I did see a certain black-haired lad that grows more an' more the image of his father each day."

"Jeremiah?" asked Catie, surprised. She'd never have believed that Jon let the boy from his sight.

"The same." Hannah nodded again as they began to walk slowly side by side. "Paid his respects to me as proper as his poor mama would've wished, may she rest in heaven. But, oh, he's thin and ragged for a child! I'd half a mind to bring him along with me for supper. Like one o' your wretched stray cats, mistress, 'cepting with a lad it would be Christian charity."

"I don't believe his father would wish him to accept your charity, no matter how kindly meant."

Hannah sighed heavily. "Nay, I don't believe his *father* would," she agreed, with pointed emphasis that stopped just short of pronouncing the Sparhawk name. "But he's a good, obedient lad, for all that he looks like some wild, rough creature now. He'll do as his father tells him."

The older woman nodded sagely, and Catie relaxed. Jeremiah *would* do whatever Jon told him to, including carrying her message. These days, it was probably the least of what Jon was expecting of him, and once again she murmured a little prayer to keep the boy safe.

"And I'll tell you one other thing about that boy, mistress," continued Hannah, warming to her subject. "He's taken with your Belinda, an' always has been. Oh, I know they're not more than babes, but mark what I say—in time you'll have a match there, see if you don't. Wouldn't Mr. Hazard have smiled on that, marrying his daughter into the gentry like that!"

"Hush, Hannah, don't be foolish," said Catie uncomfortably, not wishing to discuss exactly how close Jeremiah Sparhawk was to her daughter. "Belinda is only eight years old, and I won't have you or anyone else marrying her off just yet. Besides, I—"

"Oh, mistress, will you look at them miserable bloodyback blackguards!" Glaring fiercely, Hannah charged to the very edge of the sidewalk, brandishing her basket before her at the battalion of British soldiers that had just marched around the corner. "Look at them struttin' by so proud, like the bullyin', empty-headed cocks o' the walk that they be!"

Catie grabbed the other woman's arm. "Hannah, please! I won't have you behaving like this!"

"Then scold them, mistress, not me!" said Hannah

furiously, and to Catie's dismay the cook spat into the street at the soldiers' feet. "Wicked, filthy excuses for men! Why, I'd rather—"

"That is quite enough, Hannah!" ordered Catie sharply. "Consider the shame you're bringing to me and to Hazard's, let alone to yourself! Do you wish us all to suffer because you cannot keep a decent tongue in your head?"

"We're all shamed already, having such vermin living beneath our roof," declared Hannah heatedly. "I never thought I'd live—"

"I told you, Hannah," said Catie, her voice full of warning, "that is *enough.*"

And though Hannah jerked her arm free from Catie's hand, the older woman finally seemed to hear that warning. "Very well, mistress," she said, stifling her anger, though her eyes remained full of hatred as she watched the British soldiers. "If that is what you wish."

"It's not what I wish," said Catie vehemently as she tucked her hand back into the muff. "It's how it *is,* and how for now it must be."

"Cap'n Jon don't think so," blurted out Hannah hotly. "Cap'n Jon told me to keep a sharp eye on them soldiers in our house, and tell him what I seen. Cap'n Jon says—"

"Since when do you have such conversations with Captain Sparhawk?" demanded Catie. Had Jon set the cook to spy on her now, while she was supposed to be spying on Anthony? "I won't have you gossiping when you're meant to be working."

Hannah's lip quivered as she swallowed back her

retort. "Very well, mistress," she said again. "Very well."

Catie shot her one final glance of warning before she turned back to the parading soldiers. Inside the muff she touched the heart-shaped note, and as she did her own heart jumped. The men now marching before her and Hannah wore the uniforms of Anthony's regiment, and almost before she realized it, he was there, too, on his black gelding, with the young lieutenant riding beside him. His face was stern, a studied, official mask covering his emotions and his thoughts.

This time when he spotted her among the others on the sidewalk there was no special smile, no teasing greeting, as there had been before. But still she knew the exact moment when their gazes met, and felt the heat of that single shared look across the wide space that separated them.

Without thinking, she drew her hand from the muff and raised it, not so much to wave but to reach out to him, the pale yellow glove like a small banner in the cheerless street. His gaze shifted briefly to her hand, then back to her face, and the merest hint of a smile flickered across his mouth and eyes. Only a hint, but it was enough to make Catie's mouth go dry and her heart race.

Later, she thought as anticipation soared wildly in her breast, later I will see him alone. Later he will come to me....

Unconsciously she leaned forward as he rode down the street, unwilling to let him go from her sight. But as she did, Hannah turned and blocked her view. Catie sighed impatiently and raised her head, intent on seeing Anthony. But already he was gone, around the corner and from her view, and she sighed again, this time with disappointment.

Then, too late, she saw the look on Hannah's face before her. The anger was still there, the bitterness and resentment toward the British undisguised on her plain, guileless features. But now there was suspicion mingled there, as well, suspicion that Catie recognized and understood with a swift, sickening sense of foreboding.

Quickly she lowered her hand in the yellow glove and shoved it into her muff. "Come along, Hannah," she said briskly. "We've tarried here long enough."

But as much as Catie wanted to, she couldn't make herself meet the other woman's eye.

Once again Anthony touched the pistols at his waist, then cursed his own uneasiness. Damnation, where was Catie? He could just hear her voice from the hall upstairs, trying to soothe a querulous guest complaining about the tavern's shortage of firewood. Why the devil didn't the fool take her word for it? Anthony muttered an oath directed to all the whining old men in the world and touched his pistols again. If she didn't come soon, he'd have to leave without seeing her. He couldn't linger in this hallway all night, especially not when Peterson would soon be waiting for him below.

There. There were her footsteps, coming toward him at last. Anthony sank into the shadows of the stairwell. He didn't intend to frighten her, but he didn't wish to announce his presence to the entire inn, either. She was on the stairs now, the ring of keys at her waist jingling merrily as she hurried down the steps.

"Catie," he called softly. "Catie, lass, here."

Abruptly she stopped, listening, one foot poised above the step. Here between the two floors, the stairway bent and turned at a landing lit by day by a tall arched window. But now, at night, the only light came from the new crescent moon far above and the oil lamp in the front hall below, washing her slim figure in silvery twilight. She was dressed simply for work, in a striped shortgown and petticoats with an apron around her waist, and she'd never looked more appealing to him. But then, he thought wryly, each time he saw her, no matter what she wore, he felt the same.

"Catie," he said again. "Don't look so startled, lass. Who else do you think it would be?"

She laughed nervously, her hand fluttering over her breast. "Of course I'm startled, Anthony," she said, not really answering his question. "Why shouldn't I be, when my land is at war and my house is full of strange soldiers?"

"This one won't harm you," he said, reaching out to draw her with him into the shadows of the corner. "I promise you that."

"Will you, now?" She looped her fingers into his and let him pull her another step closer, but still glanced over her shoulder to see if they were overheard. "I've only your word on it, you see."

"My word is all I have to give you now," he said softly. "A trustworthy offering, I'm told, though not perhaps as winsome as those yellow gloves."

He saw how she laughed in spite of herself. "Bother the gloves. Oh, they're most fine, of course, very fine, and I thank you for them. But I liked the heart even better."

"You did?" he asked, genuinely surprised, but

pleased, too. The heart had been a gamble; she might just as easily have dismissed it as foolishness. "Then you must have found the sentiment to your taste, as well."

He slid his arm around her waist, gently pulling her close against his chest. But instead of curving against him the way he'd hoped, she stiffened in his embrace.

"Not here, Anthony," she whispered urgently, looking past him to the stairs. "Someone could come and find us at any minute."

"Someone could, and eventually someone would," he whispered, turning so that she was against the wall and he was shielding her with his body. How could she wave to him in the street, before his regiment and half the town, but turn skittish when they were alone? "But not now, Catie, and not yet. All I need is a moment to talk."

"Oh, Anthony, you don't understand, do you?" She searched his face in the twilight, her mouth pinched with anxiety. "You never will, will you?"

"Hush, Catie," he said fondly, stroking her cheek with the back of his hand. "I understand a great deal more than you seem willing to credit me."

She looked down, away from the powerful lure of his gaze. All day long she'd been imagining this moment when she'd be alone with him again, but now that he was here, really here with her, she didn't know what to say or do next. Against her will, the image of Anthony and Belinda together rose fresh in her mind, the sound of their mingled laughter echoing in her ears, all of it so heartbreakingly vivid that she wanted to weep all over again. How had it happened that the people she'd always trusted no longer trusted her, while the only man who seemed to care for her was the one she dared not trust in return?

"How can you understand when I don't understand myself?" she said forlornly, resting her hands on his chest. "How can you, when everything in my life—*everything*—seems turned upside down?"

"Then tell me, Catie, and I'll try—"

"No!" she cried softly. "I don't want to talk any more! What I want— What I want— Oh, Lord help me, I do not *know!*"

But she did. Swiftly, before the moment passed and she lost her courage, she slipped her hands around the back of his neck and drew his face down to hers and kissed him. She kissed him hungrily, and with a desperation that was impossible to hide. Words had failed her up to now, words had tripped her and caught her and snared her in ways she'd never dreamed of. This seemed her final hope, to lose herself in wordless emotion and find herself in the solace that only Anthony could offer. No matter how much she tried to deny it, the bond between them was there, and always had been.

Instinctively her lips parted to join with him more completely, and with a low masculine growl in his throat he deepened the kiss, his hands sliding along her back to curve her into his body. This was no gentle pledge, no promise; this was passion, raw and powerful, and she let herself be carried away on its current. His hands slid lower, from her waist to her hips, and even through the layers of her petticoats she could feel the heat of his caress. She dug her fingers into the thick waves of his hair, pulling him closer, and she felt the ridge of the paneling behind her as he pressed her against the wall.

The paneling on the wall, thought some tiny, hazy part of her consciousness, the same paneling, newly painted gray-green last autumn, that lined the stairway and the landing where one could stand and see both the center entry hall below and the hall to the guests' chambers above.

See, or be seen...

With a smothered cry, Catie pulled free, her fingers fluttering to cover her mouth, the same mouth and lips that had shamed her with such wanton ease. Over and over she'd told him how much her good name mattered, and here she'd gone and behaved like some bold, tawdry slattern.

"Oh, Anthony, what you must think of me!" she gasped, appalled by what she'd done. "If anyone had come, if anyone had seen us— Dear Lord, I've dismissed serving girls for less!"

His breathing ragged, his eyes dark with interrupted desire, Anthony reached for her again. "How could I ever think ill of you, sweet, especially for something as near to heaven as that kiss?"

But Catie shook her head, backing away toward the stairs. "I cannot stay. I must go," she said rapidly, unable to meet his gaze as she turned away. "I've many things to tend to."

"Damnation, Catie!" he said roughly. "The only reason I waited for you here was to say goodbye!"

She froze, her hand gripping the rail. "Goodbye?" she echoed faintly, the memory of how he'd left her before rising up keen and fresh. "You are leaving Newport?"

"For only a day or two, that is all. Three at most." He reached for her hand again, and this time she let him take it. But he didn't try to kiss her again. He wasn't lying; he hadn't come there for that. Besides, after what he'd put her through before, he'd respect her reluctance now, even if it left his own body aching from the sacrifice.

"Only a day?" Troubled, she searched his face for the truth. "Where could you go for only a day? And why come to tell me farewell unless you fear you will not return?"

He smiled crookedly. "Because, you know, I might not. It's always a possibility with soldiers, particularly those serving His Majesty in this war."

"Then you're going after Jon." She spoke softly, with grim certainty. "That's it, isn't it? You won't return until he's dead or in chains?"

"Don't ask me about Jon, Catie," he said quietly, his fingers tightening around hers, "and in return I'll ask no questions of you."

She nodded mutely, realizing the enormity of what he'd just done for her. He had put her first, before his orders, his general, even his king. She'd heard the rumors about what Jon and his men had been doing: stealing supplies from the British, destroying and vandalizing what they couldn't steal, luring disenchanted British soldiers into deserting and joining them. Of course the British couldn't tolerate such losses any longer, and Anthony would be the natural one to stop it. But still the notion of the two cousins so at risk from one another frightened her more than she wished to admit to Anthony.

She stared down at their linked hands, and slowly lifted his to her lips.

"Might I ask you to take care?" she asked, her whispered words brushing across the back of his hand. "If I ask that of you, Anthony, for my sake, will you listen?"

The front door opened, and the hallway filled with the sounds of men's voices and laughter and heavy shoes stamping off the snow. Yet, though he knew he must, Anthony did not draw away from Catie; nor did she release his hand as they stood there in the twilight.

"Yes, Catie, I will," he said hoarsely. "For you, sweet, I would do anything."

And through the haze of her tears, Catie smiled, and for the first time she believed him.

Anthony lowered his hand, and at the signal the men around him dropped wearily to the sandy ground, shielding themselves as best they could behind the rocks and waving grasses. The night wind from the sea was unrelenting, slicing cruelly through the men's heavy coats to settle the damp cold deep in their blood and bones. After the long march across the island, Anthony knew that what they needed most was a warm fire and hot drink, but he didn't wish to warn away the rebels, not when they were this close.

At least he hoped they were close. He'd come this far tonight depending on a mixture of what he knew and what he guessed, with an ample amount of intuition thrown in for good measure. The men had been carefully chosen, all battle-seasoned veterans who had been with Anthony since Boston in '72, and they had been picked not only for their skill with a musket, but for their reticence, as well. For Anthony's plan to work, all the elaborate lines of gossip and spying that ran like an underground stream through the occupied town would have to carry the same word: that Major Sparhawk had left Newport for the northern beaches of the island with a small party of men, their goal to capture the rebels who had been attacking the outlying British posts.

Like all the best lies, the story he'd spread in the town was largely true. Anthony's orders *were* to capture the rebels and their leaders. But instead of going north, where the rebels had always struck before and where he'd been ordered to go by General Ridley, Anthony had circled around the town to head toward the southwest tip, to the bleak, rocky point called Nantasket. He could have spent weeks trying to predict where the rebels would strike next, but he was willing to gamble his career that this was where they gathered first.

And this time Anthony's gamble had paid off. His men had already found the boats and ammunition hidden in the cave, exactly where he'd hoped to find them. Later they would burn the boats, but for now he'd ordered everything left as it was, making sure his men swept their tracks from the sand before they hid on either side of the steep path to the beach, ready to ambush the Americans.

Critically Anthony studied the rocky hillside and the sweep of beach below. How many years had passed since he was here last? Ten? As many as fifteen? So little had changed that he couldn't be certain.

So little, and yet so much...

"It's a pirate cave," said Jon with all the authority

of his nine years. "They'd bring their gold and plunder here to hide it from the navy coasters."

Anthony peered through the weeds into the narrow entrance. Being two years older, and from the country, as well, he knew better than to believe everything his cousin told him, even about something as exciting as a pirate lair. "Uncle Gabriel says your grandfather was a smuggler, not a pirate. That's not the same thing."

Jon frowned scornfully. "Well, what else would Father say about his own family? Besides, it wasn't Grandfather. It was my grandmother, too, and her first husband. He was the pirate king."

"Your grandmother?" From his first visit to Newport, Anthony could dimly recall an old lady in the plain dress of a Quaker. Certainly she couldn't have been a pirate queen. "You're daft, Jon. Likely all that's in that cave are dead crabs and bats. The same bats that are in your head."

"Are not." Stubbornly Jon raised his chin. "I bet you're just scared, Anthony. Same as my little sisters. You're just too scared to go inside."

"Am not." Before he could think too much about it, Anthony shoved aside the dead weeds and plunged into the murkiness of the cave. After the warmth of the summer sun, the sand was cold beneath his bare feet, the air around him chill and damp enough for him to imagine all sorts of evil things in the shadows beyond the daylight. Something brushed against his side, and he gasped and struggled to free himself, his arms flailing wildly into sticky cobwebs.

"Quit it, Anthony," cried Jon indignantly, "else you'll murder me!"

There was a bright little flash of sparks as Jon lit the candle in the lantern they'd brought, and in its comforting glow Anthony felt his racing heart begin to slow.

"Likely we're the first two to be in here since the pirates left," he said, striving to make his voice even for Jon's benefit. "That is, if there were any pirates."

"Oh, aye, there were, Anthony, no mistake." Jon's face was owlish in the lantern light. "Same ones as was hung, out on the Deadman's Point, their bodies left to rot from the gallows for all the terrible deeds they'd done, torturing and murdering and such."

In spite of his wish to be brave, Anthony edged closer to the lantern. "Do you think there's any treasure left inside?"

"That's why we're here, isn't it?" Solemnly Jon nodded and held out his hand. "Now swear, whatever we find we'll split even, Anthony, on account of being Sparhawks and kin and all. Swear we'll always be mates, and that you'll never slit my throat or try other base piratical acts on account of the gold."

Anthony clasped his cousin's hand. "I swear to it, Jon. I swear to it we'll be mates forever."

But forever had come to an end, thought Anthony grimly, and a great deal sooner than either of them ever expected. He looked again at the mouth of the cave, trying to see it as a soldier and not as a boy. Jon couldn't have chosen a better spot to hide his boats, and only Anthony could have found it. Had his cousin counted on that long-ago oath to protect him here, as well?

Bitterly Anthony muttered an oath to himself. What

would happen here tonight was Jon's decision, not his. He couldn't forget that.

Damnation, but it was cold. Irresistibly his mind returned to the warmth he'd found last night in Catie's kiss, and he thought, too, of how her eyes had grown too bright with tears when he'd told her goodbye. Tears for *him*. No wonder he'd been unable to tell her the same tale he'd so carefully spun throughout the rest of the town. He never wanted to tell her anything but the truth again.

And what exactly was that truth? That he cared for her, that he wanted to be with her, that he loved her? Though there had been plenty of women in his life, he'd never loved any of them, but then, Catie wasn't like the others, either. Catie was special, and with each day it was becoming harder and harder to imagine his life without her in it, war or no war.

He glanced up at the moon, gauging the time, and tugged his hat down lower on his head. If Jon and his rebels were planning a raid tonight, they'd have to gather soon, or the night would be gone.

"Lookee, sir, there!" The nearest man—Sergeant Barr, guessed Anthony—pointed up the rocky path from the beach. "That be them, sir, I'd stake my life to it!"

Five dark shadows bobbed across the open field and in and out of the scrubby low bushes. Gradually, as the shadows drew closer, their shapes sharpened into a small group of men, hurrying with their shoulders hunched against the wind and their muskets slung carelessly across their backs. Anthony smiled at that; if his men could take the Americans by such complete surprise, then perhaps they could capture the rebels without any casualties on either side.

"Hold your fire, and let them come to us," he whispered sharply, his voice rough with the cold. "Don't give the bastards a chance to scatter and run."

A low murmur of agreement rumbled through his men, and all around him Anthony could hear the little cracks and squeaks of men finally loading their muskets. As cold and tired as they were, Anthony knew the chance to avenge their dead comrades would add a raw intensity to their fighting.

"Steady, lads, steady," he cautioned, not daring to say more and risk having the Americans overhear. "Steady, now."

The Americans were almost upon them now, their hats pulled forward and their heads bent so low into the wind that they'd never see the British until they were square in the middle of the ambush. One man was singing—droning, really—a low, doleful hymn that matched the rhythm of their muffled footsteps.

Steady, steady, repeated Anthony silently, praying that none of his men would jump up too soon. His heart was pounding with anticipation, his finger tight on the trigger of his own musket. Beneath the hats, which one was his cousin Jon?

Steady now...

The second man in the ragged line caught his boot on a piece of driftwood and stumbled in the sand. His musket swung forward heavily, off his shoulder, and as he swore and grabbed for it, he suddenly noticed the red-coated soldiers in the rocks above him. He gasped and stammered—the only garbled warning he could muster.

Anthony scrambled to his feet, high on a massive rock. "In the name of your king," he roared, "damn you, surrender!"

What happened next was a blur of red uniforms rushing down the gray rocks and over the white sand, of the Americans struggling vainly to reach for their knives or to swing their muskets like clubs before they were forced to surrender. The moonlight shifting through the clouds glinted off a polished bayonet here, a torn white shirtfront there, a terrified man's open mouth as he begged for mercy.

Yet in the split second before Anthony jumped down from the rock to join the others, a movement in the distance, across the fields, caught his eye. Another man, a latecomer, scurrying from the shelter of each bush to scrubby tree as he fled the same fate as his friends.

"Halt, in the name of the king!" roared Anthony, his hands cupped around his mouth. "Halt now, you damned rebel coward!"

Still the man ran, and Anthony raised his gun to his shoulder. His orders were to take all rebels alive, but he meant to bring them, every last one of them, to the general, and he'd be damned if he'd let this last coward slip through his fingers now. With that as his only thought, he sighted the running figure at the end of the musket's long barrel and squeezed the trigger, the butt kicking back into this shoulder.

"Prime shooting, sir," said Barr breathlessly as he climbed up on the rock beside Anthony. "Especially fine, sir, since the others are sayin' that last bastard was their leader, the one shamin' your family's good name by turning rebel."

Without seeing, Anthony stared silently through the clearing gunpowder.

I swear to it, Jon. I swear to it we'll be mates forever....

Swiftly he turned on his heel. "Send two men to find the body," he said, wondering if anyone else noticed how hollow and empty his voice had become. "The general will want it as proof."

Chapter Ten

It was nearly midnight by the time Anthony returned to Hazard's. Returning to town, reporting to General Ridley, seeing the prisoners quartered in the gaol—all of this had taken time.

But what had cost him the most was the search for Jon's body. He'd watched in silent agony while his men scoured the field where Jon should have fallen, and somehow managed to keep his expression emotionless when they returned empty-handed. Not that he believed Jon had escaped—he knew his shot had found its mark—but the image of his cousin dying alone and untended like a wild animal beneath some bush or in an empty barn haunted him all through the general's congratulations and the rejoicing of his regiment. He'd saved both his career and his reputation as a brilliant officer, but the price had been higher than he could ever have guessed.

Now all he wanted was to be alone. Wearily he dragged himself up the stairs, tired in body but exhausted in his soul. He wondered if his manservant could find him a bottle of rum somewhere in the house at this hour; he wasn't usually much of a drinker, but tonight the thought of drinking himself into a senseless blank without guilt or conscience or grief seemed the best course before him.

His fingers still stiff from the cold, he fumbled with the key to his chamber. A pale light glowed from beneath the door and he frowned, thinking of the waste of wood to keep a fire blazing away while he was out. Sometimes Routt's concern for his welfare went beyond common reason, and with his mood even blacker, he threw open the door.

"Oh!" With a startled gasp, Catie jerked awake and nearly tumbled from the tall-backed armchair. Framed by the doorway before her stood Anthony, and sleepy though she was, she could see that his face didn't wear the look of surprise that she'd anticipated. Instead, he looked exhausted and preoccupied and not at all happy to find her waiting.

"Why the devil are you here, Catie?" he asked wearily. "Where's Routt?"

Still groggy, she rubbed her fingers across her eyes. "I sent him to his bed hours ago. There didn't seem any reason for both of us to wait for you."

"Indeed." Anthony wondered if she realized that his manservant usually slept in here with him, rolled up in a blanket on the floor at the foot of his bed. Trust Routt not to tell her himself; Lord only knew where he'd gone instead for the night. "It must be long past time for you to be safe in your own bed, as well."

"Most likely it is. Or was, rather," she said, not quite sure how long she'd been asleep. She slid her stockinged feet from where she'd tucked them up beneath her petticoat and shoved them into her mules, clutching the thick shawl she'd brought for warmth around her shoulders as she stood. "I overheard some of the other soldiers saying you'd returned to town, and I knew you wouldn't be long, so I decided I'd stay awake to welcome you home."

His frown deepened as he tossed his hat onto his campaign chest. "I've hardly earned a hero's welcome."

"That wasn't what I'd meant." She swallowed, realizing from his hostility that she'd have to tread most carefully. This wasn't going the way she'd planned, but she'd come too far to retreat now; nor did she wish to. "Though I overheard from the others that you were—were most successful in your venture."

"So I'm told, yes, I was." He tore at the buttons on his coat, ripping them from their buttonholes. "Most successful indeed."

She nodded, striving to understand. "Then you did find Jon."

His expression grew darker still. "Damnation, Catie, I don't—"

"No, Anthony, please, don't swear at me, but don't coddle me, either!" she cried unhappily. "I have tried to be truthful with you, and all I ask is the same in return. I know before you couldn't tell me about Jon because of your orders, but surely now there can be no harm to it."

He stood very still, the lines of weariness and sorrow etched deeper into his face by the shadows of the firelight.

"Why should you care so much, Catie?" he demanded. "What is my cousin and his misfortune to you?"

"Jon Sparhawk is my friend, a good friend, too, as are all the others of his family," she said defensively. "That includes you, as well, if you can bear it."

He turned away, ostensibly to hang his coat on the peg, but also to avoid letting her read the feelings he knew were written so large across his face. A friend— that was all his cousin was to her. *Only a friend.* Lord, how desperately he wanted to believe it!

"We captured six men—my cousin's fellow rogues—at a cave near the water, and destroyed the boats that they had hidden there," he said. "But though all of them say that Jon was their leader, he was not among those taken."

Still he kept his back to her. "It's only a matter of time, of course," he continued. "I mean to return at dawn and search every house and hayrick in the area until I find him."

"Of course," she murmured unhappily. "Your duty and your orders demand that you do nothing less."

He couldn't make himself meet her eye. She had asked for the truth, and he had given it to her. But not all of it; miserably he knew he was too much the coward to confess everything that he had done, and he despised the weakness in himself.

Catie stared at that broad, uncommunicative back in the white waistcoat, struggling to control her own emotions as well as Anthony did his.

"Were there—were any boys captured, as well?" she asked tentatively. "Was there any sign of Jon's son Jeremiah?"

"I am not in the habit of making war upon boys or

women," said Anthony sharply as he turned around to face her. "I had thought, ma'am, you held a higher regard for me than that."

"And I, sir, thought the same of you for me," she answered heatedly. "All I asked was if you'd *seen* Jon's son, not if you've taken to slaughtering innocents!"

Anthony shook his head wearily and sighed, his anger spent as quickly as it had begun. "Catie, forgive me. I am very tired, too tired to be decent company."

"I don't expect you to be," she said gently. "And you needn't apologize, else I'll have to apologize to you, too. But I'd rather thought that after all you must have been through these last days and nights, you might wish some company yourself."

"Then you were mistaken." But she hadn't been, and Anthony knew it. To tell her what had happened, to be able to pour out his fears and his grief to her sympathetic ears, was almost unbearably tempting, like a cupful of water to a man perishing of thirst.

Unable to read his expression, Catie shrugged self-consciously beneath his scrutiny, and the shawl slipped to one side from her shoulder.

For the first time since Anthony had entered the room he noticed how informally she was dressed, in a soft buttoned bodice without stays, over a ruffled shift and a single petticoat that revealed far more of the actual shape of her hips and legs than her usual layered skirts. Her silvery hair was loosely braided, the thick plait drawn over one shoulder and tied with a thin blue ribbon.

She stepped to one side to touch the little table set before the fire. "I thought you might wish some more substantial comfort, too." She smiled wryly. "It's the innkeeper in me, you see. I cannot abide to see anyone hungry or thirsty, and I'll wager you can't remember the last time you ate."

"Oh, Catie," he murmured, but still he couldn't help smiling in return. Somehow, in his own misery, he hadn't noticed the bounty spread on the table, either. Sliced ham, a round of cheese, pickled eggs, a plump loaf of bread, a squash pie with a glistening glazed crust, and a pitcher of ale to wash it all down—one look, and already his mouth was beginning to water.

"Ha, there!" she crowed softly, "I can recognize that look on any man's face! Now you sit here, Anthony, in this chair near the fire, and let me fetch you whatever you fancy. I promise you'll feel infinitely more agreeable once your belly is full."

He looked from the table to Catie eagerly holding the winged back of the armchair with both hands to offer it to him. The shawl had slipped farther down her arm, the rough dark wool baring more of her pale skin. Without the stiff armor of her stays, her breasts were round and full, and their weight pressed gently against the quilted wool of her bodice. As she leaned forward across the chair, his eyes were drawn to the shadowy valley above the neckline of her shift, and it was only with great difficulty that he forced himself to look away.

But as he did, with a shock he noticed something else. The heart-shaped locket she'd always worn without fail before was gone. Because Catie had made no secret of not loving her husband, Anthony had come to suspect that Jon's picture was tucked within the gold heart, and to find the locket missing now, for the first time, on this night of all others, made joy leap almost painfully within his chest. She'd said that Jon was just a friend, and at last Anthony began to believe it.

She tapped her fingertips on the back of the chair, unaware of his thoughts. "You needn't look so suspicious, Anthony," she said. "You *can* trust me, you know. Food is far too dear these days for me to lace all this with poison, merely for the sake of doing away with one sorry redcoat. Watch, sir, and I'll prove it."

She reached across the table and plucked one of the pickled eggs from the bowl. With a conjurer's flourish she held the egg in the air between her thumb and forefinger for him to see, placing her other hand at her waist with her arm akimbo. Then, with great solemnity, she bit into the egg, her lips very red against the gleaming white.

"There," she declared when she'd swallowed. She was on far safer ground here; hungry men were her specialty. "You can see I have not perished. Now, if you do not sit down directly, I vow I shall feel myself a perfect failure as a hostess."

"No wonder you've prospered, Mrs. Hazard," he grumbled, but nonetheless he sat in the chair, albeit somewhat tentatively, and let her push the table closer to him.

He could tell how hard she was trying to lighten the mood between them—the wry little smiles, the coaxing, even the bit with the egg that doubtless was so popular with her regular guests—and he didn't wish to disappoint her, not over something as foolish as this,

Besides, he *was* hungry. He couldn't deny that, especially not as she placed the plate of food before him.

"You're not having anything yourself?" he asked as he began to cut the ham. "Surely it's been a good long time since you ate, too."

"If I supped with every guest, I'd be stout as a barn," she said as she poured the ale into his tankard. "I'd devour all my profits, too. I know you prefer the pale rum, but at this hour you'll do better with lighter spirits."

"My, my, how you see to my welfare," he said wryly, both amused and touched by her solicitude. He couldn't remember the last time a woman had fussed over him like this, and he'd forgotten how pleasant it could be.

Even if he didn't deserve it. God help him, what would she do if she knew about Jon? No, it wasn't an *if. When* she learned about Jon.

At the thought, the ham turned tasteless in his mouth, and he reached for the tankard to wash it down. She had turned to urge more life from the fire, bending down with the poker in her hand. The single linen petticoat draped across her hips and bottom, and he liked the way her neat little feet and ankles arched up from the open mules as she bent down closer to the hearth. Had she any idea of what such simple things did to him?

He shifted uneasily in his chair. If he had any conscience left at all, he'd send her away now, the way he should have done in the first place. But instead he merely waited in silence as she dusted her hands together and perched on the edge of the other chair.

The silence stretched longer as he turned back to

the food on his plate, and Catie sighed, her hands folded in her lap as she watched him eat.

"You've never gone hungry, have you?" she asked softly. "Not just tonight, I mean, but ever in your life."

He frowned, not quite sure what she was asking. "I've been hungry, yes, just as I've been sated once I've eaten. It's generally the way of men."

She shook her head with a little shrug of her shoulders. "For those like you, who've always had money, I suppose it is. It's another of the things I've come to recognize in my trade," she said lightly, choosing not to confess how often as a child she herself had gone to sleep hungry on the rush-filled mattress under the eaves. "The way you hold your fork and knife, how you lift your food to your mouth and not the other way around, small things like that. You've always known there shall be another meal coming after this one, and the next will be every bit as fine as the last. And though you may have grown up in the wilderness, still your mama took care with your manners."

"Not my mother, no." Suddenly self-conscious, he set the fork and knife down on the side of the plate. "Both my mother and father died of the smallpox when I was a baby. I was raised in my grandparents' house, so you must lay all of the credit for my manners and none of the blame to my grandmother."

She reached across the table to touch his sleeve in unspoken sympathy. "It's all credit, that I can see."

"Ah, well, she was a true English lady," he said, his gaze growing distant at the memory. "She always expected people to call her that, too, 'my lady Dianna', on account of her being an earl's granddaughter.

Everyone at Plumstead did, even though by rights she should have put aside the title when she wed.''

"Lady Dianna," repeated Catie faintly. "How very grand."

"That she was," he admitted. "Abenaki braves lurking in the woods and the French army not far behind, yet she always saw to it that there was fine linen and silver on the table, and wine to drink the health of the king."

Wistfully Catie tried to imagine growing up in such a household, so very different from the bleak poverty of her own childhood, and failed.

"Noble blood, and silver on the table," she said, slipping her hand away from his arm. "No wonder you chose to side with the Tories. How could you do otherwise?"

Anthony shook his head. "Serving the king as an officer was my idea, not my grandmother's," he said. "It was my way to seek all the things a restless young man wants, glory and adventure and a chance to leave my youth behind. Dreams, that was all it was, Catie, the same kind of dreams you must have had yourself."

Oh, she'd had dreams, all right, she thought sadly, dreams enough for any lass. Without thinking, she touched the place where her locket usually hung, belatedly remembering that when she dressed tonight she'd wanted no reminders of herself as Belinda's mother. But Belinda and Anthony were too tangled together to be so easily put aside, and sorrowfully she looked down at the empty place on her bodice where the locket with her—no, *their*—daughter's picture should have been.

Anthony saw where her fingers rested on her bodice,

and his heart sank as he guessed the rest. Damnation, what else could he expect, blathering on about himself like some thick-witted oaf! But she'd taken the first step by removing the locket. It was up to him, now, to take the next one.

He reached across the table to take her hand. "I did not mean to make you sad, sweetheart," he said gruffly. "The dreams I had then are long gone and cast away. But I've found new ones to take their place, Catie, new ones that are much more dear to me because they include you."

Troubled, she looked up at him from beneath her lashes, her chin still low against her chest. She had never seen such tenderness on a man's face before. Yet mingled with it was fear, surely the same fear she felt herself. If she dared to dream with him, could she dare to hope and to trust, as well?

"There is nothing sure between us, is there, Anthony?" she said, her voice a rough, rapid whisper. "Nothing will last, nothing is certain. When you said goodbye two nights ago, I was sick from fearing you would not return."

"Catie, love, you—"

"No, please, Anthony, listen!" She had risen to her feet, her fingers twisting into his. "You swore you'd try to court me the way I hadn't been before. I scoffed and believed I was beyond such things, but I'm not. Oh, Anthony, I'm not, not in the least! The handkerchief, the gloves, the little paper heart, each one so dear to me now because it came from you."

His lopsided smile was almost boyish, at odds with his stubbled jaw and the weary lines around his eyes. "That's as I meant it to be, sweetheart."

"Well, yes, else you wouldn't have done it, would you?" She smiled uncertainly, her cheeks growing warm. "And because all we may have is tonight, *this* night, I wanted to give something to you in return, something to show you how I care, too."

"Oh, Catie." He shoved his chair back from the table so that he could reach for her other hand and draw her to stand directly before him. Gently he held her hands in his, stroking his thumbs across her up-turned wrists. He wouldn't promise her things that couldn't be, or insult her by telling her they'd have a long, happy life together. She knew better than that, and so did he, and the knowledge gave her offer an almost unbearable poignancy. "You've already given me a great deal more than such a sorry rogue deserves."

"But not the way I wished to." She felt oddly captive, not from the way he was holding her hands, but by the deceptively simple touch of his thumbs moving over the blue veins of her wrists. She shook her head, trying to think straight while the stray wisps of her hair drifted back and forth on either side of her face.

"I wanted this supper to be special, a surprise," she continued wistfully. "After what I heard from your men, I'd hoped you'd be happy, and wishing to celebrate. I didn't know that your skirmish or ambush or whatever it was had not gone as you'd wished."

"But that's changed, hasn't it?" he teased softly, trying to stave off the tears that he could hear in her voice. She was right; this one night might be all they had, and he didn't want her to remember it through a haze of tears. "I'd say that this skirmish or ambush or whatever it is you've planned for me is proceeding exactly as *you* wished. And I'm not about to challenge a word of your orders.''

In one easy motion, Anthony pulled her onto his lap and into his arms, and before she could think to protest, his lips had found hers, warm and demanding and certain of her welcome.

She told herself she should scramble free with a great show of indignation. This wasn't what she'd wanted, not really. The supper alone was what she'd planned. She told herself she had sorrow enough in her life without adding such wanton folly to it.

She told herself all these things, sternly, as only her conscience could. Then she told herself to stop lying, and listen to the truth of her heart.

With a little sigh of surrender, she let herself curl into his embrace, her lips parting eagerly to welcome his. She felt his hand on her hip, pulling her closer, and with only the two layers of fabric between them, she was achingly aware both of his touch and of the corded muscles of his thighs beneath her. He was so intriguingly *male,* she thought as he deepened the kiss, strong and hard where she was soft and yielding in ways she'd never realized.

She twisted toward him, instinctively seeking more of the wonderful differences between them. From the first time she slipped against him, that night on horseback, she'd yearned to touch him again. Greatly daring, she now let her hands creep up across his chest to his shoulders, over the wool of his waistcoat. Beneath her palm she felt the beat of his heart, a steady echo to her own racing pulse, and she slid her hands around the back of his neck to steady herself, his hair curling over her wrists.

She started with surprise when she felt his hand on the front of her bodice, grazing the curve of her breast through the quilted wool. Yet the gentleness of his touch reassured her even as it warmed her blood, and she slipped back farther into the crook of his arm. With deliberate and tantalizing care, he eased each button free from the loops down the front of her bodice, one by one by one.

By the time he reached the last, she was trembling with anticipation. He tugged loose the drawstring on the neckline of her shift, and when he slipped his hand inside to cup her breast, she gasped with the sheer pleasure of it. She moved up against his palm, seeking more, even though she couldn't have begun to explain what *more* might be. It was a mystery she'd carried with her for eight years, and now, at last, the secret was nearly within reach, if she dared to seize it.

Yet still she gasped again as his lips moved to where his hand had been, drawing her nipple into the wet heat of his mouth. She threaded her fingers through his hair to hold him there, crying out with the wild pleasure of what he was doing. Her whole body was growing taut and heavy with longing, the restless fire centering low in her belly, and she arched impatiently into his caress.

And then, abruptly, he stopped.

"Enough, Catie," he growled, the words hot against her skin. "I can't bear this any longer."

Her eyes flew open, her disappointment palpable as pain as she clung to him. "Please don't stop, Anthony," she whispered shamelessly. "Oh, please don't!"

"Damnation, sweetheart, do you think I'd wish such a thing? It's not you. It's this blasted *chair.*"

She laughed then from pure relief, a laugh that turned into a startled little yelp as he swept her backward onto the bed. With a soft *whoosh,* she sank deep into the feather bed, pulling him down with her. He kissed her again, hard, and she arched up against the long, lean length of his body, pressing over her.

"As if I could ever turn away from you, Catie," he whispered fiercely into her ear. "Don't you know what you do to me, lass? Don't you know how much you mean to me?"

"Then show me," she whispered in return, her cheeks hot with her own boldness. She fumbled at the buttons on his waistcoat, urgency making her fingers hopelessly clumsy. "Please, Anthony. For I want to show you how much I care for you, as well."

He raised himself up on his elbows, his green eyes so serious as he searched her face. "You are certain of this, Catie?" he asked, his breathing ragged. "I know I cannot undo the past, but God help me, I've no wish to hurt you again."

She smiled, barely holding back the tears that suddenly burned behind her eyes. What she'd say would only magnify the complications in their lives a hundredfold, but she had to tell him. "That was long ago, Anthony," she said softly. "I'm not some starry-eyed maid anymore, and now I can see you for the man you truly are."

His smile was heartbreakingly unsure. "A sorry bargain, that, sweetheart."

"Oh, no. It's the very best bargain there is," she whispered as she stretched up to brush her lips over his. "Because you, Anthony Sparhawk, are the man I love."

No woman had ever said that to him and meant it, not the way that Catie did, and for the first time he realized the power such little words could hold. In spite of the unspeakable way he'd treated her before, in spite of the red coat he wore, in spite of whatever he'd thought she felt for his cousin Jon, in spite of it all, she had chosen to love him.

Not that it was any choice for him. He had been a soldier too long not to believe in fate, and fate, he was quite certain, had spared him through battle after battle to bring him back across the ocean from old England to new, and to her. How else but through fate could they have managed to find each other again?

"And I love you, Catie Hazard," he said slowly, with infinite care. "And I love you."

He made love to her with the same care and a rare tenderness, as if this single night would last forever, as in a way it must. She might have been wed before, but no man—and he did not spare himself—had ever loved her the way she deserved. He delighted in her shy eagerness, and how she sought to please him as much as he wanted to please her. There was still a girlish innocence to her that fascinated him, and made him cherish her responses all the more. He built the passion in her body slowly, holding back his own fulfillment until he was certain of hers.

And when at last he entered her, she cried out his name with the same breathy little sigh that had become so dear to him. Again he moved slowly, reveling in the feel of her opening for him, taking him deeper. But inexperienced though she might be, she still was not as patient, and as their bodies grew more heated and slick with sweat, she was the one to quicken the pace, instinctively wrapping her legs around his waist to urge him on.

He obliged, of course, increasing both the rhythm and the intensity as she arched against him. He wanted to fill her in every way possible, not just her body, but her soul and heart, as well, until their mating became a seamless union that would bind them together forever. He shifted back onto his knees, leaving her gasping at the delicious change, and then he slipped his hand down lower, to stroke her where their bodies were so intimately connected, and she cried out his name as the joy swept her away. He joined her then, giving himself over blindly to an intense, shuddering release unlike anything he'd ever known.

Because *she* was like no one he'd ever known, his Catie, his one love. And he was home, truly home, at last.

"I love you, Catie," he murmured again, pulling her close with him as he rolled to his side. Tenderly he smoothed the pale damp curls away from the shell of her ear, watching her smile dreamily at him. He would never tire of saying the words, an incantation to keep the world away from their own paradise. "I love you, Catie."

She loved Anthony, and he loved her. It was the one thought Catie held on to as she stared drowsily into the dying embers of the fire in the hearth. His body still lay tangled intimately with hers, his arm thrown protectively around her even as he slept. She had never felt as content, or as happy, as she did at this moment.

She could not quite remember how she and Anthony

had come to shed the rest of their clothes, or when they'd shifted from lying on top of the coverlet to beneath it. But she knew she'd never forget the passion they'd shared, the way the desire in her blood had built hotter and fiercer than anything she could have dreamed of.

And when at last he entered her, there had been none of the hollow, aching emptiness she'd found with her husband. Instead, there had been only pleasure beyond imagining as the tension in her body coiled tighter and tighter and her heart raced so fast she was sure she'd explode, and then, in a marvelous, unexpected way, she had, crying out Anthony's name as the tears of joy had slid down her cheeks.

She loved Anthony, and he loved her. With a sigh, she burrowed closer to him, and let her own eyes drift shut.

She loved Anthony, and...

She heard the door open and close far away in the house. The kitchen door; that was the one that squeaked on its hinges that way. Who would come to the back door at this hour, and more importantly, who had unbarred the door to let them in? In an instant she was wide awake, every nerve on edge.

Please, God, not Jon, not here, not tonight! Catie felt her heart pounding, sick with dread from that one very real possibility. Desperately she told herself it was only that, a possibility. There must be a hundred places on this island where Jon could go to hide, and if he had any wits left at all, Hazard's wouldn't be one of them.

Please, oh, please, not this night...

She closed her eyes again, forlornly wishing she

could simply go to sleep in the warm shelter of Anthony's body and forget the door until morning. Reality and responsibility would intrude on them soon enough.

But now she could make out the murmur of voices, too, and she knew she couldn't afford to ignore them any longer. She slipped free of Anthony's arm, pulling the coverlet over his bare shoulder. He looked so much younger when he slept, his handsome face relaxed and at peace, and her heart swelled with how much she loved him. She dressed quickly, the room chilly now, with the untended fire so low, her ears straining to make out the voices downstairs. She was sure that one of them belonged to Hannah, but the other was too soft for her to distinguish, and again she prayed it wasn't Jon.

With her mules in her hand, she bent over Anthony and feathered a kiss across his cheek. He stirred in his sleep, smiled, and murmured her name with a drowsy tenderness that almost broke her heart. How she longed to climb back into the bed beside him! But, with a sigh, instead she left and quietly closed the door after her, promising herself she'd return as soon as she could, and if she was lucky, she'd be back before he even realized she was gone.

On the back stairs, she paused to slip on her shoes and listen. Again all she could hear was the gruff rise and fall of Hannah's voice, and Catie's fears began to ease. Jon couldn't possibly be here; he'd never be able to keep quiet this long. More likely it was only one of the men from the stables, or perhaps a neighbor come to see Hannah on some sort of minor household emergency. Such things happened all the time. With a final twitch to her skirts, she pushed open the kitchen door.

"Ah, so there you are, mistress!" said Hannah, her tone more than faintly accusing. From her dress, she, too, must have been roused from her bed; two long gray braids trailed beneath her nightcap, and she wore a shawl thrown hastily over her night shift. "I come looking to your room, an' I knocked an' knocked, but you never called back."

"I'm a sound sleeper, Hannah, you know that," said Catie sharply. She owed no excuses to the cook, and she wasn't going to offer any, either. Besides, the kitchen appeared to be empty except for them, and wistfully she thought again of Anthony waiting for her upstairs. "Pray, why did you wish to rouse me, anyway? What couldn't wait until morning?"

"'Twas my fault, Mrs. Hazard." A small, bedraggled figure slipped from behind the side of the tall Welsh cupboard. Clearly Jeremiah Sparhawk was trying his best to be as brave as he could, but across the dirt on his cheeks were the pale trails left by tears, and self-consciously he swiped his sleeve across his nose. "Pa said I could always come here t'you if I was in trouble."

Righteously Hannah clucked her tongue. "There now, mistress, what—"

"Hush, Hannah!" Catie stepped closer to the boy. He was trembling, and from the haunted look in his eyes she knew it wasn't from the cold alone. No child should have that look, she thought sadly, and if his back wasn't so stiff from living up to his father's notions of manhood, she would have swept him into her arms at once.

"Your father's right, Jere," she coaxed gently. "You can always come here to me, whether you're in trouble or not."

"Aye, aye, ma'am," he mumbled, and stared down at his feet. "It's just that—just that—oh, ma'am!"

His mouth crumpled, and with his head down he stumbled toward her, throwing his arms around her knees and burying his face against her skirts. Swiftly Catie disentangled the boy from her skirts and bent to his level, and now Jeremiah let her hold him tight, his cheek pressed into the hollow of her shoulder as she stroked his tangled black hair.

"Pa's—Pa's dead," he sobbed, "an' it was my turncoat coward uncle that shot him."

Chapter Eleven

"Here you go, Jere, now drink this," said Catie softly as she handed the boy the tankard of chocolate. "You won't be able to tell me anything with your teeth chattering like that."

With a shuddering sigh, the boy took the tankard, his shoulders huddled beneath Catie's coverlet. Gently she brushed the hair back from his forehead, noting how he'd fallen too far into his own misery to pull back. In a way, she wished he still could cry; that would be better than seeing him withdraw into himself.

Better, too, for her to think of the welfare of the boy, Jon's son, than to consider the grim reason he'd come to her. Better not to think of how Anthony had come to her, as well, with Jon's blood still fresh on his hands and his conscience, and once again she swallowed back the dull, sickening wave of horror and unwitting complicity.

Anthony had been able to tell her he loved her, but not this. Lying in his arms, she had forgotten the grim suffering that came from the war, and the awful, casual fragility of life. She had dared to hope that love might be enough for them both. She had changed, and so, she'd believed, had Anthony.

But not enough. Dear heaven, not nearly enough.

Behind her, Hannah sniffed self-righteously. "I'll go warm the sheets in the yellow chamber," she said. "Sleep's the best thing we can offer the poor lad now."

"Not quite yet, Hannah." Catie leaned closer to Jeremiah and rested her hands on his small shoulders. "I know it pains you to speak of it, Jere, but if you can bear it, I should like to hear what happened one more time."

"All happened so fast, ma'am," he mumbled wearily, staring down into the chocolate. "Pa and I were late on 'count of Pa going back for more powder, and so we saw the others get taken by the Britishers. Then Pa says we should run, he wasn't going to get caught in that snare like some infernal rabbit, so off we start, and then my uncle hollered at him to stop and Pa didn't and he fired and I kept running and running and running."

His head drooped lower, to his breast. "I didn't know Pa was hit until I looked back and he was gone. Then I saw the Britishers coming, too, and I kept on, like Pa says. *Said.*" His eyes squeezed shut as he fought back fresh tears. "Then I came here, Mrs. Hazard, on 'count of not knowing where else to go, and that's all, I swear to it."

"You didn't see where your father fell?" asked Catie gently. "When you stopped to look for him, did you see his body?"

Hannah gasped indignantly. "For shame, mistress!

Hasn't the poor lad suffered enough heartache without you making him tell it again?''

Without lifting her hands from the boy's shoulders, she glanced up over his head to glare at the older woman. "Hush, Hannah, and let Jere tell us. If he wants to, that is. Only if he wants to."

"I want to if you do," said Jere in a small voice. "But I—I never saw Pa again once we started to run. I heard him be struck, though. The sound of the ball, Mrs. Hazard, you know how that is. Then Pa crying out, like he couldn't help it."

"I don't expect he could," said Catie sadly. She *didn't* know the sound a musket ball made when it found its mark, and it sickened her to think that Jeremiah did. "But in the dark and all—were you quite sure it was your uncle who shouted, and not some other English officer?"

She knew she was foolish even to hope that the boy might be wrong, and the speed with which Jeremiah answered proved it.

"'Course I'm sure, ma'am," he said defensively. "Excepting the red coat and his yellow hair, he looks just like Pa. And I saw him raise the musket, clear as day in the moonlight, before I ran."

Catie sighed unhappily. "But you saw nothing more of your father when you looked back?"

Jeremiah shook his head. "No one was there except Mr. Robb and Mr. Ingraham running, too."

"You mean they were back with you and your father? They weren't captured with the others?"

"Aye, ma'am. They were with us on 'count of them being new to the cause. Pa always keeps—*kept*— the new men with him till he can trust them."

Catie nodded. "I don't believe I know Mr. Robb, but Mr. Ingraham—"

"Mr. Robb's second mate of the *Abigail*," explained Jeremiah. "One of Granfer's sloops. And Mr. Ingraham—"

"Oversees one of the windmills on the south hill outside of town," finished Catie. "He's a good man, sure to earn your father's confidence."

"But he can't now," said Jeremiah, his voice becoming barely audible. "Not from my pa, anyways."

Swiftly Catie rose and reached for the box of bandages and other surgeon's supplies from the cupboard's top shelf. The last time she took the box down had been to tend to Anthony, and now, with the tables turned, she might well be doing the same for Jon. Please God that he still lived, that Anthony had not killed his cousin, as his orders told him he must!

She traded her silk-covered mules for the thick-soled shoes she kept by the back door and wrapped a heavy shawl around her shoulders. She began to take her own cloak down from the peg, then reconsidered and took Hannah's coarser one instead. Though she doubted that the guard that Anthony had assigned to her would be waiting to follow her at this time of night, she still judged it best to be careful. With the cloak's hood pulled up over her face and in the dark, she could pass for the other woman, and she planned to slip out of the backyard and through the stable, just to be sure she'd see no British soldiers.

Fleetingly she considered leaving a message for Anthony to find when he awoke, some explanation for where she'd gone. But after what they'd shared, only the truth would do between them, and the truth was the last thing she'd dare tell him now. He wouldn't understand, any more than Jon would understand how she felt about Anthony, and all too easily she could imagine the stern frown of disapproval on Anthony's face. No, far better for her to slip away now and pray she'd return before he awoke.

"You're going out to find Cap'n Jon, then, are you, mistress?" asked Hannah. She nodded with approval. "It's well that you do that. Th' cap'n's been a good friend to this house, an' to the cause o' freedom."

Instantly Jeremiah was on his feet. "If you're going after Pa, then I'm coming with you."

"Oh, Jere, I'm not sure that's such a good idea," said Catie softly. The boy had suffered enough tonight, and she'd no wish to raise his hopes again. All she could guess was that Robb and Ingraham had carried Jon away before the British could find him. Whether they had carried a live man or a dead one was another question altogether. "You'll do better to stay here with Hannah, and I promise I'll come tell you whatever I learn when I return."

"No, ma'am, please!" The boy hurried forward, awkwardly taking the basket away from her. "Please, ma'am. If you know where Pa is, then I'm coming. I have to. My place's with my pa."

Catie began to refuse, then stopped. Every inch of Jeremiah begged her to relent, his upturned face silently beseeching. His eyes were so much like Belinda's, that same rare green that all the Sparhawks had, and inwardly she winced as she realized that for the first time she'd thought of her daughter as a Sparhawk. Anthony and Jon and Belinda and Jeremiah—

Lord, how had their lives all become so woefully tangled?

"Please, ma'am," asked Jeremiah again. "I swear I'll be no trouble at all."

She remembered how Belinda had begged to come with her, too, and how many times since she'd wished she'd agreed. How could she possibly deny Jon's son the same?

"Then come along," she said quickly, before she changed her mind. "We haven't a moment to waste."

Ingraham's mill was one of several that stood on the very crest of the hill overlooking Newport, their long, sweeping blades nearly always in motion by day as they caught the wind that rose from the water. But now the canvas sails were furled for the night and the blades lashed to the ground, their outlines rising from the hilltop like oversize spiders' webs against the sky.

"I've no guarantee your father will be here," cautioned Catie, her voice low in the silence of the night. "I'm only guessing that Mr. Ingraham and Mr. Robb brought him back to the mill."

Silently Jeremiah nodded and pushed his hat down lower on his brow. The weeks of hiding with his father showed. He moved with a stealthy ease beyond his years, sliding from shadow to shadow in the empty streets, and he'd said not a word since they left the tavern. In a way, he probably knew the odds against their finding his father alive better than Catie did. But neither of them would give up, not now.

"I believe Mr. Ingraham's mill is the one to the left," she continued. "Or have you been here before with your father?"

This time Jeremiah shook his head, but as he did his expression abruptly changed, his eyes going wild with alarm. He'd already turned to run when Catie grabbed his arm to hold him, just as the two British soldiers stepped into their path.

"'Tis either very early or very late for you to be about, mistress," said the older man, peering at her. "A strange time for you and the lad both."

Though Catie felt the tremor of fear run through Jeremiah's body, still she held him tight. If she let him go, he'd bolt, and as much as admit their errand.

"No babe ever chooses a convenient time for birthing," she said, surprising herself by how readily the lie came to her lips. "The boy came to bring me to ease his mother's travail."

Clearly uncomfortable with the notion of such women's matters, the older soldier only grunted, while the other one shifted from one foot to the other as he tried to warm himself. A good sign, decided Catie: the man was thinking less of her and more of returning to his quarters when his watch was done. She took the basket from Jeremiah and held it out toward the two men, lifting the cloth so that they could look inside.

"You can judge for yourself, sirs," she said. "Nothing to threaten His Majesty's servants at all."

The soldier inched forward, his mouth twisted with distaste as he prodded through the basket's contents. He glanced back at Catie, and suddenly smiled.

"Ah, now, why didn't you say who you were, mistress?" His whole manner instantly became deferential as he tapped his knuckles to the front of his cap. "You're the major's, ah, lady."

Catie stiffened, her cheeks growing hot. She didn't

like being linked to Anthony this way, as if she were some sort of *possession* of his. She wasn't his lady, though after tonight she couldn't deny being his "ah," which was definitely far worse.

"Major Sparhawk is quartered beneath my roof," she said with stony formality, "and thus we are acquainted, even friends. But I am no more his 'lady' than he is my gentleman."

"'Course not, ma'am," said the soldier quickly, with a little duck of his head. "Begging your pardon, ma'am."

But the knowing grin remained on his face, and the face of his companion, as well, and with a hideous sinking certainty Catie realized that the reputation she'd worked so hard to guard was now tattered and tarnished and common in the soldiers' mess. Love alone, even Anthony's love, could not protect her from that, either.

"Am I free to go, sir?" she asked, thankful that in the dark they couldn't see how she flushed with shame. "The boy's mother is in sore need of me."

"As you wish, ma'am," said the soldier, pointedly stepping to one side with his musket cradled in his arms. "You and the boy both, free as the day."

Yet freedom was far from Catie's thoughts as she and Jeremiah hurried up the cart path that led to the mill. Loving Anthony had brought her a joy she'd never found in her life before, but the price she would pay for that joy was going to be a steep one indeed. And it wasn't just her this time; Belinda would suffer, too. She'd known from the beginning that there was no future for her together with Anthony, and he'd never pretended otherwise. But now came the cold reality of what they'd done—what *she* had done—and the consequences loomed heavily before her.

She'd never intended to share his bed again. What had happened to her eight years ago should have been warning enough, and unconsciously her hand fluttered down to brush across her belly. Had the easy lie she'd told the soldiers really been some dreadful premonition from her guilty conscience?

"Pa was right, Mrs. Hazard," said Jeremiah at her side.

"About what, Jere?" said Catie, too disturbed by her own thoughts to grasp his meaning.

"About me being safe with you." For the first time, he slipped his hand into hers, self-consciously permitting himself to seek that small, childish comfort from her. "He said no matter which way the wind blew, you'd always come out on the winning side. He said you were the cleverest lady he knew, and he was right. You answered those Britishers proper, didn't you, and then you knew my uncle, too." His fingers tightened around hers. "My *damned* uncle."

She stared up at the windmill before them and didn't answer. What could she say that would mean anything to either one of them?

The crushed shells of the path crunched beneath their shoes, and the wind that powered the mills by day now sent Catie's skirts billowing around her legs. With one hand she bunched them up at her side, hurrying the last few feet up the path with the basket swinging from her arm. The mill itself was dark, as was the little shingled cottage behind it where Ingraham, a bachelor, lived alone.

"No one's home," said Jeremiah, drooping with disappointment. "They didn't come here after all."

"That's what they want you to believe, isn't it?" Still clutching her skirts in one hand, Catie walked around to the back of the cottage, picking her way through the dry stalks and twigs of last year's kitchen garden. Here the shutters were latched shut over the windows, keeping out the coldest of the wind from the north. But the closed shutters would also keep out inquisitive eyes, and a faint line of candlelight from within glimmered around the edges of the boards.

With her fist, Catie thumped against one of the shutters, sending the dry wood rattling against its squeaking hinges. No answer came, and she knocked again, harder.

"It's Catharine Hazard," she called, raising her voice to be heard over the wind, "and I've Jeremiah Sparhawk with me, too, if you'll but open the door to us."

She thought she heard a scuffling from within, and the low murmur of voices. Then came a scraping at the back door as the latch was lifted from within, and the door cracked open as Ingraham peeked cautiously outward, the glinting steel of a pistol's barrel thrust through the opening, as well.

"Mr. Ingraham!" With a gasp of anticipation, Jeremiah lunged toward the door, wriggling like an anxious puppy. "Pa's in there, isn't he? I've got to see my pa!"

"Wait, Jere, please!" With her gaze firmly on the pistol, Catie grabbed the boy by his coat and pulled him back. "We don't mean any harm, Mr. Ingraham, and I swear to you we're alone. We've only come to seek news of Captain Sparhawk, the boy's—"

"In with you now," growled Ingraham, motioning with the pistol as he looked past them and down the path where they'd come, "and be quick about it, too."

Jeremiah pulled free and rushed through the half-opened door. Catie followed more slowly, and as she squeezed past Ingraham she could smell the stale smell that was the sweat of real fear, and see how the man swallowed over and over, his throat shifting convulsively as if he could swallow his anxiety. Then she saw the scene before her, lit by a fading fire and a single lantern set on the floor, and forgot everything else.

Sprawled across the narrow low bed lay Jon Sparhawk. His coat was gone, and so was his waistcoat, and the stark white linen of his shirt's front was red with the blood that the makeshift bandage around his chest had done little to stanch. His face was pale, deathly pale, and Catie would have doubted he lived still, if his hand were not curled around the head of his son, kneeling beside the bed with his face buried against his father's arm.

"Britishers did it, mistress, the devil rot their souls," said Ingraham despondently as he uncocked the pistol and laid it on the table. The second man, Robb, sat crouched on the floor close to the fire, a bottle of rum cradled in his lap as he stared blankly into the fire. "Took us clean by surprise. Almost like they was invited. Me and Robb, we did what we could for the cap'n, but you see how it is with him. The best surgeon in town couldn't do more."

Jon groaned. "Then why don't you bury me now,

Ingraham?'' he rasped without opening his eyes. "Save yourself the trouble later."

"You've never spared anyone a lick of trouble in your whole life, Jonathan Sparhawk," said Catie softly as she knelt beside the bed. "Why should you change now?"

Slowly Jon opened his eyes, squinting up at her. "So it is you, Mistress Cate," he said. "Come to weep over me, lass?"

"Not yet, I'm not. You won't give the British the satisfaction of dying like this, Jon, and you know it." She slid her cloak from her shoulders and leaned over him. "Where were you hit?"

"Shoulder. The ball's still in there, too." Grimacing, Jon tried to ease himself higher onto the pillow. "Anthony never had much of an aim with a musket."

"He did better than you."

"A lucky shot." Jon smiled weakly. "Did he ever figure out I was the one who pegged him that first night?"

"I wouldn't know," she said, more defensively than she'd intended. She didn't like talking to him about Anthony. What they had was too precious and fragile for her to share with anyone just yet, and especially not with Jon.

But Jon wasn't listening any longer, not enough to notice. His gaze had turned inward as he wrestled with the pain, and as carefully as Catie could, she began to unfasten the bloodstained piece of linen that was serving as a bandage.

"Jere, sweetheart," she murmured as she leaned over the boy, "you're going to have to move."

"Shove along there, lad, do as the lady says." Jon winced as he stretched out to ruffle his son's hair. "She's the one giving orders now."

"Aye, aye, Pa." Reluctantly the boy slid along the edge of the bed, just beyond Catie's way and still within his father's reach.

Jon smiled, more of a grimace. "It's not so bad taking orders from a lady, Jere. Your mama made it an out-and-out pleasure."

Jeremiah swallowed. "My mama wasn't like that," he mumbled. "She never ordered anyone around."

"Oh, aye, she did," said Jon gently. "She just had a way with her that made you beg to do whatever she asked."

Catie looked up, startled by the tenderness in his gruff voice. Betsey Sparhawk had been more than his wife; she'd also been the one great love of his life, the one that could never be replaced by any other.

It was the same with her, thought Catie sadly as she cut away the last bit of the bandage, the same way she felt about Anthony.

Her lips compressed as she uncovered the ragged wound torn into the flesh and muscle beneath Jon's collarbone. She'd never had to retrieve a ball before, and she wasn't quite sure how to do it, but to leave a wad of misshapen lead and torn linen inside would mean Jon's death. He was strong as a horse and nearly as large; she was surprised he remained as lucid as he did, considering how much blood he'd lost. But all too well she knew what happened to strong men when infection and fever filled a wound. Gently she touched him again, and she saw how his whole body went rigid.

This was worse than anything she'd tended before, far worse, but she knew that sending for a surgeon now was out of the question. The British would be watching every one of their houses for just such a request, hoping to be led to Jon. His only hope now lay with her, and she prayed she wouldn't fail him.

She glanced at Jeremiah; his eyes were enormous as he watched her. She lowered her voice for Jon's ears alone. "Are you sure you want Jere here at all, Jon?"

"He's seen worse," said Jon, more sharply than Catie thought he'd be capable of. "My boy's no coward, Catie."

"I'm not saying he is, Jon. But he's still a child, no matter how much you wish otherwise, and he's suffered a great deal on your behalf this night already."

"He'll be fine, Catie. We both will." With a grunt of pain, he pushed himself up on his elbow so that he could smile at Jeremiah. "Now go ahead, lass. Do your worst. That's why you've come, isn't it?"

Ingraham handed him the bottle of rum. "Here, Cap'n, you'll be needing this."

"Thankee." Jon drank deeply from the bottle as Catie tore away the rest of his shirt. Without being asked, Ingraham brought her a basin of water, and gently she eased Jon flat onto his back.

"Would you mind holding the lantern up for me, Mr. Ingraham?" she asked, and the man quickly obeyed. She was glad that he didn't seem squeamish; she wished she felt equally sure of herself. As carefully as she could, she began to search for the ball, and she felt how Jon again stiffened beneath her touch. Only once did he begin to swear, an oath that broke off midway into a groan, and without a word Ingraham stepped forward to hold Jon steady. She realized they'd all seen and done such things before, helping a surgeon with a wounded companion like this, from Jeremiah on up. She was the only one to whom this business of war was a ghastly new experience.

Yet this was what Anthony faced every day as a soldier, a life where the single certainty was death. A life where there'd be little place for love, and less for her.

With an effort, she forced her thoughts back to the task before her. To her relief, the ball was not buried as deeply as she'd feared, and once she'd drawn it free with her fingers she cleaned and dressed the wound as quickly as she could. When she was done, Jon lay pale and sweating, his eyes still squeezed shut against the pain but his breathing less ragged. He'd sleep, God willing, and she sighed with relief and weariness.

"Best to let him rest now," she said softly to Ingraham as she drew the coverlet over Jon's bandaged chest. "But as soon as you can arrange it, you must all leave Newport for Providence."

Jon's eyes flew open. "Why?" he croaked.

"Hush, Jon, don't trouble yourself over—"

"The devil take your care, Catie," he said thickly. "Tell me what you know."

"Only if you promise to heed me." She knelt beside the bed, her face close to his and her voice urgent. "Your luck's done, Jon. As soon as it's daylight the British will be looking for you, and this time they're not going to stop until they find you."

"Not just the British," said Jon. "Anthony."

Catie sighed unhappily. "Yes, Anthony. He's sworn

he'll search every house and barn near to where you were last night, and I doubt he'll stop there.''

"Let him." The rasped words were defiant, a dare. "He'll find nothing at Nantasket except Piper's house."

"Nantasket!" Catie gasped with dismay. "But that's where Belinda is!"

"And what of it? Anthony doesn't want your daughter."

"You don't understand, Jon. You can't possibly know what—"

She broke off abruptly before she betrayed herself, turmoil twisting within her breast. She couldn't let Anthony find Belinda, not like this. Her greatest secret would be torn away the moment he saw their daughter, and when others saw them together. The resemblance would be far too clear to ignore, and she couldn't do that to Belinda.

"I must go to her now, Jon, before the British find her," said Catie, the sick dread she felt giving her words a frantic urgency. "I must go bring her home *now!*"

Jon frowned. "You know she's safe with the Pipers. Likely safer than she'd be in town."

"That's not it, Jon, that's not it at all!" she cried with anguish. "Oh, you can't possibly understand!"

"But I can, Catie." He glanced down at Jeremiah, who was sleeping with his head on the edge of the bed, and the love in his gaze was unmistakable. "How could I not? If you want Belinda back with you, then you shall have her. And I'm coming with you."

"Don't be foolish," she said, chiding him. "You're not fit to go anywhere."

With a great, determined effort, he pushed himself up to sit on the bed. "You came here for me, Catie," he said, "and now I will do the same for you. If you go, you won't be going alone."

"We could take them now, Major," whispered Sergeant Barr. "We two could do it, you an' me, sir, no mistake."

"We could, Sergeant," said Anthony curtly, "but we won't. We'll wait for Topham with the others."

"But, sir, seeing how that's the one you wounded an' all, an' we're—"

"I said we'll wait," repeated Anthony, and the tension in his voice immediately silenced the other man's eagerness, a tension that Anthony was scarcely aware of. Instead, his whole being was concentrating on peering through the crack in the run-down little cottage's shutter, and watching what passed within.

He hated himself for spying on Catie like this, just as he'd hated trailing her through the dark streets, and yet he couldn't help it. He wasn't supposed to help it; she was aiding and comforting his enemy, and it didn't matter that the enemy was his cousin, as well. He was simply following orders.

As if they were miming actors in a silent play, Catie smiled at Jon, touching her fingers to his cheek. Their relationship was undeniably close, their fondness for one another unmistakable. Still smiling, she leaned forward and kissed his cheek, touching her lips to the place her hand had been, and Anthony felt his heart crash apart in his breast.

He loved her, and this was how she returned his love. This very night he had lavished that love upon her, treating her like the rare treasure he judged her to be, giving her the pleasure he believed she'd never had, and giving her, too, his own heart with it.

And yet it hadn't been enough. She had listened to him babble on about his past, his family, his dreams. She had encouraged his kisses and welcomed his caresses, and she'd even whispered that she loved him in return, making him the happiest fool in Christendom.

But she hadn't asked for anything beyond that, and he'd been too besotted to think beyond the haven of her curtained bed. He didn't doubt that she loved him—Catie couldn't lie about something like that—but for her, that love alone didn't seem to be enough. The moment she thought he was asleep, she'd left his side and come here to Jon.

To *Jon.*

How wrong he'd been to trust her, and to believe she cared for him more than for these infernal notions of freedom! No doubt she'd already relayed to Jon and the others every last word Anthony had carelessly confided. Hanging in the shadows as he followed behind her with Topham and Barr, Anthony had heard her use their relationship as protection when she was stopped by the two British soldiers. A friend, that was what she'd said he was to her, a friend and nothing else, the same way she'd described her connection to his cousin Jon.

"Lor', Major, sir, looks like they're leavin'!" whispered Barr excitedly. "We could take 'em one at a time, sir, soon as they come through th' door!"

"I've made my decision, Sergeant," said Anthony

firmly. "We shall wait for Topham with the reinforcements."

"Yes, sir," agreed Barr miserably, until frustration forced him to speak up one more time. "But what if they leave th' windmill before Topham returns?"

"Then we'll follow," replied Anthony. "Perhaps they'll lead us to one more of their dens."

"But, sir, I—"

"I am decided, Barr," said Anthony with the perfect, icy distance of an officer of the king, a distance that could cover anything where an enlisted man was concerned. "We wait for reinforcements, and follow these rogues as necessary. But I want them alive, Barr. All of them, especially the woman and the leader, alive."

Chapter Twelve

"My husband is drunk," said Catie to the British sentry. "But then, I expect you can see that for yourself."

Warily the soldier approached the pale, dirty man slumped over the saddle, just in case this bedraggled little family was one more rebel trap.

"I should not get too close to him, if I were you," advised Catie with an ill-disguised disgust. "He was thoroughly ill in the street when I hauled him from Madame Bella's house, and I can't promise he won't spew again. He's quite rank as it is."

But the soldier had already stepped back, turning his head from the smell that clung to the man. "Madame Bella's, you say? At this hour o' the night?"

Catie sighed mournfully and nodded. She herself had always kept a decent house, but she'd always judged it good business to have a fair notion of her less reputable competition, as well, including Madame Bella's brothel.

"'Tis no place for a decent woman, I know," she said stiffly, hugging Jeremiah before her on the saddle, "nor for our boy, either, but I vowed to follow the man for better and worse when I wed him. And who can guess what mischief he'd have fallen into if I didn't come fetch him home?"

"Seven years' service in the king's navy, if the press had plucked him up," said the other guard, spitting over his shoulder for emphasis. "Better for you if they did, eh, mistress?"

Catie didn't smile. "His Majesty's officers are welcome to any service they can get from him at all, if they know the secret of separating him from his rum," she said curtly. "'Tis more than I've been able to do in nine years of marriage."

"Then may the good Lord watch over you through your trials, mistress," said the soldier, touching the front of his cap. He swatted the first horse's rump hard with the flat of his hand. "On with you, now!"

Her heart pounding, Catie forced herself to wait until they had gone beyond a hill and the sight of the sentries before she turned to look at Jon.

"Are you all right?" she called softly, twisting in the saddle with one arm around Jeremiah's waist. "You did very well there, you know."

Jon raised his head and did his best to smile. "And you lie very well yourself, Mrs. Hazard," he teased, but his speech was labored, and the way he still sat hunched over the horse's neck did little to reassure Catie. By the first gray light of the coming dawn, she could see the deep lines etched on his face, etched by pain, and how his sailor's tan seemed to rest uneasily over the pallor of his cheeks. Pretending to be a man too sick to care what happened to him had come with alarming ease.

Catie drew her horse closer to his. "We should go back," she said, worried. "I should never have agreed to take you with me."

"You couldn't have stopped me, lass," he said hoarsely, and this time he didn't even try to smile, concentrating instead on clutching the horse's reins. "I wouldn't have let you go otherwise."

Unhappily Catie knew he wouldn't have been able to stop her from doing anything, not as weak as he was. As part of their ruse, his legs had been lashed to the stirrups to keep him from sliding from the saddle, just as she'd liberally doused his coat with rum to make him reek like the drunkard he was supposed to be. Now she was thankful for those same lashings, and the lead that connected his horse to hers. Without them, she wasn't sure Jon could have managed the horse on his own.

"She wouldn't have done it, Pa," said Jeremiah stoutly, though the way his knuckles were whitened where he clung to the saddle horn showed Catie he had no more illusions than she did herself about his father's strength. "I wouldn't have let her go, not without you."

"True enough, Jere," agreed Catie softly, tightening her arm around the boy. "Hold fast now. I've no wish to lose you, either."

Yet as she urged the two horses onward, Catie wondered how much of her hastily made plan would work. If luck was on her side, she would reach the Pipers' house with Jon and his son before the British search parties, and urge Owen to escape with the Sparhawks in the little sloop he used for smuggling. It was the only reason she'd agreed to bring Jon with her, and she hoped he'd be too weak to protest. In Providence with his parents, he'd have time to recover, out of harm's way, and Jeremiah might have the chance to be just a boy a bit longer.

The rising sun was already clearing the horizon, and wearily she dug her heels into the horse's sides. She hadn't realized it was so late. They had to reach the Pipers' house before the British did, or none of this would matter.

And Anthony. Anthony would be coming here soon, as well, too soon for her, and her heart grew tight in her chest. Perhaps she and Belinda, too, should sail for Providence with the others, for what hope did she have of any mercy, let alone love, from Anthony now?

She had never intended to disappear into the night the way she had. She'd thought she'd only be gone a few minutes at the most, so few that he'd never know she'd been away. But now—now too much had happened for her to be able to explain it away. She had made the choice to go to Jon when he needed her, a choice she'd make again without hesitation. She owed that much and more to his family. But the choice, once made, was like a rock tossed into a smooth pond, with consequences endlessly rippling outward.

It didn't matter that in the warm shelter of his bed he had said he loved her; he was an officer of the king and she was still his enemy, and helping Jon escape had only made it worse. To him she was a rebel, a spy, a traitor. However could Anthony love her after that? Tears pulled straight from her heart stung her eyes, tears of longing and loneliness that she struggled to blink back.

"There's the Pipers' house," said Jeremiah excitedly, and he twisted around to see his father. "Pa, look, you can see the chimneys!"

But by the time they reached the Pipers' door, Jon was slumped over his horse's neck, and it took Owen and Abigail together to ease him from the saddle to the ground.

"They were ambushed last night by the British," explained Catie breathlessly as she slipped down to the ground herself. Jeremiah had clambered down before the horse had even come to a halt, and was now hovering around the Pipers and his father.

"When?" asked Owen curtly as he slipped his shoulder beneath Jon's uninjured arm to lead him inside the house. "He was here last night, and all was well."

"It was later in the evening, near a cave on the beach at Nantasket." Her breath was coming in rapid gulps now, and she held her hand to her breast to try to calm herself enough to speak. "Jon and Jeremiah escaped back to Newport with two other men, but all the others were captured and Jon was shot—you can see that yourself—and though I tried to—oh, I tried—"

Her voice began to waver uncontrollably, and she broke off, not wanting to cry before them. If she began, she was so afraid she'd never be able to stop. "I tried, you see—"

Abigail came to rest her hand on her arm, her weathered face filled with sympathy. "That's all right, lamb," she said kindly. "You've done right well to do this much, a lady such as yourself, and we thank you for it. We'll tend to Jon an' the boy now."

"Not yet, Abigail, because...because..." Helplessly Catie shook her head, swallowing her tears as she looked past Abigail and down the road they'd come. Before this, before there had been anyone else to depend upon, she hadn't realized how frightened she was.

"Because the Britishers are coming back, Mrs. Piper," said Jeremiah, his child's voice curiously unemotional. "Because they want Pa so bad, they're coming back to find him."

Searching for confirmation, Abigail turned swiftly to look at Catie. "It's true, all of it," said Catie raggedly. "When they didn't find Jon last night, they swore they'd search every house on the point until they found him, and they—"

"Nay, ma'am, not 'they,'" put in Jeremiah softly. "'Twas my turncoat uncle Anthony."

"Mama!" With a wild shriek of delight, Belinda raced from the house and into Catie's arms. She had come straight from her bed in her shift and nightcap, and as Catie pressed her face against her daughter's cheek she breathed deeply of the warm, sweet smell of her still-sleepy daughter's skin and hair.

The way Belinda fit her coltish body against hers, so close Catie could hear and feel her heartbeat, how she nestled her cheeks against Catie's breast and closed her eyes with a sigh of contentment—all of this, thought Catie, was what she'd missed these long weeks they'd been apart, and once again she felt tears welling up. Tears of joy, true, but tears of sorrow as well, regret for missing even this small part of her daughter's life.

"Here, you silly little goose, let me look at you. You'll turn into an icicle, dressed like that." Tenderly

Catie wrapped her own cloak around Belinda's shoulders, and tried not to see how much she resembled Anthony. She was glad to see the girl hadn't suffered or pined; if anything, she'd grown taller, and with another pang Catie thought again of how three or four weeks in the life of her daughter could seem like an eternity.

Belinda smiled, her face still plump with sleep, and Catie touched the spot in her grin where there had last been a gap.

"That new tooth's come at last," said Catie. "You're quite done with your baby teeth, aren't you?"

Proudly Belinda stretched her smile to an overwide grin. "That's because I'm not a baby any longer," she said importantly. "I'm almost nine, Mama. You can't have forgotten that."

Her grin expanded even further, to include Jeremiah, standing uncertainly to one side of Abigail. "I'll be nine in March, Jere, nearly two whole months before you will."

"Not that he cares, either," said Catie, with an unspoken warning in her glance that made Belinda instantly contrite. "Jeremiah doesn't need your chattering this morning, and neither do I. Now come, I want you dressed as fast as you can. Hurry, lass, be quick!"

Belinda's bare feet danced across the frozen ground as she rushed ahead of Catie and through the kitchen door. "We're going back to Newport, Mama? You're really, truly going to take me home?"

"Nay, little lass, she's not," growled Jon, and Belinda scuttled back behind Catie's petticoats. Jon sat on the bench before the fire, a tankard full of rum-laced coffee steaming in his hand. His face was ashen and he scowled with fatigue and pain, his beard and long black hair making him even more forbidding. "You'll clear off, aye, but not for Newport."

"And why not?" demanded Catie. "Where else would we go, Jon? Newport's my home."

"Used to be mine, too, once." Jon coughed, a strained bark that sent the coffee dashing back and forth in the tankard. "But think on what you've done, Catie. If Jeremiah and I can't go back, well then, neither can you and your daughter."

"He's right, ma'am," said Owen gruffly. "Soon as the cap'n here finishes his brew, we'll be heading off upriver. You'd be wise to join us, you and your girl both."

She stared at the two men, stunned that they'd actually suggest what she'd only thought on a whim. "It's one thing for Jon to go. What else can he do? But for me to leave Newport now—why, I won't even consider such a notion! I cannot simply abandon Hazard's because you say so. I have guests that depend on me, customers who expect me to be there."

Jon glanced up at her sideways. "The way I've heard it, about the only customers you've been entertaining lately have been wearing red coats."

Catie gasped indignantly. "That's not fair, Jon," she snapped. "I've been forced to quarter British soldiers under my roof, just like everyone else in Newport, and if you believe that—"

"Don't bluster at me, Catie Hazard," said Jon, interrupting her. "All I'm saying is that you'll have to decide whether to throw your lot in with me now, or trust yourself and your daughter to the hands of my bastard of a cousin. Your choice, sweetheart. Me, or Anthony.''

Catie went very still, unable to answer. On the surface, for the sake of the others here in the kitchen, Jon was merely telling her that Newport was too dangerous a place for her to remain, and that she and Belinda should consider fleeing in Owen's boat, too.

But Jon was offering her more than advice alone, and both of them knew it. He'd always teased her about what a good wife she'd make and how well they'd suit one another, the widow and the widower joining households.

Yet he'd never meant it the way he did now. Now he was actually asking her, Catie Hazard, to marry him.

He looped his uninjured arm around his son, standing beside him. "I know which way Jeremiah would want you to go, Catie," he said. "Mightily fond he is of you, and Miss Belinda, too. Isn't that right, lad? And there's nothing my daughter Desire would like better than having another lass about to play with the doll-babies and such.''

For the sake of their children—that was his main reason, then, for asking. And it wasn't such a bad one, either, not by half. A widower left with three young children needed someone he could trust to take care of them, and a widow with a daughter of her own would know how to be a mother, as well as a wife. She was fond of Jeremiah, too, and though she knew Jon's younger two children less well, she was certain she could come to care for them. She loved children, she always had, and with Jon there'd be a good chance she'd bear more of her own. His wife, Betsey, had been brought to bed five times during the eight years they were wed.

There'd be other advantages, excellent ones, too, to such a marriage. Before the war the Sparhawks had been one of the wealthiest and most influential families in Newport, and Catie didn't doubt that they'd be so again when the British finally left. He wouldn't be marrying her solely with an eye to the value of Hazard's. As a ship's captain, Jon was known as a fair master, sober and evenhanded, and she was sure he'd be the same as a husband. He was considered handsome, too, and if he wasn't as lighthearted as he'd once been, well, then, what man in his prime was?

He wasn't even pretending to love her, not the way he'd loved Betsey. Nor would Catie have to pretend, either, not for a second time with a second husband she respected but would never love.

Not the way she would always love Anthony...

Left waiting too long for her to answer, Jon shifted uneasily on the bench, wincing with the pain.

"'Tis not so great a question, Catie," he said, his voice sinking down once again to a low growl. "After last night, I'd have thought your mind was pretty well made up."

She knew Jon was referring to the way she'd chosen to come to his aid, but still her cheeks flushed with guilt. She couldn't help remembering how, in that same last night, she and Anthony had made love, too.

And it had been love, she thought sadly. The lopsided paper heart that Anthony had sent her, the red ribbons he'd wrapped around her hands in the snow-filled garden while his lips were warm upon hers, the smile that had lit his eyes with tenderness when his fingers brushed over her cheek and the fire that had burned in her blood with his caresses—oh, aye, it had been love, and even if it was done, she'd never forget it.

Or Anthony.

Owen cleared his throat impatiently. "Not a great question, Mrs. Hazard, but one that's keeping us all too long in this place. The tide's due to turn on the hour, and if we're not sailing with it, we might as well go welcome them redcoats on the road and save them the trouble of finding us here."

"Forgive me, Owen, I didn't mean to keep you," murmured Catie swiftly, avoiding Jon's eyes. "Come, Belinda, we must get you dressed. Hurry now, child, hurry!"

Grateful for the excuse to flee, Catie hustled the girl before her up the winding stairs and to the back bedchamber where she'd slept. The room had been used by the Pipers' two daughters, long since grown and married with households of their own, and though the floor was swept and the coverlet and sheets on the low bed were patched and clean, there was still a mournful emptiness to the chamber, a sense that the true inhabitants would never return. Even Duchess, propped up regally in her best crimson sateen gown against the bolster, could do little to dispel the melancholy of this room tucked beneath the eves, and Catie felt one last pang of guilt at having abandoned her daughter here.

But no longer. Tonight Belinda would sleep in her own snug little bed, and Duchess in her own, as well, and the certainty of it warmed Catie's guilt away.

Briskly she began untying the strings of Belinda's nightcap. "Wear the green linsey-woolsey gown," she said, "and because it's so cold I want you to wear the quilted petticoat, too, if you can find it quickly enough. We don't have time to dawdle."

"Yes, Mama." Belinda smiled, standing uncharacteristically still while Catie untied the knot, blissfully content to bask once again in her mother's attention.

Catie whipped off the cap. "Come along now, find the petticoat. We'll have Mrs. Piper send your things later. There isn't time to pack now."

Belinda scampered across the bed, Catie's cloak still billowing around her.

"We don't have to pack," she said, hopping off the side of the bed. She knelt beside her traveling trunk and flipped open the lid. "Everything's ready."

Catie followed her around the bed, frowning. "I thought Mrs. Piper said you could put your things in the drawer."

"Oh, she did," said Belinda, carefully easing the green gown from the neat stacks of folded clothing. "But I wouldn't do it. I wanted to be ready, you see, for when you came to take me home. I didn't want to have to waste a single minute packing."

She sat back on her heels and looked up at Catie, her smile wobbling. "You said it wouldn't be for long, Mama, and every day I looked for you to come. And today you did."

"Oh, lamb." Catie bent down and hugged her close. "I wanted to, but it wasn't safe."

With a loud sniff, Belinda pushed back to search Catie's face. "And it is now?"

Catie nodded, though the lie weighed heavily on her conscience. If anything, Belinda would be in more danger now than before, and it was going to take considerable planning each day to keep her from Anthony's sight. With a sigh, she smoothed Belinda's hair.

"I've missed my girl too much to be apart from her any longer," she said softly, and that much, at least, was achingly true. "You're coming home with me, as soon as you're dressed."

"Good!" Belinda wriggled free, shrugging off the cloak and pulling up first the quilted petticoat and next the gown. Catie reached out to help her, steering her flailing arms into the sleeves, and the girl's muffled voice came from somewhere inside the fabric. "I didn't want to go with Jeremiah Sparhawk anyway."

"I thought you liked Jeremiah," said Catie, tugging the gown's waistline down so that Belinda's head popped free from the top.

"I used to," said Belinda as she shoved her hair back from her face. "But he's too serious now."

"He has a great deal to be serious about," chided Catie, thinking of how much the boy had seen and suffered in just this night alone. "Remember, he has no mother to watch after him or his brother and sister."

"He has his father," said Belinda wistfully, "just like I have you. You're *my* mother."

"And you're *my* daughter. Not that there's ever been any question, has there? Come now, hold still so I can lace you up."

Swiftly Catie threaded the laces through the gown's eyelets, thinking how difficult it would be to convince Belinda to accept Jon's children as siblings. Even before Ben died, the bond between her and Belinda had been closer than that between most mothers and their children. Each had been, quite simply, all the other had.

"There now," said Catie, giving Belinda a little pat. "I'll braid your hair more neatly later. There's not time now. Fetch your stockings and shoes while I latch the trunk."

"And Duchess," said Belinda, crawling across the bed to retrieve the doll. "We mustn't forget Duchess."

"Heavens, no." Catie tied on her cloak and held Belinda's out for her. "Though Duchess would fare better with the redcoats than we would. She'd make them all bow down and call her 'Your Grace.'"

Belinda giggled, shoving her feet into her shoes without bothering to unbuckle them, so that the heels collapsed. Catie sighed with exasperation.

"No wonder you wear holes in the heels of all your stockings," she said as she bent down to fasten the shoes properly. "You'll have ones in your feet to match if you keep to such slovenly habits."

The tongue of the second buckle kept slipping away from the hole as Catie struggled with it, and the leather of the shoes was stiff with mud, making her task all the harder.

"Faith, Belinda," she scolded, "I've never seen such a mess. You took such care with your other things that I can't imagine why—"

"Who's Anthony?"

"Who's Anthony?" repeated Catie, too quickly, and she felt her face grow warm as she busied herself with the shoe buckle. At last the buckle slipped into place, and she stood, dusting the dried mud from her hands. "Who's Anthony, you ask?"

"Yes, Anthony," said Belinda, her face solemn and

anxious as she gazed up at Catie. Clearly she could
see that her mother wasn't telling all she knew, and it
worried her. "Captain Sparhawk said that was your
choice. Him, or Anthony."

"Your ears are quick, lamb, aren't they?" Catie
sighed uneasily, considering all the layers of meaning
in Jon's seemingly simple question. "Anthony Sparhawk is an officer in the king's army, a major, and he
and some of his men are quartered at Hazard's. He's
in the green chamber, to the front."

"A redcoat officer?" Belinda's pale brows puckered with confusion as she hugged Duchess more
tightly. "But Captain Sparhawk said he was his
cousin. They have the same last name. So how can he
be a Britisher, too? And how could you have chosen
him? Chosen him for what?"

"Captain Sparhawk was exaggerating, that was
all," said Catie carefully, fastening the pewter clasp
on Belinda's cloak beneath her chin. "I didn't really
have to make a choice between him or his cousin. And
though Anthony Sparhawk has chosen to serve with
the British, he was born in this country, in Massachusetts. I suppose that makes him a Tory, but not quite
English."

"It makes him a traitor to his own people," declared Belinda fervently, "and worse than any Britisher ever could be."

"Even if he believes what he's doing is right? If he
believes that he's here to protect us regular folk, and
not to harm us?"

Belinda frowned, her eyes accusing. "You sound
like a Tory, Mama."

Sharply Catie returned the frown. "And you, missy,

sound like an outspoken little girl who listens at doorways to conversations she doesn't understand."

"But, Mama, Mr. and Mrs. Piper say—"

"I don't care what Mr. and Mrs. Piper say, Belinda," said Catie firmly. "Nothing, and no one, is as simple as they seem, Belinda. You'd do well to remember that. Now come along, help me take your trunk down the stairs."

Together they bumped the trunk down the winding stairs and into the kitchen. Abigail rushed to help them, taking Belinda's place.

"Oh, here you are at last, Mrs. Hazard!" she said breathlessly. "Owen and the cap'n have already gone down to the water. Owen's the very devil where his tide's concerned, and he wouldn't hear of tarrying another moment. But we can catch them still. You'll see! Between us we'll manage this trunk over the dunes, see if we don't."

Catie let her end of the trunk drop with a thump to the floor. "You're most kind to offer, Abigail," she said, "but Belinda and I won't be sailing with Owen today. Instead I mean to ride back to Newport as soon as we've seen your husband and Captain Sparhawk off."

Now Abigail let her side of the trunk fall, as well. "Do you really think that's wise, ma'am?" she said doubtfully. "Considering what the cap'n said, and all? Perhaps if you let him take little Belinda up to Providence with the other children—"

"No," said Catie, more sharply than she'd intended, sharply enough that Abigail drew back with a stiff, stricken look on her face.

At once Catie regretted it. With a weary sigh, she

reached for her daughter, looping her arms protectively around her daughter's shoulders.

"Oh, Abigail," she began. "It's not that I don't appreciate what you've done for Belinda and for me, because I do. Truly. And I know the dangers, too, even without Jon to point them out to me. But it seems now there's danger everywhere, and I might as well keep Belinda with me as send her away."

"Very well, ma'am. You're her mother, and you'll do what's best for the little lass." Abigail's smile was tight, and her gaze lingered fondly on Belinda. "That's how it should be, you know, blood with blood and families together. But we'll miss the little lass, Owen and me both."

Impulsively Belinda eased free of Catie and ran to hug the older woman.

Abigail colored with a mixture of pleasure and embarrassment. "There now, Belinda, you come back to visit whenever you please," she said. "Those worthless cats in the barn'll welcome you too. They've never eaten so fine as when you've been here. But along with you now, back to your mother, where you belong."

"Thank you, Abigail, for everything," said Catie softly as Belinda slipped her rough little fingers back into her hand. "Though I've decided not to go with Jon, I'd like to wish him and Jeremiah farewell. Do you think we'll be too late?"

Abigail shook her head. "Nay, ma'am, not if you hurry. Through the kitchen garden and past the stone wall, then over the dunes." Her eyes gleamed with challenge. "And if them lobsterbacks come calling, they'll have to answer here to me first."

"I know the way to the beach, Mama," said Belinda, tugging Catie's hand to lead her. "It's easy."

Catie smiled. "Then show me, lamb."

They walked swiftly along Abigail's neatly swept garden path, the wind whipping their skirts around their legs. They slowed as they trudged up through the whipping grass and toward the crest of the dunes. There was no path here—a smuggler like Owen had no wish to make the way easier for others who might follow—and the loose sand of the dunes was almost like drifts of snow, pulling at their shoes with every step.

They paused at the top to catch their breath. The new day was fair, the sky cloudless, and the long sweep of the bay and ocean beyond mirrored more deeply the blue overhead. Beyond the rocks, not far from land, lay Owen's sloop, tugging at her mooring. With high tide, the beach was only a narrow band, and a little ways down stood the men—Owen, Jon, Jeremiah, and the two men from the neighboring farm who served as Owen's crew—gathered around the longboat drawn up on the sand.

With a joyful whoop, Belinda jumped and bounced down the steep dune, poor Duchess swinging at her side by one jointed arm. In unison the men turned at the sound, and Jon came forward to meet them as Catie came more carefully down the dune.

"I was half-feared you wouldn't come," he said gruffly. They were shielded from the view of Owen and the other men with the boat by an outcropping of stones, but still he stopped a pace away from Catie and Belinda, holding his hat in his hand. Self-consciously he swiped his hand across his hair, as if that would have much effect against the wind that blew from the water. "Owen wanted to shove off directly, but I said to give you and the lass another moment. Can't rush the ladies, I said."

"Oh, Jon," said Catie sadly. "I only came to say goodbye."

"Goodbye, Cate?" he asked uncertainly. He tipped his head to look at her. He stood bent awkwardly to one side, favoring his wounded shoulder, but at least the wind had brought more color to his cheeks. "You won't be coming with me?"

"I—we—can't," said Catie, her hand resting on Belinda's shoulder to include her, and lessen the sting of her rejection. She didn't want to hurt him, even if it seemed inevitable. She would spare him the truth: that because she'd married once without love, she'd never do it again. "Our place for now is here in Newport."

"Ah, Newport." He stared down at his hat. "I know I've not as much to offer you as once I might have, Catie, but I'd hoped that—"

"It's not you, Jon, and it's not what you might or might not offer," she said quickly. "But to begin such a—such a venture in these times, when so much in both our lives is unsettled, seems to me an unwise course."

"Unwise, you say. Unsettled," he repeated bitterly. He tossed his hat on one finger, still looking at it rather than at her. "I thought we were better friends then that, Mrs. Hazard. How long did it take you to learn that pretty piece of nonsense, eh?"

Catie reached across the distance between them,

laying her hand gently on his arm. "It's not nonsense, Jon. It's the truth, and I believe—"

But what she believed was never said. Instead came the snuffling sound of a laboring horse, the jingling of harness, and then, outlined against the sky, rose Anthony on his black gelding. On either side of him stood soldiers, soldiers frozen in place, with their muskets aimed straight down at Jon and Catie and Belinda, who clung in terror to her mother's petticoats.

Without a word, Anthony dismounted, his face a hard-edged mask that hid the keen blow of the pain he felt now. To find them here together on this lonely beach, Catie and his cousin, her hand resting so tenderly on his arm as they prepared to flee, was the cruelest joke of his life. As he walked down the dune toward them, his boot heels sliding deep into the sand, he told himself he shouldn't be surprised. He'd warned her himself that he'd be here today with a search party, and it was perfectly natural that she in turn would warn Jon.

Perfectly, hideously natural.

He could see nothing beyond her face, her rosy lips parted so slightly with surprise, pale silver strands of her hair dancing unchecked in the wind across her face, everything frozen by surprise and fear.

Dear Lord, he didn't want to frighten her. No matter what she'd done to him, how she'd betrayed him, he hadn't wanted that. Fool that he was, he loved her still. Yet as he came to stand before her now, his mouth was as dry as the sand beneath his feet, and he hadn't the remotest notion of what to say.

He brought his heels together, his hand resting on

the hilt of his sword. "Ma'am," he said at last. "I wish you a good morning."

"'Good morning'?" repeated Jon, standing forgotten beside Catie. He laughed—a harsh, mirthless sound that echoed against the rocks. "The devil take your good-morning, Anthony! No wonder Catie wouldn't have me. How could she, with your daughter hanging on her skirts? I'd never marked the likeness before, but now, to see you all together, I'd be a blind fool to miss it."

Anthony frowned, wondering if at last his cousin had lost his wits. Impatiently his gaze flicked down to the child that clung to Catie, and he felt the bottom drop from his heart.

His hair, his eyes, his mouth.

His daughter.

Chapter Thirteen

His *daughter.*

Swiftly Anthony looked back to Catie. The color had bleached from her face, her eyes silently beseeching him, and with the smallest possible motion of her chin she nodded.

That, and no more. Not that he needed even that much confirmation. The little girl's face, so closely an echo of his own, was proof enough. In a moment's time, so many questions had been answered: the reason Catie had married so swiftly, how she could have married a man she hadn't loved, her insistence on keeping their shared past secret, and why she'd taken such care to keep her daughter from his sight.

Yet now one question loomed even larger between them. He could understand perfectly why she'd clouded the facts of Belinda's conception when she was married to Hazard and he himself was in England. But once he came back to Newport, once he told her he loved her, why then hadn't she told him about her daughter?

No, not her daughter. He couldn't call the girl that any longer. *Their* daughter.

Unless she'd never meant to tell him. Unless she was so tangled in the rebel cause that she would have had to flee with Jon and leave him behind forever.

Damnation, why couldn't he think straight?

Catie watched and waited and silently prayed with all her heart that he'd understand. For nine long years she'd both imagined and dreaded this moment, playing it through in her mind with a thousand different variations. In some of them Anthony was angry, in others severe but forgiving. In her favorite ones he was overjoyed to discover he had a daughter, nearly as happy as Belinda was to meet her father, and as in all the best stories, they'd all lived together happily ever after.

But not once had Catie dreamed they'd be standing on a beach on a blindingly bright winter morning with a half-dozen British muskets trained upon them; nor had she ever pictured the expression that was now on Anthony's face, or, more precisely, the expression that wasn't there. His officer's face, she thought miserably, the one she knew he used to shut out the world.

But not me, she prayed. Even after all that has gone wrong between us, please, please don't let him reject me now, not me and not Belinda. "Blood with blood and families together": That was what Abigail Piper had said, and she was right.

Dear Lord, how will I find the strength to bear it if he scorns me now?

Anthony turned around, squinting up at the men still lined along the top of the dune. "You, there," he called. "Williams, you stay with my horse. The rest of you are to join Sergeant Barr's men and continue your search. I shall deal with these people myself and join you directly.''

He sensed their reluctance, saw it in how slowly they lowered their muskets and how they hung back, waiting to see what would happen next. Blast them all, they were questioning his orders for a chance to ogle his private affairs.

"Did I not make myself clear?'' he roared. "Dalton, there. Did I order you to stand there gaping like a clod-pated goose?''

"No, sir,'' said the hapless Dalton, snapping to attention. "No gapin' like a goose, sir.''

"Very well. Then I have made myself clear enough?''

The agreement rippled raggedly through the men, but at least now they moved on as they'd been ordered, and with a sigh Anthony bent down to make himself nearer to his daughter's height.

She was a pretty enough little thing, he'd grant her that, and with those great green eyes, she was a Sparhawk through and through. In a few years she'd have the men flocking around her, no mistake. Being her father wouldn't be easy. He frowned at the prospect, and in response the set of the girl's mouth grew more stubborn still.

What the devil did one say to a child, anyway?

"What's your name, miss?'' he asked gruffly. There, he couldn't go wrong with that.

"Belinda Hazard.''

He caught the slight shuffle behind the girl as Catie prodded her into a more polite answer.

"Belinda Hazard, *sir*.''

"Ah. Belinda." He cleared his throat self-consciously. He might not know a fig about children, but he knew a mutineer the instant he saw one. "That's a pretty name for a pretty lass."

The hostility in her eyes didn't waver, not a fraction. Well, he thought grudgingly, that was her Sparhawk blood, too, as much as the green eyes. She wouldn't back down, but neither would he.

"Captain Sparhawk said I was your daughter," she said. "But he's wrong. Sir. You're not my father. My father's dead."

Hell, she wasn't going to grant him any quarter at all.

"Mr. Hazard, you mean." Desperately he looked to Catie for help, but all she granted him was a silent shake of her head. All right, then, he wouldn't pursue their newfound relationship. Even if the girl was having only half the trouble he was in accepting it, she'd have an excellent excuse for her behavior.

"That's a pretty dolly you have, too," he said, grasping at the obvious like a drowning man. "What's her name?"

Belinda put both arms around the doll, squeezing it tight against her chest, almost daring Anthony to try and take her. "Her name's Duchess. Sir."

Anthony smiled, wondering what had happened to all his much-vaunted charm with the fair sex. "Duchess, is it? Duchess of what?"

"Her name is Duchess, sir," she said again, pointedly, as if he weren't quite bright. "You're Anthony, aren't you, sir?"

"Why, yes, I am." His smile widened, for he was pleased she'd volunteered something at last. "My name's Anthony Sparhawk. Your mama must have spoken of me, then.''

"Yes, sir, she has," she said promptly. "I know all about you. You're a Tory and a damned traitor to your country, and you're not my father and never were.''

"Belinda!" cried Catie, shocked and shamed. None of her daydreams had ever been like *this*. "I've never said such things, as you know perfectly well!''

But beside her, Jon laughed. "The little monkey has you pegged proper, Anthony, doesn't she?''

Anthony rose, thankful for the chance to consider his cousin instead of his daughter. Catie had told him he'd be surprised by the change in Jon, and she'd been right. Granted, nearly a decade had passed since he saw him last, but the time had not passed easily for Jon. It wasn't just the first streaks of white that silvered his black hair, or how he'd grown heavier and broader than the brash young sailor that Anthony remembered.

It was more in the way his eyes had grown somehow empty, as if part of his soul had faded away. Even as Jon laughed, there had been a sense of sorrow and loneliness around him, a weight that never would lighten. The death of Jon's wife had done this to him, or so Catie had said.

For the first time in his life, Anthony could understand such grief. If he lost Catie now, if she left him, as it seemed she wished to do, then he wasn't sure how he'd be able to cope with the rest of his life without her. But it would be her choice. He would give that to her. At least this time he knew better than to try to force her against her will.

To be strong when others were weak, to protect all

that he loved and cherished most: that was what his grandfather had told him so long ago, and that was what he'd believed he was doing when he returned to New England with the army. But maybe he'd been going about it all wrong. Maybe there was a better, more honorable path before him, if he'd only dare to take it.

Slowly he smiled at Jon, acutely aware of both the distance that lay between them and the closeness of the bond that still, despite the odds, seemed to remain.

"Miss Belinda can call me a traitor all she wishes," he said, falling into their old pattern of bantering. "'Tis bound to be more honorable than whatever she'd call you. I thought last night I was rid of you forever."

"Ha! Not so easy as that." Jon waved his hand over his wounded shoulder, and couldn't quite suppress the little wince of pain that the motion caused him. "You always did pull your aim to the left."

"To the right, you mean. You're the one who shoots wide to the left." Anthony had seen the seriousness of Jon's wound through the window of the mill, and knew how closely he'd come to killing him. Enemy or not, he was fervently thankful now that he hadn't succeeded. "At least you did at Damaris Point, didn't you?"

Acknowledgment gleamed in Jon's eyes. "So it *was* you, eh? I should have guessed no other officer would be fool enough to ride out there alone."

"Seeing as how Damaris Point is Sparhawk land, I could say much the same of you, cousin. Instead I'll say we're even."

"Even?" repeated Jon with surprise. "The devil we are!"

"The devil we're not," said Anthony. "You know, cousin, you look like some raggedy-arse old tinker with that beard."

With a snort, Jon squashed his hat back onto his head. "I won't say what you look like, Lord High Officer Jackanapes of His Blessed Majesty's bleedin' lobster circus. Least I won't say it before the ladies."

He tried to smile, but managed only to twist his mouth to one side in a lopsided grimace. "So follow your orders, Anthony. Do what you've come here to do. You've caught me fair and square, and I'm ready to be marched in irons back to town."

"I haven't caught anyone, not yet," said Anthony evenly. "My orders are to capture the leader of the rebels in these parts. But I do believe I've been mistaken. The man I seek is a bold, fearsome, black-hearted rogue. You look too feeble and weak to walk ten paces, let alone lead half the rebel raids this man's claimed. Yes, I must have been mistaken."

Catie's eyes narrowed with disbelief. "Anthony, what are you doing?"

He looked out at the ocean, unable to meet her eye. What was he doing? He was letting Jon escape to Providence. Any one of the them could see that. His orders had been to put an end to the rebel raids, and to his mind that could be accomplished just as easily by sending Jon away as by capturing him.

But that wasn't all. Though she might not realize it, he was giving Catie her freedom, too, the freedom to decide her own destiny. He'd learn soon enough whether he'd have a place in the rest of her life or not.

"I'm following my orders, Catie," he said, his voice clipped and, to Catie's ear, even more London-English than usual. "Nothing more."

"No, you're not," she said, disbelief now fading into desperation as he still didn't look her way. She knew how important the army was to him, how much its righteousness and sense of honor, however misguided, was a part of his life. Could he really be so willing to put all that in jeopardy, even for Jon's sake? "You're not following your orders at all. Oh, Anthony, what will happen to you if you do this?"

Impatiently Jon stepped forward, his long black hair tossing in the wind. "Listen here, Anthony. I don't expect any favors like this from you, and I don't want 'em."

"What makes you think this is a favor, you great fool?" demanded Anthony, slicing his hand through the air before Jon's face. "I'd call it settling the score between us, for once and for all. I'll admit to being mistaken about you here today, if you in turn agree to leave this island and not return."

But Jon shook his head fiercely. "I can't swear to that, Anthony. You couldn't, either, in the same place, and I—"

"Halt right there!" shouted Jeremiah. He stood at the edge of the water, his feet widespread and both hands together to steady the long-barreled pistol he held aimed at Anthony. "You just stop, right there!"

Jon swore under his breath. "What the devil do you think you're doing, boy?"

Jeremiah tossed the hair back from his eyes, but the pistol never wavered.

"He nearly killed you, Pa," he shouted, his voice

going shrill with excitement and emotion. "I'm going to make sure he won't have another chance to try."

Jon rumbled with anger. "That's a damned fool thing to do, Jeremiah."

"Why, Pa? You said yourself the only good that comes from redcoats comes from killing them." Jeremiah raised his head defiantly, his finger poised on the trigger. "Better him than you, anyways."

"What, and let that one shot of yours bring every blessed one of his men running back here to pepper you with shot for your trouble?" demanded Jon. "Use your wits, boy, not the gun."

"Oh, Jeremiah, listen to him, please!" cried Catie, her anguish real as she shoved Belinda behind her. She didn't doubt that the boy was capable of firing the gun; that was exactly what his father had trained him to do so well. Not only would Anthony die, and her hopes and happiness with him, but Jeremiah, too, would suffer the rest of his own life for this one, impulsive action. "You can't do this! Look at him! Anthony is your uncle, your kin! You cannot kill him, Jeremiah!"

She saw how the pistol's barrel trembled, the bright sun glancing off the polished steel, and saw, too, how Jeremiah swallowed hard, swallowing his uncertainties.

"I don't care, Mrs. Hazard," he said, but the belligerence had slipped from his words. "I'm not allowed to. He's not my uncle anymore. He's a Britisher, and he's the enemy."

Swiftly Catie glanced at Jon, who'd gone very still. Could he see what his bitterness, his hatred, had done to his son?

Yet it was Anthony who spoke first. "You're right,

Jeremiah," he said, with a calmness that stunned Catie. "I am a Britisher, and your enemy. If you shoot me now, I'll die honorably, a good soldier's death. What more could I want? But you won't, not at all. It won't matter one whit to my general that you're a boy. He'll see you tried and hanged as a traitor and a murderer anyway, and leave your body in the gibbet to rot as an example. Do you truly think that your father wants that?"

It seemed to Catie that Jon had aged another five years in the same number of minutes, his face haggard and pale.

"Listen to your uncle, lad," he called hoarsely. "Taking his life's not worth yours."

The pistol wavered, a match for the question on Jeremiah's face. "But, Pa," he said plaintively. "You *said...*"

"Come, Jere, and give me the pistol," said Jon, holding out his hand as he began walking toward his son, one slow, cautious step at a time. "Just give me the pistol."

Closer he came, and finally Jeremiah let his hands droop, and the pistol fell to the packed sand with a heavy, harmless thud. His face crumpled with the tears he could no longer hold back, and he wheeled around toward the water to hide his shameful weakness. When Jon rested his arm across his shoulders, the boy roughly shrugged himself free. But when Jon tried a second time, Jeremiah slumped against him, his arms around his father and his face buried against his side.

"The boy and I will be clearing off now," said Jon heavily. "If Owen hasn't given up on us, that is."

"You will leave Newport, then?" asked Anthony, purposefully noncommittal.

"Aye. Though I'll swear to no more than that."

The two men looked hard at one another, a wealth of feeling unspoken between them.

Anthony nodded. "You've a good son there, Jon."

"You've a good daughter, too, if you take care not to misplace her again." Jon sighed wearily. "And you have Catie."

"Good luck to you, Jon," said Catie, struggling with the tears that knotted her throat. "And may God keep you safe."

Jon shrugged, then winced. "God will do what he pleases, especially with the likes of me." His face softened. "You keep safe, too, Catie, you and Belinda both. I only wish I'd found you sooner myself."

She nodded, not trusting herself to speak further. She might not love Jon Sparhawk, but she would miss him, and Jeremiah, too. She felt Belinda come to stand beside her, slipping one hand into Catie's while she silently waved goodbye to Jeremiah. Another time, she thought sadly as she raised her own hand in farewell, and she and Jon might have been happy together. Another time, and how different their lives might have been!

Not until then did she realize how closely Anthony was watching her, his face once again a chiseled, dispassionate mask that revealed nothing. The bullion lace on his jacket and the polished brass gorget around his neck glittered in the sunlight, and his hair was another kind of shining gold, all so bright and grand it almost hurt her eyes to look up at him.

"You're not going with Jon?" he asked, with a disinterest so patent that it chilled her heart. "Why come this far only to turn back?"

"He asked me to, but I told him no," she said, unable to hide her wistfulness. "I came with Jon to the Pipers' house because I didn't believe he'd manage on his own, and to fetch Belinda, as well. I followed them to the beach only to say goodbye. But I never would have gone with him. I belong here in Newport with Belinda."

And with you, Anthony. The words froze, unsaid, at her lips. *I belong here in Newport with you.*

Anthony wanted to believe her. How could he not? He wanted to believe, more than anything he'd ever wanted in his life, and now that he let himself at last look at her, really look, and see the love that shone so desperately from her eyes, he knew he'd be the greatest fool under heaven not to.

There were so many fences to mend with her and their daughter both that he didn't know where to begin. But the one truth remained that Catie loved *him*— not Jon, not the rebel cause—but him, Anthony Sparhawk, maybe almost as much as he in turn loved her.

He tugged off his glove and held his bare hand out to her. "Come, sweetheart," he said softly. "High time we went back home."

Catie sat curled in the little armchair in her bedchamber, sipping her cup of chocolate while Belinda played with Duchess and the new tea set before the glow of the fire. They'd retreated here for an early supper together and for a few quiet moments before Belinda was put to bed and Catie returned to the taproom downstairs to welcome whatever guests Hazard's might have that evening. It was the kind of simple evening they'd shared more times than Catie could remember, the hour of the day she enjoyed and relished the most. But tonight the closeness she and Belinda had always shared seemed missing, and, sadly, Catie knew the reason why.

She watched her daughter play, carefully arranging the tiny cups and dishes as she murmured little singsong conversations between Duchess and an imaginary guest on the opposite side of the tea table. Though it was still two days until Christmas, Catie had decided to give Belinda the tea set early, as a kind of homecoming gift.

At least that was what she'd told Belinda. What she'd secretly hoped was that the tea set might become a peace offering between them, a bridge that Catie might use to breach the hostile silence that Anthony's presence had dropped between her and her daughter.

So far, as a gift, the tea set was an overwhelming success. Belinda hadn't let it from her sight. But its role as a peacemaker was far less certain.

Catie sighed, setting her empty cup on the table beside her. She had not seen Anthony since this morning, when he left them to report to his general and tend to the other business of his regiment, but he could be expected to return to the tavern at any time. If she was going to speak to Belinda, she'd best do it now.

"Belinda, lamb," she began softly. "We must talk about Major Sparhawk."

Though Belinda's hand paused over the tea table, she didn't lift her head. "Don't want to," she muttered rebelliously. "Don't *ever* want to."

"Well, then, I shall do all the talking, and you shall

do the listening,'' said Catie quietly. ''No matter how you might wish it were otherwise, Belinda, Anthony Sparhawk is your father.''

''But he can't be!'' cried Belinda plaintively as she rocked back on her heels, hugging Duchess tightly in her arms. ''My father's dead!''

Catie nodded, trying to remember the explanation she'd been composing all afternoon. This wasn't going to be easy for either of them, especially when others began to take notice, the way they inevitably would. She was surprised that Hannah hadn't already.

''You're far more fortunate than most children, Belinda. You've been blessed with two fathers instead of one,'' she said carefully. ''Mr. Hazard was the one you remember, and he loved you very much, and was proud to call you his daughter. But Major Sparhawk is your father, too, the one most people will now call your real father.''

''How can he be my real father when he isn't even married to you?'' Belinda's voice trembled uncertainly. ''Besides, I only want one father, like everyone else.''

''Oh, lamb...'' Catie held her arms open and Belinda flew to meet her, wriggling until she found her favorite place in her mother's lap. ''I know it's hard to understand. But I do believe that Anthony wants to learn to love you, too, like a proper father, if only you'll let him.''

Belinda sighed, a ragged, sobbing hiccup of a sigh. ''How can I let him, when he's a Britisher?''

''You must try, that's all,'' said Catie gently as she stroked her daughter's silky hair. ''You might find he's actually a very nice gentleman, no matter what color his coat. And I don't think he knows any more of what to do with you than you do with him.''

For a long time, Belinda considered this, tracing her fingers back and forth across Duchess's painted face while she did. ''Do you love him, Mama?''

Catie smiled fondly. ''Yes, lamb, I do, and I believe he loves me, as well.''

''Oh.'' Belinda burrowed more deeply against Catie. ''Then will you still love me?''

''What a question, sweetheart!'' exclaimed Catie gently, her arms tight around her daughter. ''Of course I'll still love you, even more than I love you now, if such a thing is possible. You'll always be my sweet Belinda, and that will never, ever change.''

The girl sighed again, and unhappily Catie knew her doubts remained.

''If you love him, Mama,'' said Belinda slowly, ''and he loves you, then you must marry him. Otherwise he can't be my *real* real father.''

''Oh, Belinda.'' Catie was grateful that Belinda couldn't see how she flushed, for this was one question she had no answer for. ''That's not something we ladies can decide. We have to wait for the gentleman to ask.''

The knock on the door came then, and Catie's heart beat faster with anticipation. It must be Anthony; at this hour, who else would it be?

''Down with you now. I must get the door,'' she said as she disentangled herself from her daughter. She smoothed her skirts and hurried to the door, still conscious of how Belinda hung back. Poor baby, thought Catie with concern. How hard this all must be for her!

Anthony bowed when she opened the door, his

smile warm and his eyes filled with the pleasure of seeing her again. Yet he looked worn and tired, too, and when he bent to kiss her cheek—a chaste, genteel salute for Belinda's benefit—Catie squeezed his hand in silent empathy.

"I've missed you," she said, her words quick and low. "Very much."

"And I you." His smile turned wry, and she knew from the way he was studying her mouth that he wished he could kiss her there next. "After a promising beginning, my day proved most tedious and filled with vexation."

Her smile faded. "You're in trouble, aren't you? Over Jon?"

"Faith, no," he said lightly. "Only a dozen different reports to make to the colonel and the general both, and a score of explanations to be written as to why the sun did rise this morning with due honor and why it most likely will set again this night with same. The sort of taxing nonsense that fills any soldier's days in camp. But where is Miss Belinda?"

He swept past Catie and into the room, and as he did, Catie's uneasiness grew. Anthony's breezy cheerfulness might reassure Belinda, but she herself feared the explanations to the general had had a great deal more to do with Jon's escape than with the sunrise.

Carefully Anthony set the willow basket he'd been carrying on the floor. He'd noticed how Belinda hadn't greeted him—how could he not?—and how she clutched that hideous cross-eyed doll as if it were a talisman against him. Well, so be it. He was willing to begin again with her, and this time he was determined to win her over. As in any sort of battle, he'd reasoned, victory was all in choosing the proper weapon.

The basket lurched to one side, rustling strangely. Curious, Belinda leaned closer, close enough that she could hear the faint mewing from within, and her eyes lit with excitement.

"Go ahead," said Anthony. "Open it."

Eagerly Belinda crouched beside the basket and unfastened the pegs that held the lid in place. Even before she'd finished, a small gray nose had thrust itself from beneath the lid, and with a squeal of delight Belinda pulled the kitten from the basket.

"Oh—*oh!*" She giggled as the kitten clung to her, using its tiny claws to climb up the front of her gown. "Oh, sir, what a *beautiful* little kit!"

"I had the very devil of a time finding her, you know," explained Anthony seriously, bending down beside her. "I hadn't realized that kittens of any sort were quite out of season. But I guessed you'd be a kitten kind of young lady, and so persevered until I found this little beauty."

He wasn't being quite truthful on several counts. The kitten was no beauty, but instead a scrawny gray wisp with its eyes too close together and a shivering tail better suited to a rat. Routt was the one who'd scoured the town for out-of-season kittens, and who'd had to pay dearly for this sorry little example, too, though he'd done it on Anthony's orders. And as for predicting that Belinda would want a kitten more than anything else—that hadn't been much of a guess, either, not after Anthony overheard the tavern's cross-tempered cook complaining about how the mistress and her daughter insisted on feeding strays from the kitchen door.

So he'd not been entirely truthful, perhaps, but he was eminently successful. The ecstatic look on Belinda's face told him that, and the quick glance over his shoulder to Catie confirmed it.

Gently he stroked the kitten's ears, and was rewarded with a rumbling purr far bigger than seemed possible from so scrawny a body. "Of course, it will be up to your mother whether or not you can keep her," he said seriously, as if he didn't already know Catie's answer. "She's going to take a great deal of feeding and care."

"I can do that, sir," said Belinda promptly. "I know I can."

To prove it, she jumped up and scraped what was left from their supper onto one plate, and carefully set it before the hungry cat before she looked back to her mother. "Mama? You will let me keep her, won't you? Please?"

The scene before Catie now was so exactly as she'd pictured it that she could do little but grin foolishly. The two people she loved best in the world, sitting side by side on the floor, their heads bowed together over the cat as she gobbled the scraps, their golden hair nearly identical in the dancing firelight. If it had taken an underfed little stray to bring them together, then as far as Catie was concerned, the cat was forever guaranteed a place of honor on her hearth.

"If you tend to the kit as you say, Belinda," she said as she knelt to stroke the animal's ruffled gray fur for herself, "then yes, you may keep her. But you must feed her and keep her from mischief, and clean up after any messes she makes. You'll have to name her, as well.''

"You have a Duchess already," said Anthony, mentally giving himself additional credit for remembering the doll's name. "Why not name the kitten Princess?''

"Princess?" Catie wrinkled her nose, coming to kneel beside them. "Faith, that's hardly proper for a decent American cat.''

Belinda rubbed her cheek against the kitten's back. "I don't care. I shall call her Princess, the Princess of Cats, so that when she grows up she can be the Queen of Cats, too.''

Anthony leaned back against the seat of the chair behind him and linked his fingers around his bent knee, enjoying his victory more by the minute. He liked watching the little girl cradle the kitten, and listening to her giggle as the animal crawled over one shoulder and onto her back.

She was a winsome little creature, his daughter, and his smile widened with pleasure at the sound of that. His daughter. Strange how much this sudden fatherhood had changed the way he saw the world.

Throughout this very long day, his thoughts had constantly been here with Catie and Belinda, and he'd turned down an invitation to dine with the other officers in his regiment to come back to the tavern instead. It wasn't the wisest move, perhaps, especially not after the endless stream of questions from Ridley that he'd had to face down this afternoon. For the first time in his career, he hadn't been entirely truthful with his commanding officer, and his conscience was far from easy. But by letting Jon escape, Anthony had done what he believed was for the best, and sitting here in Catie's bedchamber, in the glow of her happiness, he found it impossible to regret his decision.

How could he? After being rootless with the army for so many years, this small, plainly furnished room was, because of Catie, the closest thing to a home he'd had for a long, long time. In a way, he felt as if he'd finally come full circle. If his grandfather had taught him the honor to be found in protecting and defending what he loved most, then now, at last, he felt as if he'd found it.

"I danced with a princess once," he said lazily. "At a great ball in London, though I disremember who or what was being honored."

"Truly, sir?" Once again Belinda's eyes lit with curious interest. "Was she very grand?"

"Hardly. She was one of the king's poor relations, from Hanover, and she spoke not a word of English. Short and stout, and laced so tightly that she wheezed as she danced. Trod on my toes, too." Somehow he kept his face serious, even though he could hear Catie laughing. "But she *was* a full-blooded princess."

Disappointed, Belinda shook her head. "That's not how princesses should be."

"No, I can't say she was," he agreed. He looked to Catie, their shared gaze lingering over the top of Belinda's head. "But your mother, now, she'd make a most admirable princess. Drape her in silk and jewels, and shc'd have every gentleman in the court bowing at her feet."

"Oh, stuff and nonsense," scoffed Catie, yet still blushing clear to the top of her bodice. "I've no wish to live in some grand, drafty palace and wear a crown.

Besides, what could I possibly have that some silly princess might covet in return?''

He raised one eyebrow, just a fraction, but more than enough to suggest an entire world of wickedness to tempt any princess, and enough, too, to make Catie's blush deepen further. She could say nothing to scold him, not with Belinda there, but then, scolding wasn't entirely what she wished to do with Anthony right now, anyway.

The little Dutch clock on the mantel chimed eight. Catie bustled to her feet, smoothing her skirts to hide the warm rush of longing she'd felt when Anthony merely looked at her.

''Time for bed, Belinda,'' she said briskly. ''You know I'm due downstairs. Come along now. And before you ask, yes, Princess may sleep with you.''

''Thank you, Mama!'' Impulsively Belinda threw her arms around Catie, hugging her awkwardly, with the little kitten mewing her protest while sandwiched between them. Then she turned toward Anthony, and bobbed a shy, jerky curtsy, with the kitten still in her arms. ''Thank you, too, sir. For Princess, I mean.''

She skipped off to her own room before Anthony could answer, and Catie followed to help her change and tuck her into bed for the night. But Anthony hung back, not sure where he figured in all this yet. Clearly Catie and Belinda had managed quite well on their own without a man in their house, and until he'd resolved things further with Catie, he didn't want to push his welcome too far.

Catie appeared in the doorway and beckoned. ''You can say good-night to her, too, if you wish,'' she said. ''And to Princess.''

Anthony nodded and cleared his throat self-consciously as he went into the little room adjoining Catie's. A tall candle—tall enough to last far into the night—burned in a tin lantern beside Belinda's low bed. The little girl herself lay beneath a soft wool coverlet, the cross-eyed doll tucked beside her on one side and the kitten curled against her on the other.

"Princess looks comfortable enough," he said. "So do you, for that matter."

"I am." For the first time, Belinda smiled at him, freely showing the gaps left by lost baby teeth. "That is, I am, sir, thank you."

Anthony reached out to stroke the kitten's head. "Do you think we could do away with that 'sir'?" he asked. "That is, if your mama thinks it's not too ill-mannered."

"She won't mind." Belinda shifted to her side, leaning her head on her hand as she curved herself around the sleeping cat. "Mama told me that you truly are my real father, and that everyone will know because I favor you so."

"Well, it is true," he said uncomfortably. "On both counts. It's only that I've been away, that's all."

"Nine years is a great long while to be away," said Belinda. "But you're here now, and that makes Mama happy, so I suppose Princess and I shall be happy, too. Even if you are a redcoat." She flopped back down on her pillow with a drowsy, contented yawn. "Good night, Papa."

"Good night, sweetheart," said Anthony gruffly, surprised by the lump that seemed to have swelled in his throat. He bent down to brush his lips across his daughter's forehead, and found it the most natural thing in the world to do.

"The kitten was a masterstroke," said Catie as he rejoined her in the larger bedchamber. "You couldn't have chosen a better way to please her."

"A lucky guess," he murmured, once again glancing back to the sleeping child. "I don't really know where to begin."

"You're managing admirably," said Catie, smiling fondly as she smoothed her hair beneath a fresh linen cap, this one becomingly ruffled around the front with lace. "Continue as you've begun, and she'll quite forget I exist."

"Will she be safe alone in there?" he asked with concern. "She looks even younger when she's asleep."

"She'll be fine," said Catie, both amused and touched by his interest. "You forget that she's only known a mother who must toil in the evening. When she was a baby she slept in a cradle in the kitchen, where Hannah watched her, too, but she's slept up here since she was five. I lock her in, of course, but I leave another key tied to the latch on her side, as well, so she can come out to find me if she needs to."

She hooked the ring of keys once more to the string inside her pocket and looked to Anthony expectantly. "Do you wish to come with me now, or shall I meet you later?"

Anthony's face fell. "I'd rather thought we'd stay here, sweet," he said, reaching for her hand. "Together."

Gently she touched her fingers across his lips. "I can't, Anthony, not yet, as much as I wish to," she said regretfully. "I must see to my guests in the tap-room, the way I do every night."

"There aren't any guests," he said, his voice low and suggestive. "At least there weren't any when I came in earlier. And even if there were, they could spare you this once. Don't forget that I'm a guest, too."

He pulled her closer, near enough to kiss her lightly, and the sound she made was suspiciously similar to the little cat's purr.

"Stay," he told her. It was almost an order. "I haven't given you your gift, you know."

"Later," she breathed, and somehow slipped free. "I swear to it."

In the hall, her fingers were trembling as she locked the door after them, and he kissed her again, enough to make her resolve melt away to near nothingness. Near, but not quite. If she'd come this far without giving in, her beleaguered conscience reasoned, then continuing the rest of the way downstairs to her responsibilities in the public rooms would be easy.

But her conscience had forgotten that between her chamber and the public rooms lay the chamber that was Anthony's, a chamber with a feather bed and a fire and the sweet, heady memories of the night before, and as he latched the door after them, Catie's conscience at last fell helplessly, obligingly silent.

Chapter Fourteen

"Have you forgotten to ask for your present?" asked Anthony, his voice little more than a raspy whisper so close to Catie's ear. When she didn't answer, he ran his fingers along the shallow valley of her spine, stopping to caress the full roundness of her bottom as she lay sprawled on top of him. She sighed then, satisfied, and shifted so that she could prop herself up on his chest to smile sleepily down at him.

"I thought that *was* my present," she said, shoving the damp tangle of her hair back from her forehead. "And a wonderfully fine present it was, too."

He pulled her down to kiss again, leisurely savoring the taste of her mouth. "A present is something special. Making love to you should be a considerably more commonplace occurrence."

Her laugh was husky and dark with suggestion. "Frequent, perhaps, but never commonplace," she murmured as she stretched and rubbed herself languorously against him. "Faith, Anthony, I'd never dreamed how wondrous it would be with me above and you beneath. Do you think we can try that again?"

"That, and many others." Already he felt his own interest quickening, growing hard again, and his idle touch became more of a caress. "You are quite the cleverest woman I've ever met, Catie, but there remain certain aspects of your education that need improvement."

She laughed. "Then you must promise to be my special tutor."

"I wouldn't trust any other. We've nearly ten years between us to make up, you know." He groaned with the pleasure of her movements, and only with great reluctance did he hold her still. "But first your present, love."

She pouted most enchantingly. "Can't it wait?"

"A little patience is a wise thing," he said, even though he wasn't overly inclined to wait himself. "Can you reach my waistcoat?"

"If I must." She slid to one side and fished her hand over the side of the bed to reach the waistcoat where in their haste it had been dropped, along with the rest of their clothing. She rolled over to face Anthony, lightly touching the silver Sparhawk trade-piece still pinned to the waistcoat's breast as she handed it to him.

"That brought you luck enough today, didn't it," she said softly. "When I think of how you faced down poor Jeremiah, my blood still runs cold."

Anthony pulled himself up against the bolster. "The boy couldn't have done it. I've seen others who would have fired without a thought, but Jeremiah isn't one of them, no matter how much his father has tried to teach him otherwise. Pray Jon has learned that lesson."

"Amen to that," said Catie sadly. "But I say you were brave, and lucky, too. Spare a bit of credit for that little hawk."

She pulled the coverlet over her bare shoulders, watching him as he searched through the waistcoat's pockets. They'd left the curtains open at the end of the bed for light from the fire, and by its embers his untied hair was a dull gold. The broad planes of his chest and arms stood out in strong relief in the shadowy light, the curling hair on his chest glinting, and against the rumpled white linen he seemed even more intriguingly male. What a beautiful man, thought Catie, a beautiful, brave, charming man she loved more than she'd ever thought possible.

He ran his thumb across the silver piece and smiled. "Of course I'll give my hawk credit. He's kept me alive this long, hasn't he?" He hesitated for a moment, watching her face. "Just like that little heart you always wear."

"You mean my locket?" She shrugged, embarrassed that he'd noticed. "'Tis hardly the same. Inside is Belinda's portrait, done for her birthday two years past. When she was away with the Pipers, I wore the locket as a way to keep her close to me. A mother's whim, that's all."

He grinned outrageously. "Belinda's portrait? Oh, Catie, love, I thought— But no, it doesn't matter. Here, come closer."

Gently he pulled her closer, the coverlet sliding forgotten from her shoulders. "I *am* most fortunate, you know, luckier than any man has a right to be," he said. "Avoiding musket balls and bayonets is one thing. Coming back to Newport to find you again is quite another.''

He opened his hand to show a small, silk-covered box, and he smiled at her uncertainly. All his carefully rehearsed speeches, all the sweet poet's words he'd wanted to say to her, evaporated like morning mist.

He sighed, tapping his thumb against the top of the box. ''I don't know where to begin, sweetheart,'' he admitted. ''After all the ways I've wronged you, I know I've no right to expect any favor in return. And when I think of what I've done to Belinda, of the kind of scorn she could have suffered because of me—damnation, I can't believe what a scoundrel I've been to you both.''

He was rambling and he knew it, rambling like an idiot, but because she said nothing to stop him, he couldn't stop himself. ''Then look at the way I finally return, part of an army that you call your enemy. I still am. Even though I want to try to set things to rights as best I can, I know I won't be able to. It doesn't matter how much I love you, or that I never want to leave you or Belinda again. I'll bring the devil's own luck to your trade. But maybe after this wretched war, when the rebellion's put down and the king's back in Newport where he belongs, then maybe it won't matter as much if you and I—''

''Yes,'' said Catie softly. ''Yes.''

Drawn up short, he frowned. '''Yes'?'' he repeated uneasily. ''Yes, you say?''

''Yes, yes, yes, you great ninny,'' she said, smiling though her eyes shone brightly with tears. ''That is the answer you want, isn't it?''

He shook his head, almost afraid to believe her.

"How can you give me an answer when I haven't properly asked the question? I've done so many things wrong with you. Let me do this one right."

He flipped open the lid to the box and took out the ring nestled in plush within, a slim gold band crowned by a flower of garnets and pearls. Gingerly he held it poised between his thumb and forefinger, the little ring looking impossibly dainty by contrast.

"Will you marry me, Catie? Here, now, in Newport, as soon as can be arranged?" he asked, his voice thrumming with emotion. "Marry me and be my wife, my one love forever?"

This time Catie found it impossible to speak, her hand clamped tight against her mouth as she fought her tears. She'd never dreamed she'd live to hear such a question asked of her; nor had she ever imagined how much these simple words could mean. How could she possibly say anything that could begin to express the joy that filled her now?

But she could still nod, and nod she did, and with a great sigh of satisfaction and relief, Anthony slipped the ring onto her finger.

"There now, and it even fits," he said as he lifted her hand to kiss it. "I had to guess."

"It's perfect," whispered Catie as his lips grazed across her skin. "And so are you, Anthony."

"Not quite," he said gruffly. "But I'm trying damnably hard to be better."

At last she found she could smile. "Then we shall make a most excellent pair, love, always striving to improve ourselves."

"Ha! I'd say we make a right fine pair already." He curled his arm around her waist and pulled her, giggling, up against his chest. "But I suppose I could show you again exactly how well we suit."

And to her infinite pleasure—and his own, as well—he did just that.

Catie woke slowly, dragged unwillingly back to consciousness. Hanging halfway between sleep and waking, she'd no wish to leave the warmth and security that still surrounded her, nor did she bother overmuch with wondering what had brought about this blissful condition. Yet once again she heard the voices from downstairs, men's voices in the taproom, and at last the habit of responsibility dragged her reluctantly from the sweet disorientation of sleep.

She should dress and go downstairs and see to her guests. There might be a score of them waiting, from the sound of their voices, more customers than she'd had for many nights, and she couldn't afford not to welcome them, not to laugh at their jests and smooth over their arguments and see that their tankards stayed full throughout the night. She needed to check on Belinda, as well, and make sure her daughter was still sleeping as soundly as when she and Anthony had left her earlier.

She should go, yes, but in a moment. She curled herself more deeply against Anthony's body, relishing the warmth and the intimacy of being here with him. He murmured unintelligibly in his sleep and circled his arm around her waist, holding her there. Another moment, she told herself, another precious moment was all.

She lifted her hand with the new ring so that she could admire it again, the dark red stones sparkling in the last light of the fire. Catie Sparhawk—she liked the sound of that. Her husband, Anthony. She liked that even better. She'd been married nearly five years to Ben before she stopped calling him Mr. Hazard. But being Anthony's wife would be nothing like *belonging* to Ben had been, and she smiled with sheer, unbridled joy. She couldn't decide which was better: loving Anthony as much as she did, or knowing he loved her equally in return.

Her *husband* Anthony. Major and Mrs. Anthony Sparhawk, of Newport and late of London, and their daughter, Miss Belinda Sparhawk. Oh, it all sounded very fine indeed.

He'd said he wished to wed as swiftly as was possible. Given the circumstances, Reverend Wentworth might be persuaded to waive posting the banns. They could be married by Twelfth Night, or even New Year's Day. They'd have the wedding in the parlor downstairs, a small wedding, but then that would be best. So few of her closest friends remained in Newport and the ones who did might not come to wish her joy for marrying an English officer.

But there'd still be joy enough; she'd see to that, with her own special punch for all of Anthony's friends after the ceremony and Liam and his fiddle to play for dancing. Anthony would wear his dress uniform with the gold lace and the silver spurs, and if there was time, even two days, she'd have a new gown made for herself, silk taffeta or even a Spitalfields damask. For once she wouldn't choose by what was most reasonably priced. She was going to marry Anthony, and for him she wanted to be as beautiful as she could. And Belinda must have a new gown, too, kerseymere instead of silk, of course, but still very—

What were the men doing on the stairs? She pushed herself up on her elbows, tensing as she listened. One man was speaking, saying things she couldn't make out, but from the footfalls on the bare steps, there were others with him, and a woman, too, her voice rising with indignation. Not just a woman, realized Catie, but Hannah. Why wasn't the cook in the kitchen, where she belonged? What was Hannah doing here, coming upstairs with a crowd of men?

"What is it, Catie?" asked Anthony, instantly awake beside her. "What's happening?"

"I don't know," she said, fear rising in her throat as she saw him lean from the bed to reach for his pistols. "It doesn't sound like—"

But it was too late. The passkey was already scraping in the lock and the door was flying open and soldiers were filling the room, surrounding the bed, British soldiers, all of them staring down the long, gleaming barrels of their muskets at her and at Anthony as they shoved aside the bed's curtains.

With a little cry of terror, Catie grabbed the coverlet to hide her nakedness and shrank back behind Anthony. She knew why the soldiers were here. There could be but one reason, but she didn't want to hear it.

"What the devil is the meaning of this intrusion?" demanded Anthony. "I'll see you all broken, every last man of you, for breaking in here like this!"

But it was Hannah who answered first, pushing her way to the front of the soldiers. In her hand was the ring with the passkey from the kitchen, where it was kept for emergencies, and her gaze as she stared at them blistered with hatred alone.

"Don't you devil me, you foulmouthed traitor!" she shouted at Anthony, practically spitting the words. "'Tweren't enough that you come here an' ravage our town! You had to come first an' cuckold my poor master, an' leave him to raise your bastard as if 'twas his own! An' you, mistress, aye, did you think I was so blind I wouldn't see it, th' proof o' your slatternly whoring—"

"Enough, you old witch," ordered General Ridley as he stepped forward. He waved his hand impatiently, and two of the soldiers seized Hannah and pulled her aside. "Sparhawk has more to worry him now than siring bastards."

"General Ridley, sir," said Anthony, his words clipped with anger. "Perhaps you can explain why—"

"There is nothing whatsoever to explain," snapped Ridley. "At least not to you. In the name of His Majesty King George III, I hereby arrest you, Anthony Sparhawk, of His Majesty's Twenty-third Regiment."

Catie gasped, but Anthony's expression didn't change a fraction, nor did his voice lose the heat of his anger. "Am I to be told the charges against me, sir?"

"Treason," said Ridley. "High treason, and default of your duties as an officer. And may the Lord have mercy upon you, sir, because I surely will not."

Anthony dragged himself upright at the sound of the footsteps coming down the hall, the shackles around his ankles and the irons hanging from his wrists nearly as heavy as his heart. Two days ago they'd shoved him into this dank, dirty cell by himself, where the only comforts were the moldy straw piled on the floor for his bed and a bucket in the corner. There was no candle or lantern, no fire for warmth, and only the weakest of daylight managed to filter through the tiny slits high in the wall. The brick walls and floor held the damp and the chill, as well as the less tangible scents of the fear and desperation of its former occupants. The good men of Newport had built their gaol well, and since the first pirates who went from its cells to the hangman, no man—or woman, either—had managed to escape.

The footsteps were coming closer, their echoes louder, and Anthony lumbered to the door. It was too early for the guard to bring the evening meal, and until now he'd had no other visitors. He leaned close to the heavy battened door, straining to make out the voices on the other side, concentrating so hard that he barely had time to stagger back from the opening door when he heard the scrape of the gaoler's key in the iron padlock.

The gaoler, a bilious man named Foulk, came first, holding a lantern that made Anthony shield his eyes from the unaccustomed brightness. After Foulk followed an infantryman Anthony recognized by now as one of his personal guards, none of them from his own regiment. The man spat at Anthony, making his contempt as clear as he could, and raised the butt of his musket, as if to strike him with any provocation.

Not that Anthony intended to offer any. He still bore the angry bruises from the first night, when Foulk and the guards had been as rough as they dared in bringing him here and putting him in irons. Yet it didn't matter that his cheek and brow were battered and swollen, or that his shirt and waistcoat were torn and filthy; he was still an officer of the king until proven otherwise, and he would not be intimidated, and before the guard he stood as proud and straight as he could.

But that hard-earned composure vanished as soon as he saw who else had come.

"Ridley, by all that's holy," he said furiously. "Where's Mrs. Hazard? What have you done with her? Damnation, if you've hurt her in any way—"

Now the guard swung the musket, striking Anthony so hard in the shoulder that he staggered, gasping, back against the wall.

"You'll do exactly what, Sparhawk?" asked the general, his smile thin. "I vow that in your present condition you'd do better to look after your own affairs than those of the chit who brought you down."

Slumped against the wall, still struggling to catch his breath, Anthony let the first edge of desperation creep into his voice. "The—the devil take you. Where—where is she?"

"Oh, Mrs. Hazard's safe enough," said the general lightly. "Still snug under her own roof, if you must know. We wouldn't want any ill to come to her before she must testify against you. Irregular, that, swearing in a woman for a court-martial, but given the circumstances, I intend to use everything against you that I can. After that, of course, she'll be tried herself in a civil court on charges much like yours. Spying, treason. She'll hang, too, if that's any comfort to you."

Still breathing hard, Anthony fought against the bleak sense of helplessness that threatened to overwhelm him. He knew that every word the general said

was true. There was no possible way he'd be found
innocent in a court-martial, not when he'd be judged
by the same peers he was charged with betraying.
He'd done what he believed was right, but with Ridley
against him, no one would stop to listen to his reasons.
Now every order he'd ever given, every action that
had depended upon his judgment, would be reviewed
and questioned and finally discredited, until the career
that had been his life would be dishonored beyond
redemption.

And then there was Catie. What Ridley had said
about her was true, too. She would be forced to testify
against him, and the prosecutor would not treat her
with the gentleness she deserved. Everything she'd try
to say in Anthony's defense would be twisted about
and turned against them both, and by the time she
herself was tried, there would be nothing left of either
her credibility or her good name.

It was bad enough for a man to be hanged, but for
a woman it seemed somehow even more horrifying,
more shameful. Once he'd seen three women, a trio
of thieves, executed at Tyburn, and the memory had
stayed with him long after. To know that Catie would
die in such an unspeakably cruel and painful way was
beyond bearing, and the thought of poor Belinda left
orphaned and friendless in that appalling manner only
compounded his sense of rage and powerlessness. The
best that Anthony could hope for was that in the two
nights they'd spent together, Catie had conceived another child by him, for then at least her life would be
spared until the baby was born. But as best hopes
went, it was a grim one indeed.

His head bowed, he let the despair sweep over him.

Once before she'd been nearly ruined because of him. Now he'd returned, and instead of the wedding he'd promised her, she faced death. All because of him, all because of what he'd brought to her.

Slowly he glanced back at Ridley, raising his hands just enough for the irons to clink together. "Why did you come?" he asked. "To mock me? To gloat?"

"Why did I come?" Musing, Ridley dabbed at his nose with the scented handkerchief that he was using to mask the stench of the gaol. "I suppose I'm here to teach myself a lesson. I trusted you, Sparhawk. I believed you were one of us, that you were British, no matter where you'd been born. But I was wrong to trust, wasn't I, eh? In your heart, you always remained one of these lawless savages, and even wearing the king's colors couldn't change you."

A lawless savage, thought Anthony. Lawless savages like Jon and his uncle Gabriel and his grandfather, too, good men, strong men, men who didn't need a faraway king to decide what was right. He looked down, his eye drawn to the glint of silver as the lantern caught his lucky hawk, somehow still pinned to his waistcoat. The only luck he had now was ill, but perhaps there was more of a message to be found in the little hawk than luck alone.

"I have never once brought shame to my uniform or my regiment, sir," he said as he touched the silver piece. "Though you will not believe it now, I have always done my best to obey my orders and follow my duty to the people I'd sworn to protect."

"But you couldn't deny your blood, could you, Sparhawk?" said Ridley sharply. "When the final choice came, you sided with the rabble. Now you've destroyed yourself for the sake of this pointless rebellion, and for your misguided devotion to that whoring little tavern wench. You couldn't have done worse if you'd held a pistol to your own head. In the end, you followed your own kind.''

"Aye, that is true," said Anthony slowly, "and for the sake of my soul, I thank God that I did."

"Then your soul will go straight to the devil, where it belongs, Sparhawk, and welcome he is to it." Curtly Ridley motioned to the gaoler to lead the way from the cell. "I should have known better than to expect any sort of contrition or regret for your actions from you. What could your kind know of a gentleman's honor? The court will convene in two days. I expect their decision to be swift, so you will do well to prepare yourself."

Anthony watched them leave in silence, his chained hands hanging heavily at his sides. There was nothing left for him to say, not now.

But in the doorway, Ridley suddenly turned again, his dark cloak swirling around him.

"Oh, and happy Christmas, Sparhawk," he said with a mocking smile. "Enjoy the day however you can, for you know it's bound to be your last."

The door swung shut on the general's laughter, and the darkness that surrounded Anthony was complete.

With a sigh, Catie drew the grimy coverlet around her shoulders and stared up at the beams overhead, as if she could see beyond them to the room above. The taproom, that would be it, and from the stamping of feet and the whooping and cheering of men tumbled far into their cups she was certain they'd broken the lock on the bar to reach the liquor kept inside. At least they hadn't come down here yet in search of more. Or perhaps the British soldiers simply hadn't realized that this cellar room that they had turned into her makeshift prison was really the storeroom for her best rum, Sparhawk rum, hogshead after hogshead of it, stacked against the outside wall to keep cool.

Tonight that cool had shifted to outright cold, and when Catie blew out her breath in a little puff she could see it, a tiny cloud that hovered before her lips. She curled herself more tightly for warmth on the worn straw mat, and wrapped herself as best she could in the single old coverlet she'd been granted. At least they hadn't left her in the dark. The tallow candle in the pierced-tin lantern smoked badly and gave off only tiny pinpricks of light that scattered across the rough stone walls like a hundred flickering stars, but as small as those flickers were, at least they helped keep the awful loneliness at bay.

The men upstairs were roaring Christmas songs now, songs for a day that had lost all its special joy for Catie. One more time she turned her hand toward the lantern to see the garnet-and-pearl betrothal ring, Anthony's Christmas present to her, and one more time the red stones blurred before her in the tears she couldn't hold back.

She had thought they'd never again be parted. She had believed that their love for one another would be strong enough to carry them through anything. She had imagined Anthony as her husband and she as his wife, and Belinda at last with the two loving parents that every child deserved. She'd pictured other children, too, happy, gurgling babies with Anthony's green eyes and golden curls. She'd dreamed of this house filled with laughter and with love, in a Newport that was again as it once had been, at peace and prospering.

All this she had dreamed; but as with so many other dreams, Catie had seen hers crushed ruthlessly and forever in the brief moments that the British soldiers had needed to drag Anthony away from her. He would never be her husband now, and never again would she know the sweetness of his kisses or the passion of his embrace. She would never even see him alone again, not in this life. For in those same few moments, her own fate had been inexorably changed, too. No more could she dream of being a wife, a mother. Now she was only a rebel spy with bound hands, destined to be dropped and to dance her life away on the end of a rope.

With trembling fingers, she opened the locket for the heartbreaking torment of seeing her daughter's face. Belinda, too, had been torn from her, with no hope of return. The soldiers had told her that the girl was not to be found, that her little bed had been empty when they searched for her. But Catie didn't believe them, and with the sickening dread that only a mother could feel, she thought of all the misfortune that might have befallen her innocent daughter.

Nothing was right in her world, nothing was as it should be, or ever would be again. Nothing could help her now, and with a frightened, desperate sob torn straight from her soul, Catie buried her face against the musty straw mat and wept as if her heart would break.

For, in a way, it already had.

* * *

"*I* get to hold the basket, Jeremiah," whispered Belinda as she yanked the handle away from the boy's hand. "Your father said so."

"What Pa told *me*," hissed Jeremiah in return, "was that I was supposed to watch over you, and that means carrying the basket if it's too heavy for you."

Belinda raised her chin the same way she'd seen Mama do when she expected to be obeyed. "Well, it's not," she said firmly. "And if you keep looking so grim and grumpy, the gaoler will know in a minute that you intend to cause him mischief. We're supposed to look meek and innocent. Your father said so."

Jeremiah swore with exasperation—a fine, fulsome oath that made Belinda gasp with indignation. "You mustn't say such things before ladies, Jeremiah! Your father would thrash you good if he heard you!"

"I'll say what I want, Belinda," he said with an equal measure of indignation, "and if you tell me one more time what my own pa said or didn't say, why, then you can see what it's like to walk into that old gaol by yourself."

"I wouldn't mind at all," she said promptly. "It's my mama and papa that I'm going to rescue."

Jeremiah glared at her. "*We're* going to rescue them. You can't do it by yourself."

"See if I couldn't," warned Belinda, her eyes narrowed. "I haven't forgotten, Jeremiah, that you were the one who wanted to shoot Papa, and leave me without a father all over again."

Jeremiah swore again, the only answer he could think of. He didn't like arguing with Belinda, not the way she always seemed able to turn what he said wrong side out, and besides, they were within sight, and hearing, of the gaol itself. Nervously he looked over his shoulder one last time, peering into the shadows where his father had promised he'd be waiting. Saucy-mouthed girls like Belinda didn't know what real danger was, not the way he did.

"Where's that wretched doll of yours?" he whispered.

Silently Belinda pulled Duchess from the basket and cradled the doll in her arms. She felt so much better now that she had something to *do* to help her parents. Jeremiah's father—she still couldn't think of him as her uncle, not yet—had promised her it would be like that, and he'd been right. She was still a little afraid of him, even though he was the one who'd found her after the soldiers came and she hid in the stable. But Captain Sparhawk was far kinder than he looked, and what was more important, he'd understood why she wanted so much to be here now. Bringing Duchess had been his idea, too, and she smiled as she smoothed the doll's elaborate satin skirts, imagining how surprised her father was going to be.

Neatly she tugged the checkered napkin back into place over the top of the basket, and handed it to Jeremiah.

"Now you can carry it, if it pleases you," she said. "But remember I'm to do the talking. Your father said so."

They walked boldly up to the gaol door, flanked on either side by two soldiers. Without hesitating, Belinda reached up and pounded her mittened fist on the door.

"'Ere now, what do you think you're about, missy?" asked one of the guards, his manner not unkindly. "Go on, back 'ome t' your mama. A gaol's no place for little lasses like you, nor for your brother, neither.''

Gracefully Belinda bobbed a curtsy, the way Mama had taught her, or at least with as much grace as she could manage with Duchess clutched in her arms.

'''Tis no place for my father, either, not on Christmas,'' she said sadly. ''If it pleases you, sir, I'd like to see him, if only for a moment. His name is Major Anthony Sparhawk.''

The two soldiers exchanged uncomfortable glances. Though the whole town, British and American, now knew the scandal of the major's bastard, there hadn't been any orders given regarding her. ''It's not for me t' decide, missy,'' said the first one. ''Christmas or no, your father's not a regular sort o' prisoner.''

The pleading in Belinda's gaze was genuine, and could have melted all the snow in Newport. ''Please, sir,'' she begged softly. ''What harm could come of it, especially on Christmas?''

But before the soldier could answer, the door opened and the gaoler himself appeared. Clearly Mr. Foulk had come from the comfort of his fire, with worked slippers on his stockinged feet and a stiff cone-shaped cap covering his shaved head instead of his usual brown stuff wig. He'd been in charge of Newport's gaol for almost ten years now, and when the British came he'd kept the post, his experience overriding his questionable loyalty to the crown.

''Mr. Foulk, sir.'' Belinda made another quick curtsy on the snowy step. ''If it pleases you, I wish to bring my father Christmas dinner.''

The gaoler frowned to hide his discomfiture. Drunken sailors and desperate thieves were nothing to

him, but a solemn little girl in a red hooded cloak was
something altogether beyond his experience.

"Belinda Hazard, isn't it? Mistress Hazard's daughter?" he asked, then cleared his throat as he recalled
the details of the scandal. "Or is it Belinda, er, Belinda
Sparhawk now?"

"If it pleases you, you may call me just Belinda,
sir," she said primly. "That's easiest. Now would you
kindly take me to my father?"

Uneasily Jeremiah shifted from one foot to the
other, convinced they would be sent off on their way.
His father *had* said to let Belinda speak to Mr. Foulk,
on account of men favoring girls more than boys, but
it was hard, damned hard, to stand here behind her
petticoats. The gaoler opened the door more widely,
and Belinda sailed through with her head held high as
a queen's. But as Jeremiah began to follow, Foulk
thrust out his leg to block his way.

"Here now, not you, too, boy," he growled. "The
lass can see her father alone."

"But I have to come along with her," said Jeremiah
anxiously. He'd no wish to return to his father without
Belinda. He lifted the basket for Foulk to see as proof.
"I'm her cousin, an' I have to. Besides, I'm bringing
her father's supper."

"Then I will take it from here," said the gaoler,
grabbing the basket before Jeremiah could stop him
and then slamming the door in the boy's face. He
turned and bent down to smile at Belinda, his breath
sour in her face. "You don't need that nasty rogue of
a boy, do you, lass? Nay, not a pretty little mite like
you. How old are you, anyway?"

As Foulk's smile widened into an outright leer, Belinda would have very much liked Jeremiah's company with her, and his father's, as well. But she'd bragged that she could do this alone, and she was determined to prove it. Her father and Mama were depending on her.

"Nearly nine, sir," she said, as imperiously as she could. "If you please, I should like to see my father now."

"Only nine?" The gaoler's smile wavered and fell. "Where's your coin then, you impertinent little baggage?"

From her pocket Belinda drew the Spanish dollar that Jeremiah's father had given her, and even before she held it out, Foulk had snatched it from her and stuffed it into his waistcoat.

"On with you, then," he growled. "Go see that worthless excuse for a father. Little enough he can do for you now, turncoat gallows bait like that."

As he spoke, he rummaged through Belinda's basket, searching for weapons or anything that might be used for an escape. Finding nothing but the food she'd said, he flipped the basket back toward Belinda, forcing her to scramble to catch it with her free hand before it fell to the floor.

Without a backward glance, Foulk led Belinda through the parlor and bedchamber that were the sum of his dingy quarters, down a narrow hall where their footsteps echoed ominously, and toward the double-walled brick cells designed to hold the most dangerous prisoners. They passed two more guards, tossing dice to pass the time with a squat bottle of Christmas rum between them, and when they rose to join Foulk, he waved them back, not wanting to waste the show of another guard on a mere girl.

Even though Belinda didn't trust the gaoler, she still kept as close to him and the lantern in his hand as she dared, her heart pounding as she skipped to keep up. The prison smelled worse than any barnyard, and behind the barred doors locked with heavy iron padlocks, men yelled and swore at Foulk as he passed by, and at her, too. In the tavern she'd overheard tales of the wicked things that men did to land in the gaol, but these men must have done things that were even worse to land in such a nightmarish place. Yet her father and mother, her mother who hated dirt and untidiness and coarse language, were here, too, and she clutched Duchess all the more tightly as she thought of what she must do next.

Foulk stopped before the last door, fingering through the keys on his ring. "Up with you now, Sparhawk," he called, thumping his fist on the door for good measure. "You've another visitor."

Chapter Fifteen

On the other side of the cell door Anthony was already standing tensed and waiting, drawn by the sound of Foulk's footsteps long before his call. He had mentally raced down the short list of possible "visitors"—Ridley, his regiment's chaplain, a handful of officers whose friendship might still be strong enough for them to dare a visit—and had found none who'd come here now, on Christmas night. Yet as cruel as Foulk was, he wasn't clever enough to make such an announcement from sadistic spite alone. If he said there was a visitor, than a visitor there was, and Anthony squared his shoulders as best he could to meet him.

But the visitor wasn't a *him* at all.

"Happy Christmas, Papa," said Belinda, her voice barely higher than a whisper as she hung back in the doorway. "I came to see how you were faring, and to bring you supper."

Filled with shame, Anthony could see how battered and loathsome he must look from the expression on her face. He had never wanted her to see him like this;

he didn't want to see *her* here in a place like this at all.

"Happy Christmas to you, too, sweetheart," he said softly, willing to give the world for them to have met in another place. "How is your mother?"

He saw the pain flicker across his daughter's eyes as she shook her head, and cursed himself for having brought it both to Belinda and to Catie, too, wherever she was. When Ridley told him Catie was a prisoner beneath her own roof, he'd prayed that she was only under house arrest, that she'd been confined but was still able to see Belinda and have the comforts of her own rooms. One look at his daughter's face, and he realized how much in vain those hopes had been.

"I am with friends who care for me," said Belinda, with a woodenness that convinced him she spoke from rote. "I am well, as you can see."

She in turn could see that he was not, her gaze shifting inevitably from the irons to the bruises and cuts that marked his face. But as ghastly as he must look, she still came toward him, tipping her face up to be able to kiss his cheek. With mingled sorrow and tenderness, he kissed her in return, the chains that joined his wrists making it impossible to embrace her the way he wished.

She took a step back and held the doll up to him. "You must kiss Duchess, too," she said. "She's missed you, you know."

Anthony stared down at the doll's unpleasant face, wondering what in blazes could make Belinda so attached to it. Not that he'd ever tell Belinda such a thing, not tonight, and dutifully Anthony reached for Duchess to lift her to his lips, looping his linked wrists around the doll in a way he hadn't been able to with his daughter.

Was it the weight of the irons alone that made the doll feel so heavy? He frowned a little, his fingers spreading to support Duchess's body, and as he did he felt the shape of the pistol's butt beneath the satin skirts. Swiftly he slid his fingers higher, following the barrel that was tucked snug along Duchess's stuffed back.

"Duchess likes you, Papa," said Belinda, her face even more angelic as she smiled for the first time. "She always has."

Suddenly her face twisted with shock as she clutched at her pocket, and she looked fearfully to the gaoler. "Oh, Mr. Foulk!" she gasped. "I had another dollar piece for you, sir, and now it's gone! I know I had it just a moment ago—it must have fallen in the straw, here!"

She dropped to her knees, frantically running her hands through the straw to look for the missing coin. With a muttered oath, Foulk crouched down beside her, holding the lantern over the straw.

"Calm yourself, missy," he said as he bent low to help her search, greed barely masquerading as concern. "Silver pieces don't just go missing."

For an instant Belinda's gaze, eager and excited, met Anthony's over the gaoler's head, just long enough for Anthony to realize the lost coin was for his benefit, too. His daughter, he thought with a surge of pride, his brave, clever, little daughter, had done this for *him.*

Swiftly he dropped the doll and the pistol, wrapped the iron chain taut around one wrist, and with the heavy cuff struck the clean-shaven back of Foulk's head as hard as he could. With a startled grunt, the gaoler toppled over into the straw and lay still.

Belinda stared wide-eyed at Foulk's lifeless body. "Is he dead?"

"No, but he'll wish he was when he wakes again," said Anthony as he tore the big ring of keys from the clasp on the gaoler's belt. "I'll need your help again here, sweetheart. One of these little keys should open the irons, but we'll have to keep trying until we find the right one. Hurry now, as fast as you can!"

Belinda scrambled closer as he held the lock steady for her to begin testing the keys. "You didn't use the pistol."

"Didn't need to," he said, his thoughts already racing ahead. "But most likely I will before we're clear from here. I can't begin to thank Duchess enough."

She glanced up without lifting her chin and smiled shyly, so much like her mother that Anthony caught his breath. "I've powder and balls in my pocket. Duchess wanted to help."

"Well, Duchess can help as much as she pleases. There!" The lock on the manacles fell away with a clank and Anthony shook his hands free, rubbing his wrists where the heavy iron had chafed the skin raw. Finding the key to the leg irons was even easier; the second one that Belinda tried fit the lock. Swiftly Anthony rolled Foulk over and clasped the irons around his wrists, pinning the gaoler's hands around his back before he used the unconscious man's own neckerchief to gag him, as well. Next he took the little pouch with the powder and balls she'd brought and loaded the pistol.

"I'd say we're done here, Belinda," said Anthony as he held out his hand to the girl to help her to her feet. "Best we leave before anyone notices Foulk's gone."

"But what about Mama?" cried Belinda plaintively. "We can't leave without her!"

Anthony sighed. "She's not here, sweetheart. Do you truly think I'd leave her behind if she were?"

"Then where is she?" asked Belinda, her voice squeaking upward, and very close to tears. "Jeremiah's father said she was here in the gaol, too."

"Well, he's wrong, then." He should have known that Jon was behind this. Freeing an important prisoner was exactly the sort of thing Jon and his men had been doing to the British ever since they landed in Newport. This time, though, Anthony was going to do everything he could to see that Jon succeeded, and that meant leaving this cell with Belinda at once.

He bent down and put his arms around his daughter's shoulders, surprising himself by how naturally he did it, and how readily, too, Belinda in turn clung to him. She'd seemed so self-assured when she tricked Foulk that he almost forgot how young she was, and how frightened she must be, until she buried her face against his shoulder.

"There now, we'll find your mama," he said gruffly as he patted her back. "I love her, you know, and I've no intention of losing her—or you—now. Besides, I've a notion where she is already."

Belinda pulled back to look at him, rubbing her eyes with her sleeve. "You do?"

"I do indeed," said Anthony, rising to his feet.

"But we have to hurry now. I promise I'll tell you on the way."

She nodded and snuffled loudly as she tried to smile.

"Good lass," said Anthony, kissing her quickly on the cheek. He pinched out the candle in the lantern, leaving Foulk in the same murky darkness he'd endured, and slipped the ring of keys around his wrist. "Now fetch Duchess, and we'll be gone."

Belinda hurried to retrieve the doll and her basket. "Jeremiah's father said you're to meet him near the northwest wall, in the far corner of the yard, and he'll toss you a rope. He said you're to cry like a gull twice, the way you used to. He said you'd know what that meant."

"And I do, too." Anthony took Belinda by one hand and the pistol with the other. "You'll hear it yourself soon enough."

"Not now," she said, shaking her head. "Jeremiah's father said I must leave the same way I came, by the front door, so the guards won't suspect anything. I'm to tell them that Mr. Foulk's gone to the privy so they'll let me out. Jeremiah's father said—"

"Oh, the devil take what Jeremiah's father said," said Anthony gently. "You'll listen to what your own father says now, and I say you're coming with me, where I know you'll be safe."

She flashed the shy smile again, though now it wobbled with the tears she was trying so hard not to shed. "Very well," she said. "I will."

Anthony shut the door after them, locking Foulk inside for good measure, and they hurried to the far end of the narrow hall, to the door that opened to the outside yard. The long key was easy to find, and Anthony eased the door open just far enough for him to peek outside, the pistol ready in his hand. From his cell he'd heard guards patrolling this yard late at night, but tonight the small walled court was empty, at least for now.

With his fingers across his lips to warn Belinda to be quiet, he tossed the ring of keys into the snow behind the privy and led her swiftly across the yard to the wall. After the narrow, oppressive blackness of the cell, he felt perilously exposed in the moonlight, as if every suspicious eye in Newport might be turned their way, and he pressed himself flat against the thin band of shadow cast by the wall. Through the linen of his shirt, the bricks were rough against his arms, and only then did he remember that he wore no coat, the edge of excitement and fear enough to keep away the chill of the December night.

He took a deep breath and mimicked the mewing of a gull, the high-pitched call bouncing back at him from the brick walls. As boys he and Jon had practiced so much that they could confuse real birds into flying toward them, and Anthony knew he hadn't forgotten any of the finer points. But no answering call came from the other side of the wall, nor did the promised rope come flying over the top.

What if Belinda had mistaken the directions? What if Jon had been captured himself while waiting on the other side of the wall, or what if he and Belinda had simply taken so much time inside the gaol that Jon had given up on them? What if he'd come this far only to be recaptured again, and this time Belinda with him?

And what if he never saw Catie again?

"Maybe you should try again," whispered Belinda. "Jeremiah's father said—"

"Silence now," ordered Anthony, far more sharply than he'd intended. He strained to hear any guard or alarm over the painful thumping of his own heart. Over and over in battle he'd faced down death itself, but never before had the stakes seemed so high. His mouth was dry and he swallowed hard, then cupped his hands around his lips to repeat the gull's call. The familiar mocking mew, halfway to laughter, rose again over the wall.

Anthony waited, concentrating everything on willing Jon's reply to come. Jon *had* to be there. He couldn't have abandoned them, and he couldn't—

The answering cry rolled into the night, more raucous than any gull had a right to be at this hour, even at Christmas. Anthony looked up just in time to see the knotted rope's end arc gracefully over the top of the wall to swing with a dull thump against the bricks. Anthony grabbed the rope and jerked on it hard to test its strength. The rope was so clearly from some ship, a mariner's line still daubed with old stains of tar, that Anthony had to smile, imagining Jon commandeering it from some unsuspecting vessel in the harbor. But the rope would easily bear his weight, and that was what mattered most to him now.

Swiftly he tied the checkered cloth from the basket around his waist into an impromptu sash and thrust the pistol into it to free his hands, then held the rope out to Belinda.

"Sling that basket over your shoulder," he whispered, "then climb hand over hand up the wall. I'll be right after you. Easy enough, eh?"

But Belinda shook her head, her arms wrapped tightly around Duchess, and glanced longingly over her shoulder back to the gaol. "If you please," she said in a small voice, "I'd rather go back the way I came."

Anthony groaned at his own callousness. "You don't know how, do you? Because of the petticoats, and being a girl and all?"

Too ashamed to answer, Belinda stared down at her feet.

Anthony sighed. "Well, you've been brave enough before this, but I'll be damned before I let you go back in there. Now give me Duchess. Be lively, lass, Jon's waiting!"

Reluctantly Belinda handed Anthony the doll, and he stuffed it into the front of his waistcoat, leaving only Duchess's head, with her frizzled hair, to peek crossly out from between the buttons.

"Come along now, onto my back," he ordered, bending so she could climb up. "And try not to throttle me, mind?"

He could feel her fear by the way she clung to him, using her legs, as well as her arms, to keep herself from falling. "Hang on, sweetheart, that's a good lass," he said as he braced his foot against the wall. "You mama will expect to see us both whole."

But Belinda was heavier than he realized, and the two days in the gaol had already taken their toll. The muscles in his arms quivered with the strain, and he was close to gasping from exertion by the time he reached the top. Yet not once did Belinda cry out or fight him, and he thought again, with pride, that she really *was* a Sparhawk, through and through.

It wasn't until they'd reached the ground and Jon had lifted her from his back that Anthony saw she had kept her eyes squeezed shut the whole time, and had them shut still. He grabbed her hand and followed Jon and Jeremiah, running away from the wall and the gaol and not stopping until they'd reached the burying ground, all four of them dropping down into the protective shadows of the tall stone wall that surrounded it.

"There, Belinda, it's done," said Anthony breathlessly as he hugged her close. "I'm proud of you, sweetheart, and your mama will be, too. Look here."

He tapped the little silver piece pinned to his waistcoat. "That's my spar-hawk, Belinda, and the luckiest of lucky pieces. No harm would dare come to us with that keeping guard."

"Fine enough, Anthony," said Jon impatiently, "but where's Catie? Should I go back and cast the line again for her?"

Quickly Anthony rose, his hands remaining protectively on Belinda's shoulders. "Catie's not in there, Jon. Ridley told me she's still at Hazard's."

"Hazard's?" Jon swore with disbelief. "Damnation, Anthony, we don't have *time* to search all over Newport for her!"

"We have time to search Hazard's," said Anthony softly, and again he touched the little hawk pinned to his breast. "You can come or not, as you please, Jon. I'm not leaving Newport without Catie."

"That general was lying, Papa," whispered Belinda. "Look. Mama can't be in her bedchamber.

There's no light in her window, and besides, she'd never leave the shutters open like that at night, not when it's this cold.''

Anthony nodded, drawing his shoulders more deeply into the anonymous old coat that Jon had brought for him. From where they stood across the street from Hazard's, hidden in the ruins of a house half torn down by the British, Catie's darkened window did stand out conspicuously amid the blaze of candlelight in the others.

The British officers had chosen Hazard's as the site of their Christmas celebrations, and even without a hostess to oversee the festivities, they were managing to entertain themselves most royally, and noisily, too, their shouts and singing spilling out into the otherwise silent street. Even the guards at the front door were sitting sprawled on the step, passing a bottle between them. As an officer himself, Anthony was appalled by the slackness, even as he realized he'd once have been a part of it. No wonder his escape hadn't been noticed yet.

"Belinda's right, Anthony," said Jon beside him. "No one's seen or heard a glimmer of Catie since they captured you both. You know well as I do that Catie wouldn't sit quiet and peaceful. If they'd locked her up in there, she would've been calling from the window like a preacher from a pulpit. I side with Belinda. Catie's not there.''

"Then she must be elsewhere in the tavern," said Anthony. "Ridley liked the notion of keeping her a prisoner in her own house too much to move her. He's hidden her somewhere else, that's all. Think, Belinda.

Is there some servant's chamber or storage room under the eaves where he might have put her?''

Belinda shook her head. ''The attic's full of soldiers, and the maidservants' chambers don't have locks.''

''The cellar,'' said Jon excitedly. ''That's it. There's a special storeroom down there where she stows her wine and Father's rum. Catie had a padlock big as a hillside put on the door to keep everyone but her out.''

''And now it's keeping her in,'' said Anthony, hating the image of Catie locked away alone in some dark, cold cellar. ''Of course, Ridley would have taken her keys when they took her, but maybe we could force the lock.''

Belinda began hopping up and down from the cold and from excitement. ''You don't have to force anything. Mama keeps another ring of keys hidden in a little door in the paneling outside her room.''

''Then I'll go fetch them,'' declared Jeremiah. ''No one will notice me, and I can be back again in no time.''

Belinda scowled. ''*I'll* go. I know where they are, and you don't, and I—''

''Neither one of you is going,'' said Anthony firmly. ''Not with the place full of British officers. It's too dangerous.''

''No, it's not, Papa.'' Belinda's hopping grew more insistent, the hood of her cloak bobbing up and down over her head. ''I can go in through the stillroom door and then up the back stairs, the old twisty ones that only Mama and I used. Hannah was too fat, and you're probably too big, too. Then I can come back and let you in by the cellar door. Please, Papa, let me help!''

Anthony sighed unhappily. He should be keeping Belinda close to him, not sending her off alone among the British like this. Catie would have his head when she learned of it. But what choice did he have, really? The girl was the only one who knew where her mother had hidden the second, secret set of keys, just as she was the only one who could find her way through the back stairs and passages of the rambling tavern.

"All right, then, sweetheart," he said quickly, before he could change his mind. He reached inside his borrowed coat to unfasten the silver piece, and then bent to pin it on the front of Belinda's gown. "You wear this for luck, and let me have Duchess. But if you're gone more than ten minutes, Jon and I will come after you, understand?"

Belinda nodded, her eyes shining as she handed Anthony the doll and touched the silver piece. Then she turned and disappeared, darting off into the night, and as Anthony watched her go he wondered if he'd lost any shred of sanity he might still have. What had he done, trusting so much to an eight-year-old girl?

Jon pulled out his pocket watch, holding it cradled in his palm so that Anthony could read it even in the shadows.

"You said ten minutes, and ten minutes she'll get, cousin," he said with gruff sympathy as he rested his hand on Jeremiah's shoulder. "You must trust her, Anthony. None of us could do what she can. And Catie will understand, too, if that's what's plaguing you. Likely she'd do the same for you, given the choice."

Anthony sighed, not at all convinced, as he tucked the doll into his coat pocket. Catie had sent Belinda to live with the Pipers rather than have her near the

British soldiers, and now he'd sent her smack into the middle of an officers' party. He glanced at Jon's watch, then again, and yet again, and each time less than a minute had passed. Why the devil had he let her go on such an errand, anyway?

His gaze never leaving the front of the tavern, he ran his fingertips restlessly back and forth across the barrel of the pistol, each minute stretching longer and longer. Each minute was another chance for something to happen to Belinda, another moment when the British could learn he'd escaped and raise an alarm. He let himself steal another glance at Jon's watch. What exactly *would* he do if Belinda didn't return? There must be thirty or forty officers in there, and as for the others—

"Here I am!" whispered Belinda breathlessly, dodging in through the broken timbers behind them. She'd lost her cap, her pale hair half-unpinned and trailing from her hood, but her face was radiant with triumph as she held a lumpy pillow slip like a trophy in both hands before her. "I had to wait and go round through the stable because there were two nasty soldiers being ill in the snow in the yard."

"You're all right?" demanded Anthony. "No one tried to harm you?"

"Of course I'm all right. No one even *saw* me. Where's Duchess?" Quickly she hugged the doll, then reached deep into the linen pillow slip. "Here are the keys, right where Mama left them. This one—here— that's the one to the cellar room."

"You're a wonder, lass." Anthony slid the key from the ring and tucked the rest into his pocket.

"What else is in the bag? General Ridley's sword and watch chain?"

Belinda giggled with excitement. "Only some things from Mama's room that I thought she'd want, seeing as how we'll be leaving for good tonight in Jeremiah's father's boat."

For good. Anthony hadn't thought of it like that—he hadn't looked beyond finding Catie at all—but with a jolt he realized Belinda was right. There was nothing left for any of them in Newport now, at least not as long as the British were here. His career with the army was over, and so was hers as the keeper of Hazard's. They'd have to begin all over again, whether in Providence or elsewhere. But whatever came next, they'd face it together, not only as husband and wife, but as a family, as well.

Together, that is, once he'd rescued Catie.

"As precious as those things must be, Belinda, you're going to have to leave them behind with Jon," he said as he checked the pistol to make sure the powder was still dry. Jon had also given him a long-bladed knife, now hidden at the back of his waist, that would probably prove more useful for fighting in close quarters. "And I'm afraid you'll have to trust him with Duchess, too."

"I don't mind," said Belinda. "He's already taking care of Princess, too. She's waiting for me on the sloop."

"But we're coming, too!" protested Jeremiah indignantly. "Isn't that right, Pa? I'm not going to be left behind again, 'specially not with some double-blasted, double-damned *doll!*"

"Watch your speech before Belinda, son," warned

Jon mildly. "And aye, we'll be letting Anthony and his lass go without us. Mrs. Hazard don't need us all thumping down into her cellar after her."

He smiled at Anthony as he took the pillow slip and doll from Belinda. "We'll be waiting here for you, cousin, for you and your two ladies. Mark that, Belinda. If you find yourself alone, you come find Jeremiah and me, and we'll see you're taken care of."

Anthony clasped Jon's shoulder. He knew well enough what Jon was offering. It wasn't just that Belinda could return here to Jon if she was separated from her parents tonight. But if both Anthony and Catie should die or be recaptured—very real possibilities—then Jon was promising to give their daughter a home.

"Thank you, Jon," he said softly. "For everything."

Jon shrugged free of Anthony's hand, embarrassed by the emotion that both of them felt. "Just so we're truly equal, eh, cousin?" he said, swiping his sleeve self-consciously across his eyes. "Shove off now, both of you, and be quick about it. Doesn't do to keep a fine lady like Mistress Cate waiting."

"Amen to that, Jon," said Anthony quietly as Belinda slipped her hand into his, ready to leave. "Amen to that."

Chapter Sixteen

It was the same dream again, the same place one more time, but knowing she'd been here before didn't make it any easier for Catie to bear.

A dark place, dark as midnight without any stars, black and deep as new velvet. Catie didn't like the dark. It frightened her, not knowing what was hiding there around her. What could be seen could be tended to, bargained with, reckoned or considered. What hid in the darkness was forever secret, determined to swallow up everything she was or had been in its endless, empty mystery.

But she would fight it, and when the dream began she was always poised to run, her petticoats gathered in her hands and the darkness chilly on her bare legs. Then she'd hear Anthony call her name, his voice faint and far away, and Catie would begin running toward the sound. Her arms and legs were heavy in the darkness, nothingness pressing down upon her, stealing her breath, as she struggled to find the man she loved.

But Anthony's voice never came closer, never grew

nearer. "Catie, love," it called, rough and wild with loss. "Catie, where are you? Why don't you come?"

As she ran, Catie tried to answer, but the words stuck in her throat, mired in more darkness, like cold molasses. She could not speak, she could not stop, and the harder she tried to reach Anthony, the deeper the darkness became around her.

"Catie, sweet, where are you?"

Catie woke with a strangled cry that she knew as her own, her heart pounding and her legs tangled in the coverlet. A dream, she told herself as she pressed her hand over her racing heart to calm it, only a dream, only a nightmare. She sat upright, trying to control her panic as she stared into the scattered light of the tin lantern.

Only a dream...

"Catie, are you there?"

Catie gasped. She was awake and the dream was done, and yet Anthony's voice was unmistakable, more dear to her than any other. Fearfully she looked around the walls of the storeroom, forcing herself to see reality as it was, not as she wished to dream it.

"Catie, sweet, can you answer?"

"Anthony?" She couldn't help herself. The voice was too real, the ache of her loneliness too raw, for her to ignore. She threw off the coverlet and stumbled to the door. "Anthony, is that you?"

The door swung open before she reached it, and Anthony was there, really there, sweeping her into his arms with such fierce possession that her feet left the floor. She laughed through her tears and kissed him, his cheeks and his nose and his chin and his lips, each kiss all the more precious for having nearly been lost forever.

"I dreamed you'd come for me," she whispered joyfully. "I dreamed you'd come back, but this is so much better than the dream! Oh, Anthony, how much I love you!"

Anthony held her tight, almost afraid to let her go now that he'd found her again. Only two days had they been apart, yet he'd never been able to remember the exact feel of her in his arms, the scent of her hair and the taste of her mouth.

"I love you too much ever to leave you, sweetheart," he murmured, "and God willing, I never will again."

"Mama, Mama," cried Belinda impatiently as she danced beside them. "I'm here, too, Mama!"

"And so you are, lamb!" Catie slipped free of Anthony's arms to hug her daughter, fresh tears of joy beginning all over again. "Oh, you can't know how I've missed you both!"

She reached for Anthony's hand again, weaving her fingers into his. "But that's done now, isn't it? If you're here, then the general's seen fit to drop the charges against you, hasn't he?"

"He hasn't seen fit to do any such thing," said Anthony grimly, "and though I promise to explain it all to you later, we'd best leave now. Hurry, love. I can't say how much more time we'll have before they raise the alarm."

With the first glow of their reunion passing, Catie belatedly noticed the shapeless old coat and hat he wore instead of his spotless uniform and, worse, the pistol that he'd held in his hand even as he embraced her. There was a fresh wariness to his eyes, as well, a kind of suffering that had little to do with the angry bruises that marked his cheek and forehead. But as he'd said, she also knew the time to ask questions was later, not now.

"Then I'm ready," she said, grabbing the coverlet to use as a makeshift shawl and the lantern for light. "Come along, Belinda, no dawdling!"

Yet before they were even in the passageway, Anthony heard the change from upstairs. Though the fiddler continued to play and his audience to bellow along with him, the sounds of other, more serious voices could be heard, too. A clipped order, the stamp of boots, and then came a man's footsteps on the narrow stairs to the cellar.

One rapid nod was all that Anthony had time to exchange with Catie. But it was enough to make her duck back into the storeroom with Belinda, silently shutting the door afterward, while Anthony melted into the shadows beneath the cellar stairs.

The man was a young lieutenant, gorgeous in the gold-laced and scarlet dress coat of his regiment, his only weapon his dress smallsword with an enameled hilt. Impatient to rejoin the festivities upstairs, he barely rested his hand upon the storeroom's door to test the padlock before he turned on his heel.

But that half second was enough for Anthony. With ruthless efficiency he stepped from the shadows and struck the lieutenant on the back of the head with the brass-plated butt of the pistol. The young man crumpled to the floor unconscious, his smallsword clattering on the bricks and his powdered wig slipping from his shaved head.

For another half second Anthony stared at the scarlet uniform on the man sprawled at his feet. Now he *was* the traitor they'd accused him of being, an undeniable disgrace to his regiment and his king. But he had saved Catie and Belinda, and for their sake he would strike King George himself.

"Come, Catie, now hurry!" he ordered softly as he shoved open the door to the storeroom once again.

Catie gasped with surprise when she saw the lifeless lieutenant, but she didn't flinch, lifting Belinda over the man's body when it blocked their way. Too much was now at stake for niceties, and she was practically running as she and Belinda and Anthony rushed toward the narrow back stairs that would lead to the stable yard and safety.

But suddenly Belinda pitched forward with a yelp of pain, her shoe catching on the worn brick floor and her ankle twisting beneath her. The yelp turned into a muffled sob as the girl collapsed in a tangle of petticoats to clutch at her ankle.

"Oh, please, lamb, not now," said Catie anxiously as she set the tin lantern down and knelt beside Belinda on the bricks. "You must try to walk, Belinda. I know it hurts, but you *must!*"

But without waiting for his daughter to try, Anthony scooped one arm beneath her and lifted her up against his chest.

"You didn't think I'd leave you behind, either, did you, sweetheart?" he said with gruff tenderness as Belinda curled herself into his arms, her mouth pinched and her cheeks wet with tears. "Not my own little lass?"

"Oh, my, my, what a pretty scene!" called General

Ridley scornfully from the stairs behind them. "'Not my own little lass?' 'Not my own little bastard' has more the ring of truth to it. But what would a traitor like you know about separating truth from lies, eh, Sparhawk?''

Slowly, with infinite care, Anthony set Belinda down beside Catie before he turned to face Ridley.

"General Ridley," he said, his voice deceptively mild. "You may call me what you please, but I won't hear you dishonor my daughter."

Ridley snorted with disdain. "I can call the little chit whatever I please, just as I can call her mother the whore that she is."

Stay calm, Anthony told himself as he fought to control his outrage. *Use your wits, and not your heart. What matters most is that Catie and Belinda escape.*

The general stood on the front stairs, an aide beside him. Because both officers were dressed for evening, they carried no weapons beyond the fancy small-swords that hung at their waists. That was good, decided Anthony, very good for him. Even if he'd been able to draw his pistol and fire first, he'd only the single shot for two men, a shot guaranteed to bring a swarm of men from upstairs. But swords in a close space was altogether different, his own skill making an even match of one against two, especially when the two were flushed with drink and the one was as desperate as a man can be. All he needed now was a sword of his own.

In a single swift movement, Anthony grabbed the fallen lieutenant's sword, the sound of scraping steel echoing in the passage as he tore the blade from its scabbard. He held it lightly in his hand, familiarizing himself with the weight and balance, while the two other men froze on the stairs.

Never breaking his gaze from theirs, he tore his arms from the sleeves of his coat to free them, tossing the coat to one side. He thought of how he must look to them, with his bruised face and rough clothing, his hair untied and tangled about his shoulders as he taunted them with the sword in his hand: a wild man, a savage, a rebel and a traitor, not to be trusted.

"Should I go sound the alarm, General Ridley, sir?" asked the aide nervously. "Shouldn't I fetch the guards, sir?"

"What, and admit we cannot tend to this sorry rogue ourselves?" said Ridley, his face purple with rage below his snowy wig. He ripped his own sword from its scabbard, flicking it in the air before him, and heavily jumped the last three steps to confront Anthony. With more reluctance, the aide drew his sword, as well, and followed the general down the stairs.

Anthony shifted back and forth on his feet, every muscle tensed and ready to fight. "Catie, love," he said, not daring to look back to where she still stood. "You must leave now, while you have the chance. Jon is waiting for you. Belinda will show you where."

He heard the little catch in her breath. "I can't leave you here, Anthony, not like this!" she cried. "I love you too much to abandon you now, and I won't do it!"

"You must, Catie," he said roughly. "For Belinda's sake, if not for your own. I must know you're both safe. I swear I'll come to you as soon as I can."

"But, Anthony—"

"Damnation, Catie, if ever you loved me, you'll go now. *Now!*"

Suddenly the aide lunged forward, pressing past Ridley. "I'll take him first, sir!" he shouted, his sword poised. "Damned dog of a rebel!"

Coolly Anthony raised his sword to meet it, the two blades crashing together, the impact vibrating clear down his arm. But Anthony was ready, all his concentration focused now on the fight. With a deft twist of his wrist, he deflected the aide's attack and turned it into an attack of his own, forcing him to step backward, then backward again.

Yet Anthony didn't ease, his sword lashing across the aide's chest. The front of his waistcoat was at once stained and spreading crimson. With a yelp of pain he couldn't suppress, the man retreated again, this time stumbling over a basket of dirty linens left for the laundresses outside the door to the storeroom. His balance lost, he fell back hard, his feet flying upward as his head struck the brick floor, and he lay still.

"Worthless puppy," sputtered Ridley with disgust as he lunged toward Anthony. "You won't have the same from me, Sparhawk!"

And from the first blow, Anthony realized the general was right. Ridley was no callow young officer with swordsmanship better suited to a dancing master, but a seasoned old warrior, and the ruthless way he answered each of Anthony's attacks with an attack of his own proved it. Whenever Anthony tried to use his size against him, Ridley pushed back, the two of them forcing one another to fight harder and harder.

Anthony's shirt soon became soaked with sweat, his sword arm heavy and his breathing ragged, as the past two sleepless nights in the gaol took their toll. Damnation, why wasn't Ridley slowing, too? With a great effort, Anthony lifted his sword to slash crossways, but as he did the general darted beneath and caught Anthony's upper arm with just the point of his blade, and a stinging line of pain raced from his shoulder to the inside of his elbow. At once the white linen of his shirt turned red, the sleeve damp and sticky on his skin.

Grinning at his success, Ridley lunged to one side, seeking to find a new angle of attack, and as he did his foot kicked the tin lantern that Catie had left behind, sending it skittering across the bricks on a lopsided path.

But Anthony didn't notice, too caught up in battling the pain and weariness, in addition to Ridley. Laboring for breath as he circled around Ridley, he caught a glimpse of movement from the corner of his eye, enough to break his concentration and make him look. Huddled in the back stairwell were Catie and Belinda, their arms wrapped tightly around each other and their faces rapt with horror.

"The candle!" cried Catie. "Behind you, Anthony!"

He dodged another blow from Ridley and glanced swiftly over his shoulder. The latch on the door of the lantern had given way, launching the still-burning candle into the pile of rumpled linen. Already the first smoldering sparks had blossomed into crackling flames, the smoke beginning to cloud the narrow passageway.

"Remember the rum, Anthony!" cried Catie frantically. "The storeroom is full of it!"

"Then, for God's sake, leave now!" he shouted hoarsely, his voice thick. "Take Belinda and run!"

Catie's heart wept as she watched Anthony, so close to exhaustion that he was nearly weaving on his feet as he barely deflected one more of Ridley's thrusts. She didn't want to see Anthony die, not like this, yet she could think of no other way for it to end. For Belinda's sake, she knew, she must go now, as he'd ordered, but though she'd already slipped her arm around the girl's waist to help her up the stairs, still Catie hesitated for one last, precious moment, the last glimpse she might ever have of him.

"Oh, Anthony, I love you," she whispered miserably, though she knew he wouldn't hear her. "I love you, and I always will."

With the smoke stinging their eyes and burning their throats, Catie half carried Belinda up the narrow, winding stairs, through the cellar door and into the back of the stable yard. Already men were spilling from the tavern's doorways, some clambering out the lower windows as smoke from the fire filtered up from the cellar, and the street was already filling with curiosity-seekers drawn by the noise. No one noticed her and Belinda as they tried their best to hurry from the burning tavern.

"Over—over there," gasped Belinda between coughs. She pointed toward the abandoned house where Jon and Jeremiah were waiting, and as Catie crossed the street, Jon himself rushed forward to help, lifting Belinda to carry her back to their empty house.

"You'll be all right, lamb, I promise," murmured Catie, taking Belinda's hand in hers as Jon carefully set the girl down. "You'll be all— Oh, dear Lord in heaven, how did you come by this?"

Lightly she touched the silver hawk pinned to her daughter's bodice, the rush of memories threatening to overwhelm her.

"Papa—Papa gave it to me," she said, her coughs now changing to sobs. "He said—he said it was a spar-hawk, and would help—help keep me safe. Oh, Mama, where *is* he?"

Anthony's lucky piece, thought Catie wretchedly as she stared back at the burning tavern, the one talisman he was never without. Never, that is, until now, when he'd given the piece to protect his daughter, and had luck abandon him forever.

Oh, Anthony...

"What has happened?" asked Jon urgently. "Where's Anthony?"

"The fire," she said, her voice high-pitched and incoherent even to her own ears. "He was—Anthony was wounded— Oh, Jon, the fire's right where he was—is—and it's right beside the storeroom with the rum. He made us go, Jon. He wanted Belinda and me to be—to be safe."

Jon swore, squinting back at the fire. "I can't guess how many hogsheads you had stored there but when that fire reaches them, then—"

But the fire had found the rum already. The first explosion was muted, no more than a dull thud, but the next was loud as a warship's broadside, thunder and lightning combined, ripping through the back of the tavern. Bits of burning wood and cinders hurled through the air as the fire crackled to white-hot life, lighting the night sky as bright as day. The terrified shouts and cries of men mingled with the shrill, high-pitched screams of the horses trapped in the stable, and one by one the windows burst, tiny, dry pops of glass that gave way before the heat and clouds of acrid smoke.

Her grief and shock beyond tears, Catie stared at the burning building, her hand pressed tightly over her mouth. For nearly ten years, Hazard's had been her home, her livelihood and her life, but as she watched the fire devour it all, her one thought was for the man who had perished within, giving his life to save hers and Belinda's. But still the awful irony of his sacrifice tormented her, as it would until the day she, too, died. Without Anthony to share her life, what could it possibly be worth to her now?

"Come with me," said Jon gently, his hand on her arm. "Best we head for the sloop now, while no one will miss you."

She stared at him blankly, her heart at once too empty and too full to answer.

"It's what Anthony wanted, lass," he said. "For you and Belinda to come upriver to Providence with me."

What Anthony wanted.

Yes, that was what Anthony wanted, and mutely Catie nodded her agreement. With Jeremiah hovering at her side and Duchess cradled in her arms, she followed Jon and Belinda; it was a grieving, somber, little procession as they made their way through the empty streets to the water, down Long Wharf, to board the last small sloop tied to the very end.

"I'll take the lass below," said Jon softly, not wanting to wake Belinda, asleep from exhaustion in his arms. "There's a second bunk there, if you'd like to rest, too, Catie. God willing, we'll catch the tide, and be in Providence before you know it."

But Catie only shook her head, looking back at the orange glow on the hill that marked the fire, and what was left of her hopes and dreams and the fleeting promise of love. Everything was turned to ashes now. *Everything.*

The breeze from the water was cold, and as she shivered she pulled the old coverlet higher over her shoulders. If only she could cry, then maybe she'd feel less numb, less empty. If only she could feel something inside beyond this raw, aching emptiness where her soul and heart once had been.

"Catie, lass."

She shut her eyes and bowed her head against the memory of his voice. He was gone forever, and with him the sound of her name on his lips.

"Catie," he said, a heartsick rasp of doubt and fear and desperate hope. "Say it's you, love. Say it's you."

She spun around with a frightened gasp. He stood at the gangway, swaying unsteadily, as if the breeze alone could carry him away. His shirt was torn and stained dark with blood, his face and hair were blackened, his green eyes were red-rimmed from smoke, and nestled in the crook of his uninjured arm slept a gray kitten remarkable only for its homeliness.

He swallowed hard. "I love you, Catie," he said hoarsely. "I love you, and I always will."

And with a cry of boundless joy, at last she ran to him.

Epilogue

Providence
Six weeks later

Through the tall arched window of Mariah and Gabriel Sparhawk's house lay a view meant to be admired, with the whole neat city spread along the hillside like children's toys as it swept down to the river and the harbor below. But on this chilly February afternoon, Anthony wasn't interested in admiring the ships or houses or churches. Instead, he leaned close to the glass and breathed gently on it until the square pane clouded and the much-praised view was obscured. Then with his forefinger he carefully traced first one half of a heart, then the other, and smiled at Catie, standing beside him.

"Well?" he said, cocking one brow expectantly. "Should I put your new initials inside, or keep to plain Catie?"

"'Plain Catie'? How wonderfully gallant of you, Anthony," she said, her eyes silver-gray in the pale winter light. "We've been wed not even an hour, and already I've become plain Catie, the dull and dutiful wife."

"As long as I've known you, you've never been plain, and I don't imagine you'll become dull or dutiful, either," he teased, drawing her into his arms. The pale blue silk of her wedding gown rustled against his legs, and he eased the sheer linen kerchief away from her neck so that he could brush his lips across the side of her throat. "Particularly not dutiful."

"At least you realize it, so you won't be disappointed later." Catie laughed softly as she relished the pleasure of his arms around her. The fiddler's music began again in the crowded parlor downstairs, and she knew they should return to their guests and the celebration in their honor. Gabriel and Mariah had gone to such lengths to give them this lovely wedding that the least she and Anthony could do in return was to attend it.

She touched her finger to the cool glass and drew her new initials, *CS,* inside the heart, and beside them Anthony's. Then, for good measure, she added wings, arched like an angel's, to either side of the heart.

"There," she said, leaning back against his chest. "Now we'll always be lighthearted."

"I wish it were that easy," he said ruefully. "It won't be, you know."

She slipped her hand over his, understanding all too well. Though these past weeks had been a time of healing, both in body and spirit, neither of them had been idle, either. Anthony had offered his years of experience to the newly raised Rhode Island Regiment, and he now wore a colonel's splendid blue-and-buff uniform.

And thanks to Gabriel Sparhawk, Catie had begun running a tavern here in Providence, a small public house abandoned when its Tory owner fled back to England. It wasn't Hazard's, not by any means, but she'd begun with next to nothing before and she wasn't afraid to do it again, especially now, with Anthony beside her.

"We have each other, love," she said gently. "That's enough for me. And for Belinda, too, if you hadn't noticed."

Anthony smiled, thinking of how their daughter had blossomed in the glow and security of her parent's love. "Where is the wicked little creature, anyway?"

"Somewhere with her cousins, and Princess, too, most likely. She's never been part of a family before, and she still finds it altogether fascinating. Even Jeremiah." Gently she eased their joined hands lower, over her belly. "And it will be excellent experience for when she must be a big sister herself."

Anthony grew still. "Is this another one of your secrets, Catie?"

"By spring, it certainly won't be," she said shyly. "We'll have the gossips counting the months all over again."

"Are you sure?" he asked with confused concern. "That is, it seems so early."

"As sure as I can be." Catie laughed softly. "There are a number of things we do quite well together, Anthony, and making children seems to be one of them."

"Then you must give up the tavern," he said firmly.

"You must rest, and take care of yourself and the child. *Our* child."

"Oh, stuff and nonsense," she scoffed. "You said I'm not plain or dull. Well, I'm not frail or fragile, either."

She turned around to face him, smoothing the lawn ruffles on the front of his shirt. For their wedding, Belinda had returned his silver hawk pin, newly polished, and she touched it, smiling to herself at all it signified to him, and now to her, as well. "Neither dutiful nor dull, frail nor fragile. But it's very nice of you to care, just the same."

"Oh, Catie, how could I not?" He chuckled, holding her protectively. "Have you any notion of how much I love you?"

"A notion, yes." She stretched up to kiss his cheek, the joy and happiness she felt on this day greater than she'd ever dreamed possible. "For you know I love you, too, Anthony Sparhawk."

He smiled then, his world complete. "Amen to that, my love," he said softly. "Amen to that."

* * * * *

And the Winner Is...
You!

...when you pick up these great titles
from our new promotion at your
favorite retail outlet this June!

Diana Palmer
The Case of the Mesmerizing Boss

Betty Neels
The Convenient Wife

Annette Broadrick
Irresistible

Emma Darcy
A Wedding to Remember

Rachel Lee
Lost Warriors

Marie Ferrarella
Father Goose

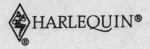

HE SAID

SHE SAID

Explore the mystery of male/female communication in this extraordinary new book from two of your favorite Harlequin authors.

Jasmine Cresswell and Margaret St. George bring you the exciting story of two romantic adversaries—each from their own point of view!

DEV'S STORY. CATHY'S STORY.
As he sees it. As she sees it.
Both sides of the story!

The heat is definitely on, and these two can't stay out of the kitchen!

Don't miss HE SAID, SHE SAID.
Available in July wherever Harlequin books are sold.

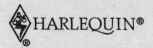
HARLEQUIN®

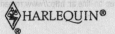

It's hot...and it's out of control!

Beginning this spring, Temptation turns up the
heat. Look for these bold, provocative,
*ultra*sexy books!

#629 OUTRAGEOUS
by Lori Foster (April 1997)

#639 RESTLESS NIGHTS
by Tiffany White (June 1997)

#649 NIGHT RHYTHMS
by Elda Minger (Sept. 1997)

BLAZE: Red-hot reads—only from

Harlequin Romance®

Delightful

Affectionate

Romantic

Emotional

Tender

Original

Daring

Riveting

Enchanting

Adventurous

Moving

Harlequin Romance—the
series that has it all!

HROM-G

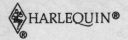